Praise

"Tense and Exhilarating. It'll take you on a whirlwind of twists and turns, all while you flip the pages to find out what happens next. A real treat for anyone who likes a little adrenaline from their reading."
Adam Cantu, Amazon Review of *Fabricated Lies*

"Great book, awesome twists, loved the plot. A real page turner from a talented author. Highly recommended!"
Amazon Review of *Fabricated Lies*

"I absolutely loved the transformation of the main character."
Venus, Amazon review of *The Creation of Marla Adams*

"A thrilling crime novel that follows the story of a female police officer as she tracks down a notorious serial killer in a small town, this book is a must-read for any mystery fan that will keep you guessing until the very end."
Sylvia C. Hall, Amazon Review of *The Creation of Marla Adams*

"Marla is such a complex character that I fell in love with. Her surrounding cast is well developed and adds a great deal of depth to the story. Lots of mystery, suspense, and plot building. I'm hooked."
Amazon Review of *The Creation of Marla Adams*

The Desperation of Marla Adams

A Stem Cell Medical Thriller

Patrick Hanford

Savoy House Publishing

Copyright ©2023 by Patrick Hanford
All rights reserved. No portion of this book may be reproduced in any form without permission from the publisher, except as permitted by U.S. copyright law. For permissions contact:

Cover design by KJ Waters Consultancy (kjwconsultancy.com) and Jody Smyers Photography JodySmyersPhotography.com.

ISBN: (eBook) 979-8-9856939-4-2
(paperback) 979-8-9856939-5-9

Sometimes people just want to tell their story. We should listen.

Also By Patrick Hanford

Fabricated Lies
The Creation of Marla Adams

Chapter 1

He should have picked up the heroin on the outskirts of Erina, Texas, fifteen minutes ago. Eighty miles north of Laredo, the unincorporated community had a paved intersection with a two-pump gas station and a restaurant serving dinner plate-sized chicken fried steaks with all-you-can-drink, sweet-iced tea. DEA Special Agent Crosby Adams had been undercover for months and was ready for the big buy.

The clock in his blue 2018 Camaro changed to 5:14 p.m. With extra dark tinted windows, previously owned by a convicted drug dealer, Crosby drove bumper-to-bumper on I-35. He texted SAC, Special Agent in Charge, Roger Davies' burner phone, *had to jump through too many hoops to get the cash for the buy. Running late, still a go?*

Davies replied with a quick *yes.*

For the last decade, I-35 leading in and out of Laredo had been stuffed with vehicles whose drivers thought the speed limit of seventy-five was ridiculously slow. Oversized tires on SUVs and raised pickups rumbled past him on his right side. He needed to change lanes and exit this mass of metal and humanity to a two-lane strip of asphalt as straight as a tight string. A fuel truck crept closer to him on the right. Crosby flipped his turn indicator and lurched into the next lane. A horn blew long and loud as the Camaro veered across the road to the exit ramp and left the lunacy behind.

The light at the intersection turned red, with no one near him. Run it? The last thing he needed was a city cop pulling him over and wasting ten minutes. At twenty-four minutes late and sixty-two miles away, he looked both ways at the empty road, "Screw it," and floored the accelerator, making a sharp turn.

He glanced at the clock again. "Damn it." The speedometer raced past one hundred.

Four miles from Erina, he slowed near an entrance to a small slaughterhouse with a lengthy white metal fence surrounding it. He scoffed at the baby blue color of the building. "Stupid color for a killing floor." Three semi-tractors pulling livestock trailers had backed to the unloading gates inside the fence.

◆

Several months of DEA training in Quantico, Virginia, kept Marla Adams from Crosby, and all she wanted for the next week was sex and sleep. Internally, she couldn't contain herself as a new member of the Drug Enforcement Administration and last month's upset win at the Virginia State Women's Quick Draw Competition. She checked her phone at the airport for any reply to her texts over the last few days. Nothing. Her calls went immediately to, "Leave a message."

Standing in line to board the plane and ready to return to the Texas heat, she tapped, *Home this afternoon. Meet you in the bedroom.*

Four hours later, the bell dinged overhead, and the attendants went through their routine of seatbacks up and tray tables in locked positions. Recirculated air blew from the vent above Marla's head. Thirty inches of rainfall soaked Bexar County yearly, but this summer was brutely dry. She rubbed the seatbelt latch as turbulence rattled the plane and slowly lowered toward the airport.

The captain spoke on the intercom, "The tower informed us there is a plane stalled on the runway. Sorry for the delay."

She gazed out the window. Jets hung in the air, circling the airport like seagulls waiting for food. From the ground, a single string of black smoke rose.

After twenty minutes, the bell dinged again, and the captain announced, "We have received our clearance. Flight attendants, prepare for landing."

The wheels bounced on the runway while the brakes ground hard and the thrust reversers roared. On a nearby runway, remnants of a single-engine aircraft smoldered on the tarmac. Lime green fire trucks surrounded the black twisted metal covered in fire-retardant foam. Body bags lay on the stretchers as the medics loaded them inside the ambulances. Her last assignment as a Hildebrandt cop was inside a burning barn with bodies broken and burned beyond recognition. She thought of Crosby and wondered why he hadn't replied.

◆

The building had no name, but Crosby knew it as Azucena Azul. "Crazy name for a slaughterhouse." Crosby snapped a picture of the trucks with his phone before turning toward the gate. DEA could track down the license plates later. He pulled to the entrance and came to a stop in front of the cattle guard.

A man with a tight t-shirt and a gut hanging over his low-slung belt holding baggy-assed jeans. He wore black sunglasses and a bushy ponytail and pointed his semi-automatic rifle at the driver.

Crosby lowered his window. "Jorge, let me by."

"You're an hour late."

Patting an envelope on the dashboard, Crosby said, "I got the cash, man. Let me in, and everyone gets what they want."

Jorge gazed over the car's front and back seats. "How do you know what I want?"

"I know what everybody wants. Money. How much do you want?"

Jorge shook his head. "I don't need that shit. If I want something, I take it. I don't buy nothing." He slammed his fist onto the roof, leaving a dent. "And I don't need your shit."

"Yeah, I can see that. You want something nobody else has and nobody can take away. What's that?"

"I want every gringo out of Texas. You stole it." Jorge gestured his hand in a northerly direction and said, "Go back to where you came from."

"I came from Texas, born eighty miles from here. Where'd you come from? Three miles south of the Rio Grande River? How about you go back to your momma and suck on her tit?"

Jorge stuck the rifle barrel into the car. "How 'bout I stick this up your ass?"

Crosby pushed it to the side, grabbed Jorge's shirt, and jerked him forward. His forehead hit the roof. The startled man dropped his rifle and staggered backward.

"Come on, Jorge. I didn't mean to hurt you."

Jorge snatched the gun off the ground. "You can't hurt me."

"Well, the blood on your face and shirt says otherwise." Crosby picked a couple hundred dollar bills from the envelope. "Here, take this. All good?"

He snapped the cash out of Crosby's hand.

"Can I go in?"

Jorge wiped away the blood from his forehead. "Get out of my face."

When Crosby eased by the trailers, something caught his eye. After the last of the cattle hoofed down the shoots, rows of young teenage girls proceeded toward a Ford F-350 pickup hitched with a seventeen foot, white, unmarked, enclosed trailer. The back doors were wide open, with several humans piled inside. Smuggled immigrants? Sex trafficking? Crosby discreetly aimed his phone toward the girls while taking pictures.

Crosby's phone vibrated—a message from Marla, his wife, *Home this afternoon. Meet you in the bedroom.* He couldn't contain his smile. Shoulder length hair, athletic, smart, sexy when she wanted to be, mean as a cobra when angry. He should congratulate her for completing her three-month DEA training and was definitely ready for a long weekend with her, but he decided to answer later. She might reply, and a buzz in his pocket while buying dope would not go well.

Chapter 2

The Camaro eased past the unloading docks and stopped near a prefabricated building painted baby blue with DRUG FREE ZONE printed in broad black letters above the door. That was a lie. Marijuana odor floated in the air.

A sun-weathered man lumbered out of the doorway wearing a western shirt, jeans, and boots, with mud and hay stuck on the sides of the heels. Crosby knew the man, Arturo, his drug connection.

Crosby should send the pictures and location to his superior, but Arturo reached the car too fast. He shoved the phone into his jeans pocket.

The Camaro's car door creaked as it opened. Crosby's once close-cut golden curls, now colored raven, hung below his shoulders. Narrow silver rings pierced each earlobe. He hated the earrings. He scratched the three-day-old stubble on his neck and wished someone would invent a cream to permanently stop facial hair from growing. The South Texas humidity was jungle thick, causing his aviator-style sunglasses to fog when he stepped out into the afternoon heat. He cleared his throat and mentally tried to slow his heart rate. Be cool, he thought. You've done this before, many times.

Arturo called out in Spanish, "You're late."

Burn scars on Crosby's back ached from the sun beating on him. It had been years since he saved two girls in a natural gas explosion. They lived untouched while he underwent months of skin grafting therapy and daily oxycodone. Crosby responded in Spanish, "Good to see you again, my friend." He fished out a reclosable, clear plastic bag from his front pocket before snapping it open. After popping two pills into his mouth, he held the bag open toward Arturo.

"No."

Crosby shoved the bag back into his pocket, then laid his hands on the Camaro's roof and clanked the metal with his skull ring. "Nice looking cattle...and your other livestock."

"Don't worry about what doesn't concern you." Arturo glanced at the pickup and trailer, then back to Crosby. "You never saw nothing, right?"

He shook his head once. "Nada."

"Good. Is it the same as last time?"

Crosby held folded bills between his fingers. "Ready to step up to the big leagues."

Arturo waved toward the office. "We don't do nothing outside."

"Lead the way." Crosby held the cash in his fist as he glanced at the pickup truck and trailer heading north. *San Antonio*?

Standing at the gate, Jorge took a photo of the American and his car.

When Crosby entered the office, it looked the same as last week, with a simple folding card table and chair in the center of the room. He raised his arms as he had done several times before. Two teenagers behind him held automatic rifles across their chests, like soldiers on X-Box games. "I know the drill. No guns for me, everyone else, yes."

A mousy looking man sat in the chair wearing a large turquoise squash blossom necklace over a black shirt and a toothpick between his lips. "You're late. I don't like late."

"Emilio, my friend, I'm late because, you know, I had to get more cash." Crosby waved folded hundred dollar bills in the air. "I'm ready to buy more heroin."

Emilio leaned back, pulled the toothpick away, and smiled, revealing a gap between his two front teeth. "How much?"

"I want my regular ten ounces today, just like every week, but I could handle a kilo."

Emilio aimed the toothpick at the man standing in front of him. "That would be twelve thousand. You got that kinda cash?"

"Tell your boss I can move much more." Crosby dropped the cash for the ten ounces on the tabletop. "When do I get the kilo?"

Emilio flipped the toothpick to the floor before removing his phone from his shirt pocket. He tapped a number and waited for an answer. "He wants a kilo this time." Emilio eyed the walls and ceiling. "When...where...if he wants it, he'll do it." Emilio put the phone on the table, withdrew a baggie from a backpack beside his chair, and dropped it on the table. "Here's the ten."

"What about the kilo?"

"Midnight." Emilio snatched the money. "Have it then."

"I'll be back." One teenager grabbed Crosby's forearm when he reached for the drugs.

Emilio stuffed the bills into his backpack. "You stay with us. I have a job for you."

Crosby frowned at the boy holding his arm. "Kid. You got two seconds to let go."

The boy pressed the muzzle of his gun against Crosby's ribs. "Or what?"

Crosby spun around and elbowed the kid's nose. Blood gushed from his face as he fell backward and dropped the rifle on the floor. Crosby stood over him. "Don't fuck with me." He kicked the weapon to the corner of the room and glared at Emilio. "What do you want me to do?"

◆

The sun broke through and inflicted a stagnant ninety-five degrees with ninety-five percent humidity. Marla squinted at the sun's glare through the terminal's plate glass windows. After she passed through the baggage exit, a man dressed in a dark blue suit, with salt and pepper hair, held a sign like a limousine driver waiting for vacationers.

DEA SPECIAL AGENT MARLA ADAMS

She held out her hand. "Hello, I'm Marla Adams."

"No, ma'am, you are not." He shook her hand. "After all you went through, you are officially DEA Special Agent Marla Adams. Remember that. I'm Special Agent Quinton Wales, but you can call me Quinton." He shoved the cardboard sign into the wastebasket. "We need to get to the office."

Marla stared at yellowed grass and limp trees as they rode on the inner loop of San Antonio. "Has it rained much since I've been gone?"

"Nothing. It's been drier than ten-day-old biscuits." Quinton watched a pickup speed toward them from his side mirror, then zip past them on the left, with another tailgating and changing lanes. "Where's a cop when you need one?"

"Do you know my husband, Crosby Adams? Excuse me, Special Agent Crosby Adams?"

Quinton smiled at her when she corrected herself. "No. We've never met. Your husband is undercover, so he doesn't come to the office."

Marla squirmed back into the passenger seat. "He never spoke to me about what he's doing."

"As expected." Quinton changed lanes and subjects. "Heard you're a quick draw competitor."

"Right. I won a competition while in Virginia. Learned as a kid, but improved when a cop in Hildebrandt."

Quinton continued to stare at the road. "What happened in Hildebrandt is still talked about all over the city. You saved that town from utter destruction."

"Hmm. I'm past it."

"And the kidnapping issue. How are you doing with that?"

Marla glared at him. "I said I'm past it."

"Right, which brings me to your first assignment. Assistant Special Agent in Charge Ronald Borland thinks the Los Zetas Cartel is transporting girls across the border this week. He wants you involved and me to train you. How's your Spanish? Need to be fluent in this job."

She flipped her dishwater blond hair past her shoulders. "Can't pass as Colombian, but I understand it well enough to know when to get the hell out of the way."

Chapter 3

Inside the office, Crosby stuffed the baggie of heroin into his front jeans pocket. "I'm listening."

Emilio leaned back against the chair. "I need a driver."

"Drive where?"

"You drive to a place and then you stop and sit and then you return."

Crosby rubbed his nose. "What's in the car?"

"You want the kilo?" Emilio leaned forward. "Shut up and do what I tell you."

"At least tell me where? I have commitments." Crosby patted his pocket with the heroin. "I got people waiting."

"Arturo will tell you where to go and when to come back."

"And then the kilo?"

Emilio fluttered his hand toward the door. "Get out. Follow Arturo."

When the two stepped outside, Crosby watched the semi-trucks turn past the gate and head south. *Back to the border?* "I need to go to my car and grab my cap. Be right back." He needed to get his pistol from under the seat.

"No. Stay with me." Arturo kept walking past a row of cars and touched the rear of a tan colored minivan. "We go in this." He opened the passenger door.

"This ugly piece of crap?" Crosby held out his arms. "Who lost a bet?"

"Let's go," Arturo said.

Crosby closed the door and noticed Arturo holding a revolver. "Two things." Seatbelts snapped in place. "One, don't point that at me, or two, I'll take it away from you like I did with that little shit inside. Got it?"

Arturo slipped the gun barrel between his leg and the car seat. "Head toward Cedarville."

Crosby glanced behind his seat at three five-gallon yellow storage containers. "What's in those?"

"Get going. We need to get back before midnight."

Crosby drove down the two-lane road. Heat waves rolled over the blacktop. The sun's glare pounded through the windshield, and the temperature inside the vehicle quickly rose. When Crosby reached for the a/c fan knob, Arturo reached for his gun.

"Easy now. It's getting hot in here." Crosby turned the knob. "You look sleepy. Take a nap. I'll wake you when we get there."

"Shut up and drive. I'm not sleepy."

After a wide turn, Crosby spotted a minivan identical to theirs parked catty-corner off the road near open fields of scattered cedar trees and scrub brush.

"That's one of ours. Stop behind it."

Slowing behind the vehicle, the tires ground over gravel on the shoulder.

Arturo slipped his gun out from under his leg. "Come on. Let's check it out."

Crosby opened his door and scanned both directions of the empty road. "Hey! I don't have a weapon."

Arturo motioned him toward the driver's side of the vehicle.

Crosby decided not to pull out his knife from inside his boot. He wasn't ready to release that bit of information yet. Blood splattered the driver's door, with no one inside.

"Over here!" Arturo yelled.

Running around to the other side, Crosby found a yellow container lying sideways on the ground. Large bags of white powder had spilled out. Two other sealed containers sat inside the vehicle. "Looks like an attempted robbery, but where's the driver?"

Crosby caught sight of a man looking like a two hundred pound WWE wrestler rushing out from behind the trees, holding an AK-47 in his hand. He fired a burst into the air. "Get your hands up."

Both raised their hands. The man took Arturo's pistol and gun-butted him between the shoulders, dropping him to his knees. He pitched the pistol into the creek twenty feet away and then pointed the rifle at Crosby.

"Hold on." Crosby looked down. "I got no beef with you. Take all of it. I don't give a shit. Take it and go."

The man gestured the gun barrel toward the containers as he spoke Spanish, "Put those in your car." When he turned away, Arturo darted toward the trees. The shooter chased after him. Gunfire erupted.

Crosby ransacked the glove compartment for a weapon. "Come on. Got to be something here." Feeling under the seat and inside the console, he stopped after hearing another burst of gunfire above his head.

"Get your ass out of there."

Crosby stood and raised his hands. "What happened to the other guy?"

The gun muzzle hit Crosby in the chest. "I said, get those bins and put them in your car."

"What did you do to Arturo?" Crosby reached for a container, surprised by the heaviness. He carried it to the vehicle and placed it beside the other three. Thoughts spun through his mind with ways to get the rifle. "Did you kill the driver? Is that why I saw blood on the door?"

"Shut the hell up."

The gun muzzle shoved against Crosby's back, giving him his chance. He swung his arm blindly and hit the man's forearm, pushing the rifle away. Crosby's fist bashed into the man's face before throwing an uppercut, knocking him off-balance. Crosby ducked as the rifle butt swung near his head. He felt a sudden pain in his ribs and gasped for air when shoved against the vehicle. A fist smashed into Crosby's mouth.

His tongue felt a loose tooth, and a coppery taste spread across his mouth. *This guy is going to kill me right here.*

The gun butt slammed into Crosby's chest, and he dropped to his knees. His heart pounded as thoughts turned toward Marla's smile. His hand grasped a handful of dirt and flung it in the air. Crosby ducked when the machine gun fired over his head. He looked up at the weapon pointing at him.

"I should kill you right now, but I need a gringo. Get up and grab the other two bins."

Crosby rubbed the blood off his swollen lip. "Sure. I'm your gringo." After loading the containers and closing the side door, he sat in the driver's seat and glared at the rifle pointed at him. "Where's Arturo? I should check on him."

"Go."

The engine started. Somehow, he had to take this guy out. And Arturo? Vultures would feast tonight.

Crosby felt the gun barrel against his side. The bruised ribs made him wince.

"I told you to get going."

"Yeah, yeah, okay."

They drove in silence until Crosby asked, "What's your name?"

"Don't matter what my name is. Just shut up and drive."

"Okay, all right. I'm calling you Bob."

His eyebrows scrunched. "Stupid name."

"Okay, then what?" With no response, he said, "What about Diego?" No response. "Miguel? Lorenzo? Pablo? Javier?" That's when Crosby noticed a slight facial twitch. "Javier. I'm calling you Javier."

"No. Don't call me by my...don't call me anything."

"Javier? Where we going?"

Javier nodded toward the containers. "Where were you taking those?"

"Not sure...Javier." Crosby could tell it got to him. The man's nostrils flared. "The guy we left behind—"

Javier jabbed the end of the rifle against Crosby's shoulder. "I said, where were you going?"

"How the hell do I know? You killed the only guy who knew where to go."

Javier pulled out his phone and dialed a number. "I got six boxes," he glanced at Crosby, "and a Los Zetas screw-up. I'll call you when we get close."

"Bullshit, man," Crosby said. "I am not with them."

"This belongs to Los Zetas, so you're Los Zetas."

Crosby had to play this guy. "I'm going to be honest with you. I came to buy kilos. Do you hear me? Lots of drugs."

"You're American, right?"

"Yeah, so what?"

"Why is an American working for Los Zetas?"

"I told you, I'm not part of them."

"From now on, you buy from me."

"I don't have any cash on me. Gave it to the other guys."

The man laughed. "You left your money with those scumbags? You'll never get it back, and you'll get no drugs from them, either."

"Yeah, probably so."

"I should kill you, but a gringo could do me good. Turn right on that road up ahead."

Crosby slowed and turned onto a dirt trail where a house sat between two metal barns about a quarter mile to the right. "There? What's there?"

"Shut up." Javier called on the phone again, "We're here."

Crosby turned toward the house, and a barn door slid open. A multitude of bright lights lit the inside of the building. He rolled his window down, and the odor of marijuana filled the air. Hundreds of hay bales lined up on one side, except it wasn't hay. On the other side, money counters flipped bills. Men wrapped currency straps around stacks and placed them in the same type of yellow containers sitting behind him. Crosby felt a shiver. He hit the motherlode. After stopping the vehicle, he opened the driver's door and stepped out.

A weathered man with a Pancho Villa mustache aimed his gun at him. "Back inside."

"Hey, man, come on, I'm with him. I got to take a piss. Bathroom?"

He nodded toward the outside.

"Yeah, thanks," Crosby said. He headed out and turned the corner while slipping his phone from his pocket. Pressing the map app, he took a picture of the screen's location.

When the minivan's side door slid open and clunked, men removed the containers of drugs and replaced them with others full of cash. Like a NASCAR pit crew changing tires, it was a smooth operation. Returning inside, Crosby made an exaggerated effort to zip his pants up before climbing back into the vehicle.

Javier sat in the passenger seat. "Let's go."

Crosby shifted the transmission to reverse. "Where to?"

"Laredo."

Chapter 4

Marla opened the glass front door and took in the round DEA logo imprinted on the lobby wall. She felt proud. Quinton entered behind her and pointed toward the reception desk where two men sat. He signed the electronic register and Marla did the same. After cordial introductions, they headed up the stairs to the second floor. A multitude of animal pictures from the San Antonio Zoo covered the walls. She thought, *all right, DEA supports wildlife.*

"It's noisy inside, and there is a pecking order. Be ready." Quinton opened the conference door, revealing a jungle of intermingling people.

The correlation to zoo animals hit her with hyena laughs, predator growls and groans, and the most exposed, vulnerable species, the newbies bouncing around like impalas trying desperately to look important.

Quinton glanced across the large rectangular table with folded placards of names and found theirs aligned with each other.

Assistant Special Agent in Charge (ASAC) Ronald Borland charged through the side door toward the head of the table. Marla raised her eyebrows. *Lion in the jungle.* He sat with his back toward the wall, capturing the attention of every agent at the same time. "Everyone, sit."

The room went quiet. Trained animals hunkered in their chairs.

In Quantico, Marla learned Borland had been an undercover agent for ten years and recovered more heroin than any person in the agency's history, but when he dove deep into the life of the cartel, he lost his self-worth, his wife, and children. After a suicide attempt,

HR pulled him from the field and ran him through the wash and dry cycle of the psych department.

Suzie Moore, a woman in her mid-twenties with short purple hair, wearing tortoise-shell eyeglasses with rose-colored lenses, sat alongside Borland. A long, green fingernail tapped a single key on her laptop.

A page with four police sketchings of men lit the whiteboard on the wall.

Borland popped the cap off a red marker. It squeaked across the board as he wrote *Alejandro Torres-Hernandez*. "He's back in Texas." After snapping the cap back on with his palm, he dropped the marker on the table.

"El Pajaro," an agent called him.

Marla leaned toward Quinton and whispered, "The Bird?"

"Right, part of the Los Zetas Cartel. This guy has escaped capture so many times; legend says he turns into a bird and flies away. Rumor is, he easily slips out of handcuffs and ropes around his wrists and feet." He drummed his pen against the table. "There's no photos of him, only four police sketchings of the same man from witnesses who survived his torture."

Marla studied the sketches. The top left, a mid-forties Hispanic man with uncombed hair, heavy bags under ebony eyes, and thick leathery skin that looked like it avoided sunscreen, lotion, or soap. To the right, a man the same age with Oakley style sunglasses, bald, and days old beard. Below, a younger man with shoulder length hair, a weak mustache, and a wide nose, and the last sketch had Brad Pitt curly hair and a heavy black goatee. Marla leaned back in her chair. *If nothing else, this guy is good with makeup and facial masks.*

Borland continued speaking. "Intelligence reports he's crossed the border and near San Antone. Remember, Torres-Hernandez is smart. Smarter than anyone in this room. Frickin Einstein IQ." An image of Yale University lit the screen. "Ivy League grad. Somehow, his face had been scrubbed from the admissions office, and no student ID at the security department can be found." Another image popped up. "Master's at the Vienna University of Business and Economics. No pictures there, either. Smart son of a bitch. Scotland Yard wants him for trafficking and a string of murders."

The picture changed to two houses. Both lay in decay. The first, an old Victorian style house with second story windows broken or boarded, and the entire building leaned like the Tower of Pisa. The second house, a third the size, had a weather-beaten wraparound porch and thin columns. Sad roof lines yielded to inclement weather.

A rush of adrenaline shot through Marla. The houses were only a few miles from her ranch in Hildebrandt, on the edge of Bexar County. Several years ago, as a police officer, she helped rescue families at both places when a hurricane slammed into the Gulf Coast, dropping almost twenty inches of rain in a few hours. South Texas weather rapidly aged the vacant homes. She focused back on Borland.

"Intel reports Torres-Hernandez is bringing drugs and girls into Texas." He stood and pointed at the house pictures on the whiteboard behind him. "We think these are where they will stay tonight, arriving sometime after midnight."

Marla leaned into Quinton. "I'm familiar with these places."

Borland continued. "I want him alive. The US Attorney's office agreed they would strike a deal with him to move further up the food chain and inside the Central and South American production plants." He tapped his finger on the board. "At the western house, Orozco and Zapata. At the eastern house, Valdez, Wales, and Adams. The rest of you are on your computers. This needs to be a clean takedown." Borland stood and pointed at Marla. "Everyone be cognizant this is Special Agent Adams' first outing."

Marla mumbled to herself, "Great. I'm a fricking impala." She focused again on Borland.

"That is all." Everyone stood and ambled toward the door. Borland slipped between people and stopped in front of Marla. "Special Agent Wales is your trainer. You stay beside him, and everything will work out great."

"Yes, sir, stuck like glue."

Quinton said, "We're heading to the house to check it out. Never been there, and I want to see it before dark."

Borland replied, "I don't trust this guy. Be careful."

"Any of ours around there?" Marla asked.

He shook his head. "The sheriff's department is grumbling we won't let them on the front line. Rumor is Los Zetas may have a mole inside their office, so I didn't let them know every detail."

"You think it's a deputy?" Marla asked.

"More likely, an office worker that hears everything."

"What about the Border Patrol?" Quinton asked.

"They backed off this morning because of the massive influx at the Laredo Port of Entry. I'll have Valdez meet you there, but he informed me before the meeting he had to check on his grandparents at the nursing home."

Quinton flashed a quick salute to Borland. "We'll be careful."

Marla turned to her new trainer. "Now what?"

He raised his eyebrow for a second. "First, I need to say something to Ms. Moore. I'll be right back." He coursed around the table and bent beside her. "Hi, Suzie. You look exquisite today."

She smiled while gazing into Quinton's eyes. "You think I look exquisite?" She laughed, "Quinton Wales, you are such a liar."

He put his hand on her forearm. "May I take you to dinner tomorrow night?"

She scoffed. "Like a few nights ago? I know what you mean, and food is not what you want."

"Just trying to be nice."

Suzie patted him on his hand. "Bring a bottle of wine when you come over."

Quinton returned while Marla stared at what she was watching.

"A little young for you, don't you think?" Marla didn't expect an answer. "Now what, Casanova?"

"Her?" Quinton asked. "Just trying to be friendly to everyone."

"Hmm. I'll ask again. Now what?"

Quinton moved toward the door. "We head to the house and check the area. Wait and hope."

She looked at her wristwatch. "It's an hour before dark and four hours before they arrive. I can tell you what's there. As a Hildebrandt police officer, I've been there, and there's not much to see. A thousand-square-foot house, single bathroom, two bedrooms, front and back door, and an unattached one-car garage."

"Still, I want to see it."

Minutes later, they climbed into the Chevy Tahoe and closed their doors.

Marla glanced in the back. "What's the dolly for?"

"Had six boxes of clothes to donate to Goodwill, so I borrowed a company hand truck. I'll put it back tomorrow."

The engine rumbled. From the parking lot, she watched the cars creep by on I-10. "Traffic is heavy."

"San Antonio has heavy traffic 24-7." Wales glanced at the fuel gauge. "Damn. I'm almost empty. I'll have to throw in a few gallons before we head out."

Chapter 5

Crosby flipped on the bright lights of the minivan while driving down a straight black ribbon. Night approached with an orange and red sunset quivering between trees.

Arturo was weak and small and would have been easy to overtake anytime, but this guy, who looked like a cartel veteran, would be an odds-on favorite. An AK against a knife is not much of a fight.

Crosby needed to screw with this guy's head, irritate him, speed up, slow down, and get the idiot's mind off the weapon. "Always heard if you put drugs in a big bag of coffee beans, dogs couldn't smell it. I'll bet there's a convenience store somewhere close. We could steal all the bags and pour them inside those containers."

Javier turned his head toward Crosby. The gun barrel moved slightly away from Crosby's side. "That's stupid. Coffee don't work."

Working, Crosby thought. He lifted both hands off the steering wheel and raised his voice. "You know, when we get to the border, the dogs will smell the drugs on the containers. Those guys had powder on their hands." He pointed behind him. "They touched those boxes back there. Even the cash has bits of drugs on them. We'll never make it across."

"Put your hands back on the wheel and shut up."

"Just trying to help you out." Crosby placed his hands on the steering wheel. "You know, keep you...us out of prison." *I'm going to throw your ass in jail for twenty years.*

"You talk too much."

"Wait. Just remembered; I can't cross. No passport. They'll search me, and you, and the vehicle."

Javier aimed the gun at the windshield. "We're not going to Mexico."

All right, finally. Point that somewhere besides me. "Then where? Every dog in Laredo knows what cocaine and heroin smell like. They've been sucking on tits full of drugs since birth. I bet you've been sucking on tits. Tell me, when's the last time—"

"Shut your face. I ain't talking about no tits. Turn right at that flashing yellow light."

Laredo lights gleamed up ahead. "Up there? Small road. What if we get a flat? Long way to walk. A cop might drive by. A Sheriff or a Constable. What are you going to say to them? Can't shoot them...they've already sent in what you look like before they exit their car. You'd be on the run. What about the stuff in the back?"

Javier swung his fist, hitting Crosby on the side of the head. "Shut your fucking mouth." He fired a single shot into the floorboard.

Crosby jerked his feet up and the vehicle slowed. "Okay. Point that thing somewhere else." He stepped on the accelerator again.

After crossing a bridge with no water underneath, they entered Laredo city limits. "Which way?"

The brute directed him through several side streets to a warehouse with a single light shining above the overhead door, then called a number on the phone. "We're here." The long metal door rose, and he clicked the gun barrel on the windshield. "Go."

Crosby perused the area as the minivan crept in. Totally different setup, with hundreds of yellow containers on pallets. He stopped the vehicle.

Men surrounded them with their rifles in hand. The side door slid open, and others took the containers almost as fast as a Formula 1 car pit crew changing tires.

Crosby sat still behind the wheel while counting the rows of containers. He checked the side mirror when a man pulled on a chain to close the metal door. Things just turned sideways.

The driver's door swung open. A kid, not more than sixteen, wearing a gray Tecolotes de los dos Laredos baseball t-shirt, motioned with his head for Crosby to get out.

As soon as he climbed out, he felt a gun barrel against his back. The teen shoved Crosby away from the vehicle.

"Sit."

He sat on the ground and waited for the teen to disappear, then squirmed behind the pallets, pulled his phone halfway out of his pocket, and snapped another location image from the map app.

Javier came around the corner and surprised Crosby. "What are you doing over here? Get back to the vehicle."

Crosby turned away from him as he shoved the phone back into his pocket, then started to stand, but Javier pushed his shoulder down. "First, you tell me where you were going?"

"Promise, man. I don't know." Crosby sat and held his hands above his head. "I'm here to buy large amounts, and if you got the drugs, I'm all in." *Why am I not dead?*

The man shoved his foot into Crosby's side, rolled him onto his back, and pushed the muzzle of an AK-47 against his forehead. "You got the cash?"

"Yeah. I can get it." He slapped the barrel away. "Get that thing away from me."

"You don't buy shit from anyone but me."

"Sure. Whatever you say." *I'm definitely sending your ass to prison.*

Crosby and Javier climbed into the front seats, and three men entered the minivan through the side door. It slammed shut.

"Drive," Javier said.

"What are they doing here?" Crosby asked.

"Shut up and drive."

"Where?"

"Erina, back to the ranch."

"How do you know about that place?"

Javier waved his gun at Crosby. "You are one dumb son of a bitch."

Chapter 6

Quinton turned off a county road to a dirt path and stopped five or six hundred yards from the abandoned house. "Between gas and traffic, it took longer than expected. This is where we get out and walk."

With a gentle nudge, Marla opened the door of the Tahoe. The interior stayed dark as she stepped out into the thick, humid air. She gazed at the orange glow of the city lights miles away, with dusk permeating the landscape and heat refusing to relent its hold.

"It's getting dark." The evening heat parched her throat. She reached for a bottle of water, but the liquid, almost as warm as the night, curbed her thirst. After wiping her lips with the back of her hand, she closed the door. "And still hot."

Quinton stood on the driver's side of the vehicle and slipped on his disposable gloves. "No shit." He reached for his radio when it squelched. "Wales here."

Borland said, "You mentioned heading to the place early. Are you there?"

He stared across the hood at Marla while she slipped on blue disposable gloves. "This is not going to be good. He never calls unless something bad has happened." He pressed the mic button. "Just entered the area, about five hundred feet from the property."

"Stop. Intel says they arrived an hour ago."

"Not supposed to be here for another three hours," Quinton said.

Borland scoffed. "Guess they caught the early flight."

Quinton knew the answer to his own question. "Are the Sheriff's deputies coming?"

"No."

"Got it. Out." He dropped the mic on the seat and eased the door closed.

A voice to the right of Marla called out in Spanish, "What are you doing here?"

A thin Hispanic man with a sweat laden shirt and a grimy kerchief around his neck came out of nowhere with a rifle pointing at her. It looked like an M-16.

In the dark, he struggled to see who she was. "Who are you?" he asked.

Quinton knelt and duck-walked around the front of the Tahoe.

Marla bent on her knees and spoke in her best panicky Spanish voice, "I no run no more. I'm sorry. Please take me back to the house."

"Shut up, whore. How did you get away?" He glanced at the vehicle. "Whose car?"

She tried to hide the large yellow DEA on the back of her jacket. "A friend left it for me to escape."

He pushed the muzzle against Marla's shoulder. "Stand up, bitch."

She snatched the barrel and jerked it out from his hands in a single motion.

He growled and showed his teeth at her like a mad dog. "I'm going to kill you."

Quinton grabbed the man's collar from behind and swept his feet off the ground. The man fell flat on his face. With handcuffs on his ankles and hands and the kerchief stuffed in his mouth, all the guy could do was grumble.

Quinton yanked the magazine out of the rifle and pitched it to the right, then slung the weapon as far as he could in the other direction.

"We might need that rifle," Marla said.

"Are you kidding? Shooting someone with a stolen gun, a potential murder weapon? It would give me a mountain of reports to file. No, thank you."

A barrage of rapid gunfire erupted near the house. A woman screamed.

"Time to go to work." Quinton opened the passenger door, reached for the microphone, and called out on the radio. "Gunfire at the east house. Need backup ASAP."

"Sending now," Borland replied. "Proceed with caution."

Marla asked Quinton, "Just the two of us?"

He nodded. "Can't wait for reinforcements."

They advanced toward the house with Spanish music blaring inside and a weather-beaten NO TRESPASSING sign nailed to a porch column. To Marla, it seemed the outside walls leaned inward, like a house of bent cards ready to collapse at any moment. Silhouettes in the windows slipped through the soft white glow. A Ford F-350 pickup truck sat in front with an enclosed trailer to the left of the boarded-up garage.

Quinton whispered. "Normally, I'd send you around to the back door, but Borland would kick my ass if you got yourself killed the first day on the job."

"Right. That would be bad for you—and I'd be dead."

"We should check if anyone is sleeping in the truck. I'll take the driver's door, and you take the passenger side. Stay low; aim up at a body." He patted his vest. "Don't shoot me." He waited for her to tiptoe around.

Marla held her weapon straight ahead while focusing on the windows, expecting the door to open and a barrage of bullets charging at her. A hot wind gust slapped hair across her face. While kneeling near the passenger's door, her heart pounded in her chest. She drew a deep breath and called out, "Ready."

Marla grabbed a handle and flung the door open. Nobody inside. On the other side, Quinton smiled at her. She had never been so happy in her life not shooting someone. They quietly closed the doors.

He snapped open a pocket knife and stabbed a tire. It hissed as it flattened. "Let's keep the bastards from riding off in the sunset."

She chuckled. "It's dark."

The music stopped.

"Move up," Quinton said.

Two men yelled at each other inside. Angry voices increased. A single gunshot exploded, and Marla instinctively ducked. It sounded like a body fell against the wooden floor.

With both on each side of the door, Quinton called out, "DEA. Open up."

They heard boots shuffling and glass breaking.

"DEA. Open up."

Gunfire erupted inside. Bullets splintered the front door. Quinton kicked the door open. "DEA." He charged right toward the bedrooms.

Marla entered and turned left toward the kitchen. Fast food paper sacks and canteens sat on a table, with scattered glass on the floor near broken windows.

A man lay flat on his back in the kitchen with a sucking chest wound. Several bullet holes littered a dead woman's body a few feet away. Marla checked the man for a pulse. "Pulse thready." She holstered her pistol, ripped the man's shirt open, and pressed her gloved hands on the wound.

Quinton came around the corner. "The place is empty. They must have escaped out the window." He knelt beside Marla, but seconds later, he heard a laugh behind them. Quinton spun around and aimed his pistol at two men, one in his early twenties with not a whisker on his face, and the other, much older, looked like life had stomped on him a few times. They had their rifles pointed at Quinton.

The young one read the yellow letters on the back of Marla's jacket. In a heavy Mexican accent, he said, "DEA."

A siren wailed in the distance.

The older one said in Spanish, "Drop it."

Quinton shook his head and replied in Spanish, "Hear that? Sirens. Many more DEA coming and will kill you if you don't give up."

Marla kept her hands on the chest wound. "This man is dying. He needs help."

"Shut up, bitch," the older one said.

The old man swung the gun butt toward Quinton's face but missed when he ducked. He pointed the muzzle at Quinton. "Give me your pistol."

"I'm not giving you my weapon."

Marla took her hands off the man on the floor. "He's dead."

The older man aimed the rifle at Marla and yelled at Quinton, "Drop the gun, or I kill her!"

Quinton looked at Marla and said in English, "Virginia state championship?"

"Right." She stood and snapped the gloves off.

"Okay. Prove it to me." Quinton bent down and pitched his pistol toward the door. Both men's eyes followed the gun.

In a fleeting second, she drew her pistol and shot both men in the chest before either fired a shot.

The young one, flat on the floor, coughed once before he stopped breathing. The other never moved. Quinton kicked the weapons away from them. "Yep. That's fast." Sirens came closer.

Valdez entered the house with his pistol aimed at Marla before lowering his weapon. "Got here as quick as I could." He glanced back at the front door. "More help coming."

They heard muffled sounds outside. Marla and Valdez spun around, aiming their pistols at the broken front door. Quinton said, "Valdez and I will double check these two guys. Adams, you check the noise."

The trailer not far from the garage wiggled side to side, and sounds came from inside. She yelled at Quinton, "Need help." She ran to the back, unlatched the lock, flung the doors open, and shined her flashlight into the trailer.

Over forty girls crouched together as far away from the door as possible, bodies trembling and clothes soaked from sweat.

One girl lay on her side, eyes closed, lifeless. When Marla jumped in, the girls screamed and squeezed closer together. She rolled the emaciated girl onto her back: no breath or pulse. She pumped on the young girl's chest.

Quinton ran to the trailer as sirens closed in. He yanked his phone out of his pocket. "Calling Borland. We need a dozen ambulances. I'll check inside for any water."

Three vehicles charged toward the house, lights swirling, sirens blaring. Quinton bolted past the door with the dead men's canteens in his hands as three white Crown Vics with Sheriff printed on the side slid to a stop. He pitched the canteens toward Marla. "Ambulances on their way."

Valdez glanced behind him. "And we have the Sheriff's department here."

The deputies jumped out of their vehicles with flood lamps pointed at the trailer. Deputy Jeffrey Keene aimed at Quinton and called out, "Put your hands up where I can see them."

Quinton and Valdez raised their hands and turned their backs to show the large yellow letters on the jackets before turning back toward them.

Valdez called out, "DEA Special Agent Wales and Valdez."

Quinton pointed at the badge on his belt. "Four dead in the house, one alive and tied up in the field. We discovered girls inside this trailer. Need help."

Jeffrey opened the trailer doors wider and shined his flashlight inside. A young girl, leaning against Marla, sipped from a canteen. All the rest, eyes wide open, arms wrapped around each other, huddled closely behind their savior. Marla gazed at the deputy without uttering a word. Her emotions: rage, sadness, and hope, entwined together. Annie Leibovitz or Da Vinci couldn't have asked for a better pose.

"Marla Adams? What are you doing here?" Jeffrey asked. He snapped a picture from his phone.

Chapter 7

Crosby left Laredo driving the minivan and carrying three malnourished, half-drunk men with automatic weapons in the back and a man who could pass for a WWE wrestler in the passenger seat. The muscles in his back tightened, making a long day longer while plodding north into a black oblivion. The three men had no idea Crosby understood Spanish. He listened to each man speak about how they would exact revenge on Los Zetas men at the slaughterhouse.

At two hundred seventy pounds of mostly muscle, Crosby couldn't take Javier in a fistfight. Even if he could get lucky enough to kill him with his knife, the three men in the back held automatic rifles and would rip him apart.

The clock on the dashboard read 11:52. With the slaughterhouse five minutes away, Crosby had to figure out how to survive this outing.

When they approached their destination, Javier motioned with his head. "Turn off your headlights and stop."

Crosby looked out his window toward the building with lights on. Three semi-trucks hooked to livestock trailers, different from earlier in the day, sat in the dark, with a few men rambling around without worries. "And what do you think you are planning to do?"

The side door glided back and locked.

"Whoa there, guy," Crosby said. "I'm not getting involved in a drive-by shooting."

The men racked their weapons. Javier raised his rifle toward Crosby's head. "Drive, or you're dead."

"Not doing this." Crosby floored the accelerator and yanked the steering wheel side to side. One man fell out, and the other two rolled to the back of the van. *Might as well get a little laugh before I die.*

Crosby felt a gun barrel against his temple.

"Stop," Javier yelled.

He slammed on the brakes and pushed the gun barrel away. Javier's head cracked the windshield. The two in the back rolled forward and smashed against the passenger seats.

Crosby opened his door, ready to jump out, when a hand grasped the back of his collar. He raised his hands above his head. "Okay, okay. Just checking on the guy who fell out. Hope everything is okay."

Javier said evenly, "Shut the door and drive in, nice and slow."

Crosby closed his door and drove.

After passing the entrance gate, Javier said, "Stop and get out and go over there."

When Crosby exited the minivan and walked between the trucks, he winced from the flashlight shining on his face. Arturo stood with arms crossed in front of his chest.

"What is going on?"

Arturo smiled. "Had to make sure you were with us."

"And now I know two of your places," Crosby said. "Why don't I go back and steal it from you."

"Because it's gone. Cleaned out. You go back and find nothing." Emilio sat behind a fold-out table and held out a kilo of heroin wrapped in plastic. "You're a good man. Got that twelve K?"

"All this was bullshit?"

"A test, man." Arturo chuckled. "All good. You didn't rat on anyone. Played the game and stayed true. Hell, you even tried to jump out of a moving car."

Emilio jokingly pushed Arturo's shoulder. "I don't know if I could have done that." He stopped smiling. "Where's my money?"

"In my car, unless you've already ransacked it."

His fingers rubbed the turquoise on his necklace. "No way would I steal from someone who buys my product. That'd be like stealing from Bird. You wouldn't steal from Bird, would you?"

Crosby waited a moment. "No."

"Good. Get your ass over to your car and get my money." He waved his hand toward the car. "Go on. Get. I'll wait."

A few minutes later, Crosby returned wearing a black leather jacket with a small pistol in his right pocket. "Got chilly out here." Sweat lingered around his neck.

Emilio placed the heroin on an electronic scale sitting on the card table. Crosby read the digital amount, 1.02 kilos. He used the back of his hand to push it off the stand.

"If you don't mind." He held a small, round weight in his hand. "Thought I might need this." Placing it on the scale, it read 1.00 kilo. "Good." He reached for two bundles of hundred dollar bills from the left pocket and dropped them on the table.

Emilio flipped through the bills and smirked—a gun hammer cocked behind Crosby.

A voice said, "You did well, my friend."

Crosby stuck his hand inside his jacket pocket, touching the trigger. He spun around and focused on the end of a suppressor attached to a .22 caliber revolver aimed at his forehead.

Elvis style glasses dominated above the man's black soul patch. The man had curly Brad Pitt hair. Wearing an expensive navy blue suit, a matching colored tie, and a crisp orange shirt, he looked like a fat oriole.

Crosby smiled. "You must be the notorious Senior Torres-Hernandez."

He scoffed and lowered the gun barrel to Crosby's chest. "Notorious? I am only an entrepreneur in a dangerous world."

Crosby had found him; Torres-Hernandez, Bird. He changed the subject. "What's with the outfit? Expected trashy clothes like the rest of your crew."

"The world needs a little more fashion. More culture, don't you think?"

Crosby laughed. "Not with cow dung on your shoes."

Bird waved his pistol casually up and down Crosby. "And what do you wear? Black jeans, black shirt, black jacket. Not very original."

"Comfortable. I can run faster with loose clothing."

Bird's smile disappeared. "You purchase from me ten ounces a week. Too much for personal use. What have you been doing with all my Mexican horse?"

"Your horse? You mean my heroin? You sold it. I bought it. When I buy it, it becomes mine." Crosby shook his head. "Don't worry, I'm not selling it here." Inside his pocket, he aimed his pistol at Bird's crotch. "Why do you care?" He looked at the end of the suppressor. "Aim that somewhere else."

Arturo said, "He doesn't like guns pointed at him."

Bird lowered his pistol. "Canada, that's where you sell it, right? I have watched you jump on a plane without luggage and head toward Seattle every month. You must tell me how you get the drugs on the plane. Perhaps an associate from an airline? Baggage handler? How much does he charge?"

Crosby expected the question. He had to buy enough over several months to be noticed by Los Zetas and Torres-Hernandez, but the DEA needed a place he couldn't check. "Right, Calgary and Edmonton. No competition with the cartel, and you don't need to know how I do it."

"I want in," Bird said.

Crosby scoffed at him. "Los Zetas wants in, or you?"

"I sell five kilos for sixty K to my dealers, but for you, fifty and ten percent of your profit. You bring Arturo with you to Canada and show him your operation."

Bird was smart. Capitulate too soon, and this entire scene might go south. "You want to be my partner? My BFF? Hang out together, grill a steak, and knock back a few tequila shots? Ten percent is too much. Four percent and thirty-five K for the five kilos."

This would be Crosby's biggest bust if he confiscated five kilos of heroin and put Bird in a cage.

"Eight." Bird tapped Crosby's shoulder with the suppressor. "You have that much cash in your car?"

Crosby imagined the worst-case scenario: fire two rounds into Bird's scrotum, drop, and spin around to hit Arturo before he emptied a full mag of bullets. Emilio would disappear behind the trucks and run like the little chickenshit he was and tell the cartel—if he lived.

"Five kilos for thirty-seven, and you get six."

When a thud hit the table behind Crosby, he turned to see a cellophane-wrapped eleven-pound package of brown powder, Mexican heroin. He withdrew his hands from his pockets and placed the package on the digital scale. It read 4.99 kilos.

Another man stepped behind Bird, clean-cut, not looking like a cartel man. The man whispered in Bird's ear. His lips pursed, and he nodded once before waving at the driver sitting in the semi-tractor cab. The diesel engine cranked on.

Crosby touched the powder with his index fingertip and pretended to taste it with his fourth finger. "Good enough."

"Change of plans." Bird raised the pistol.

Emilio forced Crosby's head down on the tabletop and took the pistol from his jacket.

"What the hell are you doing?"

Bird shoved the suppressor against Crosby's scalp. "Someone just told me who you are."

"I'm a guy buying drugs."

Crosby jammed his heel on Bird's shoe, and he stumbled backward. Reaching for the knife inside his boot, he stabbed Emilio in his side before spinning around to stab Bird, but Arturo gun-butted him in the back of the neck. Crosby's legs wavered and then a hand pushed his head down on the table again.

Bird shoved the gun barrel against Crosby's head. "You're a fucking narc, and the DEA killed my brother."

Crosby flinched when the gun barrel hit the back of his head. "Give it up, asshole. Killing a DEA agent will bring the federal government down on your entire operation."

"I'm not going to kill you here. I've done these enough times to know where a bullet will kill you instantly, behind the ear and through the eye. The top half of the brain is where you will suffer the most hours of misery before death. That is what I will give you, a slow, miserable death, and let you think about my brother." Bird nodded toward the truck driver.

The engine revved high, and Bird pulled the trigger.

Chapter 8

Crosby vomited. Blood poured from the hole in his scalp. His head spun a thousand miles an hour while lying inside the back of a minivan. Tires ground against gravel—Spanish words mushed together; creek, blood, Narco.

"This is not good, man." Emilio knelt over Crosby. "He's a Fed." He pushed his hand against the knife wound on his side. "I need a doctor."

"Shut up." Arturo turned the wheel onto a narrow road. "I know what he is."

"The Feds will come after us when they find him." Emilio winced when the vehicle bounced. "We have to get back to Mexico."

"We are not going anywhere until Bird tells us."

"No. I don't want to spend the next thirty years in jail."

Arturo raised his firearm. "You see this? You need to worry about today, not the next thirty years. Today."

"I'm going to ask Bird if I can go home. Come with me. I will buy a bottle of Patron, and we can dance with the whores every night."

Just ahead, Arturo saw the arched brick bridge built over a century ago. He said, "We stop at the middle and wrap the chain around his legs, then drop him into the water."

"We do this and go back home to Mexico tonight?" Emilio asked.

Arturo saw headlights approaching a few hundred yards away from the bridge. "Stay down. I see a car."

"Where?" Emilio stuck his head up over the passenger seat. "What are we going to do? We can't have witnesses." When Emilio slapped the back of the seat, pain shot through his side. "Turn around and get out of here."

"No," Arturo said. "Got a better idea." He trailed off the road toward the waterline. The oncoming car's engine sounded louder, and tires bounced over the uneven concrete on the bridge. "Here. We dump him here." Another vehicle tracked over the bridge.

While lying on the floor of the van, Crosby's mind wandered to smiling parents, childhood dog, and Marla lying on top of him in bed. His stomach spasmed, and he tried not to vomit again. His head pounded in pain with each heartbeat. He held his breath when the vehicle stopped.

Arturo motioned to Emilio. "Stay here. Let me make sure no one is around." He rushed around to the other side before banging on the side door. "Clear."

Crosby winced when the side door banged open. Hands grabbed his jeans and yanked him out by his ankles, bouncing him on the ground.

"Come on," Arturo said. "Drag his ass over to the water."

"I can't do much. My side hurts too much. I'm telling you, none of this is good."

"You're worthless." Arturo grabbed Crosby under the armpits. "Wrap your good arm around his legs, and let's go."

Emilio knelt and wrapped one arm around the ankles. He groaned when he lifted the legs. "We were supposed to drop him off the bridge and sink in twenty feet of water. Someone will find him over here."

"Shut up. I got this figured out." Arturo looked at the shoreline where tall grass grew. "Over there."

"How is that going to help? Anyone can see him from the bridge. I have to get back to Mexico before someone finds this guy."

The two struggled with the almost dead man.

"This guy is getting heavy," Emilio said. "I have to drop him."

Crosby rolled through tall weeds before stopping with his legs and feet in water. Frogs croaked in the black night. Mosquitoes attacked. His head throbbed—hammer-size pain.

"Let's go." Emilio rushed toward the vehicle.

Arturo said, "Get in the back and wipe up that blood as best as you can."

Emilio leaned inside and looked for a towel. He turned back toward Arturo. "There's a lot of blood and nothing to clean with."

Arturo aimed his pistol at Emilio. "That's okay. There's going to be more." He fired twice, hitting Emilio in the chest. Arturo slid the door closed and drove away.

With every bit of effort, Crosby felt for his burner phone and slipped two fingers inside his jeans pocket. It clacked against rocks. His hand swept the ground in the darkness. *Where?* He touched hard plastic, and the display lit up the early morning blackness. Muscles felt like warm gelatin; arms too heavy to move, legs with no sensation. The coppery taste on his lips wouldn't leave. Trying to keep his thoughts clear, he brushed over the number pads on the phone. *Count two right, two down.* He pushed a number and the phone beeped. His fingers were too weak to push again. The universe swirled around him when he turned his head toward the phone. Fuzzy, out of focus. *Is it a 6 or a 9 on the screen? Is the phone upside down, the screen above the numbers or below? Screen above, right?* His thumb felt the pads again. *Top left for 1. Push it, do it.* He rolled his hand toward the phone and forced his thumb down. The phone beeped again. *Rest before...pushing again.* Blood filled his ear canals. He never heard a third beep.

Chapter 9

At eight o'clock in the morning, Marla sat in the empty employees' break room wearing a dark blue jacket and pants with a white blouse. With legs tightly crossed, her foot wiggled a thousand times a minute. Crosby didn't come home last night or call, and she wondered why. She ceaselessly rubbed her badge hanging from a lanyard before flipping it over and reading it upside down. She thought of the little boy smiling and the plane burning. It hadn't been one full day, and she was at the principal's office. In high school, it took a month for her to be sent to detention.

She finished her third cup of coffee and pitched the flimsy paper cup into the wastebasket. Her muscles quivered from caffeine overload and lack of sleep.

Attached to a wall, closed caption words on a television rolled in a line at the bottom of the screen:

DEA SAVES GIRLS FROM SEX TRADE

Local broadcasters spoke of last night's raid. Deputy Jeffrey Keene's picture of her and the rescued girls in the trailer popped on the screen. They praised the new DEA agent. A thousand positives and red hearts filled Instagram, Facebook, Twitter, and graffiti on the lavatory walls.

Quinton stuck his head inside the break room and glanced at the television. "He's ready for you."

Ready to walk the plank. Marla nodded and stood before snapping her jacket lapels tight. "Right." She lumbered into the office with Quinton behind her. As expected, everything sat perfectly in its place, no paper turned sideways, no coffee rings on the desk. Even a spotless wastebasket sat empty.

Borland sat at his desk. "Shut the door, Wales." While never looking up, he closed a manila folder. "Sit, Adams."

"Yes, sir." She eased onto the stiff metal and cloth chair across from his desk. Her hands rested on her knees, and toes curled inside her shoes. Quinton stood near the door.

"We have a problem, Adams."

"I have one as well, sir."

Borland raised his eyes toward her. "What?"

"My husband didn't come home last night. Do you know where he is? Why did he not call me?"

"He's undercover," Borland said. "By definition, he's out there, somewhere, and I don't know exactly where."

"Then I am requesting for a report where he is. Something is not right. He would have called me."

Borland knocked the manila folder against his desk. "I don't have the info about where each undercover agent is. Not my position."

"Then who does...sir?"

"SAC Davies."

"May I contact him?"

"You want to jump command over me?"

"No, sir. You said you did not have the intel I am asking for, so I want to ask who does."

Borland glanced at Quinton for a few seconds and then back to her. "Allowed. Now, may I explain why you are sitting in my office?"

"Sorry, sir. Yes, of course."

"The raid was unsuccessful."

"Sir, we recovered cash, drugs, and all those girls."

"But Bird didn't show at either house, so he is still out there somewhere." Borland passed a picture to her of one of the two men she shot. "Did you know this was Bird's brother?"

"No, sir."

"The word on the street is you killed him in cold blood." He turned his laptop around showing the same closed caption words from the breakroom television. "Hell, the world knows what you did. It's all over the news." He tapped his knuckles once on his desk. "And you can be sure Bird is coming for you."

"I did what had to be done. I didn't know who the guy was."

"Torres-Hernandez is now listed as the number one priority in the district. He'll be on a rampage. We've seen what he does to traitors, so don't expect anyone to flip on him. Innocent bystanders are at risk until he's caught, or you're dead."

"Is that all, sir?"

He glanced at the television again, then back to her. "Do you know Deputy Keene?"

"Yes, sir. Short time."

"Is that why he took the picture and plastered it for the world to see?"

She shifted her butt in the chair. "Unsure, sir."

"I don't like showboating."

"Neither do I. Not my intention."

"Have a strange way of not doing just that." His finger drummed the desktop. "I hope this will have a positive edge to it. Someone out there knows where Bird is, and a picture of you and those girls will tug at someone's heartstrings. Possibly get a lead, but don't count on it."

"Is that all, sir?"

"No. I read your first report as a DEA agent, and it's incomplete. That bothers me. Was that standard operating procedure in Hildebrandt? Filing incomplete reports?"

Borland picked up the manila folder and pitched it into the 'File Out' basket.

She cleared her throat. "Is this where you tell me I'm strapped to a desk? Am I out? Am I being released?"

"Is that what you think? If I released every agent who screwed up, I'd have no one here, including myself. Just don't go rogue on me."

"No, sir. I'm here to be part of the team."

Borland stood and walked around the desk. "What about your incomplete report?"

She cleared her throat before staring ahead. "I don't believe I left anything out, sir."

"As your trainer, agent Wales read your report and said you did."

Marla glared at Quinton, then turned back toward her boss. "What part, sir?"

Borland folded his arms and leaned against his desk. "Inside the house, the two perps had their AKs in hand, and you shot both."

"My report stated I fired two times."

Borland unfolded his arms. "The two men had automatic weapons. You didn't say you drew your weapon and fired twice before they had a chance to pull their triggers?" He laid his hand on her shoulder. "Are you that fast?"

Her breaths shortened. Three and a half months ago, at the Briscoe Barn in Hildebrandt, a perp stood less than ten feet away and challenged her. He died in less than a second.

"Yes, sir. I am."

◆

Eleven o'clock at night, inside the lobby of the ICE detention center, Marla checked for messages and missed calls, but nothing from Crosby. She was not liking the life of a deep undercover agent's wife.

Marla and Deputy Jeffrey Keene entered the interrogation room and sat on brown metal folding chairs. She placed a small spiral notebook and two drinking cups on the small square table.

"I'm going to just listen," Jeffrey said. "It's you she has the connection with. Not me."

The door opened, and the girl she saved in the trailer came through the doorway wearing the same clothes, trailed around the table, and sat on the chair. She rubbed the sleep from her eyes as Marla smiled and pushed one of two small cups with a lid and straw toward her. They both spoke in Spanish.

"It's a Coke with ice," Marla said.

The girl scooted up in the chair, took the cup, and sipped through the straw. She smiled back.

Marla opened the notebook. "What is your name?"

"Kata."

She wrote the name down. "I have some questions I would like to ask you."

Kata wiggled in her chair before taking another small sip. "Okay."

"Were you in Mexico or Texas when transferred to the trailer?

"I do not know the place, but I think after we crossed the border."

"How did you do that?"

"A tunnel."

"How many girls were with you?"

Kata raised her shoulders. "Twenty? Twenty-five?"

"How old are you?"

"I am not sure. Sixteen, I think."

You look thirteen or fourteen. Marla wrote more in her notebook. "Could you find this tunnel if we took you back to the border?"

"I don't think so. When we climbed out, we were inside a building where men worked on trucks. I never saw the outside."

"And that is where you entered the trailer?"

"They put us in the back of cattle trucks."

Marla wrote more. "Kata, do you mean a livestock trailer?"

She shook her head. "I do not know what that is."

"A big truck carrying many cattle in a long trailer."

Kata nodded and sucked more coke from the straw. "Yes. Stuffed inside a small area on the top floor."

Jeffrey hadn't planned on saying anything, but he remembered two empty livestock trailers driving south out of town late yesterday evening—an odd time. Too late in the day for pickup or delivery, but he ignored it. "You mean the doghouse?"

Kata wrinkled her eyebrows. "We did not have a dog."

Marla drew a picture in her notebook and spun it around. "Ranchers call the upper level back corner of the trailer the doghouse. That is where they put the calves."

"Yes. They locked us inside and told us to be very quiet, or they would kill our families back home."

"No cattle?" Marla asked.

"After they shoved us in the trailer," she half smiled, "the doghouse, as you say, they drove to a place with many cattle and put the animals inside the trailers. That is when it smelled very bad."

"How long did you ride in the trailer before stopping at the cattle pens?"

She shrugged her shoulders. "I fell asleep."

"When did you change to the trailer where I found you?"

She thought while sipping her coke. "An hour or two."

Marla wrote the time. "Tell me what happened."

"They forced us out of the doghouse and into a smaller trailer. The men were very mean and pushed us very hard. It was dark inside when they closed the doors."

"I'm sorry for that, Kata. Could you describe the place?"

"A blue metal building with many cows. I saw a white fence and green grass."

"This has been immensely helpful. Is there anything else you saw where you changed vehicles?"

"A man drove a blue car by us."

"What kind?"

"I don't know names of cars, but when he got out, he was a nice looking man. He went into a small building close to us."

"I want to make sure I understand everything." Marla read her notes. "You went from Mexico to Texas through a tunnel. You came out into a closed building with three cattle trailers inside, and the girls forced into the doghouses. The trucks drove to a cattle pen, and men loaded cattle inside the trailer. The trucks moved on and eventually stopped at a blue building with green grass, cows, and a white fence.

That is where you and the girls were transferred to a different trailer. Is that about the gist of it?"

"Yes."

"I have one more question for you, Kata. You have seen Torres-Hernandez, right?"

Her expression turned sour. Both hands wrapped around her cup while she sucked two gulps from the straw, then nodded.

Marla pushed her coke to the side and gently placed the page with the four sketches from the DEA conference room on the table. "Does he look like one of these men?"

Kata touched the drawing of the man with curly hair and a black goatee before pulling her hand back to her cup.

"Has he ever looked like any of the other drawings?"

She hunched forward and looked down at the table, keeping the straw between her lips.

Marla asked, "Did you know the other men who took you from your home in Mexico?"

Kata kept the straw between her lips and glanced around the room before nodding.

"The people here say you have no family." Marla turned her notebook around. "What happened to them?"

She let go of the straw and jabbed her finger at the sketch. "I saw him kill my Poppa and Mamma and my brothers."

Marla rubbed her forehead in disgust. "If immigration sends you back, where will you live?"

Ice swished inside when Kata shook the cup. She eyed Marla's before looking back at her. "Nowhere. I die there."

Marla saved the girl's life, and now Kata could help with the investigation. Before Marla went to the detention center, she visited the courthouse, and an Immigration Judge granted a special request.

Marla slid her cup toward the girl. "I can take you away from this place. If you would be a material witness, you could stay with me at my house."

Kata latched onto the second cup. "Please. I go with you. I cause no problems. Please. Please."

✦

Marla's truck crossed over the cattle guard as she turned onto her property late at night. The girl's eyes stared at the largest house she had ever seen. She placed her hands on the side window, wanting to touch the barn and chicken coop.

"You have chickens? And eggs?"

"Yes." Marla smiled at the simplicity. "Would you like to eat some eggs? Fried or scrambled?"

"Oh, yes, please."

Marla stopped near the garage and cut the engine off. She reached across the console and touched the child's arm. "Are you ready?"

"This is where I stay? It is wonderful." She opened her door, raced around the truck, jumped onto the porch, and landed at the front door.

Marla caught up to Kata and unlocked the door.

When they entered the house and Marla turned on the lights, Kata dropped to her knees and cried.

Marla bent down near the girl. "What's wrong?"

Kata wiped her eyes. "It is so beautiful. Please let me stay forever."

Marla helped her to her feet. The clock on the wall read 1:04 a.m. "Let's have an early morning breakfast."

She'd been in San Antonio a day and a half and still had not heard from her husband. *Where are you, Crosby Adams? Please call me.*

Marla forked the sizzling bacon from the large cast iron skillet and placed them on paper towels.

"I love the smell of bacon," Kata said. "It is the best."

It's Crosby's favorite, too. "I'm so glad you like it."

Marla cracked open four eggs, and the grease popped around them in the pan.

"I love the smell of fried eggs. They are my favorite, too."

Marla laughed. "You are too funny." She placed two eggs and several slices of bacon on each plate and carried them to the dinner table. Before she could stop herself, she put them where she and Crosby ate every morning. "Tell you what, let's eat at the counter."

Marla decided not to drill the girl about her life and the last twenty-four hours. Instead, she asked about school, boys, and after-school activities—big mistake. The girl's family had been killed, all her girlfriends had been raped or kidnapped, and the boys became mean men.

After eating, Marla picked up the plates from the table and placed them in the sink. She gazed out the window into the night before checking her phone for any messages. *Where are you, Crosby?*

Kata followed her. "I can clean for you. I wash all your dishes and glasses."

Marla chuckled. "I keep a clean kitchen. These are the only things dirty." She squirted soap into the sink and turned the water on. "You must be exhausted. Lay on the couch, and I will be there in a few minutes." Marla washed a plate and laid it on the drying towel.

"I dry them for you. Okay?"

Marla chuckled. "Okay. I wash, you dry."

Marla handed the girl another plate. "One rule here. You stay inside, out of sight." She pointed toward the living room. "I will show you how to turn on the television and radio. South Texas has many Spanish stations."

"I help you clean your house."

Marla scoffed. "My house is clean, Kata. You relax, and we will talk later about what happened to you."

"Do you have a phone?"

"No calling." She wiped her hand on a towel and held up her cell phone. "I keep this with me at all times."

"I could play games on an iPad. Do you have one of those?"

"Let's keep it simple, Kata. You stay here with no contacts outside. If not, then you go back to the detention center. Understand?"

"Yes, of course. Thank you for letting me come here."

Marla disappeared into her bedroom and then returned with her laptop and tablet. "I'll keep these in the truck."

She felt something off-kilter. *Can't stay at the house and do nothing.*

"You understand? Inside the entire time."

"Yes. I promise."

Marla returned from the truck, walked into her bedroom, and called the DEA office at two o'clock in the morning. "This is Special Agent Marla Adams. Who is the supervisor of the undercover agents?"

"I'm sorry, but that information may not be discussed over an open communication line. If you come to the office after eight o'clock, ASAC Borland could help you."

She shook her head. *I'm presently not on his 'I'll do you a favor list.* "Eight, you say? That's great. Thank you." She hung up, hit the Find My Phone app, and typed in Crosby's number. It said BLOCKED. She slipped her phone back into her pocket.

Chapter 10

S uzie Moore had been typing on her laptop for over an hour. What started as a fictional short story turned into a tell-all nonfiction novel. After sending what she had to her agent, she poured more hot sauce on the last bite of her taco salad. She read the quick reply, *Dealing with a Mexican cartel, sex trafficking, drugs, and money laundering is always headline news but very dangerous.* Suzie raised her eyebrows for a second before closing her laptop.

She glanced at the wall clock; well past midnight, and Quinton would come over in twenty minutes, not the least bit interested in dinner. She poured the last of the wine into her glass and headed for her closet. After picking out earrings and lingerie, she stood facing the mirror, fluffed her new hair coloring, blonde with black tips, and held a very short dress in front of her, which could easily slide off her shoulders. Two fingers hooked strappy shoes on her feet. After dressing, she checked her makeup and applied a lipstick color that screamed, look at my mouth and make a wish.

A knock on the door made her smile.

When she opened the door, Quinton's eyes bulged wide. "Wow. Look at you." While holding a bottle of wine, he reached in for a hug, and she complied. He ran his hand down her back to her buttocks. "Love the hair."

She playfully pushed him back, straightening the back of her short dress while moving around the couch. She sat and crossed her legs. Her hand patted the cushion by her side. "Come in and sit beside me."

Quinton placed the bottle on the coffee table and sat down. He gently laid his hand on her knee and slid it up her thigh. She put her hand on top of his, stopping his movement.

"I'm not really hungry. Are you?" Suzie smiled.

"Hmm. No, not too much. What do you have in mind?"

"Good." Suzie uncrossed her legs. "I have a nice bottle of champagne in the fridge. Would you open it?"

When Quinton stood to go to the kitchen, Suzie tugged at his coat tail. "Take your jacket off and stay awhile."

It slid passed his arms. "Absolutely." After pitching it onto the arm of the couch, he eyed her laptop on the breakfast table.

"I have a block of Havarti in the cheese drawer. How about a slice for both of us?"

Quinton turned into the kitchen. "Sure, I can do that."

When the refrigerator door opened, Suzie snatched his phone from his suit jacket and downloaded an app to record his conversations and calls. It startled her when the champagne cork popped.

Moments later, Quinton came around the kitchen corner, balancing two glasses, the bottle, and two cheese slices in his hands. He stopped and gawked at Suzie's dress lying on the edge of the couch.

She wore black lingerie and stockings and wiggled her toes at him. "I decided not to wear that dress after all."

"I completely agree." Quinton placed everything on the table, then wrapped his arms around her.

She smiled. "Not yet."

Surprised at her talent for making him want to wait and take it slow, he sipped champagne before leading her to the bedroom.

The morning light pierced the window. He squinted while reaching for Suzie, but his hand felt an empty sheet. Metal pans clattered in the kitchen, so he spun his legs out of bed, stood naked, and closed the bathroom door behind him.

After showering, he slipped on his clothes, grabbed his jacket, and exited the bedroom to the kitchen. The champagne bottle and glasses had been removed from the coffee table.

"Great night," he said.

Suzie wore a below-the-knee bright green dress. The black tips of her blond hair skimmed across her shoulders. "I loved it." She poured two cups of coffee. "I need to get to work soon. A lot is going on."

Quinton sat at the breakfast table and swept his hand over her laptop. He remembered it being in a different position last night. Did she use it this morning? "I might need your help," he said. "Our new agent has me concerned."

"What do you mean?" Suzie placed a cup near him with steam stretching into the air. She sat and sipped her coffee. "How can I help?" Lifting the laptop off the table, she set it on the floor against her chair leg.

"Marla Adams' personnel file. It would help if I had a chance to review it."

"Quinton? I shouldn't do that. I could be fired for handing over files to employees."

He moved his coffee to the side and stroked her fingers holding her cup handle. "It would be easy. Have it on your desk, and when Borland is out of the office, I can look at it for a few minutes, and then I'm gone. The folder would never leave your desk."

She placed her palm on his cheek. "I could, but it would cost you."

Quinton raised his eyebrows, dug into his trousers pocket, and pulled out a money clip. "How much?"

She brushed her hair from her face. "I get cold at night when I'm alone." She nodded toward the bedroom. "A little more often?"

"I could definitely do that."

A few minutes later, Quinton climbed into his black Tahoe and closed the door. He immediately squirted a glob of hand sanitizer in his hand and rubbed vigorously. "Not sure who's playing who in that house."

◆

Ninety miles from San Antonio, early morning motocross riders ripped over narrow trails through hills and valleys near the Frio River. A dozen high-pitched engines whined in the air. Two kids crossed halfway over an arch bridge. One stopped when he saw something at the water's edge.

"Is that a body over there?" He raced his bike to the water and jumped off.

"Hey, man," the other one said. "Don't go there. Call the police."

The first rider touched a loose shoe sticking out of the grass. He inched closer and noticed a body on its side with water rolling over legs.

◆

Red and blue lights bounced off the Frio River. Birds chirped on tree branches. Turtles sat on rocks with necks extended. A bright sun hovering in a cloudless sky had already raised the temperature by fourteen degrees after cresting the horizon.

An ambulance sat with open back doors, and five police cruisers surrounded the area. Every radio turned to the max, squawking relentlessly into the morning air. Mosquitoes swarmed the EMTs as they pushed a gurney through tall grass.

Sunshine beat on Crosby's face. He wanted to pull the oxygen mask off but couldn't move. His head throbbed from the uncomfortably tight cotton gauze. Electric shocks surged through every pore of his body with each bounce across the gravel until all movement halted. He heard a click below him and metal scraping across metal as the gurney slid into the ambulance. His mind slipped into a black cloud.

Bexar County Community Hospital Emergency Department entrance buzzed with a half dozen police officers and medical personnel ready. The ambulance back doors swung open, and the EMT yelled as he jumped out, "Mid-twenties male with a bullet wound to the head, unconscious, bleeding stopped. BP sixty over nada, heart rate thready, respirations sixteen. Has an IV in the arm."

Ambulance attendees rushed the gurney down the hall with two nurses leading and yelling at anyone in front of them to move. They swung a curtain open. ER techs grabbed each corner of the sheet under Crosby. "Ready, go." They swung him over to the hospital bed. Seconds later, when the nurses connected clamps, wires, and a BP cuff to him, a monitor screen came alive with multiple colored lines and beeps declaring the patient's vital signs. Another nurse pushed an IV pole near the bed with two bags of clear fluid hanging from spiraled hooks.

A doctor wearing gloves unraveled the cotton gauze off Crosby's head. He pushed the bloody hair out of the way and felt the hole in the scalp. He called out to the paramedics from the ambulance, "Any exit wound?"

"Didn't find one, Doc. Just a single entry shot to the head."

The doctor turned toward the nurses. "Roll him over and check his backside. Do we have a name yet?"

A man in a dark suit stopped at the foot of the bed and said, "This man is DEA Special Agent Crosby Adams. Take extra care of him."

The doctor glanced over the facial overgrowth, long black hair full of coagulated blood, and dirty clothes. "Thought this was a homeless guy, robbed or something."

"No, an undercover agent."

"And you are?" the doctor asked.

"I'm his boss, DEA Special Agent in Charge Roger Davies."

A nurse called out, "No other wounds."

The doctor focused back on the monitor. The BP dropped, and the pulse increased. "I need type and cross O negative and use a rapid infuser. Get that central line ready. Large bore IVs in each arm. Get radiology here, ASAP." He checked for breath sounds on both sides of the chest. "Where the hell is the neurosurgery resident?"

The cardiac monitor clanged when the heart rhythm jumped from a regular rate to a jagged line.

"V-fib," a nurse declared. Without being told, she opened a packet of defibrillator pads and stuck them to the patient's chest.

The doctor grabbed the paddles, placed them on top of the pads, and yelled, "Clear!" He pushed the button on each paddle and a jolt of electricity shot through Crosby's chest.

The erratic line didn't change on the monitor.

"Everyone clear!" The doctor pushed the buttons again. Electricity surged.

A rhythmic beep came from the monitor. A nurse called out, "Heart rate 112."

Another nurse pumped up the BP cuff. "86 over 44."

The surgical resident swung the curtain away and adjusted his glasses. "What do you have?"

The emergency doctor smiled while peeling his gloves off and dropping them in a red hazard container. "Hey, buddy." He jokingly backslapped the resident. "Glad you could join the party." The doctor pointed at the bloody hole in the skull. "There's a bullet hiding inside. Think you can pull a rabbit out of a hat?"

Chapter 11

The odor of fragranced hand sanitizer, alcohol, and bleach lingered in the hallways of the hospital. Sunlight sparkled through plate glass windows in the surgical waiting room. Outside, a world of people had their own worries.

Marla clasped her hands in her lap while sitting in a chrome and cloth chair a thousand others had sat in before. With one leg crossed over the other, her ankle wiggled back and forth a hundred times a minute. Special Agent in Charge Roger Davies sat next to her. They had talked about San Antonio, state politics, weather, his kids, and anything else except Crosby. They waited for the surgical double doors to open and the doctor to present himself like the Messiah to tell them the news, good or bad.

She stood up and patted her hips twice. "I wonder what's in the machines."

Roger dug into the front pocket of his trousers and found a ten-dollar bill. "I could use a cup of coffee. On me." They crossed to the other side of the waiting room and stared at the packaged food inside the vending machines. "Wouldn't suggest the sandwiches. Not sure how many days they've been there. On the other hand, I don't think you can hurt a Milky Way or Three Musketeers."

Marla nodded. "Musketeer."

"Agree."

Two candy bars plopped into the holding spot. He dug them out and handed one to her. "Coffee?" Davies asked.

The machine was the type where the cup dropped down and coffee poured for a few seconds. Marla's lips broke into a smile, then quickly returned to nothing. "Bet the coffee has been sitting longer than the sandwiches." She pushed the coffee with cream button. "I'll have to tell Crosby about this machine." The cup clattered in place, and a burnt-smelling liquid poured inside with a little splattering around it. "He would be happy if it was three or four days old." Her finger wiped across her lips. "Sorry. Stupid of me to say that."

"No, no. You're right," Davies said. "He liked—likes it strong."

The hydraulic arms swished the double doors open. A man wearing a green surgical cap with images of Texas bluebonnets on each side, blue scrubs, and a long white coat strode directly to Marla. He didn't smile but held out his hand. She dropped the full cup of coffee and candy bar in the wastebasket and grasped the surgeon's hand. His grip was firm when they shook.

"Mrs. Adams, I'm Dr. Wilson, your husband's neurosurgeon." He released Marla's hand. "He's alive, but there is extensive damage to the brain."

Her lips tightened as she stared at the ceiling, then asked, "May I see him?"

"They are transferring him to recovery, changing dressings, IVs, starting antibiotics; all that stuff we do. Give us thirty minutes, and I will let you back there." He gently put both his hands on her shoulders. "Mrs. Adams, the bullet entered his temple." He pointed near his ear. "His face is swollen, and we shaved his head. He doesn't look like the man you saw yesterday."

She swiped the hair back from her face. "I didn't see him yesterday."

Davies asked, "Is he awake?"

"No. Not sure when...if ever."

Marla clamped onto Davies' forearm. "How long will he stay in the ICU?"

"Let's get him stable first." Wilson spun around and waved at them as he reentered the surgery unit. "Thirty minutes. You can see him then."

Marla followed the hospital bed, her hands filled with bags of Crosby's clothes. The rubber wheels wiggled, each demanding to go a different direction. The long, narrow hallway had patients in their own disrepair, separated by glassed-in rooms and large square windows soaking in sunlight. A man lay flat on his back, a young woman sat sideways on the edge of the bed with bandages on her abdomen, and an elderly man hunched over in a chair with Jell-O cups sitting beside him on a food tray. She stopped looking with too many to count beeps, bells, and dings from the rooms. Crosby's bed slowed and turned into a room. After the nurses shifted him from one bed to another, they tucked the sheet around him like they were putting a five-year-old to bed.

A nurse smiled at Marla as she picked up the remote control attached to the bed. "Bed controls, television channels, and volume are here, and the red button is for an emergency. Only for an emergency, not for nurse calls. We run in here, guns blazing...sorry, insensitive of me. We come in here in a hurry if you push that button."

Marla put his clothes in the corner of the room before looking back at the nurse. "May I stay here tonight?"

The nurse looked behind her, then back at Marla. "I'm pulling a double tonight and taking care of your husband. We're not supposed to let the family stay after nine o'clock, but my brother is a police officer in Dallas, and I know what you guys put up with. You can if you promise to be quiet," she smiled again, "I'll make sure you have a dinner tray."

When the nurse left, Marla stared at her husband lying flat in the hospital bed. Sharp-witted, energetic Crosby Adams had left her. Only the body survived. His swollen face blanched with thick white gauze wrapped around his scalp. Shirtless, a white sheet covered him to mid-stomach with wires stuck to his chest, leading to a large monitor above his head. Did he have clothes under the sheet? Did they give him a little respect? Attached to the head of the bed, an IV bag hung from a pole with a transparent plastic tube snaking to the skin near his neck. Her eyes shifted to a bag half full of urine clipped to the bedside. Who put their hands where no one should be—handling him in ways he would never consent to if conscious, except he wasn't conscious, and the doctor said he may never be conscious again.

She took a step closer, wanting to lift the sheet and climb in next to him, hold him, have him hold her like they did the night before she left for Quantico. Her lips touched the back of his hand. "I'm sorry."

People make decisions in their life, work, and family. For a second, she wondered if their decision to join the DEA was wrong. Yes, of course it was. She should have made him stay in Hildebrandt. She should have kept him close, closer, but she didn't. Instead, she left him for three months to do what? Find another job? Another job to do what?

Marla kissed his hand. "I promise I'll do anything to make you better. We will figure this out." She squeezed tighter. "Crosby, please hear me. I promise."

Hours later, after the sun gave way to the night, distant building windows lit up like fireflies. White headlights and red taillights wormed the roads. While finishing lukewarm hospital food in the only chair in the room, Marla researched head wounds on her phone. There were too many words she couldn't pronounce, a foreign language only medical people understood.

A doctor's name, Reginald McCollum, kept popping up for gunshot wounds to the head, Traumatic Brain Injuries. With his explanations closer to layman's English, she understood a little more about inflammation, tissue damage, bleeding, and swelling.

He mixed stem cells with an unnamed metal and his own proprietary protein solution given daily, whereas other research centers injected once and waited. He declared ninety percent brain regeneration within a week, while other research clinics asserted success with any regrowth over months, if at all.

British broadcasters named him Dr. Stem Cell Hell after performing fifty procedures in England. Thirty-nine patients died days later from excessive brain growth, four never woke from their coma, and five died months later from multiple organ failure. Dr. McCollum declared a complete success after two men recovered, smiling and fully functional like nothing ever happened. His social media pages touted his life-saving procedures while denouncing a mesh of slander from the traditional medical community and their repression of his experiments.

After typing his name in a search tab, Marla found the British General Medical Council had struck his registration, leaving him no license to practice medicine in England, and moved to Baton Rouge, Louisiana.

◆

At four o'clock in the morning, Reginald McCollum sat alone at a small round dining table in his third story apartment two blocks from the Mississippi River. A water-stained mattress lay on the wooden floor. Several published articles, with him as the principal investigator, laid on the edge of the kitchen table; Stem Cell Manipulation Within Brain Tissue, Injection of Platelet Rich Plasma Into Peripheral and Central Nerve Tissue, and Primary Inoculation of Double Stranded RNA Into Acute Cerebral Injuries, and his most recent and promising one, Addition of Proteins, Metals, and Ultraviolet Light as Catalysts to Stem Cell Proliferation.

He snorted a line of cocaine before emptying the last of the Beefeater Gin into a glass. Outside the dust-speckled window, a slow train rumbled a block away. The front door, desperately needing a fresh coat of paint, shook when the horn blared long enough to wake the dead.

He adjusted his heavy, light brown-tinted glasses with thick lenses on the bridge of his nose and reread the first sentence of a letter from the Louisiana State Board of Medical Examiners. *We are sorry to inform you that your application for a medical license has been rejected.* After downing the rest of the gin in one gulp, he gently folded the letter, stuffed it back inside the envelope, and tapped it on the table twice, hoping magically it would change to acceptance tomorrow.

The alarm clock on the kitchen countertop rang. It had been three hours since the last injection. Dr. McCollum had repeated this so many times over the previous two years that he could do this in his sleep: open the refrigerator door, remove two glass test tubes, each holding one milliliter of stem cells, then add two drops of a protein extract solution and one drop of a transition metal catalyst into each tube before putting them inside his specially designed tabletop centrifuge with ultraviolet light in the lid. After spinning at a low speed for three minutes, he would aspirate the solution from the test tubes and place them into separate syringes.

On a metal card table, a raccoon and an opossum, unconscious with half their brains removed, laid flat on their backs. Their legs splayed out, each with a short stainless steel tube sticking out of their skull. Cats and dogs would be better experimental animals, but he had both as pets and couldn't let himself use childhood friends. He pushed the solution into the animal brains before placing them in separate cages. After snorting another line of cocaine, he fell asleep. Three hours would come soon enough.

◆

Bright light speared through the windows of Dr. McCollum's apartment. Two women screaming at each other down the outdoor hallway woke him. Already, yesterday seemed better than today, and tomorrow could be undeniably worse. The alarm buzzed continuously with the clock showing 7:34, a half hour late for the next stem cell injection. He slammed his hand on the alarm, flung the sheet off, and put his glasses on. Trouncing to his front door, he opened it and yelled at the women two apartments down the hallway. "Shut up, you ninnies."

Inches from each other's faces, the two women stopped yelling and turned their heads toward his door. One woman had a saucepan in her hand. "You shut up!" She threw the pan toward him, clanking down the hallway, as he ducked back into his apartment and slammed the door.

"Everyone in this building is bloody crazy! I must find another flat soon." He rushed into the kitchen and snorted two lines of cocaine before flipping the gas stove knob to high and sliding the tea kettle over the burner.

Both animals lay in different positions from last night. The raccoon had chewed on its bloodied left leg, and the stench from the bottom of the opossum's cage, wet with a black mass of diarrhea, hit him.

Their eyes had frozen open and dried, with black tongues slightly protruding from their mouths, but both had moved for the first time during the night. Better than the two animals last week. He draped a worn blanket over their cages. He would dissect the animals after breakfast. *Too much protein? Too little? Catalyst too fast? Should I return to every six hours?*

The tea kettle whistled, declaring a new start for the day. He lifted the kettle and poured boiling water over his previously used tea bags from yesterday. After stirring a teaspoon of sugar into the light brown liquid, he pushed his glasses up and reread the letter. It hadn't changed.

Chapter 12

Marla trudged down the hospital hallway and entered the main cafeteria with a long, dark buffet line. The linoleum flooring had scuff marks where chairs had been pulled back thousands of times. All the square tables were empty except two. A young couple sat across from each other, and the other with a thin man with sun-damaged skin and an oversized nose wore a green baseball hat with a tractor implement company logo printed in the center. His hands clasped together, elbows resting on the table. Was he praying for his wife upstairs? The cashier sat on a stool in front of the register, ignoring everyone and everything while reading a magazine.

Marla stopped at the fountain drink counter and grabbed a large cup from the dispenser. Ice clunked into the cup. She filled it with Pepsi Zero. When she turned around, Dr. Berghoff, the Bexar County Medical Examiner, stood a few feet from her.

"Dr. Berghoff? It's nice to see a friendly face in this big hospital."

"Officer Adams, I am deeply sorry to hear about your husband."

"Thank you, and please call me Marla."

"Yes, of course, Marla."

"What are you doing here?"

"I drop off the pathology slides from yesterday's autopsies. I don't usually come into the cafeteria since they don't have my drink at the fountain. Big Red is my preferred addiction. I come in occasionally to check the selection."

They moved to a small table and pulled the chairs back, scratching the linoleum.

"I'm sure you are devastated. I can't imagine what I would do if my wife laid upstairs in the ICU."

"It's the hardest thing I've ever had to do." Marla sipped her drink. "You're on staff at this hospital?"

"Yes, the pathology department."

"Dr. Wilson, Crosby's neurosurgeon, gave him no chance of recovery. He won't say it, but I can tell he's...if I may say, just watering the flowers. Would you look at him and tell me if my husband could ever be himself again?"

"Marla, I'm a pathologist, not a surgeon. I don't have the proper training to answer that."

"Would you do me...us a favor and just see him?"

Berghoff rested his elbows on the table and clasped his hands together. "Let's go upstairs. I can make sure his pathology reports are on the chart. But I can't give you an official opinion."

Crosby lay on his back in the ICU bed. His breaths steadied, heart rate regular, eyes closed, with no extremity movement. Flowers filled the room. The odor of blooming carnations, roses, and lilies permeated the air.

"Crosby, look who I found downstairs. Our friend from the medical examiner's office, Dr. Berghoff."

The doctor opened the patient chart. His facial expressions never changed while reading the surgical, radiology, and pathology reports. After closing the chart, he gently grasped Crosby's hands, then checked reflexes. He touched the skull and the softness where Dr. Wilson had removed a three-inch diameter section of the cranium. Crosby never moved.

"Unofficially, Marla, I never said this to you, but I don't believe he will recover like you want him to."

Marla sniffed and rubbed her nose. "Thank you, Dr. Berghoff. Crosby appreciates you being here."

"I'm very sorry for everything."

They shook hands, and she watched him stroll down the hallway. Marla returned to the room and turned a vase, aiming the flowers toward Crosby. With a sad smile, she said, "If you get any more, we'll need to upgrade to the Presidential Suite."

An employee handed Marla a stack of square envelopes. She wondered how all these Get Well cards arrived so quickly. Morning sunlight prickled her eyes as she sat on the edge of his bed and opened each, reading them aloud. Some funny, some serious. The last was not a card, but a single white envelope unsealed with no return address, and CROSBY ADAMS, ICU typed in the center. She pulled back the envelope flap, unfolded the page, and read it to herself.

CONGRATULATIONS. YOU ARE STILL ALIVE. MAY YOU SUFFER FOR ETERNITY. AND TO YOUR WIFE, WE WILL MEET SOON ENOUGH. BIRD

Dr. Wilson entered the room. "Mrs. Adams, how's he doing?"

She folded the letter and stuffed it under her leg. "No change." She glanced at the monitor screen. "He's breathing well, but no movement."

Wilson nodded in agreement. "Don't expect much for a while. The massive amount of inflammation must subside before the healing process begins."

"How long will that be?"

He pursed his lips and stared directly at her. "I don't know, Mrs. Adams. Nobody knows."

Marla stood and stuffed the letter into her back pocket. "Have you ever heard of Dr. Reginald McCollum?"

Dr. Wilson crossed his arms. "He's a man who experimented with animals and humans before the British government became smart enough to ban this butcher. He preyed on people at their most troubled times."

"And he brought two men back from being near dead," Marla said.

Dr. Wilson unfolded his arms. "Look, Mrs. Adams, that may or may not be true, but what is true is he killed forty plus others. Every neurosurgeon has read his story and research papers. He's an example of a man with NO medical ethics, and you need to stop reading about this madman."

She grasped Crosby's hand. "This hospital does research, right?"

"Yes, of course we do."

"Any on stem cells and damaged brains?"

"Mrs. Adams, there is more to medical research than pouring a liquid inside a brain. It's not like fertilizing a plant and watching it grow."

Marla put her hands on her hips. "There seems to be enough manure in this place to fertilize anything."

Dr. Wilson stuck his hands in his lab coat pockets. "I'll check on Mr. Adams tomorrow."

"And I'm sure he'll be the same."

A nurse entered the room after Dr. Wilson left. "Mrs. Adams, visiting time is over."

"Oh, Jeez." Marla stormed out of the room and shoved the ICU metal door wide open.

A few hours later, when visiting hours returned, Marla stopped at the nurse's station with a paper coffee cup in her hand. "Listen, I'm sorry for my outbreak."

"Understandable. I can't imagine all the stress you have right now."

"Thanks." Marla took a sip while looking at the bank of closed caption monitors behind the nurse. "Who's in with Crosby?"

The nurse didn't look up. "Shouldn't be anyone. Rest time for the last forty-five minutes."

Marla rapped her knuckles on the counter in front of the nurse. "There's someone in the room."

The nurse turned around. "I don't recognize him."

Marla charged into the room. A man held a pillow over Crosby's face.

She yelled, "Hey! What the hell are you doing?"

The man released the pillow, flipped open a switchblade knife, and rushed toward her. She threw her hot coffee in his face. He raised his arms, and she slammed her fist into his side, then his stomach. The knife rattled on the floor. He backhanded her, knocking her down, then bent to reach for the knife, but she kicked it across the room. His hand wrapped around her collar, and she heard cotton ripping. He lifted her and spun her around. She dodged his punch and slapped a plastic cup full of water off a food tray toward him. Liquid sprayed in the air. His fist smashed into her cheek. Dazed, she collapsed to her knees. He threw the sheet from the bed over her head and pounded her face again. Double fisted, she threw an uppercut between his legs. He staggered backward while Marla flung the sheet from her head.

"Freeze. This is the police." A uniformed security officer stood with his gun aimed straight ahead.

The man grabbed Marla's wrist and twisted her around, wrapping his arm around her neck. "I'll kill her. Let me go." His arm squeezed tighter.

Marla stretched for the food tray on the table. Her fingertips inched toward it and grabbed the tray, swung it above her, and bashed it against the top of the man's head. He released his grip. She spun around, and the edge of the tray thrashed across his throat. He bounced backward on the floor, grasping his bleeding neck.

Marla dropped the tray, letting it bounce between the bed and the cabinet, as she rushed to lift the pillow off Crosby's face. He took a breath as if nothing had ever happened.

Chapter 13

Inside an executive conference room, eighteen swivel chairs surrounded a long rectangular table. Marla sat in the middle chair facing the windows of a grassy knoll with a view of a reproduction Italian fountain flowing with crystal clear water. She thought about the extravagant display of hospital money.

The door opened, and two men entered, trying to smile, looking like their mouths irritated their faces. The door automatically closed on its own.

"Hello, Mrs. Adams. I'm Mr. Dawkins, CEO of the hospital, and this is Dr. Conner, our Chief of Staff."

Marla shook each of their hands. The two sat opposite her like offensive lines on a battlefield.

Dawkins loosely clasped his hands on the table. "How may we help you?"

"You have heard about the attempted murder on my husband in your ICU?"

"Yes. We are sorry and concerned."

"Why is there no security at his door?"

"That would be a police matter. We have increased the number of hospital security officers around the facility, but they are not trained for individualized security."

"I have contacted the police department. Seems to be a bit of a circle of denial. With the attempted murderer dead, they won't send anyone else, and you are concerned, but not enough to prevent another attack."

The CEO unclasped his hands and laid them flat on the table. "I am sorry. Try calling the police again." He stood. "If there is nothing else, I will see you to the door."

Marla leaned back in her chair. "Did you receive my letter?"

Dawkins' lips tightened, and he sat back down. "Yes. We received your request to allow Dr. Reginald McCollum to see your husband. Let me emphasize that he does not have a Texas medical license. Have you spoken to him?"

"No. I have read his research and would like his opinion."

Dr. Conner leaned forward and laid his palms flat on the table. "His medical opinion? This butcher, this embarrassment to the medical field, cannot do anything without a license."

"He's still a doctor, and I would like him to look at my husband's record."

Dawkins' lips tightened for a moment. "I have spoken to our legal team, and I am sorry Mrs. Adams, but they won't allow Mr. McCollum to see your husband or his records."

Her eyebrows furrowed. "You said, mister. He's still a doctor, right?"

"Doesn't matter," Conner quickly retorted. "He can't come here."

"That's all right." Marla straightened in the chair. "I'll have the doctor come into the ICU during visiting hours."

Dawkins kept his hands on the table, but his fists tightened. "I'm sorry, but only family is allowed in the ICU, and he is not part of your family. Dr. Wilson is Mr. Adams' neurosurgeon. Have you spoken to him about this?"

"Yes."

"And what did he say?"

"It doesn't matter what he said. I'm here, not him. I want a second opinion, and you deny this."

Marla lumbered past the hospital's automatic sliding glass doors and sat on a park bench near the fountains. Through the second-floor window where she had been a few minutes ago, she watched the two men who denied her request stand and talk to each other. She wondered if they were reconsidering or laughing.

She opened the LinkedIn page for Reginald McCollum, rolled down to the contact link, and called the number.

❖

The doctor's phone rang. He rubbed his nose hard after sniffing a line of coke and then spun the phone around to find a number on the screen he didn't recognize. He touched the speaker button. "Hello."

"May I speak to Doctor Reginald McCollum?"

"This is him."

"My name is Marla Adams, and my husband has been shot in the head. He's unconscious in an ICU bed. Can you revive him?"

He rubbed the last of the white powder from the table onto his gums. "That depends. I must first examine the patient."

"He's in a hospital ICU bed, and they won't let you come in."

Everyone seems to be against me. He smiled as he poured more gin into a glass and sipped it. *Speak nicely about the mugger and get money from her.* "I see. Where is your husband?"

"Bexar County Community Medical Center, downtown San Antonio. What type of food do you like?"

"English. Fish and chips."

"Closest to that in this town is Long John Silver's. How about Mexican?" She heard a sigh before he said anything.

Is that all they have in Texas? "I prefer English food."

"We have pizza and burgers. Take your pick."

He groaned. "Fine."

"Which do you prefer?"

He changed the subject and threw out a number. "I need ten thousand for the procedure."

"Meet me tomorrow morning at Casa Verde on Culebra Road, 11:30. Enchiladas are on me."

"San Antonio is a seven hour drive."

"I can help you get your medical license."

At 11:27 the next morning, Marla watched a man, alone, enter the restaurant. It had to be him. With thick, light brown-tinted glasses, a bushy handlebar mustache, and a week-old beard, he looked like a hairy nearsighted Peter O'Toole holding a thirty year old medical bag. He twisted his slightly off-center tie, knotted loosely halfway up his wrinkled white shirt. She raised her hand in the air and smiled. Without reciprocating, he plodded toward her.

She shook his hand. It felt like a weak, wet Gummy Bear. She rubbed her hand on her pants. "I'm Marla Adams."

"Dr. Reginald McCollum. Pleased to meet you."

"Thank you for coming. Please, sit."

A waitress immediately showed up at the table when they scooted across from each other. "Hi, Marla." She placed two glasses of water on the table and asked McCollum, "What do you want to drink?"

"Gin martini," he said.

She tried to look into his eyes, but the eyeglasses were too thick to get a realistic view of his pupils. "A little early for alcohol," Marla said.

"I left Baton Rouge at four o'clock this morning. To me, it's the middle of the afternoon."

Marla nodded. "Fair enough." She took a sip of water from her glass. "I read your papers. Interesting."

He scoffed. "Probably understood very little. All my writings are quite technical."

"The people at the hospital said you're a madman. Scotland Yard wants to talk to you. Your passport is blocked from entry into most European countries. You've tried, unsuccessfully, to get a medical license in Europe and the United States. How do I know you can do what you say you can do?"

Another server placed his martini glass on the table. He didn't answer but instead sipped the drink.

She nodded toward the bag on the floor. "What's in there?"

He lifted the bag and put it beside him on the other side. "A solution I developed to stimulate stem cells at exponential speed. I can do what normally would take months for stem cell growth and repair damaged tissue in days, if not hours. I go nowhere without it."

"You mean the protein catalyst you developed? I told you I read your articles. And the centrifuge with the special invisible light? Did you bring it?"

"In the boot of my car. I brought all my equipment." He put the olives in his mouth and slid them off the toothpick. "Did you bring money?"

She slid a white envelope toward him. "Half. Five more when my husband is cured."

He opened the medical bag and dropped the envelope inside. He now had five thousand forty-seven dollars to his name. "I read the news articles about your Mr. Adams before I came. I must examine him and review the ancillary reports before I can give you a complete medical decision."

"Ancillary?"

He readjusted his glasses. "Radiology, lab, neurologic tests."

"All that's inconsequential. You took my money, and now I expect results."

The waitress returned. "Ready to order?"

Marla pushed the menu away. "I come weekly. The number one lunch special is their best dish."

"What's that?"

"Chili Relleno and a fried avocado with beans and rice on the side. You should try it."

"No." He finished the martini.

The waitress tapped the menu on the table with her pencil. "Pick something."

"I don't like Mexican food."

"You agreed to Mexican?"

"I agreed to meet you here."

"What do you want?" Marla asked.

"Roast lamb, pork pie, some curry." He pushed the empty glass to the edge of the table. "Forget it and bring me another one of these."

Marla nodded at the waitress, who looked at her for approval, then waited for her to leave. "I can get you inside the hospital, inside the room, and look at his chart. You need to be sober. I don't want any screw-ups. Ten minutes max in the ICU."

When the second martini arrived on their table, his fingers wrapped around the stem of the glass. "You mentioned a medical license."

"I have contacts at the Louisiana Medical Board." She knew no one at the Medical Board. "I can get you an interview."

"And who is that?"

"You want an interview to explain your views and why you're not a deranged doctor? You save my husband, and I'll get it."

"When do I see the patient?"

Marla looked at her watch. "ICU visiting hours start in forty minutes. You have a white coat?"

He scoffed. "Of course, not. White coats are an ego trip."

"I have one in my truck. Every doctor in that hospital wears a white coat," she nodded once, "and a massive ego on their shoulder."

Chapter 14

Marla stood outside the open ICU doors. From the stairwell, Dr. McCollum gazed through the small door window at the opposite end of the hallway. Nurses and family members buzzed in and around the rooms.

Marla entered the ICU holding a cup of water and strolled to the end of the hallway. She eased the door ajar, and Dr. McCollum kept it from closing. After returning to the ICU entrance, Marla dropped the cup and slid on the water. When she landed on her back and cried out, the staff at the nurse's station hurried to help, and McCollum quietly opened the stairwell door. With his hands stuffed in his buttoned-up white coat pockets, he strode to the empty nurse's desk and took a chart from the rack before heading down the hallway to Crosby's room.

"My back. I think I hurt my back," Marla called out.

A doctor came out of a nearby room. She stared at Dr. Conner, the Chief of Staff, the man who rejected her request for Dr. McCollum's consultation. He recognized her.

"Lay still, Mrs. Adams. Let me check you."

After her wincing and groaning each time he touched her, Dr. Conner called for a gurney to transport her to the emergency department on the first floor. Marla tugged on his white coat when he tried to stand, bringing him back down on his knee.

"Don't leave me, Doctor. My legs, they tingle, and my feet feel numb." Her grip tightened on his coat.

"Everything will be fine." He gently tried to remove her hand. She groaned again and tightened more. "Mrs. Adams, please let go of my coat."

Marla turned her head and watched him sneak out past the stairwell door. She released the coat and relaxed. "I'm better. It must have been a muscle spasm or something." Sitting up, she fluffed her hair as the elevator doors opened with two attendants pushing a gurney toward her. "I'm okay." She stood and brushed herself off. "I'll go see my family doctor. He's down the street. Thanks everyone for your help." She trekked into the elevator and pushed the lobby button.

The doctor's car sat beside Marla's truck in the parking lot. He leaned against the grille with the chart in his hand. Marla unlocked the doors, and they both climbed inside.

"I need to return that before they notice it has disappeared," Marla said.

He nodded while turning a page. A few minutes later, he closed the chart. "I won't go into the medical jargon, but he has extensive damage and will never wake up. Not, of course, without my help."

"When will you do this thing you do?"

"Today, tomorrow, sooner the better."

She drew in a breath before saying anything. "Dr. Wilson wants to keep him in the ICU for a few more days and wait for the brain swelling to go down."

"Of course, he does. He's a control freak." Dr. McCollum impersonated the neurosurgeon with wide animation of his arms and hands. "I control what happens to my patients. I am the greatest doctor in the world." He clamped his hands on his thighs. "What are they doing for him now? Nothing. He has an IV to hydrate him, like a gardener watering his lawn and a therapist bending and stretching arms and legs. They'll keep him in the most expensive room in the hospital until insurance tells them differently."

"You want me to remove him from the hospital today?" Marla asked. "What about supplies, meds, all that IV stuff? He needs nutrition. I can't stuff a hamburger down his throat. He doesn't eat, remember?"

"He won't need to eat. I will have him sitting and talking to you in three days." After writing a list on a piece of paper, he handed it to her. "I need all these things before I see him again, so get cracking." He opened the truck door.

"Where are you going?" Marla asked.

"To find decent food and a gin martini. Tomorrow, are you taking your husband to your house for recovery?"

"No, not there," Marla said.

"We need a place as large as an ICU room."

"I have a place, a thing, not as big as a hospital room, an enclosed horse trailer."

The doctor shook his head. "No. We need a clean environment. It's too bloody hot outside for that. We'd burn up."

"It's fourteen feet long with sleeping quarters in the front and air conditioning throughout. I'll pressure clean the back part tonight."

"Why not your house?"

She started the engine. "We need to hide from Bird."

"Who?"

⚜

Marla's truck bumped across the cattle guard at her home, stopped near the barn, and backed to the trailer hitch. After power washing the inside of the trailer, she heard Daisy and Blackie in the barn. The horses smelled her and whinnied.

During the fiasco, her neighbor cared for them and the chickens. Marla slipped her work gloves on, grabbed a hay bale, and entered the barn.

Daisy pranced and stuck her head out past the gate.

"Hi, girl. Miss me?"

The horse snorted and shook her head. Blackie edged to the end of his stall.

"Is Mrs. Hawthorne taking good care of you and your boyfriend? I see she left some carrots in the bucket." She grabbed one, snapped it in half, and held it near Daisy. The horse's lips wrapped around the orange veggie, and it disappeared into her mouth. Blackie did the same. Marla rubbed Daisy's forehead. "I have missed you while in Quantico. And...and now I must be gone a little longer." She pitched half a bale of hay into each of their stalls. "As soon as this is over, we'll ride every day. I promise." When she opened their gates, they pranced to the corral and trotted in circles.

Marla's phone dinged with a text message. "Well, speak of the devil."

Hi, Marla. This is Mrs. Hawthorne. Let me know if you need me to come over today to take care of the animals. Hope you are doing fine.

Marla texted back, *Thanks, Mrs. Hawthorne. Maybe for a few more days if that is all right?*

With the horses out of the stalls, she shoveled horse manure, cleaned the tools, and hammered a few loose nails back into the wood. She left the barn and noticed all the chickens gathered near the chicken wire, waiting to be fed.

"You guys miss me, too?" Marla laughed, grabbed a bucket of chicken feed, and entered the coop. After spreading their meal on the ground, she gathered the eggs in a basket. A blue jay perched on the peak of the henhouse and turned its head a dozen times, seemingly watching every move she made.

With the eggs in hand, she closed the gate behind her and stared at the house. A shiver ran through her, remembering she always showered after working the animals. Crosby would join her, but that may never happen again.

✦

Marla's truck pulled up to the Hildebrandt Pharmacy drive-through window with the trailer behind her. A woman in her late teens smiled through the glass and slid the small window open. "Hi, Marla. Oh, excuse me, Mrs. DEA Marla Adams." She chuckled. "Are you coming back to stay? Please come back. Say yes."

"Hi, Brittany. Thanks. Is Richard somewhere close?"

"Sure. He's on the phone with our new doctor, Dr. Yung. Fresh out of his residency. He looks younger than me, and I'm in high school."

"I'll pull over to the waiting area."

Brittany looked past Marla's truck at the horse trailer. "Our overhang is nine and a half feet high. Richard did that for all the farmers and ranchers. I'm pretty sure yours is low enough."

"I guess we'll find out in a second. Send him out to me, please."

"Okie Dokie. Come back real soon."

Marla stopped at the waiting area and unlocked her doors. A minute later, the pharmacist, Richard Black, opened the passenger door.

"Hi, Marla. Can I help you?"

She smiled. "Come on in."

He looked back at the pharmacy and then at her. "Are you here on official business? Am I in trouble?"

"No, no. I need a favor and hope you can help. Climb in."

After closing the door, she handed him the list of medicines and supplies. He read the front, flipped the page, and read the back. "This is a big favor. Are you performing surgery on someone? I could get in trouble with all this."

She smirked. "No, you won't. I know someone in the DEA regional office. How much for all of it?"

"I can't take money. I'd have to show who I sold this to. It will have to be listed as a loss, considered breakage, something." He patted his pant leg several times. "This is for Crosby, right? Absolutely terrible what happened."

"I need all this ASAP," Marla said.

"You sure I won't get in trouble?"

"I'm sure. One more thing."

Richard tilted his head. "Anything. What?"

"You still have that hospital bed in your storage unit?"

Chapter 15

A mid-morning sun rose steadily in the cloudless sky, hurling heat waves in every direction. High humidity stifled human life while encouraging plants to grow.

Marla stopped her truck with the trailer attached beside the doctor's vehicle in the hospital parking lot with his hood raised and steam rolling out of the radiator.

She noticed his unshaven face, looking more like an 'I don't give a crap how I look' fashion statement. After lowering her window, she asked, "Problems?"

He slammed the hood down. "It needs a new something," he kicked a wheel, "and tires, petrol, and more bits and bobs." He opened the trunk and piled everything into Marla's truck.

"Are you leaving your car here?"

"Yes. I'll buy a better one with the money you gave me."

Marla thought five thousand wouldn't buy much of a vehicle. "We're not coming back here. Are you sure you have everything you need?"

She pulled the truck and trailer to the ambulance entrance at the emergency department and stopped. The sliding glass doors opened, and they entered.

A hospital security officer recognized Marla as the DEA agent rescuing the Mexican girls on the news and waved at her. She waved back as they marched down the hallway to the hospital CEO's office. Marla knocked on the door and entered, with Dr. McCollum following. They passed the desk with a woman drinking coffee and eating a donut. The title on her desk proudly stated ADMIN. ASSISTANT. She pressed a button on the telephone as the two passed her.

When Marla opened Mr. Dawkins' office door, he called out, "You can't barge in here."

McCollum closed the door behind him.

Marla laid her palms on the desktop. "I want my husband released from the hospital."

Dawkins bolted around his desk. "Mrs. Adams, your husband is seriously ill. He's unstable and can't be moved from the intensive care unit."

"He's already had one attempt on his life while here, and you are doing nothing to prevent another. All I see anyone doing is IVs and moving his arms and legs twice a day. I can do that at home. He's stable. Let him go."

Dr. Wilson entered the office. "What is going on?" He looked up and down at the man he didn't recognize. "You must be the one who killed all those poor people in England. A man with a tenuous grasp on reality."

"I'm taking my husband out of this hospital," Marla said.

Dr. Wilson stepped between Dawkins and Marla. "Mr. Adams is in critical condition with massive brain damage. His brain is still very swollen. I performed a craniectomy, and that needs to be monitored closely."

"What is that?" Marla asked.

With his arms crossed and leaning against the wall, Dr. McCollum said, "He cut out a section—"

"Shut up." Dr. Wilson shoved his finger into the doctor's chest. "You are no one. Nothing. A farce who kills people. You're not allowed to give a medical opinion in this hospital." He turned back toward Marla. "I removed a part of his skull to release pressure. That piece of bone is in a medical freezer, and I will reattach it when the pressure drops."

"Keep it. I'll come back for it later." She turned back to Dawkins. "I have a safer place for him. No one will stick a pillow on his face and try to suffocate him like they did upstairs." She pointed at Dr. McCollum. "And he will do more than push water in his veins and stretch his muscles. Release my husband."

"Mrs. Adams," Dawkins pleaded, "for your husband's sake, let's keep him in the ICU for now. We can talk about a transfer to another facility in a few days."

"If you don't release him, I will call the police and the news media. It doesn't matter what happens, except you will get adverse publicity for the hospital."

Dawkins backed up. "If you have a facility that will accept him, I will call for an ambulance to transfer."

"No transfers. I have a trailer. Do it now!"

Dr. Wilson sliced his hand through the air. "Do it. Have her sign the AMA form."

Dawkins begged her. "Mrs. Adams, please reconsider."

Dr. Wilson left the office before returning a minute later and slapped a printed page on the desktop. "Sign here and take him, AMA, against medical advice. Once you leave, I will not be his doctor again."

The elevator lowered to the first floor, and Marla led the way to her truck as Dr. McCollum walked beside Crosby lying flat on the hospital bed. Two attendants pushed the bed down the hallway while a nurse followed, pushing an IV pole with wheels. The glass doors slid open, and Marla opened the back doors of the trailer, lights shining bright, walls and floor clean, and a freshly made hospital bed. She worked all night building a counter with a small refrigerator underneath, hanging a hook for IV bags above the bed, and a twenty-inch monitor on the wall. The rooftop air conditioning blew cool air inside.

With the help of the hospital employees, Marla transferred Crosby to his new bed. She checked and locked the wheels before closing the door with the doctor sitting beside the bed.

The attendants returned inside after watching the truck and trailer disappear down the road.

Chapter 16

Pulling the trailer behind her truck, Marla drove down a two-lane road with a Janus-faced ecosystem of infinite mesquite and prickly pear – full of thorns that cut and dig deep on one side, and thousands of acres of cultivated wheat fields on the other. She snapped the microphone button on the handheld 2-way radio. "How is Crosby managing the ride?"

McCollum sat in a chair beside his comatose patient, happy there were no potholes or bumps in the road. "Stable vitals. Breathing well. I need to change an IV bag but can't do it while the trailer is moving. How much longer?"

"We're here." She slowed. In her rearview mirror, a semi-truck hauling a livestock trailer changed lanes to pass her. She thought, *why is there no police officer with a radar gun when you need one?* It zoomed by her with two more passing by only a few yards between them. "Hang on, wind gust."

The trailer wobbled, and the doctor lost his footing, toppling off the chair. "What the bloody hell was that?"

"Three cattle trucks. All looked empty, except the dung left inside." She shook her head.

He covered his mouth and nose with the crook of his arm. "They smell horrendous." The trailer turned off the road before stopping. When the truck door opened, the doctor gazed through the small side window in amazement at endless fields of chest-high wheat. They flowed in the wind like tides rolling across his Atlantic shores. His soul longed for his London home and the shores of Newhaven.

He had never seen such massive machinery before. Combine harvesters moved at a funeral's pace, cutting through the horizon of brown wheat. Long tubes aimed into the sky, spewing grain in an arc and landing into dump truck beds.

He dug into his pocket and retrieved a small vial, opened it, tapped white powder on the crook of his hand, and sniffed it up his nose. The truck engine increased while his feet shifted, trying to keep his balance.

After they stopped, the trailer side door opened, and Marla waved her hand at him. "This is it, the place where you heal Crosby."

From a cool temperature inside the trailer, he glanced over the thirty foot tall, two-sided prefabricated metal shed with both ends open. When he stepped out past the door, the heat of the day slapped him across the face. "What use is the building for?"

"Hold strippers and combines."

"I haven't the foggiest what you just said."

Marla chuckled. "Large farm equipment."

"Nothing in here," he pointed to the corner, "except an orange extension cord and that thing."

"Right. The cord connects to a generator you called a thing. You sleep in your own bed at the front of the trailer. Limited water for showers and toilet. No need to use the stove. I'll bring food every day."

"How considerate."

"You're welcome." Marla looked around the shed. "The place has been in probate for a few months, so attorneys try their best to suck as much money from the estate before it sells. It should be another few weeks before anyone can buy this place." She gripped the doctor's shoulder. "Crosby will be better, and he can walk out of here by then, right?"

He realized what he got himself into, isolated in a foreign land with no gin and little cocaine. "Right. Three days." He turned back toward the trailer. "I need to assess the patient and get my equipment ready, then prep him for the first injection in an hour." He patted the vial in his pocket, knowing it was almost empty. "Tomorrow, I must return to town and gather more medical supplies." He knew no one in San Antonio, but he could call his dealer in Baton Rouge. He wondered if drug dealers were connected with other dealers from one town to the next, like car salesmen or Chick-Fil-A restaurant owners.

Marla didn't reply. She unhitched the trailer from her truck, plugged the extension cord in, and strolled back toward him with a pen and pad in her hand. "Here, write what you need, and I will get it this afternoon. You're staying here."

"No. I'm a doctor, and I know exactly what I need."

"And who stays with Crosby? No one? Not happening. Do you want a medical license in the United States? You keep your ass right here until my husband can walk out of here on his own." She opened the back door of the truck. "I have sandwiches for lunch, sliced barbecue beef or turkey. I'll let you choose."

Sweat beads formed on his forehead and neck. He rubbed his hand over the vial inside his pants pocket. "Neither."

"Then I guess you get yourself inside the trailer and cure my husband."

Dr. McCollum stared at her through thick lenses before opening the side door. The cool air chilled his neck and sweat-ladened shirt. Crosby lay on the hospital bed with eyes closed, lips sealed, motionless, except for the steady chest movement with each breath. Like the twenty-inch monitor in the ICU, the squiggly red, blue, and yellow lines across the screen with random beeps announced the blood pressure, heart, and respiratory rate.

He opened his medical bag, pushing his bent spoon and disposable lighter to the side before removing sterilized packages of a 50cc syringe, a needle the size of a number 2 pencil, an eyedropper, a handful of 5cc syringes, and a three-inch, small bore stainless steel tube. He placed two small bottles, one labeled Protein Extract Solution and the other Transition Metal Catalyst on the table near the centrifuge in the order of his needs. After slipping on disposable gloves and unwrapping the bandages from Crosby's head, Dr. McCollum revealed his patient's shaved scalp. On the left side above his ear, sutures held a half-circle incision closed. With his fingertip, he felt the softness under the skin where a round, three-inch diameter section of the skull had been removed, Dr. Wilson's craniectomy. This will be where he injects the stem cells into the damaged brain.

Marla opened the side door and entered with a bottle of water and a barbecue sandwich on a paper plate. "Here, you need to eat." She placed them on a small fold-down table at the rear of the trailer.

The doctor glanced at the plate before returning his focus to Crosby. "I need your help."

"Happy to."

"Help me roll him to his side. I'm going to remove a sample of stem cells."

"How?"

"The stem cells are in his bone marrow. I stick a large needle in his hip bone and withdraw the solution."

"Do I need gloves like you?"

He scoffed at her. "No."

Dr. McCollum cleaned the upper buttock, stuck the pencil length needle through the skin and muscle into Crosby's hip bone, and aspirated 50cc of red slush into the syringe. He handed Marla a square bandage. "Put this over the hole and lay him on his back." The doctor squirted an equal amount into two 50cc plastic conical tubes and placed them into the centrifuge, then pushed the high-speed button and waited for the stem cells to separate from the remaining bloody solution. He snapped his gloves off like a surgeon finishing a procedure and pitched them into the wastebasket.

"If I must stay here, then you go to town and pick up more IV bags. The patient needs fluids in him for the stem cells to grow."

"Where am I supposed to get that? I don't think Walmart has it on the shelves next to the vitamins."

"Same place where you got all the other supplies. Hurry up. I'm starting today."

A few minutes later, when Marla's truck turned off the dirt road onto the asphalt and disappeared toward the city, he called his dealer in Baton Rouge.

"Speak," someone said on the line.

"You know who this is?"

"Yeah."

"Brilliant. I need two grams."

"Two? You always want a half. Leaving town?"

"I'm in San Antonio or somewhere close by."

"Can't help you. Too far."

"Don't you have someone nearby? I'll pay more."

"Got a cousin there. Wait at the corner of—"

"I don't have access to a car anymore. He needs to bring it to me."

"The guy won't know you."

"You know me." He hit his chest as if the man on the other end of the call could see him. "Vouch for me. I said I'll pay more."

"Where are you?"

He looked out past the metal building to flat fields. "Bloody hell, I don't know. I'll send you coordinates from my phone."

"Coordinates? You think I'm some kinda pilot? I don't know nothing about co—ordinates."

"I'll send you my location on Google Maps. Three hundred for two grams, that's a hundred more for your troubles. Two seconds and the dealer's gone with a big bonus for coming out here. And I need it now."

✦

Dr. McCollum opened the trailer door, entered, and locked it behind him. The centrifuge had stopped. The screen continued to beep and produce multicolored lines. He tapped the vial, and the last of the drug fell on the tabletop. After using a scalpel to push the powder into a straight line, he snorted it, bringing instant elation. He rubbed his nose in victory.

After gloving and again with the ease of an experienced surgeon, he removed two sutures where Dr. Wilson had performed the craniotomy. Thick yellow mush oozed out of the hole.

"Look at this mess. That idiot surgeon didn't clean the wound very well and left a mess inside." Before inserting the metal tube into the damaged brain, he removed as much yellow discharge as possible, then gently stuffed gauze around the tube to hold it in place. He glanced at his watch, time for his cocaine delivery.

While standing alongside the two-lane road, the sun beat down on the nape of his neck and shoulders. A mile away, the grille of a car wavered in the heat. A vehicle the size of a small dumpster with different colored quarter panels slowed to a stop in front of him. The engine sounded like it came out of a riding lawnmower. A thin, shirtless driver with almost every rib visible leaned over and spoke through the open window of the passenger door.

"What the hell is going on with those thick glasses, man?" He looked behind his buyer. "You staying in that building?"

"No," McCollum said. "You got what I want?"

The driver glanced at the tire tracks behind the doctor. "Something heavy came down the trail. Whatcha hiding, man?"

"Nothing you should care about."

The driver shoved the stick shift into Park. "Let's go check out what you got."

"You carry a spare in the boot?"

"A what?"

He held a scalpel in his hand. "Do you have a spare tire?"

"No."

"I'm going to cut your tire, and you can walk back to town."

The driver jerked out a revolver from under the car seat. "And then you die."

"Give me the cocaine and leave before someone drives by and writes your license plate down."

The driver shoved the gun under his leg. "Four hundred."

"I agreed to three."

He held the plastic bag in the air. "Four or I'm gone."

Reluctantly, McCollum pulled out another hundred from his pocket and dropped the bills on the passenger seat before taking the bag. "Better be all two grams in this."

The driver turned the compact car around and drove off.

Dr. McCollum's phone rang. "Hello?"

Marla said, "I've got twenty IV bags. Need anything else?"

"Fish and Chips."

"Eat the sandwich I left in the trailer." She hung up.

From inside the plastic bag, he scooped white powder onto his fingertip, snorted it up his nose, then shook his head and smiled. "Blimey."

✦

Inside the trailer, multicolored lines waved in a sinusoidal fashion on the monitor. Dr. McCollum tapped out powder on the tabletop and snorted a row. Laughing aloud, he rubbed his nose hard. "Blimey, that's good."

The locked trailer door rattled. "Hey, Doc?" Marla called out. "What are you doing?"

He pushed his glasses up the bridge of his nose and looked at his watch. Thirty minutes had passed since they spoke on the phone, and he hadn't started on the first injection. "Be there in a minute. I'm in the middle of something."

He opened the centrifuge lid, removed the conical tubes, and transferred the stem cells into two glass test tubes, placing one inside the refrigerator. With the second test tube, he aspirated two milliliters of stem cells and emptied the syringe into a small stainless steel cup before adding two drops of his protein extract and one drop of the catalyst. He carefully mixed it before pouring the liquid into a clean test tube. Slipping it into the centrifuge, he closed the lid and turned on the ultraviolet light. When he pushed the low-speed button, the motor whined.

"I'm waiting."

"Then bloody wait. You can't come in during my procedure." When the centrifuge stopped, he aspirated the solution into a syringe.

"Open this door right now," Marla called out.

"Keep your bloody knickers on. I'm almost finished." He held the syringe near Crosby's face. "You are a lucky man." He meticulously injected it down the tube into his patient's brain cavity.

Crosby's eyelids, lips, hands, arms, or legs never moved. His chest rose effortlessly with each shallow breath.

Marla yanked on the door again. "Unlock this door. I don't like you locking it."

After checking the position of the stainless steel tube, he removed his gloves and patted his leg, confirming the plastic bag in his pants pocket. It startled him when the door opened. "How did you open the door?"

She held her key in her hand. "I got tired of waiting. Don't lock this door again." Marla reached past him, placed a small sack on the table, and headed to the bed. When she reached for Crosby's hand, she flinched at the tube jutting out of the scalp. She knelt beside him and whispered, "You can do this. You're strong—stronger than me." She kissed his lips. "Back home, at the barn, the horses could tell something offbeat. Blackie shoved his nose at me. I know he wants you to ride him again."

She turned back to the doctor. "Your box of IV fluids is outside the door."

"Good. The patient must wash the toxins from that repulsive surgery out of his system." He remembered the dead animals in the Baton Rouge apartment. What killed them...removing half their brains or the every three hour injections? "I will repeat the stem cell injection every six hours."

"For how long?"

"Until we don't need to anymore."

Marla stood. "Your three days start now. I'm staying the night with Crosby, but I'm working tomorrow morning. You sleep in the bed up front, then tomorrow, you'll be here all by yourself.

"What's in the box?"

"Fish and chips from Long John Silver's."

✦

The early morning heat rapidly passed eighty-four degrees and eighty percent humidity. Marla opened the glass entrance door to the DEA bureau and felt the air conditioning on her face. She lifted her badge toward Michael and Jason, the two security guards that have been behind the desk for years, and signed in on the entry page.

"Agent Adams," Michael said, "it's not necessary to report today. We have you down as FMLA."

"Thanks for the info, but I have someone watching my husband. No problem with me going upstairs?"

"My info says you are not required to be here. Nothing about blocking you."

"Thanks." She headed toward the stairs.

"Oh, wait." Jason bent down and held a small box in the air. "You had a delivery. I scanned it, and it's clean." He placed the box on the countertop. "But a reminder, we are not supposed to accept personal items delivered here. I'll let this one go since you're new, but no more."

She took the small cardboard box. "Thanks." Turning away, she noticed no return address but opened it anyway. Inside was a photograph of Crosby looking to the side with his sunglasses perched atop his curly black hair. He had a two-day-old beard and an infectious smile as he stood beside a blue Camaro. A small corner of a light blue painted building stood behind him. He looked lively, dynamic, different from what she saw this morning. Her eyes welled up. It hit her. Kata mentioned a man in a blue car. Was it Crosby who Kata saw? Marla sniffed before stuffing the picture into her pocket and dropping the box into a wastebasket near the security desk.

Chapter 17

At a small Mexican store west of downtown San Antonio, Torres-Hernandez always bought his groceries where they knew who him and knew to stay quiet. Mozart's opera, Don Giovanni, blared from the speakers of his two-door Lexus. He slid his access card through the card reader at the entrance of an underground parking garage. The wooden security pole rose, and the vehicle banged over the metal drainage cover.

As the car turned into the parking spot, music bounced off the walls and tires squealed on the concrete. When the engine and the music stopped, he opened his door, reached for the peach colored jacket from the back seat, and slipped it on over his mint colored tie and matching shirt. His hands swept invisible dirt from his lapels, attempting to copy high-society sophistication. He grasped six plastic sacks before pushing the car door closed with his butt. The locks chirped. The elevator doors were open and ready. Lucky him. At the press of a button, the doors whisked closed. He hummed the opera as the elevator rose to the fourth floor.

At the bottom corner of his front door, a small piece of paper was stuck in the hinge. A low-tech trick, but it still worked. When he opened the door, the alarm beeped until he typed in his code. The door automatically locked behind him. Stuffed birds perched on small branches peppered the kitchen countertop and dining table. A five-foot-wide painting of Frida Kahlo with a bird on her shoulder hung on a vibrant red wall, dominating the other blank white walls.

He placed five sacks near the refrigerator and put the sixth beside a fake fireplace in the living room. On the mantle sat a framed picture of him smiling beside his twelve-year-old son at a restaurant table in Chihuahua, Mexico. He cradled the photo and kissed the image of the boy. "I promise everything will be okay, and we will be back at Mama's restaurant soon enough." He swung a hinged cabinet out from the wall, turned a combination lock on a safe three times, and opened the steel door. Taking bundles of cash out of the sack, he placed them inside the safe. After closing the door and spinning the dial, he pushed the cabinet back in place.

No one had ever entered his apartment, but that didn't mean he was alone. He always had associates available to him. In the living room, three naked mannequins sat on white leather chairs around a circular white coffee table with a weapon placed neatly in front of each.

French Lieutenant Allard's picture was taped over the face of the first mannequin. It leaned against the back of the chair, arms to its side, and one leg crossed over the other with five thin puncture wounds in the chest. On the table, an eight-inch dagger pointed toward the mannequin. Bird stared at the picture and laughed. "I never found out which killed you...the poison in your drink or the blade."

The mannequin next to Allard was slumped forward in the chair with Spain's Deputy Inspector Iglesias' photo attached to the back. Bird touched the two bullet holes in the rear of the fiberglass head. "You were too full of yourself, never expecting I carried a gun." A .22 caliber revolver pointed toward it on the table.

A third mannequin sat erect in its chair, feet flat on the floor, arms crossed in its lap. On the table, another .22 caliber revolver with a suppressor pointed away from the mannequin. A picture of DEA Special Agent Crosby Adams lay beside the gun. "You have surprised me, but not for long."

Torres-Hernandez removed his black rimmed glasses before pulling off his latex nose and heavy under-eye bags. From the bar, he poured himself two fingers of tequila. As he loosened his mint colored tie, he sat on the only empty chair around the coffee table, saluted the mannequins with his glass, and sipped his drink.

"Allard, Iglesias, it is good to see you both again. I am so glad you could be here with me." He placed the glass on the table. "Soon, you will have another to talk business with while I am away." He leaned forward and held the photograph of Crosby Adams over the face of the third mannequin. "I almost made a fool of myself by showing my face to a DEA agent. I would have been in prison for a long time. And who would care for you, my friends? The police would come and knock down my door and take everything. Take both of you. You are the only ones I trust, and soon, Mr. Adams will join you." Bird raised his glass. "Salud."

After drinking the last of the tequila, he removed his phone from his coat pocket and typed a message.

Marla's phone dinged as she entered the elevator on the first floor of the DEA building. An unknown text. Her face flushed when she read it.

TO SPECIAL AGENT MARLA ADAMS,
I HOPE YOU ARE ADJUSTING TO YOUR NEW ENVIRONMENT. IT CAN BE LONELY WORK WITH NO ONE YOU CAN TRUST. DO YOU TRUST THE DEA WITH YOUR LIFE? WITH YOUR HUSBAND'S LIFE? I HOPE YOU RECEIVED MY GIFT. A NICE PICTURE, DON'T YOU THINK? WHEN I CAME BY THE HOSPITAL, I WAS SAD TO HEAR YOUR HUSBAND HAD BEEN DISCHARGED. WHERE COULD YOU HAVE TAKEN HIM? I WILL SEE THE TWO OF YOU SOON.

Marla held her phone tightly. With no name at the end, it had to be the shooter. Bird? If she told Borland about Crosby's picture in the package and this, someone contacting her, almost admitting he shot Crosby, would he believe her? Would she be transferred to the outskirts of nowhere? The elevator doors opened, and her boots stomped down the hallway toward the conference room. She muted her phone before gently opening the door. Every agent listening to ASAC Borland turned around to see who entered. Borland stopped talking and stared at her. Marla inched the door shut and stood in the back corner.

"Agent Adams, why are you here?" Borland asked. "You're on family medical leave."

Quinton pushed back his chair and stepped in front of her. He spoke in a low tone, "Let's go out and talk."

"No." She moved around him. "This bird-shit person is a sex trafficker and a murderer, and I'm here to help capture the son of a bitch." She glanced across the crowd. "Just like everyone else in this room wants to do."

♦

Three livestock semi-trucks headed north on State Highway 16, carrying cattle from Mexico. Aquelio, the lead truck driver, kept the cruise control at 60MPH. They passed the intersection where they usually turned.

Doroteo, the second driver, spoke on the radio, "Why did you not turn?"

"Azucena Azul Slaughterhouse is full. We will go there next time. Today we unload at Schmidt & Schmidt Slaughterhouse in San Antonio."

"That is much farther," Doroteo said. "What about the girls in the trailer? That is too far for them."

"Who cares about them?" Aquelio snapped back. "You do what you are told, and tomorrow you live to do it again."

Santos, the third driver, said, "I like San Antonio. I drink a few beers, dance a little, then go home to Benita."

They passed an intersection with a flashing yellow light. A Texas Highway Patrol vehicle sat positioned off the road. As soon as the third truck passed, its emergency lights lit up.

Santos called out on his radio in Spanish, "I have a police car behind me."

Aquelio replied in Spanish, "What did you do?"

"Nothing. I did nothing. I'm following you."

"You should be fine," Aquelio said. "Do everything the cop says. See you in San Antonio."

Santos stopped his truck, and a Texas State Trooper ambled past the trailer full of cattle. The animals shuffled inside, reeking of ammonia and hydrogen sulfide. As he reached for his papers in the glove box, two knocks on the door of the cab startled him. When he opened it, the Trooper gazed inside. "You were traveling too close to the truck in front of you."

In his best English, he said, "Sorry, sir. I have a full trailer and am driving to a slaughterhouse in San Antonio. They need water very soon."

"Let's see your license, insurance, and logs."

Forty-five minutes after the other trucks arrived at the slaughterhouse, Santos pulled his truck into the lot. He helped unload the cattle into the pens before aligning near the other rigs.

Arturo stood at the driver's door with his phone to his ear. "All three are here."

Bird held a small glass of tequila while studying his beautiful painting by Frida Kahlo and listening to the Vienna Philharmonic. "Who's the problem?"

"Same as before, Santos," Arturo said.

Bird glanced toward the mannequins. "Just him. Make sure the other two know what happens to a screw-up."

When the engine shut down, Santos stepped down and closed the truck door.

"What happened?" Arturo asked in Spanish.

"I was scared. The cop asked a lot of questions, like where I was going. Where did I start? Where am I staying tonight? How many cattle? Why is my truck so dirty and smelly?"

"Did he inspect the rig?" Arturo angled toward the end of the trailer. Santos followed. "And the girls? Did you have any problems with them in the trailer?"

"No, nothing with the girls. The cop looked at the tires and lights. He gave me a ticket for following too close."

"A ticket? We must be careful." Arturo laid his hand on the nervous driver's shoulder. "They have your name and your picture."

"I will be careful. Maybe I should stay in Mexico for a while when we drive back."

A man quietly appeared behind Santos.

Arturo nodded. "That would be a good idea," he removed his hand from the shoulder, "but too dangerous."

A wire garrote slung around Santos's neck. He kicked and jumped. His fingers struggled to grasp the wire until his arms and legs eventually stopped moving.

Arturo pointed at Doroteo and Aquelio. "Head down to the canyon and bury him." He flipped his phone open and called a number.

Bird answered, "Speak."

"Taken care of. I'm sending this truck back down tonight on a different road."

Bird sipped his tequila. "What about our packages?"

"The girls and the heroin are safe."

Bird held Crosby's picture over the mannequin's face. "You're a good man."

Chapter 18

The air conditioning kicked in from the ceiling, and coolness swirled inside the trailer. The screen above the bed beeped a steady eighty times a minute while Crosby lay still. When Dr. McCollum exited and closed the door, the heat caught him off guard. His glasses fogged for a moment. Stepping out from the metal shed, sun rays hit him like a furnace, and he longed for his cool London rain. He raised his hand over his eyes and glanced at the empty field where farm equipment had reaped the wheat yesterday, leaving a residuum of leaves and stalks carpeting the ground. Sweltering heat waves danced above the dirt and played havoc with his vision.

How did I get here? The world should be awed by my discovery. The British Medical Association should draw a standing ovation, neither castigate nor criticize nor condemn me.

He yelled toward the heavens, "I will be exonerated, you bloody bastards!"

The heat humiliated him. He staggered and stopped before dipping his little fingertip in the plastic bag of cocaine and snorting it.

Cotton ball clouds languished in the polished blue sky. He held the bag above his head, trying to blot the sun from his eyes. When a jackrabbit shot across the dirt and startled him, he stumbled and fell, scattering white powder across the ground.

"Bloody hell." Trying to scoop the cocaine back into the bag, he pushed in more dirt than drugs.

An engine slowed. Marla's truck turned off the road and headed toward the shed. He jumped up and hurried back inside the trailer.

The cool air crawled across his sweaty neck as he yearned for another hit.

The alarm rang. Time for another treatment, but he didn't have the solution ready. McCollum removed the vial of stem cells from the refrigerator and vigorously rolled it between his palms, trying to warm it before she came into the trailer. His heart raced, and his mind tried to focus. He bent down to Crosby's ear. "You should feel lucky I am here. I am saving your life." He felt the chill of the glass in his hand. "This will return my reputation to where it duly belongs."

He placed the vial on the counter. "This. Is. Your. New. Life." Holding Crosby's chin between his fingers, he stared at the silent man. "I am the only one who can bring you back." Dr. McCollum covered Crosby's face with his hand and felt the brain's healing; stem cells twisting, turning, building, growing new tissue at double, triple the speed anyone else could imagine. Exultation shot through his cocaine-infused brain. "God, I need another hit."

The door opened, and Marla stuck her head inside. "Who are you talking to?" She placed a sack of food on the table.

The doctor turned away from her, trying to hide his cocaine dilated eyes from her. "Myself, the patient. I talk to my patients. Leave us alone. I'm mixing the solution." He pushed his thick glasses up before adding the protein extract and catalyst to the stem cells.

"Aren't you supposed to have on gloves?"

He stopped and looked for the box of gloves. "Yes. Of course, you're right. I'll put them on right now." His head felt like a helium balloon ready to explode.

Marla shut the door and squeezed past him. Clasping Crosby's hand in hers, she whispered, "I love you and miss you. Come back to me." She held his hand against her cheek. "We have too many things we must do together." She chuckled. "You planted enough okra, tomatoes, and jalapenos to feed Texas twice over, and they are getting close to being ripe. Chickens need a new coop, Blackie needs riding, and I need you back in our bed."

After mixing the solution, he placed the tube in the centrifuge and hit low speed. It rumbled for a few seconds before spinning. He stared at the machine with the purple light and waited for the bell. It felt like hours to him. His eyelids became heavy. Rest, that's what he needed, if only for a second. He remembered the first time he snorted cocaine years ago in London. The sky opened, rain clouds separated, the sun glared in his face, warmth, exhilaration, a life worth living if only to feel the same again. But it never did. The first was the best. More didn't give him the same. It gave him chills, headache, crawling skin, his heart jumping out of his chest, brain screaming it wants more, demands more. The bell on the centrifuge dinged, and the motor slowed. He opened his eyes and recognized his predicament, incarcerated inside a trailer. After aspirating the solution into a syringe, he was ready to inject his patient.

Marla stared at the odd glasses, trying to see the man's eyes. She wondered about his sight. "How many more times?"

"That I must be forced to ingest your American food?"

"No. How many more injections?"

"Unknown. Move. You are in my way." He placed the syringe tip in the tube and pushed the plunger, feeling back pressure for the first time. It meant the brain grew. Crosby's heart rate increased to 110, and his blood pressure jumped to 148/92.

"What's happening?" Marla asked.

"The stem cells are working."

✦

Both sat at the table at the back end of the trailer. Marla stared at the squiggly lines and listened to the multiple beeps from the monitor. "When you pushed that stuff inside his brain, he reacted. That's good, right?" She bit half a French fry.

"Yes." The doctor hadn't touched the hamburger on his plate. "Yank food has an abhorrent taste. Did you bring any malt vinegar?"

She wrinkled her nose and shook her head. "Good God, no. What would you put that on?"

He pinched two fries between his fingers and stared for a moment. "The chips." Grunting once before he shoved them past his bushy mustache, he chewed with a wince. "No taste. Nothing."

She pointed at her plate. In a terrible British accent, she said, "These? You mean the fries?" She twisted her fry in ketchup and held it in front of her. "Sorry. It just came out."

"I had a dog that spoke better English than you."

"Are you sure he can be healed this week? I can't keep him here much longer. Bird will find us."

"Who is Bird?"

"Don't worry about it." It bothered her that his eyes were out of focus behind the glasses. "I sort of remember college chemistry class, but remind me what is a catalyst?"

"An accelerant. It makes chemical reactions move quicker. It makes new brain tissue grow much faster. And who is this Bird you are talking about?"

Crosby's heart rate jumped to one hundred eighteen, then quickly back to his usual seventy. His left index finger twitched.

"Did you see that?" Marla jumped up from her seat and rushed to him. She held his hand.

"His finger moved. That's good, right?"

Dr. McCollum took the penlight, raised Crosby's eyelids, and flashed the light across the eyes. "They're sluggish, but the pupils constrict faster than yesterday."

"He's responding?" She looked up at the doctor. "You did it. All those people were wrong about you. This is working." Her palm grazed over Crosby's face. "You come back to me. You can do it. You're strong, stronger than anyone I know." She looked toward Dr. McCollum again. "Should you give him more? More would make him heal faster."

"No. The stem—"

Marla stood close to his face. "Why not?"

He stepped back. "Because the stem cells must have time to grow. Putting in more won't help."

Crosby's heart rate jumped again to 110.

Marla studied the screen. "Everything is higher. Even his respirations. Is he trying to talk to us?" She knelt again and grasped Crosby's hand. "Are you talking to me? Come on. Show me."

All the vital signs dropped back down.

"What just happened?" Marla asked.

"Everything went back to his normal range. He might have been trying to correspond with us, but he has no reserve energy. It wore him down, and he fell asleep."

She stood. "When is the next injection?"

"I injected him just before we sat down. We have six hours before the next one."

"You said you wanted to move faster. Faster than every six hours?"

He sat back down at the table to keep her from looking at his eyes. "Right." He remembered injecting the two human survivors every five hours. "I could try sooner."

Marla paced the short distance inside the trailer, then grazed her fist across the table. "You do what you need to do. I'll bring all the supplies you want. Anything. Name it. Anything."

Sniffing and rubbing his nose, he wanted to say, bring a bag of coke. "How serious are you about...anything?"

She glanced at Crosby before nodding at the doctor. "What do you need?"

He cleared his throat. "I could use some non-medical things."

"What? Like fish and chips? Bangers and whatever? I'll get it. What do you want?"

"Right. That's a start."

Crosby's pulse jumped to over 130, and his blood pressure shot to 200/124. Then his breathing stopped. The monitor bell clanged every half second. His arms and legs quivered, body shaking like an earthquake.

Marla dropped to her knees and laid her arms over his chest as he bounced on the bed. "What is this?"

"A seizure." Dr. McCollum fished in his bag for a vial of Valium. On the monitor, Crosby's blood pressure rose higher.

She pressed her arm down on his jerking legs. "Do something."

"I am." He injected the medication into the IV line.

The seizure stopped, and Crosby took a breath. The monitor quieted with all the vitals returning to normal.

Marla jumped up. "What was that? If he dies, you don't get a license. You get that?" She pushed the doctor's chest. "That scared the crap out of me. You make sure it doesn't happen again. You understand me?" She wanted to rip the glasses off his face and glare into his eyes. "I said, do you understand?"

He turned away and decided now was not a suitable time to bring up the cocaine.

Chapter 19

Borland called a meeting of all the DEA agents to report the findings of Special Agent Adams' undercover activity, and what went wrong. Everyone except Marla waited in the conference room.

Inside his office, Borland asked Marla, "How is your husband?"

"Everyone thinks Dr. McCollum is a quack, but he's not. Crosby responded to me last night. It's a miracle."

Borland nodded, not sure whether to believe her. "Good." He changed the subject. "You understand why you cannot be in the conference room, right?"

"Yes, sir."

He left his laptop open on his desk with several crime scene pictures of Special Agent Crosby Adams on the screen. "You keep me informed of your husband daily...and where he is."

"I will let you know about his status, but I can't tell you where he is."

"I expect you to tell me, I'm your superior."

"Yes, sir. You are. Somehow, the cartel found him in the hospital, and Torres-Hernandez is probably involved somehow. Crosby is safer hidden as the doctor does what he does."

"You're bordering on insubordination and the collaboration of illegal medical practice."

"I'm not doing anything but hiding and protecting him."

"Tell me about this doctor."

Marla shook her head. "I shouldn't reply to that, sir."

Borland looked her over. "I have enough on my plate. Are you on FMLA or not?"

Marla nodded while looking at the crime scene pictures. "No, sir. I want to work. What do you want me to do?"

"Leave the investigation of your husband's attempted murder to others." Borland closed the laptop. "You are assigned to human trafficking with Special Agent Wales and nothing else."

"Yes, sir. I understand."

All the DEA agents, except Marla, surrounded the conference table. ASAC Ronald Borland entered through the same side door he always did.

Suzie Moore followed close behind, sat beside him, and connected her laptop to a projector. A row of pictures from Agent Adams' crime scene lit the whiteboard behind Borland; the riverbank with a black-clothed body halfway in the water, a gravel trail, clouds of mosquitoes hovering over tall grass, and the back of an ambulance with the doors open and a man on a gurney.

Borland scanned the crowd. "Special Agent Adams had planned to meet with Los Zetas members for a drug purchase. It didn't go well. Instead, found shot in the head and dumped along the banks of the Frio River with his identification, phone, and weapon missing. A DPS Trooper found his car abandoned under an overpass twenty miles from where Adams had been found."

Suzie added another photo to the whiteboard of Crosby's blue Camaro parked under a bridge.

"Forensics says the lack of blood spray indicated the shooting occurred outside the car." Borland pointed to Suzie, who zoomed in on the picture of the gravel trail below the bridge and near the waterline. "Forensics also said they found multiple footprints from two sets of boots or shoes and fresh tire tracks with a width of 225. Too narrow for a full-size pickup or van, possibly a minivan." Borland nodded at Suzie again, and she clicked on an image of tall grass on the board. He pointed at the photo. "Here is a wide row of grass bent toward the water. The two dropped Adams, and he rolled to the waterline." Borland pointed at Suzie. When she widened the following picture, everyone saw Adams on the gurney with an oxygen mask over his face and his head wrapped in gauze. "With the car easily found and Adams not at the bottom of the river, the cartel left a message to undercover agents trying to infiltrate Los Zetas. Adams condition is critical."

A picture of a boot popped up behind Borland. "Forensics reported ryegrass and cattle feces on the soles of Adams' boots." The images on the whiteboard disappeared. "I want the guy who shot a DEA agent. Bring me that man and shut his drug business down. Go find him."

After the meeting, Quinton rushed out of the room and headed to Borland's office. When he opened the door, Marla sat on the couch against the wall, reading something from her phone. He closed the door behind him. "Are you okay?"

"No, I'm not." She turned the phone off.

Quinton sat down. "Marla, you shouldn't be on this case. Your husband's attacker? Borland assigned you to kidnapping and human trafficking, not murder investigations. If you don't like that, you'll get assigned the desk job nobody ever wants."

"He told me to stick with human trafficking, and I will, but I can't sit back and ignore what happened to my husband." She put her phone down on the couch. "I have a few ideas."

"Borland would have my ass if I let you do anything."

"Let me? You think you can stop me?"

Quinton ran his fingers through his salt and pepper hair. "All right, between you and me, this is unofficial."

"Agreed," Marla said.

He glanced behind him, making sure Borland wasn't within hearing distance. "You've lived in this area longer than I have. What ideas do you have?"

Marla stood and stuck her phone in her pocket. "Do we have a detailed map of Texas? Businesses, homes, farms, ranches."

"Sure. The main computer," Quinton said.

"Come on." She headed out of Borland's office and charged toward her desk. "Dr. Wilson, the neurosurgeon, estimated Crosby's wound at one to two days old. He laid in the grass for a full day and lived."

"Amazing man."

Marla nodded. "Yes, he is. He had cow dung on his boots. Kata, the girl at my house, said they forced her from a livestock trailer to the one we found her in. Her description sounded like the switch was near a building or field with cattle dropping patties on green grass. Crosby had ryegrass on his boot."

Quinton said, "If they unloaded the livestock and exchanged the girls into different trailers during the day, maybe your husband took pictures and that is why they stole his phone."

She remembered the picture Bird sent her of Crosby standing alongside a blue Camaro with the corner of a light blue building behind him. The same place as Kata? "There must be a hundred ranches in South Texas dealing in cattle."

"Besides a ranch, where else would you unload cattle? Slaughterhouses or auction houses?" Quinton asked.

"Not sure about an auction house. Sell cattle the same day you bought them? Not much profit in that. A slaughterhouse is a possibility. I'll talk with Kata again and ask her more detailed questions about where the exchange happened."

At her desk, she logged onto her computer. The DEA had the address of every business in the United States. She clicked the icon for maps and typed in cattle ranch. "I'm wrong. There are thousands of cattle ranches in South Texas."

"Try cattle auction houses within a ten-mile radius from where they found your husband," Quinton said.

She typed it in and pressed enter. "Nothing."

"Try a fifty mile radius," Quinton said.

One popped up. "It closed last year."

"Okay, try slaughterhouses within ten miles," Quinton said. The computer showed none. "Try a fifty."

When she hit enter, one flag popped up: Schmidt & Schmidt Slaughterhouse outside Bexar County.

Marla hit the link, and pictures of cattle, hogs, and goats filled the screen. A sign declared it open every day, 7 a.m.-9 p.m.

"Crosby was shot on Wednesday morning," Marla said. "We should check this place."

✦

With the slaughterhouse close by, a distinct odor wormed its way inside their Tahoe, pig farmer perfume. Quinton turned onto a gravel lot past a neon sign flashing OPEN with no livestock trailers, pickups, or cars in the lot. A few cattle bellowed and yawped in the pens.

"Odd to have nothing here."

"Why?" Quinton asked.

"Slaughterhouses run every day," Marla said, "but there's no action."

"I live in the city, so I've never been to one." Quinton put the transmission in Park and killed the engine. "Let's check it out."

Marla opened her door and exited with the wind swirling a mild fecal odor in the air. She smelled worse. After closing her door, she adjusted her service belt. Her vest felt like a Vise-Grip. She noticed wide tire tracks with flattened green animal feces on the gravel.

"Why is there dung out here?" Quinton asked. "Cattle out here?"

"No. Feces fall off the trailers as they backed up to the unloading docks.

Quinton pulled on the glass front door to the office, but it was locked with a sign taped to the glass: Man in Back.

They heard wood being sawed behind the office. Quinton turned toward the noise. "Must be the man in the back."

They turned the corner, with a guy wearing a San Antonio Spurs cap cutting a long piece of wood with a hand saw.

"Excuse me," Quinton called out.

The man turned around and peered at Quinton's and Marla's badges. His eyes opened wide. "Can I help you?"

"DEA Special Agents Wales and Adams. We wanted to ask a few questions."

"Hey, I'm just a carpenter fixing some broken boards. I don't know anything, man."

"Don't worry, you're not in trouble. Where's the manager?"

"Arturo? He should be back soon. The electricity shut down, hence," he aimed the hand saw toward a breaker box, "Arturo's out trying to find out why." He pointed to the animal pens. "He's got all those cattle needing to be processed."

"Cattle come every day?" Marla asked.

"Mostly. They run 'em through pretty fast."

Marla's eyebrows furrowed. "They don't hold them for a day before slaughter?"

"Beats me. The only thing I know about cattle is that I like a thick, juicy steak."

"What about this Arturo guy? He here every day?" Quinton asked.

"Oh, sure, all day during working hours."

"What is Arturo's last name?" Marla asked.

"Hmm, not really sure." He pointed to the sign. "Schmidt, I guess."

She aimed her pen at the billboard. "Schmidt, of course. You got his phone number and address?"

"No. I'm just a carpenter."

"Mind if we look around?"

"No skin off my nose." He pushed the saw back against the board with metal teeth ripping into the wood.

They strode toward the last loading dock connected to the pens. Two Chrysler Town & Country minivans sat under a metal carport with weathered red and white For Sale signs taped to the right passenger windows.

"Interesting," she said. "I'll check to see if they're locked."

"We don't have a warrant," Quinton said.

"I'm car shopping." She bent down and inspected the black sidewall of the tire. "225 by 16." She checked the other vehicle. "Same."

"Probably the standard size on every Town & Country," Quinton said.

Marla opened the driver's door, and stale tobacco odor rose in the air. Dried mud and specks of cattle dung covered the floorboard. She closed the door, coursed to the other side, and opened the side door with hay and dirt covering the floor.

"Adams. May I remind you we have no warrant?"

"May I help you?" A voice came from behind them.

They saw a mid-thirties man in jeans, a Western shirt, and a hat approaching them.

"Yes," Marla replied. She stopped at the second vehicle and slid the side door open. It looked like someone had power-washed the inside. She knew all about power washing. "I saw this for sale. How much?" She knocked on the roof. "How much for both?" Coursing to the front of the vehicles, she noticed the clean one had the windshield cracked on the passenger side, which she surmised could be from someone's head. "Got a name?" she asked.

"Arturo."

Marla asked, "Is your last name Schmidt?"

"No. That's the owners. I work here."

Quinton glanced behind the man. A white Ford F-250 crew cab sat near their SUV. "Did you just get here?"

"I'm sorry, but I should have removed the sign. Both sold yesterday. Anything else I can do for you?"

"What do you do here?" Marla asked.

"I, um," Arturo crossed his arms in front of him, "Sorry, I have some work to do in the office."

"Convenient," Quinton said. "I mean, we came out here, and you arrived a little after we did."

"Didn't catch your names," Arturo said.

"Didn't throw them out," Quinton replied. "DEA Special Agents Wales and Adams."

Arturo smiled. "Well, honored to have law enforcement around. Sorry about the vans."

"Right, thanks," Quinton said. "We'll be leaving now."

"I would say come back anytime, but not much out here for Drug Enforcement. We sell livestock. Haven't seen any drugs around here."

"Right," Marla said. "Guess we should be on our way."

They both climbed into the Tahoe, and Quinton started the engine.

"That sack of shit is lying," Marla said. "One clean and the other filthy? Why clean? And one with a broken windshield. Nobody would buy those."

"You're right. If Crosby had been in that minivan, there would be blood, hair, and bone frags," Quinton said.

"And we're ninety miles from where he was found. Still, it's odd, one clean and one not."

"By the way, how is Crosby?"

"I have him hidden from Bird."

"I'd like to see him. Give my respects."

"He's stable but not ready for visitors." Marla snapped her seatbelt. "How about we get in a little range practice? I need to blow off some steam."

Quinton moved the shifter to drive. "Okay, but I need to call and ensure there's a slot for us."

"Have a better idea. I have a practice range near my house in Hildebrandt. It's thirty minutes away with good traffic."

Chapter 20

Marla and Quinton stood under the metal canopy of her private firing range at her ranch with a long table in front of them, waist-high for ammo and handguns. A man-made hill stood fifteen feet high behind the targets to absorb all the spent bullets.

Marla opened a locked storage cabinet and laid a bucket full of loose 9mm bullets on the table.

"Let's use these. No sense burning through your personal ammo."

Quinton picked one bullet out and looked at the end of the cartridge. "What's with the black dot on all of them?"

"The whole family would come out and practice almost daily. We collected our cartridges and reloaded them. Cheaper that way." She picked up a cartridge. "I have a black mark on the back of mine. Crosby used blue, my brother used red, and Chief Searcy used green." She dropped the cartridge in the bucket. "I've lost the desire to reload, but I still have a few thousand cartridges in the house." She started loading her two magazines. "When I'm out, I'll start buying ammo like everyone else."

Quinton started loading as well. "Is that why there are so many cartridges on the ground?"

Marla felt her heartbeat quiver momentarily when she saw a cartridge with a red dot on the ground. "I should clean those up." After filling her two mags, she put her ear protection and safety glasses on and shoved a mag into the grip of her DEA-issued Glock. She yelled, "I'm hot."

"Me too." Quinton pointed his Glock at a silhouette target with a small heart in the center twenty-five feet away taped to a board.

Marla fired seven times before Quinton fired four. He glanced at her target with a grouping of seven shots in the center of the chest. He tried to keep up with her speed, but his bullets landed on a broader pattern from shoulder to waist. After emptying her second mag, Marla laid the pistol on the table and waited for him to finish before slipping her ear protection off.

Quinton laid his gun on the table and looked at her target with nothing outside the heart. "You must practice often." He slid his earmuffs behind his head.

"There are a lot of bullets in that hill." She cleared her spent cartridges off the table.

They trekked to the targets and replaced them with clean ones. She noticed half his bullets hit the center. "Let's reload and go again."

Quinton caught her glancing at his target. "I didn't use my second mag."

Marla laughed. "Sorry, I thought you had just missed the target." When they returned to the firing line, she reloaded both magazines.

He loaded his first magazine and covered his ears again. "Ready."

With her ears covered, Marla called out, "Ready." She emptied her two mag seconds after Quinton finished his first. He noticed the heart in her target had disappeared.

Quinton raised his voice. "Feeling better?"

She exhaled. "Yes, some. One more round before we go, then I need to get back to Crosby."

Quinton placed his pistol on the table and took off his safety glasses.

"What's up?" she asked.

"If you don't mind, you're much better. I'll watch."

She gazed at the targets. "I can use what is there."

After loading her two mags, she placed one on the table and shoved the other in the pistol grip. She inhaled deeply and held it for a moment before exhaling, raised her pistol, and smoothly emptied both in less than thirty seconds, leaving two tight groupings, half in the forehead and half in the neck.

Quinton paid close attention to her accuracy.

"Mind if I practice my quick draw?"

"Not at all. Go for it."

She tried to hide her smirk. "I'll use your target since the center chest is pretty clear." Marla loaded another magazine, pushed it into her gun, and holstered it. She held her breath, drew her weapon, fired twice, and reholstered it.

His eyes widened. He swallowed hard. "Never seen anyone fire that quickly."

She motioned toward the target. "Mind if I keep going?"

"Oh, for sure. I could watch this all day."

She drew, fired twice, and holstered her pistol. She did it repeatedly.

"Amazing."

"Takes practice."

"More than that. It must be in you to do that. I noticed something. You fired twice each time."

She drew again and fired twice. "That's how I have always practiced. Two bullets at heart level should stop anyone." She glanced at her watch. "After I reload, I have to go."

Quinton grabbed a handful of bullets from the bucket. "Mind if I grab a handful?"

"Not at all."

Quinton loaded his magazines. "After reading all the newspapers about you and the face-to-face shoot-out inside the burning barn, did you shoot the perp twice?"

Marla holstered her gun and looked down. Not answering, she grabbed both magazines in a single sweep and headed toward the Tahoe.

He reached for another handful of cartridges and stuck them inside his pocket.

Chapter 21

In Nuevo Laredo, weathered Mexican houses lined a narrow asphalt road two hundred yards from the Rio Grande River. Above the entrance of a neon green house stood the name Torres-Hernandez arched in red. A van stopped, and a bald man in a wife-beater t-shirt wrapped in a slew of multicolored ink climbed out of the passenger seat, moved around to the rear, and opened the back doors. Fifteen and sixteen-year-old girls piled out and marched in a line into the house.

Intricately hand-carved chairs and a coffee table stood in the small living room. A picture of a thirteen-year-old Samuel Torres-Hernandez hung on the left side of the fireplace. His older sister's picture hung to the right with eyes missing from cigarette burns. A gold-encrusted Jesus on the cross hung above the mantle.

Samuel despised his sister. She hit him, burned him, threw knives and hammers when their parents were not around, and laughed the hardest after she broke his arm. She stopped laughing when he stabbed her to death in her bed. After burying their daughter, Samuel's parents banned him from their house. Two days later, while his parents slept, he unlocked the back door, crept down the hallway, and put two bullets into each of their heads. Twenty years later, with two advanced degrees, he continued to elude law enforcement in Europe, Mexico, and the US. One thing never changed—Bird never stopped despising women.

Three men with rifles stood around a hole in the kitchen floor with a ladder leading underground. Each girl climbed down to an air-conditioned, well-lit, six-by-six-foot tunnel. One behind the other, they trudged five hundred and thirty yards under the Rio Grande River before climbing up a ladder and emerging inside a semi-trailer repair shop in Laredo. Three Schmidt & Schmidt Slaughterhouse Inc. livestock trailers backed into place and stopped. Tattooed men rushed the girls up a loading ramp into the trailers and locked them inside the upper back corner called the doghouse. Each understood speaking or making any noise would put their families and every girl in the trailer in danger.

Another man covered with tattoos climbed into one trailer and walked to the nose. He unlocked an airtight container welded to the ceiling, removed a silver metal case, snapped the latches, and opened the case revealing bundles of US dollars wrapped in plastic. "Got it," he said, then slid an identical empty case inside and locked it back. He did the same in the other two trailers. After jumping out of the third trailer, he whistled loudly and banged the truck cab with the palm of his hand. "Vamanos."

The diesel engines revved, and the three tractor-trailers headed for the cattle pens with the girls locked on the upper level.

❖

On the Mexican side of the border, livestock tractor-trailers passed through the gates at the World Trade Bridge, Port of Entry, and entered Laredo, Texas. The drivers unloaded the cattle into the US pens, and a few hours later, USDA authorities cleared the animals for release into the United States.

Nicolas Gustavo, a purchasing agent, bought sixty-seven Mexican cattle from the 612 Ranch and placed them into one pen. He leaned against his car and waited for the trucks to arrive. The Schmidt & Schmidt livestock tractor-trailers turned the corner toward the pens, then backed up to the loading ramp first.

Gustavo pounded his fist on the truck driver's door. "Why are you late?"

Miguel, the driver, climbed out. "My other shipment took too long."

"Your orders are to have your truck here and be ready to load when the cattle arrive. You wait for the cattle. The cattle don't wait for you."

"It's not my fault. Bitch at whoever is managing the other product. I sit in the truck and wait for someone to tell me to go."

Gustavo barked, "We cannot wait! When the cattle are released, we load them immediately. Do you understand?"

"Not now," Miguel muttered. "Get out of my way. I have to load the cattle."

The girls stayed hunkered inside the doghouse while the cattle filled the three trailers. Once finished, Gustavo called Bird. "We have all the cattle accounted for and loaded. Something happened at the repair shop in Laredo. I shouldn't have to wait on them."

"I will make sure it doesn't happen again, my friend," Bird said.

"You want us to go to the ranch or the slaughterhouse?"

"The ranch is expecting them."

"On their way."

The three trucks headed onto the interstate but took the first exit five hundred yards away to the less congested SH 59, avoiding traffic and potential State Trooper vehicles.

Miguel spoke into the two-way radio in his hand, "Sevino."

"Ola," the second driver said.

"No. We speak English. We have green cards."

"Fuck you. Hello," Sevino said. "What do you want?"

"We stayed at the repair shop too long and are half an hour behind. I talked to our contact in Freer."

"Where?"

"Freer, you idiot. Freer, Texas. He said no cops on the road for sixty miles, so kick it up." Miguel pushed the accelerator further down. "Stay close and tell Navarro not to get behind. He always drags."

"You know him. He doesn't like to speed. He worries about cops."

"I'm tired of talking to him. You tell him to stay close."

Sevino turned his steering wheel. "I'll call him in a minute." His diesel engine hummed in the Texas heat. He touched the warm, sun-fired side window while accordions and trumpets screeched Mexican music from his radio.

Fifteen minutes later, a red BMW passed all three trucks.

Navarro called out, "Did you see that? He had to be going over a hundred."

"Good," Miguel said. "If there is a cop, let him get pulled over, and we keep going."

About a quarter of a mile up the road, the BMW's brake lights lit, and the tires smoked as it spun a U-turn. It flew by the trucks again. Miguel looked in his side mirror as the car did another U-turn.

"I don't like this," Miguel said. "It brings attention to us. Someone might call the police on him, and we get pulled over for inspection."

Sevino looked in the side mirror. "I'll pull to the center, so he can't pass us."

"Don't do that," Navarro said. "I see cars behind us."

"Don't like this estupido Americano." Sevino moved left and drove down the middle of the road. The BMW slowed down and blew its horn. He laughed. "Hey, Puto, come suck on this."

"I don't like being this close to the backend of your trailer." Navarro slowed, leaving an open spot between the trucks.

"You idiot," Sevino yelled. "Don't slow down."

A pickup crested a hill. It drove toward them, hugging the shoulder while blowing its horn. The BMW sped up and slipped between trucks.

"You fucking pendejo!" Sevino moved to the middle again.

Miguel yelled on his radio, "Stop doing that! Let him pass us. We have other cars behind us watching."

Sevino eased off the gas and laughed. "How about I slow down to nothing?"

The BMW blew its horn and tried to pass.

"Damn!" Sevino swerved back into the right lane when another car crested a hill. It slammed on the brakes with nowhere for the BMW to go, so it slid into the ditch. All the other cars behind the trucks stopped to help.

"What the hell are you doing?" Miguel yelled into his radio. "You almost killed a man."

"Don't worry. They all stopped, and no one will bother us."

A green road sign said FREER 3 MILES. Miguel's sweaty palm rested on the stick shift. He checked the side mirror and saw no cars behind them. They had two hours before pulling into the slaughterhouse unless a trooper arrested them.

Chapter 22

D r. McCollum stood by the edge of the road and cleaned the thick lenses in his glasses with his shirt. Sweat dripped off his nose and splattered on the toe of his shoe. More drops hit the asphalt. He wiped his face with his sleeve. "Bloody Texas heat."

A mile away, a car drove toward him on a flat road. The same car as last time, with three out of four different colored quarter panels and a lawnmower-sounding engine, slowed and eased off the road. The same driver, a young teenager with hair full of gel and curls shooting in every direction, smiled out the open passenger window with the barrel of a semi-automatic pistol shoved inside the front of his pants. Several rolled paper sacks sat in the front seat.

"Hey, man. You used all that? Heavy hitter. I like it. I can come every two days and load you up."

McCollum put his glasses on and looked inside the car. "You had a revolver last time. Different gun now."

"Had to change. You know, use it once and throw it in the river." He patted the pistol. "Like this one better, more bullets."

Three semi-trucks hauling cattle roared past them toward San Antonio. McCollum's feet lifted off the ground from the wind gust. He waited a few seconds, then stuck his hand past the open window and held the folded money between his fingers. In a quick motion, the guy took the cash in one hand before holding out a rolled white paper bag in the other. McCollum grabbed it and unrolled the bag with the La Zapata logo on one side. When he opened the zip-lock plastic bag, dipped his fingertip in the powder, and snorted, an effervescence of joy filled his mind.

"What's inside your place, man?"

McCollum pulled himself back to earth. "Nothing. A trailer. I live in a trailer."

"Hey, cool, man. Let me see. Got a TV? Netflix? There's this cool show me and my old lady watch. Fatties and Skinnies. Not girls... marijuana. Get it? They talk about which weed is best for fat joints and skinny joints. And tequila. Oh, man, the best tequila. You got any?"

"I don't have Netflix or tequila. You can go now. Come back in two days."

"No Netflix?" His door creaked open. "I got this box in my trunk. I could hook you up to Netflix, Hulu, and Disney for ten bucks." He rushed around to the back of his car, stuck a key in the trunk's lock, and wiggled it a few times before it opened. Smiling, he held up a small black box. "Here, man. This is all you need. Let's go hook you up."

"I don't want Netflix. No time for that. I'm a terribly busy and important person."

The kid stood in front of the doctor. His smile disappeared. "I don't give a rat's ass who you are. You're just a hophead to me, man. You want more? We go inside."

Without McCollum having a chance to say anything, the dealer charged forward.

"Wait, stop."

The dealer kept walking.

"I said, wait. I have my father in there. He's old and sick. He has...he has...tuberculosis."

The kid stopped. "TB? He got TB? That's bad, man. One of my bros got TB in prison and died." He glanced at the building and then back at his buyer. With a big smile, he said, "Nah, man. You joking? You ain't got no one in there with TB. You'd get it. You got TB?" He charged toward the building again. "You ain't got shit, man." He strode around the shed corner and saw an elongated trailer.

"Nice, bro. Nice one." He pointed to the roof. "And you got a/c?" He nodded. "Need it in this heat."

The doctor stood at the doorway and motioned for the kid to turn around. "Okay, you saw it. Now go. Leave."

"How much you pay for this bad boy?"

Wrapping his fingers around the scalpel tucked in his pants pocket, McCollum's hand shook as he slipped it out. Watching the dealer march toward the trailer, he raised the scalpel. "You need to stop and leave."

The kid turned the handle and opened the door. His eyes widened at the sight of a man on a hospital bed.

McCollum lurched toward the kid and stabbed him in the back. Swinging around, the dealer fired his gun. The blast echoed off the walls. When the doctor stabbed the kid's arm, he dropped the gun and bolted toward his car.

The alarm rang inside the trailer. Dr. McCollum had to decide—the injection or the dealer. Charging around the trailer, he stopped. His heart pounded, and shivers shot up his neck as the car made a U-turn and sped away. The alarm continued to ring. He stopped next to the pistol lying in the dirt. "Bloody hell." Reaching for the gun, he mumbled, "He'll be back to kill me. Unless...."

He silenced the alarm. "You forced me to do this." He gazed at the restaurant logo on the sack before pulling his phone out and tapping the Uber app.

McCollum climbed out from the backseat of a gray Prius and closed the door. "Thank you." He handed the Uber driver a twenty dollar bill.

"Nice." He folded the bill in half. "You staying long? I could take you back." The driver noticed his passenger wearing blue gloves. "You okay, man? I mean, the gloves and all."

"I'm fine. Don't want to get sick. Trying to avoid nasty human infections and all. I'll need a ride back."

The driver stuck the money in his shirt pocket and held up a business card, hoping for another big tip. "Call me on my private line, and I can be here pronto."

The only word on the card made him smirk, ROBERT. When McCollum called the number, the phone on the Uber driver's dashboard rang. "Okay, I'll call in a few minutes. Be close, very close."

"Sure, man, but I got to get gas before we return." The car took off down the road and turned the corner.

Across the street, a car with three different colored quarter panels had parked catty-corner in the alley behind the La Zapata Restaurant. The driver's door stayed open. He looked inside the vehicle. Blood had pooled in the driver's seat with red fingerprints on the steering wheel and rolled paper sacks on the floorboards. Drops of blood trailed down the alley to the restaurant's back door.

The doctor's lips twitched, and his chest tightened. Standing in front of the closed door, he heard angry voices inside. Tapping the back door with the gun barrel twice produced immediate silence. An elderly woman wearing a scarf over her hair opened the door partway.

McCollum waved the pistol in her face. "Where is he?" He forced the door open.

Metal pans rattled behind her, and water swished inside a small dishwasher. Two old men shot glances at him while clumsily putting food on plates.

"I don't know," the woman said.

"Piss off." He aimed the pistol at her. "Where is he?"

"Don't shoot. I show you." She let him inside and opened the storage room door where the kid sat on the floor, leaning against the wall. Blood dripped from his arm and his back onto the concrete floor. He stared at his buyer, holding his own gun aimed at him.

"You should have let things be." The doctor aimed the pistol. The woman screamed. He fired once and dropped the gun. He turned away and ran past the alley, disappearing down the street.

◆

Dr. McCollum snorted a row of coke on the table inside the trailer. "My bloody drug connection is dead. I should have taken the other bags from inside the car." After clearing his throat, he gazed at the metal tube protruding from Crosby's skull. The growing brain tissue had pushed the tube out a half-inch. He touched Crosby's palm, and the fingers twitched. "Mr. Adams, can you hear me?" Crosby responded with a deep exhalation. Even though an hour late with the injection, McCollum had to smile. "I knew I could do this." His cocaine-spiked head buzzed. Hands trembled as he picked up the syringe and held it in front of Crosby's face. "I am going to inject more solution into your brain. Do you understand me?"

Crosby slowly turned his fist and moved his thumb up.

The doctor pushed the plunger, and the solution slid down into the crevices of the brain. Crosby moaned as the syringe emptied.

"Did you sense the solution?"

Crosby moaned again.

On the table, McCollum's cell phone rang. After peeling off his gloves, he rubbed his nose clean as if Marla could see through her phone. "Hello?"

Marla stood outside the Tahoe at a convenience store while Quinton went inside. "Running late. Won't be there until later. You hungry?"

Before answering, he dipped his little finger into the bag and rubbed the powder on his gums. "No. I want a martini."

Marla sized up Quinton, then in a faint voice, she said, "No. You need food."

He scoffed. "You don't know what I need."

She wanted to jump through the phone and smack him, but Crosby had improved. "How is my husband?"

"Thinking of increasing the injections to every four hours."

"Why?"

The police or the kid's buddies would soon be after me. "Need to finish this."

"More improvements?"

"Tell you when you get here." He disconnected the line and mumbled, "I need to get out of this bloody mess."

Chapter 23

Quinton drove the Tahoe on Loop 410 as vehicles passed them, and Marla sat in the passenger seat gazing at the stagnant buildings.

His phone rang. "Wales here."

ASAC Borland spoke on the other end. "I received a report fifteen minutes ago on three semi-trucks loaded with cattle driving fast through the small town of Freer. No reason for trucks to be on that road if they are hauling cattle to San Antonio."

Quinton pressed the speaker button so Marla could hear and motioned for her not to speak. "Yes, sir, but why tell me? Racing vehicles down a highway should be a DPS matter."

"You're not reading the connection. DPS Troopers are looking for them. Adams had cow dung on his boots, and we have cattle trucks where they are not supposed to be."

Quinton asked, "You think this is related to Special Agent Adams because he had shit, excuse me, feces on his boot?"

Borland's voice on the phone became louder. "Get down to Freer and ask questions."

Quinton raised his shoulders and shook his head at Marla. "It's a stretch, sir."

"Everything is a lead until it's not," Borland said. "Pull up a map on your phone, drive there, and find those trucks."

"I know the area." Quinton visualized a map in his mind. "About forty-five miles east of Freer is a small slaughterhouse. I think the name is The Blue Lily." He glanced at his watch. "Not sure what day of the week their auctions occur and if they could manage three trailers full of cattle. Adams and I can be down there in about an hour and a half."

"Is Adams with you?" Borland asked.

Quinton winced as he lied. "No, sir."

"Limited action with her. I may be moving her to another location soon."

Marla whispered to Quinton, "What about Schmidt & Schmidt? They could turn north and head up here."

Quinton asked, "How about we check out the slaughterhouse here in San Antone and then if we don't find what we want, we head south?"

"No. Agent Crosby Adams had been working in Laredo and surrounding counties. Check the closest place north of the border first."

"All right, I'm on my way."

Quinton hung up and tightened his lips. "What am I going to do with you? Borland says you're out."

"You can drop me off anywhere, but I will tail you at every corner, and don't think I can't be objective." She pointed to him and then to her. "We are looking for a man active in human trafficking and kidnapping, right?"

"Right, but you heard Borland."

Marla swept her fingers through her hair. "When he pulls me out of this vehicle and tells me I'm assigned to a desk, that is when I will stop. Until then, I'm hunting for this son of a bitch."

"I should call Borland back."

"All right, all right," Marla said. "Here's what I will promise. I won't shoot until he pulls a gun on me."

"The poor bastard won't have a chance."

"You're damn right he won't."

◆

While driving, Miguel called Bird. "We got a problem."

Inside his condo, Bird eased the hinged cabinet open and unlocked the safe in the wall. "What happened?"

"Sevino ran a car off the road. The cars behind us had to have seen what happened."

"Sevino is a hothead. Where are you?" Bird removed five bundles of cash from a backpack and placed them inside the safe.

"Please don't kill him," Miguel said. "We need him to drive."

"He's fine, for now. He has a cousin in finance. But you must get off the road. The DPS Troopers will search for three livestock trucks. Where are you?"

"About thirty-five miles north of Freer."

"Cancel the ranch. You will need to go to San Antonio."

"Why? That is so much farther."

"Pay attention," Bird said. "Have you passed the wind turbines on the right side of the road?"

Miguel watched the blades spin like slow-motion propellers. "We are there now."

"Go four miles and turn at the intersection where the traffic sign says San Antonio seventy-four miles." Bird closed the safe.

Miguel's heart raced. "I know that road. It's too small for us. We'll get stuck."

Bird sat at the table with the mannequins and filled a shot glass full of tequila. "My friend, you must trust me." He raised his glass toward them and swallowed the tequila. "Turn left, then eight miles, turn right. Head straight north. When you hit Loop 1604, you'll recognize your location."

"We will be very late tonight."

"I will be there waiting." The phone went dead.

Four miles past the wind turbines, Miguel slowed and pushed down the turn signal. Dusk crept forward as hills swallowed a setting sun with orangey reds coloring the underside of clouds. Green and white pumpjacks moved slothfully up and down.

The three trucks downshifted. Of all the times they had traveled to San Antonio, they had never turned onto this road.

Sevino asked over the radio, "Miguel, is something wrong with your truck?"

"No. Shut up and follow me." Miguel turned the steering wheel, and the truck managed a wide, slow corner toward a road not much wider than the truck itself. He felt the trailer wobble. The cattle complained. He slowed even more when the paved road ended, and the tires bounced over uneven roads and potholes. A hazy cloud of dust swirled in front of Sevino's headlights. At this speed, it would take all night.

Eight miles later, the trucks turned right at the intersection and rolled back onto a two-lane paved road. Dusk turned to a starless night. Miguel wiped the sweat off his forehead.

They had over fifty miles to go, and it seemed another town existed every ten miles with a single flashing yellow light at a lonesome inter-section.

Meandering turns led to another traffic light, this one red. A neon sign in the window of a small café told all they were closed. Miguel arrived two hours late, and with no thought about stopping, he sped up, passed through, and shifted again, accelerating to fifty, the fastest he had gone in almost an hour. The other two followed. He passed a pickup truck on the shoulder of the road. His headlights revealed a word he never wanted to see: CONSTABLE on the door. Red and blue emergency lights sprayed from the grille into the night.

"Damn. Oh, damn, hell," Miguel yelled.

Navarro called on the radio. "What do I do?"

The vehicle shot forward and blared the siren into the night air.

"We pull over," Miguel said. He downshifted and slowed to a stop. The other two did the same.

With the constable's bright headlights and the emergency lights swirling, the uniformed man sauntered toward the truck cab and made a hand motion to roll down the window.

"You in a hurry there, son?" He coughed once from the odor. "When's the last time you washed out this trailer?"

Cattle grunted from inside.

"I not speeding, sir."

"You ran a red light. We don't get livestock trailers through our area. You lost?"

"I follow the other trucks."

"Maybe I should check all three trucks. What are you hauling?"

"Cattle. All of us. We stay together." Navarro opened the glove box and handed his logbook out the window.

The constable glanced at the other two trucks stopped on the road shoulder. "Yeah, I see that."

Miguel watched the cop from his side mirror. He reached across and opened his glove box.

Sevino radioed Miguel. "What do we do?"

"You stay put." Miguel crawled over to the passenger side and opened the door.

"Out of the truck, mister," the constable said.

"Please, sir," Navarro begged. "The cattle are thirsty. I should get them to the stockyard."

The constable held the log in one hand and placed his other hand on top of his service weapon. "Open the door and climb out."

Navarro opened the door while Miguel crept around the back of his trailer.

Behind him, the constable noticed his headlights fluttered. He turned his head and saw a shadow move.

Miguel's arms raised shoulder high. A flash shot out of his gun barrel.

It felt like a brick hit the constable's chest, but the vest stopped the bullet. Navarro covered his head with his hands and lunged toward the passenger seat. The constable stumbled backward against the open cab door. He drew his pistol and fired, hitting Miguel in the shoulder. Miguel fired again, and the man fell on his back, moaning with a bullet hole under his left eye. Blood stains spread down the interior of the driver's door. Miguel stood over the constable and aimed his gun. "Fucking cop." Another bullet pierced the man's head.

Sevino jumped out of his cab and ran toward Miguel. The constable lay dead, blood pouring onto the asphalt. "You killed him. You fucking killed him. We have to get out of here now. You hear me? Now."

Miguel collapsed to his knees, blood drained on his shirt.

Navarro jumped out of his truck cab. "You're shot." He looked both ways down the road for headlights before wrapping his arm around Miguel's waist. "Can you drive?"

Miguel's shoulder burned like fire. Each heartbeat pumped pain in his arm and up his neck. "Have to."

Chapter 24

Across the road from The Blue Lily, Quinton and Marla sat inside their Tahoe in the Lone Tree Cafe parking lot. The sweltering heat hovered over South Texas. Their air conditioner blasted air through the dashboard vents.

"How long do we stay?" Marla asked. "I want to see Crosby tonight."

Quinton snapped open his pocket knife, cut an apple down the middle, and offered half to her. "Never know. An hour? Hours? Sometimes all night."

"Thanks." Marla bit into the apple as she gazed at the auction sign flashing tomorrow morning. "There are trucks out there somewhere, and they must unload cattle tonight. The animals will need water and food."

"Right. They should pull in and unload soon."

Marla scooted up in her seat. "Guessing you read my file, know my history, but I know nothing about you."

"Me?" He shook his head. "Not much. Nothing to tell."

"Married?"

He tilted his head a little to the side. "No."

"Kids?"

He thumped the steering wheel with his palm. "Enough interrogation. Ever watch those hunting shows on TV? This one episode has two guys tracking cougars in northern California."

"The two brothers that call themselves Bronco and Buckshot?" Marla snickered.

"Yeah. They're odd, but they know how to track."

"You think they're real?" Marla asked. "They always find what they're tracking the last thirty seconds of the show. It's all editing and setup."

"Probably right, but there is one thing they do that seems to help."

"What's that?" she asked.

"They strap motion-activated cameras on tree trunks to see if the cats, or whatever they're tracking, are nearby at night. The brothers return the next morning, hook it to their laptop, and watch for any action."

"I remember watching animals stroll past the cameras. Eerie-looking eyes."

"So, I bought one and have it in my backpack." Quinton motioned toward the backseat. "A camo green device about the size of a small tissue box. I could strap it to that telephone pole and aim it across the street. We don't need to be here all night. Come back tomorrow morning and check for three trucks."

"I like that. After we do this, I could head over and take care of my husband."

"Or I could set the camera up in about ten minutes, then head over to Schmidt & Schmidt. Check two places at once."

Marla's excitement dropped off a cliff. "Sure. We could do that."

❖

Miguel's truck slogged over a narrow paved road for miles before worsening to a winding trail.

His radio squelched. "What?" He snapped at whoever happened to be on the other end.

Navarro asked, "How much longer?"

"I don't know. Wouldn't be in this mess if you kept close and didn't let that car get between you and Sevino."

"Not my fault. I get nervous riding too close. Sevino made me nervous moving back and forth on the road. It's his fault, not mine."

"Settle down. We'll get there." Miguel heard the cattle groaning from hunger and thirst. "We'll get there soon."

"I heard that, Navarro," Sevino said. "Are you blaming me? It's all your fault. Nobody else. It's all on you, and I'm telling Bird you fucked this up."

"Both of you, shut up," Miguel said. "I see lights up ahead, thirty more minutes."

"If Bird's there, I'm telling him what went down," Sevino said.

"When I get out of this truck," Navarro said. "I'm kicking your ass and then I'm telling Bird you pushed that car into the ditch. He'll cut you up like barbecue."

"Shut up, both of you!" Miguel yelled. "I see a flashing red light about a half mile ahead. Bird said turn left on a paved road and follow it to the stockyard."

"I'm going to kick your ass right now," Navarro said.

"Try it and die, bitch."

◆

Quinton veered off the road across the street from Schmidt & Schmidt Slaughterhouse to the farm implement dealership.

He pulled in between two combine harvesters. "This looks like a suitable spot to wait."

With headlights and inside lights off, he kept the engine running to let the a/c continue to blow cool air. Quinton reached across the dashboard for the cigarette pack.

"I saw those sitting there. You smoke?"

"Used to. Quit. Now I just play with the cigs." He fished for a disposable lighter from the console. "When I have a hard day, I hold the cig up and light it. Smell it for a moment before I put it out." He shoved the lighter into his pocket.

On Marla's side, a set of headlights came into view. "Big truck coming," Marla said.

Quinton killed the engine, silencing their vehicle. They lowered their windows slightly to let air circulate in the stagnant humidity.

The truck downshifted, and the diesel engine roared as the tractor-trailer hauling cattle slowed and passed a single overhead streetlamp at the edge of the drive.

"Get the night vision camera out of the console."

She opened it and noticed a box of 9mm cartridges in the back corner.

He lowered the binoculars. "Always keep an extra box close by, just in case."

"These things are great." Marla took pictures with the camera. "Heat from the truck's hood and wheels shone bright red and yellow."

The first truck stopped, then systematic beeps blared into the night as the truck backed into the unloading dock. Two other livestock trucks downshifted with roaring engines filling the air, then backed into other unloading docks. Men came from the office to help move the animals. Miguel hopped out of the cab, wincing from his shoulder and arm pain. He rushed to the rear of the trailer, trying to ignore the man walking toward him. He asked for help to raise the trailer door.

Arturo barreled out of the slaughterhouse and growled at Miguel, "You're late."

"Don't blame me. It's stupid Sevino and Navarro's fault."

Arturo grabbed Miguel's arm. "You've been shot. What happened?"

Miguel pulled away. "Leave me alone."

"I'll have to tell Bird about this."

"No," Miguel said. "Arturo, I will. I'll tell him when he gets here."

Metal gates clanged inside the trailers, and animals bawled and yawped as they hooved down the chute.

"How many cattle do you think they have?" Quinton asked.

"Without knowing the weight, my guess, twenty or so in each trailer." She stared through the camera. "The trailers are too close together to get decent pictures of what's happening inside or be-hind them."

"So far, it sounds like the only thing going on is unloading cattle."

Marla focused more on the holes in the trailers and the motion inside. The heat from the animals lit up the camera. "The bright-ness of the cattle is blocking everything behind the trailers. I see a man on the upper level near the nose, but not sure what he's doing."

Arturo slapped the last cow hoofing down the ramp, then asked, "Got the girls up there?"

"Yeah, sure," Miguel said. "All yours."

Arturo climbed to the upper level and the doghouse. He opened the lock on the gate. "Vamanos." Six girls trotted down the ramp. "Go. Go," he said as he pushed the last girl forward.

Men along the railings rushed the girls down a walkway between cattle pens to the rear of the stockyard. An eight foot enclosed trailer hooked to a pickup truck waited for them. The doors closed after all the girls from the three trucks climbed inside.

Quinton struggled with his binoculars in the dark. "Not sure where everyone went."

Marla held the night vision camera to her eye and took pictures. "All I see now are three men standing between the first and second trailers. All the rest of the men are gone."

"The drivers?" Quinton asked.

"Should be." She took a dozen more pictures. "Looks like they're arguing."

Sevino shoved Navarro backward. "You wait until Bird comes. He's going to kill you and everyone in your family."

Navarro pulled a knife out of his back pocket and snapped it open. "I'm going to cut you and then go home and fuck your little sister."

Still hurting from the gunshot, Miguel held his arm tight to his chest and squeezed between Sevino and Navarro. "Nobody is getting cut, and no one's dying. We got here safely, and Bird will be happy."

Sevino grabbed Navarro's hand holding the knife and kicked him in the groin. Navarro threw an uppercut, connecting under Sevino's chin, then swung the blade in a wide swath.

Miguel grabbed his bleeding neck, sank to his knees, and fell forward, face first on the ground.

"You dumb shit," Sevino said. "You killed Miguel."

Marla snapped pictures as fast as she could. "Big time trouble. One man down."

Quinton scanned the area with the binoculars, but the darkness impeded his vision. "A driver?"

"I think so," Marla said.

Navarro aimed the knife at Sevino. "You need to take him somewhere."

Sevino swung his fist and hit Navarro in the face. "It's your fault. You started this. You take him somewhere." He pushed Navarro's hand holding the blade against the trailer, then grabbed his throat. "Die, you fucking motherfucker."

A silhouette of a man appeared between the trucks. Sevino and Navarro stopped and stood still.

Bird raised his pistol with a suppressor. He fired twice, and both men collapsed. He fired two more times into their chests.

"Uh, oh. Not good," Marla said. "Man with a gun came around the corner and shot the two."

"Can you ID the perp?" Quinton asked.

"No."

"Give me the camera." Quinton grabbed it out of her hand and watched the scene. Three men came from behind the trailers, picked up the bodies, and pitched them over their shoulders. A minivan pulled in front of the trucks. The side door slid open, and they pitched in the three bodies.

"Schmidt didn't sell the minivans," Quinton said while looking through the camera.

Marla glanced at Quinton. "Are you taking pictures?"

"Sorry, forgot." He clicked the shutter button several times before handing it back to Marla.

She held the button down for rapid-fire pictures. "Got three more men coming in. They're removing the Mexican license plates off the bumpers and replacing them with new ones."

"Texas plates to get them back across the border tonight," Quinton said.

Bird stuck his head inside the passenger window of the minivan. "Same place as the others." He patted the roof twice before ambling back through the pens and disappearing. The three empty tractor-trailers cranked the engines and lit the headlights. In sequence, the trucks headed toward the border.

"Who do we follow? Minivan, trucks, or man?" Marla asked.

Chapter 25

"If we stop the van with bodies, the driver could turn. Possibly get a lot of intel," Quinton said. "The trucks may have something but don't know what. We could get DPS to stop them and do a full search when they're back on the farm-to-market road. The man? He's gone into the maze of pens. We'd never find him."

"The van is our best shot," Marla said. "Let's go."

With the headlights off, Quinton pulled onto the road and followed the red taillights. "It's black outside. No moon. Let me look through the camera as I drive."

Marla passed it to him. "Sounds dangerous." She smirked. "Don't text and drive. Don't hold a camera to your eye."

The road curved several times. "Taillights way up ahead. He's moving fast. I should turn the headlights on to catch up."

Marla shrugged her shoulders. "Your decision."

"Taillights disappeared. Must be a big curve or drop-off ahead." Quinton tapped the steering wheel and stopped the vehicle. "I can't drive looking through this thing."

"Over there." Marla pointed to the right. "Red lights charging down a side road. He's either hurrying to dump the bodies or running from us." She lowered the camera. "He turned on the headlights. You think he knows he's being followed?"

Quinton turned the headlights on and firmly pushed the accelerator while negotiating bumps, divots, and rocks. Headlight beams bounced across the road as the back end slid left and right. Marla steadied herself as best as she could while watching through the camera.

"Anything?" he asked.

"Our headlights make it too bright for me to see straight ahead. Nothing so far to the sides. We lost him. Stop the vehicle."

Quinton slammed on the brakes. She opened her door, climbed on the hood, and scanned the area. "Got him. To the right, a vehicle with headlights off." She jumped down and climbed back into the vehicle. "About two hundred yards, there's a small dirt trail."

Quinton floored it. "Can you see the road he's on?"

"Slow down, almost there. Here. Turn now."

He veered right and charged down the narrow trail. The Tahoe suddenly dropped. Marla forgot to buckle her seatbelt. Her head hit the roof and then her body slammed against the door. Water sprayed in every direction as the vehicle slammed into a creek full of water and mud before stopping.

Marla looked out her side window. "There, a small bridge. He must have taken that."

"I didn't see it." A half foot of water flowed under the vehicle. Quinton said, "We might be stuck. I'm changing to four-wheel drive."

"Do whatever you got to do. We're like fish in a barrel," Marla said as she buckled her belt.

He floored it again and climbed to the top. A fire raged a hundred yards ahead. They cautiously closed in on the van, with flames roaring out the open side door.

"Guess he spotted us," Marla said. "What now? Head back to the stockyard?"

"Where's the driver?" Quinton asked.

The glass behind Marla shattered. Another bullet pierced the windshield.

"Damn." She ducked. "Where is he?"

"Stay down." Quinton floored the accelerator and spun the vehicle around.

A bullet ricocheted off the dolly. Quinton swerved left and right as two bullets pounded the side of their Tahoe. The left wheels missed the bridge again, and the Tahoe rolled onto its side and slammed into water and mud.

Bullets ricocheted off the underside.

"Get out." Quinton kicked the windshield. Water rippled over the hood. He turned and fired toward the gunshots while Marla climbed out and fired into the night.

"We need to get away from the vehicle. The guy can flank us in the dark," Quinton said.

Marla motioned back. "We have no cover if we climb up the creek bank."

He looked back and forth. "Our only out is to run through the water, down the creek."

Multiple gunshots hit their vehicle. Quinton and Marla fired back at the muzzle flashes. Mud spurted inches from Quinton's foot. He hurried around to the other side of the vehicle to find Marla. "Come on."

Their feet splashed with each step, reaching a sharp turn in the creek. Gunfire exploded behind them.

Searing pain hit Quinton, and he fell. "Hit."

"Where?"

"Leg."

Marla jumped behind a bush growing out of the creek's edge. Her pants and shirt soaked, breaths rapid, and heart pounding. She heard water splashing. Is the idiot walking down the middle of the creek? In pitch blackness, she glanced around the dead bush. Quinton moaned between stifled breaths.

Feet swished through the water forty feet away. He called out in a heavy Mexican accent, "I'm going to kill you now, you fucking cop."

Quinton stared at her. Wishing she had the night vision camera, her hand skimmed over the mud and found what she needed. When she pitched a rock over the creek, the man turned and fired. She raised her gun toward the flash and fired twice. A body splashed in the water.

Chapter 26

Marla ripped Quinton's pant leg open, cleaned the mud from the wound as best as possible, and felt for a hole. He winced from the pain. "The bullet sideswiped you. It feels like someone dug a trench in your leg. You'll need stitches."

"I need this like I need another hole in my head." He held his hand in front of him. "Sorry. I say that sometimes. Stupid. I'm sorry."

"Don't worry about it. We need to take you to a hospital. That wound is dirty, and it could get infected."

"Speaking of dirty," he held up his pistol with mud inside the barrel, "not usable. We should call 911."

She removed the phone from her pocket and pushed the on button, but there was no light. "It's soaked. Dead. What about yours?"

He patted his pockets. "Must have lost it in the battle." He lit his disposable lighter. "This still works."

Marla stood and felt the dark fingers of night wrap around her. "Can't see anything out here. Guessing we're a mile or two from the main road and thirty or forty from San Antonio city limits with half a mag, one gun, and no phones." She helped him stand. "Come on. Up you go."

Quinton grasped her shoulder and almost fell as he put weight on the injured leg. "I don't know if I can make it. You go and bring help."

"No way. Have you ever seen The English Patient?"

"The what?"

"It's a movie about a guy who leaves a girl in a cave and runs for help. When he gets back to her, she's dead. I'm not doing that."

"I'm not a weak-ass girl."

"You want to rephrase that, mister?"

"Okay. Second stupid thing I've said tonight. I meant...you know, girls in movies are always...never mind what I meant."

"Mmm-hmm, that's what I thought." She grabbed a belt loop with her arm around his waist and held tight. "Watch for rattlers and coyotes."

"You're a bundle of joy this evening."

"I don't get along with rattlers, and hungry coyotes smell wounded animals a mile away, but usually don't bother humans. They would rather catch a rabbit."

"My leg hurts, so let's get out of here."

Crickets chirped, frogs croaked. A coyote yipped and howled in the night. Marla tried to look over the top of the creek bank, expecting something staring down at them.

"Word is out," she said. "Every coyote smells blood. They don't know if it's a rabbit, cat, dog, or what, but they're hungry."

Limping through the ankle deep water and soft mud, Quinton stopped. "I have to get out of this and on dry land. Can't walk in the stuff."

Marla gestured ahead. "Have to keep going until the banks drop lower."

Quinton hopped a few steps. "Wait a bit. Let me rest before we go."

Barking in the night stopped Marla. "If we run into a wild pack of dogs, this mag won't be enough."

"You think it's one of the packs they mentioned on the news attacking people?"

Marla stood and gazed across the blackness, with the only light coming from twinkling stars a trillion miles away. She could barely see her hand. "I don't know, but we can't take on five or six pit bulls."

A dog barked to their right. It seemed closer. When Quinton pushed his back up the creek bank, he stood shoulder high to the edge of dry land. "I can roll here." He turned and grabbed handfuls of grass and tried to pull himself up. She countered behind him with a shove into his shoulder and back. With gritted teeth, she pushed.

Quinton cursed vile words as he swung his leg on high ground and rolled.

She climbed out of the creek with ease and knelt on her knees. When a coyote yelped and dogs barked incessantly, she jumped to her feet and swung the gun toward the sound.

"They ambushed a coyote," Quinton said.

She crawled near Quinton. "I can't see a thing out here."

After pulling the mag out of her pistol, she emptied the bullets into her hand and felt four cartridges before reloading them. She knew Quinton could never walk a mile or two to town. "I'm going to get the ammo box out of the console and the dolly in the rear. Back in a sec."

"Wait," Quinton said. "You should leave the gun with me. Dogs, remember?"

She wavered, but he was right. He couldn't run. If she had to face a dog, she could jump in the water and hope crazed dogs wouldn't chase her. "Here." She handed him the pistol. "Only four in the mag."

Marla scoured her hand on the ground until she found a broken branch, which meant nothing to a wild animal. She jogged along the creek bank, not wanting to run into a dead man—or worse—not a dead man.

She heard water splashing. It had to be the Tahoe in the creek. The increasing wind bit at her wet clothes. She slid down the muddy bank and felt a slow water flow around her boots. Her hand rubbed across the Tahoe's front quarter panel still lying sideways. *Do I go through where the windshield had been knocked out or where the back door side window had been shot out? Neither ideal.*

Marla lifted the back passenger door and slipped inside. Something cracked under her boot. She reached into the black water and pulled out the camera with a bullet hole through the center. It snapped in half. "Well, crap." It splashed when she dropped it in the ankle high swirling water. "So much for evidence."

The door slammed shut above her head. She spun around and looked up, but there was no one. The chilled water rose to her mid-calf. With doors closed, the vehicle sideways, and rising water, she felt the enclosure surrounding her.

She lowered her hands underwater, reached between the front seats, opened the console, and grabbed the soggy box of cartridges.

Thunder rumbled in the distance. When she gazed through the broken windshield, lightning streaked above hills miles away. She stood and stuck her head out where the side window once was. Another lightning bolt seared the sky, revealing massive clouds raining on the horizon. A blast of cool air hit her, throwing a chill through her wet clothes.

Inside, water sloshed against the tailgate. Marla climbed over the back seat and crouched against the dolly. She pushed on the tailgate, but it didn't move. She pushed on the tailgate window. It didn't move, either.

Water rose a few more inches inside the Tahoe. A loud noise rumbled like a semi-truck charging down a road. She looked toward the front of the vehicle, hoping to see something, but the black night made it impossible. Thunder rumbled like mystic lions roaring in the clouds. Lightning bolts charged into the ground, revealing a narrow tidal wave rushing toward her.

"Oh, things just got worse." A flash flood rushed at her as she ducked behind the seat back.

Uprooted trees and rocks surged in the water. A large branch smashed against the hood and jammed inside where the windshield used to be, blocking her escape. A rush of icy water slammed against her, shoving her back against the tailgate. The wet ammo box broke, spilling the cartridges into the water. "Damn." She clutched the passenger grab handle as the vehicle ground across the creek bed. Rising water lifted the Tahoe and shifted it backward.

She yanked the back door lever, but the door wouldn't open. It was useless. The child safety locks kept potential prisoners from escaping.

The vehicle turned in the rushing waters, front and back bumpers anchored into the muddy creek banks. Water white-capped over the side of the Tahoe. In seconds, the entire vehicle would submerge underwater. It rolled onto its back like a dead animal.

Marla dropped underwater and pushed against the back window again. It wouldn't budge. Raising her head above water with only a few inches of air left, she drew a deep breath, squatted underwater, and kicked the window. It opened, and the water pressure shoved her out of the vehicle and into the rising creek. Her hand grasped the dolly's handle, holding on as her body twisted upside down and over, underwater. When she floated to the top, her lungs gasped for air.

As quick as the flash flood came, it went. The rains moved toward town, never reaching them. The Tahoe sat upside down with branches and mud covering the windows and wheel wells. She coughed out water. Wet hair stuck to her face and neck, with muck covering every inch of her body and clothes. Her socks squished inside the soaked boots.

Marla gathered what little strength she had left and struggled to pitch the hand truck over the creek bank. The bloated tires bounced on dirt and rocks. Her arms reached over the bank, hands grasping clumps of grass, while the toes of her boots dug into the muddy bank. She yelled as she flung herself up to dry ground. With dirt caked onto her clothes and hair, her energy drained; she thought a minute of rest would help.

A dog growled, sounding like it had caught an animal in its limp.

Marla jumped up and grabbed the dolly with tires bouncing across the uneven terrain. Quinton yelled, followed by a gun-shot. She let go of the handle and ran. Two dogs had their heads down, showing sharp teeth, and growled two feet from him. She screamed at the animals and flailed her arms in the air. The sur-prised dogs ran off into the night.

"Quinton, are you all right?"

"Yeah." He dropped onto his back. "One snapped at my leg and caught my pants. I'm glad to see you. Thought you were dead in the flash flood. Find the ammo?"

"No. Got this, instead. Figured you could lie in it, and I could push you."

"That's right nice of you, but I weigh almost two hundred pounds."

"Didn't say it would be easy."

Chapter 27

"Do you know which way you're going?" Quinton asked as she turned right where the creek forked.

Marla held the handle while the dolly trundled behind her with Quinton lying on top. "Strictly a guess. Looks like there's a red light flashing on a tower a mile or so away. I remember passing a short bridge during the chase. We should be heading toward the road, but I could be sending us further into the abyss. It's so fricking black outside."

Coyotes yelped on their left, with dogs barking on their right. Marla gazed both ways, wishing for nothing close to them. "The coyotes are keeping their distance. We should too. You have the pistol, right?"

"Right. Guess I'm the tail gunner."

Her forearms and shoulders ached from pulling the heavy weight. Sisyphus had it better. Quinton moaned each time the tires bounced over a rock. Her foot slipped, causing her to fall and Quinton to roll to the ground.

"Oh, Jeez. I'm sorry," Marla said. She lay flat on her back with every muscle yelling to stop.

Quinton held in a scream. It took a few seconds to answer. "Leg is feeling hot."

Two dogs rammed into Quinton and ground their teeth into his arm. He screamed and flailed as best he could. "Get off me. Get off."

Marla jumped up and swung the dolly over them. The two dogs let go and paced back ten feet, with one barking like a rabid animal. The other moved its front legs side to side.

"Where's the gun?" Marla asked.

"I don't know. I dropped it." Quinton snapped open his pocket knife. "This won't go deep, but maybe it will scare them."

"Sounds like we have one to our side, along with one near your feet."

Quinton flicked his lighter on and off. "Don't know if this will help."

"Give that to me." She held it above her head and caught a miraculous glimmer of light six feet from her. "Found it." Marla grasped the cold metal of the gun from the ground.

He felt teeth snip at the tips of his shoes. Quinton bent his knees, and pain shot through his wounded leg. He threw a handful of dirt at the animals and yelled, "Get out of here!"

The pit bull lunged forward, then jumped back. It let out a low growl and barked.

"I think he's trying to bite my shoe and drag me away," Quinton said.

"The other is easing toward me," Marla said. "If I shoot and miss, a third of our ammo is lost."

The dog lunged and sunk its teeth deep into Quinton's calf. He screamed and stabbed the animal twice before it yelped and ran into the darkness.

The other charged at Marla. She fired, and it dropped in front of her. It made a death whine before it stopped breathing.

"Hold on." She spun around the hand truck to feel Quinton's leg. "You have some deep puncture wounds. Let me have your knife."

"And do what with it?"

"You don't trust me? I could leave you here, and the dogs would be happy."

He handed her the knife. "Thanks. Just remember, I gave you half my apple."

She sliced the inseam of his pants, cut the legs off mid-thigh, and made them into bandages. "We need to get out of here." She wheeled the dolly close to him. "Climb on."

"No. We stay here. Gather kindle and branches, and we'll make a fire. That should keep the animals away. They'll catch us in a few seconds if we try to run."

"Have to find some dry stuff." She handed the knife back. "I can't go out there without the gun. You good here with just the knife?"

"No, but go ahead."

The night wind swirled, drying the mud on her face and hair. She rubbed as much off as she could before bundling twigs and grass in her left hand while holding the gun in her right. She piled them near Quinton, sitting with his legs stretched out. "This should get you started. I'll go for the bigger ones when the fire is going."

Quinton lit the kindling with his lighter. "Cigarettes might have saved my life."

Marla pitched more on the fire as yellow flames licked the air.

Marla sat beside him. "Marshmallows?"

"I could go for s'mores about now," Quinton rolled onto his back as the fire raised several feet in the air. He touched the face of his digital watch, and it lit 3:46 a.m. "We should see daylight in about three hours."

"This should keep the dogs at bay. Close your eyes and rest. I'll take the first watch." She watched smoke rise above the flames into the black night, just like the minivan on fire and the plane at the airport. It never crossed her mind until now. Did the pilot survive, or was a body found inside the burning wreckage?

Coyotes howled in the night.

"Sounds like the dogs went after the coyotes," Quinton said. "Arms and legs hurt like the dickens." With his energy zapped, he rolled to his side and laid his head on one hand while holding the knife in the other. "I'll be better in the morning."

"Sure," she said.

A minute passed before he rolled on his back and said, "South Carolina."

"Sorry?"

"That's where I grew up. My father received his pension after twenty-five years as a police officer, and my mother ran the house. A sister...somewhere. Me? Four years at Auburn with a baseball scholarship. Not good enough for the Majors, so I joined the police force and then DEA."

"Where did you learn Spanish?"

"Foreign language classes at Auburn."

"Married?"

He cleared his throat. "That's why I needed the dolly. I boxed up my wife's clothes. She died seven months ago from, um...breast cancer. Hit her fast." He rubbed the leg bandage. "Being a teacher, we planned to see Europe on spring break, but, well, it didn't happen."

Marla threw another branch on the fire. "I'm sorry."

"The FDA approved a brand new drug, and her doctors wanted to give it to her, but the school insurance wouldn't pay for it." He sat up. "I called a hundred times. They didn't care. I talked to HR at work. They didn't help, and so she died." He whisked dirt from his hair. "Nothing much to do outside of work. Online gambling keeps me busy now."

"Gambling?" she asked.

"What am I supposed to do after work, watch TV? I bet on baseball, football, soccer, golf, and NASCAR. I bet on anything. Damn the insurance. Damn the government and their twisted rules."

Three dogs crept closer with guttural growls. The fire lit up their faces with icy gray eyes staring at them. The animals trekked back and forth.

"Didn't take long for them to regroup," Quinton said. He turned around and pushed his back against hers. With his knife in hand, he said, "Expect them to attack one direction and flank us from the other." He unwrapped the bandage on his leg and handed it to her. "Wrap this on a stick and torch it."

A jet roars a mile above them.

She wrapped the cloth on a stick, lit it, and returned it to him. "Think they can see our fire?"

"Too small. Besides, the pilots are looking toward the heavens." Quinton looked up at the stars. "Me too."

Marla stood, swung her arms out, and yelled, "Go! Get away!" She flung a burning branch at the predator staring at her.

She didn't see the dog lunging in the air behind her. It latched onto her left arm, its head twisting, teeth digging deeper. It dragged her across the ground like a toy doll. Quinton climbed to his hands and knees, screaming and waving his torch. Marla shoved the gun barrel against the belly of the animal and fired. The dog yelped before it dropped dead. The other two ran away.

Pain shot through her entire body as she grabbed her arm. She crawled to Quinton and lay near him. "Have one bullet left." She shook her head. "It's not enough to get us through the night."

Quinton's leg throbbed. He coughed. "Have an idea." He cleared his throat. "Build the fire up and drag the carcass on top. The hair will burn and stink to high heaven, but it might keep those animals away."

"That weighs thirty pounds, and I have one good arm."

"Make it a Viking burial. Throw grass and branches on top of it and let it burn."

She leaned back on her knees. "I'd have to go out there and get more wood."

"Screw it. Use this torch and set the beast on fire."

Dogs growled and barked nearby.

"Yeah," Quinton yelled. "We're burning your buddy. Any of you hell dogs want to join in?"

Marla said, "They're regrouping."

"You want the torch?" Quinton said.

She lit the hair on fire, then pitched grass and small branches on top.

The hair stunk up the place, but the fire snowballed with sparks flying and settling yards away, catching the grass on fire. Within minutes, the flames hovered ten feet in the air. The winds shifted toward them, and a line of fire roared as it ate through grass and weeds. Marla looked both ways. The flames grew to over twenty feet on each side and encircled them in less than a minute. She shoved the dolly toward Quinton.

"Get on."

"Only place left to go is back to the creek," Quinton said. "You can't push me with your arm like that."

She handed the pistol to Quinton with one bullet left. "Get on and let's go."

Quinton rolled on top, screaming curse words again. Marla's shoulders ached as she pulled the handle behind her. Hot winds swirled, and sparks flew.

A dog charged at Quinton's legs. "Shit." He fired. The dog yelped and rolled to a stop. "Last bullet."

Marla dodged flames erupting in front of them. Pulling hard with each stride, she charged in the direction where the creek was supposed to be. She had Sisyphus beat this time. "Where is it?"

Two dogs arced in from the side and charged toward Quinton. "Hurry up!"

She felt the balls of her feet shove into the ground as hard as they could.

The fire shifted, flanking its prey like victorious gladiators. The dogs turned away, and the flames engulfed them.

"Has to be close," Quinton said. "See anything?"

"Not yet."

The fire roared out its anger, stretching higher, devouring everything in its path. Heat dug into her neck. Her legs weakened. Her foot slipped, and she dropped to her knees. Quinton rolled off. He tried to stand but fell.

"Where the hell is it?"

She grabbed his arm and swung it over her shoulder. "Come on, can't stop." She slapped burning ash out of her hair.

Her legs ached when she sprung to her feet. The fire felt like a blowtorch searing the right side of her face. With both hands, she grasped the handle behind her. Ignoring the pain from the animal bite on her forearm, she bulldozed forward.

Quinton struggled to hold on as the tires bounced over rocks. "The fire's closing in on us."

Marla yelled as she reached the edge of the creek, her arms and legs flailing in the air, with the dolly and Quinton following. She spun around, and her back slapped into the mud. Water exploded around her, knocking her breath away.

Quinton covered his head when the hand truck crashed into him. "My leg, I think I broke something. It hurts like a motherfucker." He touched the bullet wound and winced. "A motherfucker."

Fire raged at the creek's edge, mad as hell it couldn't climb down and take its victims. Sirens wailed in the distance.

Marla asked, "Is that a cop chasing someone or, God help us, please, a firetruck?"

Air horns blared, and water sprayed on the flames.

Marla's lips curled as she laughed inside. Lying flat against the bank, her arms and legs suddenly felt too heavy to move.

Chapter 28

After the physician released Marla, she made a beeline to Quinton's room and pushed open the door. She froze. Visions of Crosby crossed her mind; the monitor beeping, IV lines draining into arms, a bedsheet neatly tucked under his sides like a mummy or a corpse, except Quinton turned and waved.

"They washed my wounds for an hour and filled me with antibiotics and morphine. Have you ever had morphine? That drug is fantastic. I want more, a bunch more."

She closed the door behind her. "Anything broken?"

"No, just a sprained knee, but they tell me I must stay overnight, and the doctors would scrub out the leg and arm wounds in the morning. After that, I come in once a day for a shot of antibiotics. I'm going to ask for more morphine. That's good stuff."

"Am I on hold until you recover enough to return?"

"No." Quinton scooted in the bed. Borland left a while ago, and I told him he should put you back into the field as soon as you get your medical release. You don't need more training. In fact, you should train the next newbie."

She sat down in the chair by Quinton's bed. "I'll report for work later this morning."

Quinton laughed. "They wrapped your right arm in gauze, and you'll need medical clearance before you return to work."

"Why? The doctors released me from here. I'm fine. Just need a few days for the animal bite to heal."

Quinton scooted further back. "Need a release from *our* medical department."

"Fine. I'll wait. I'll go this afternoon."

"Wrong again. Have to call for an appointment."

"Appointment?" She stood and flipped his small IV bags, looking for the names like she had any idea. "I'll call a taxi to get my truck at the bureau and then talk to Borland."

"You'll never make it past the security desk. Take the day off. Take two."

She glanced at her watch. "I need to see Crosby," she pointed toward the door, "but I'm calling the doctor's office straight up at nine o'clock tomorrow morning...after I buy a phone."

"Getting a replacement at the phone store would take a long time. Go down to the convenience store and get a burner."

"Yeah. Okay."

The bright morning light startled her as she squinted and covered her eyes with her forearm. After getting her truck, she drove to the store a block away. In line, a hunched-back elderly lady rested her forearms on the aluminum walker. The cashier with tattoos on his face, neck, and arms sat behind the counter, ripped off four lottery tickets, and handed them to her. She moved away and stood next to the coffee dispensers before scratching off the gray coating. In front of Marla stood a kid holding a six-pack of beer. He plopped it on the counter with a ten-dollar bill. The cashier glanced at the kid and then at Marla with a badge on her belt.

"No way, bud. Your too young."

"What are you talking about? I came here yesterday, and you sold it to me then."

The cashier glanced at Marla again. "Not me. Get out of here before that cop behind you says something."

The teenager spun around wide-eyed at Marla. "Yeah, right." He rushed out the door.

Marla pushed the beer to the side and pointed at the burner phones hanging on the wall behind the cashier. "I'll take one of those."

"A burner? Sure." He smiled. "You buying drugs or hiding a boyfriend from your husband?"

"Neither. Phone, please."

"Got some on sale." He weeded through a stack from behind him and laid a few on the counter. "Pretty cool colors. Green, orange, and yellow. They all have double minutes."

Marla pushed the colored ones to the side. "I'll take the black one."

After setting up the phone in the store, Marla hustled outside while holding her phone to her ear. "Sorry, doc. I couldn't make it last night. How is Crosby?"

"I'm stuck inside this trailer, a metal hotbox, and hungry."

"You slept in the bed, right?"

"Yes."

"Enough water for a shower and brush your teeth?" Marla asked.

"Blimey. What are you, my mum? Bring food."

"Breakfast tacos on their way."

He rubbed the back of his hand over his mouth. "You're killing me with your Yank food."

"I'll stop at the Grill House and pick up hard-boiled eggs, sausage links, and an English muffin. How's that?"

"Finally, edible food in this God-forsaken country."

"You said you had news for me about Crosby."

"You'll see, and don't forget the marmalade."

Half an hour later, Marla pulled the truck around the backside of the shed. The generator constantly ran, supplying light inside the shed and air conditioning for the trailer. While carrying the food bags, she stepped to the metal wall as sunlight poked through a small, round hole. Her finger rubbed the smoothness of the void with an exit hole on the other side. No doubt in her mind it came from a bullet. She knocked on the door and quickly opened it.

Dr. McCollum removed the stethoscope diaphragm from Crosby's chest and turned toward the door. He hadn't shaved since leaving Louisiana, and his two-day-old scruff, when he met Marla at the restaurant, had turned into a hobo mess. He snatched the food bags from Marla's hand and sat in the chair, "I'm bloody starving to death," then dug into the sack, peeled a hard-boiled egg, and bit into it.

Marla stared at Crosby's face. It seemed less waxy than yesterday. She winced at the thin steel tube extending from the skull. It looked like an antenna. She squeezed the almost full IV bag hanging from the ceiling. "Do you have enough of these?"

"Yes."

"What about food for Crosby?"

"I expect him to drink soon."

She shook her head in disbelief before reaching for Crosby's hand. "Hello, my love."

With a mouthful of egg, McCollum called out, "No. Stop. Don't touch him."

She pulled her hand back. "Why?"

"Please step back. I first must show you something."

Marla stood at the end of the bed while staring at Crosby's face. Dr. McCollum stuffed the rest of the egg into his mouth. After swallowing, he said, "The patient has improved as I expected." He took a pen from his shirt pocket and touched the point against the palm; fingers flexed.

She dropped to her knees and pressed Crosby's hand against her cheek. "You're better. You moved. It's all better." She faced the doctor again. "This is good. How soon can he talk to me?" His heart rate beeped faster. "Is that him doing that?" Crosby exhaled harder. "He's talking to me," Marla said. "I love you. We'll get you well, I promise."

The alarm blared again. "Christ." The doctor turned it off and stuffed the second egg into his mouth. "It's time for another dose. Please step back and let me do my work."

He'd become proficient in readying the stem cells, protein extract, catalyst, centrifuge with ultraviolet light, and injections through the tube into the brain. When finished, he reached for his food and took a bite of link sausage.

"How much longer with that thing stuck in his head?"

"As the brain redevelops, I pull it further out."

"When will he talk?" Marla asked.

The doctor shook his head. "I can't answer that. The patient should be able to communicate better soon, just not sure how much."

She wished he would stop calling Crosby—the patient. "What do you mean?"

"Even if his brain fills in with new tissue, I don't know if everything will work as it once did. His speech, hearing, and thoughts may not be the same."

Marla glanced at the doctor's hands as he took another bite of food.

"Why the tremor?"

He rubbed his hands together. "Hungry."

Crosby's fingers twitched more. Marla held his hand. "Come on, my love. Squeeze me." His heart rate stabilized. "Crosby?"

"I think he may have fallen asleep."

She released Crosby's hand and placed it on top of his chest. "We'll talk later."

After stepping away from the bed, she sat at the table across from the doctor. "Who was here?"

He turned his head away from her as he placed the stethoscope behind his neck. "May I finish my breakfast, please?" He pointed at a bandage on her forearm. "What happened to you?"

"Don't worry about that."

"I'm a doctor, and you have blood on the gauze. Did something bite you or tear your skin?"

Marla removed a small paper sack from inside the larger plastic bag. "A wild dog bit me. I'm all good."

Dr. McCollum chuckled. His thumb and finger spread his mustache away from his upper lip before biting into the muffin covered in marmalade. "Wild dog? Much like Yanks I know."

Marla unrolled the aluminum foil from around her soft taco. "I'll rephrase my question. Who else has been inside the shed since I left?" She stared at the doctor across the table as she bit into her food.

The orange spread on his muffin brought him back to comfortable days in London. He placed the rest of the sausage on top and folded it like a taco. "I have been terribly busy here." He took a bite. "There are farmers out there, and I don't keep track of what is happening outside the trailer." He took another bite, shoved the food into his cheek, then pointed at his patient. "He's kept me quite busy, indeed."

After finishing her first taco, she wadded the foil and pitched it into the sack. "Hmm." She wiped her mouth with a half-sized napkin, the kind fast-food restaurants hand out. "Well, staying busy is good." She bit the second one in half. After chewing and swallowing it, she cleared her throat. "You didn't answer my question. You've worked extremely hard, and I genuinely appreciate everything you've done for my husband." She ate the last of the taco and pitched the used foil into the sack. "And because of this, I will ask as nicely as possible."

He stood and held the stethoscope again.

"Who brought in a gun and fired a bullet into the shed's structure?"

Dr. McCollum dropped the stethoscope on the bed between Crosby's legs and blurted out, "A man surprised me and asked for money. Some bloody drifter, a bum, a guy alongside the road. He must have heard the generator, and he came in."

"So, a man robbed you?"

"Yes, that's right. A man robbed me."

"What did he take?"

He took a moment to check the monitor. "I had a few bills in my pocket."

"Not the five thousand I gave you?"

"No."

She rolled up the paper sack. "Why the bullet?"

His fingers twirled the ends of his mustache. "I don't know what you mean."

"There is a bullet hole in the wall of the shed."

"Oh, yes, of course. I argued with the prat. Told him to go straight away from here, but he pulled a gun on me."

"Why did he shoot the gun?"

With animated hands, he replied, "I...he pulled the gun out and swung it near my face. I pushed his arm away, and it went off."

Marla dropped the paper sack inside the wastebasket. "Never get into a fight with a thief. Give him what they want and let him get on his way."

"Right. I'll remember that the next time someone surprises me with a gun."

Crosby exhaled hard again. Marla rushed to his side and knelt beside the bed. She pressed her lips against the back of his hand.

"Are you talking to me?"

He breathed hard again. Marla turned toward the doctor. "He's communicating with us. We must figure out a way to understand him."

Crosby's index finger moved slightly.

"I think that's a yes," Marla said.

He moved again.

"Okay. Once for yes, two for no."

He didn't move.

"Crosby, come on. Move one for yes and two for no. We can work on simple questions."

The heart rate and respirations stayed steady. Dr. McCollum patted the back of her shoulder. "I think he went back to sleep."

Marla stood. The monitor beeped steadily behind her. "Come outside with me." She opened the door and exited down the metal steps.

He followed and closed the door behind him, knowing she needed him as much as he needed her. *It doesn't matter what happened at the restaurant. She must protect me.* His brain called out for another hit of cocaine.

Marla pointed at the bullet hole. Like a principal would talk to a student in trouble, without raising her voice, she spoke firmly, "You're lying about the robbery. Who did this and why?"

He pretended he couldn't see a bullet hole. "There's nothing else to say."

Marla patted his pockets like a police officer would during an arrest. "You have your phone? The thief didn't steal it, did he?"

"I have it."

"Where?"

He pointed toward the trailer. "Inside."

"Good." She opened a small storage door on the side of the trailer and removed a portable security camera. "When Crosby and I traveled to rodeos and kept the horses at night, we hung this outside." She hooked it above the side door. "Battery operated, no wires." She looked behind her. "No. Not there. I think it would be better near the generator, that way, I can see who enters the shed with an unobstructed view of the door." It took her a minute to set it all up with her left arm hurting. She showed her screen to the doctor. "Great. All set."

He needed to change the subject. "Speaking of phones and computers, I can get the patient to talk. Not with his mouth, but another way."

"What way?"

"Can't tell you. I haven't sent in a patent yet. I will make millions with this program."

"A patent? So, you've tried this thing on people before?"

"Yes."

"Do you have it with you?"

"No."

"Do you know where this program, or thing, or whatever it is, is?"

"Yes."

She was afraid to ask but did anyway. "Where?"

Chapter 29

Dr. McCollum avoided Marla's stares while trying to convince her she would be in his way staying overnight inside the trailer. Most people fall for the 'I'm a doctor, and I know what I'm doing' spiel.

Marla listened. She still had more work searching for Bird and the other girls. After several hours of sitting, standing, and kneeling beside Crosby, the time came for more stem cells and IV fluids. The gunfight, flash flood, wild dogs, fire, and dragging a man across an open field caught up to her, and she needed a night of rest in a comfortable bed. Acquiescing to the doctor's request to leave, she headed for the ranch.

Marla's eyes felt heavy while driving. She needed a deterrent and touched favorites on the dashboard screen.

"Wales here."

"Excuse me, but aren't you supposed to address yourself as Special Agent Quinton Wales?"

Quinton chuckled. "You caught me. My apologies. Did you get some sleep after leaving the hospital?"

"Not yet. Still daylight, but I'm on my way back to the ranch and a bed."

"What's at your ranch? Animals or plants?"

"Cattle. Just so you know, ranches have animals, farms have plants."

"Good to know. Someone there 24/7 watching the cattle?"

"No. The ranch hand we had for years left town after the shooting, but the cattle will be fine. Where is Torres-Hernandez?"

"Bird is Bird, and impossible to find. Is the quack doctor watching your husband?"

"Not a quack, just quirky."

"I have a friend in the DOJ who said Scotland Yard is hunting this guy. They want his ass back in London. My guess is not just for questioning but incarceration. Don't flush your brand new career down the drain protecting this doctor."

Quinton may be right, except Crosby had done something no brain trauma person had done before—improve this quickly. She needed Dr. McCollum to continue his work, no matter what. "I won't." She hoped not.

"You have the girl at your house?"

"Heading there now to check on her. I'm planning to have her review mugshots." She passed an open field with cattle grazing and envisioned Kata locked inside a livestock trailer. "It would be great if she could pick out Bird's photo."

"I can save you the time. He's never been incarcerated in the US."

"He could have been and lied about his name. Longshot, but we'll try."

"How's your husband?"

"I've been with Crosby the last few hours, and he's doing well."

"Doing well? You might need to reassess your state of reality, girl. How well could a guy with a fresh head wound be doing?"

She shouldn't tell anyone about Crosby's status. No one would believe her. "How's your leg?"

"Sore as the dickens, but I can tough it out. They want me to use a cane for a few weeks, so I must find a nice one. Don't want a wooden stick from Walmart."

Marla laughed. "And the arm where the dog bit you?"

"Sore. The doctor said it missed all the important stuff."

Sunlight glistened from the barbed wire as she drove alongside her property. "Good. I'll call you in the morning." After disconnecting the call, she noticed a section of barbed wire had fallen to the ground. She eased to the shoulder of the road and backed the truck to the spot, noticing a one-by-one wooden stake had not fallen; it had snapped in the middle. The sun hadn't risen high enough to get a good view of the land for footprints, but tire tracks on the road formed a U-turn. She walked a few feet where blood had stained the asphalt and guessed the distance to the broken fence at thirty to thirty-five feet. Did a vehicle hit a deer? Slam against the fence and break the post? A colored cotton strip hung on a barb—from a shirt. Someone came here. "Kata!"

Truck tires bounced over the cattle guard as she approached the gate. After the pickup slid to a stop fifty feet in front of the house, Marla hopped out and drew her weapon. Both horses pranced inside the corral, Birds pecked away on the feed inside the chicken wire, and the front door of the house was wide open.

Marla bolted toward the door and stopped. Inside, Mexican music played like at the abandoned house where she found the girls with a constant whine in the background. She entered with a two-handed grip on her pistol raised shoulder high.

The smell of lilac and baby powder filled the air when Marla stepped past the threshold. Music blared from the radio on the end table beside the couch. She watched the backside of a young girl move her bare feet to the music while pushing the vacuum cleaner. Marla holstered her pistol and turned down the sound. "Ola."

Kata jumped and screamed. She spun around and flipped the vacuum off. "Marla!" Running to her savior, she wrapped her arms around Marla's waist. Kata tried her best English. "I'm so happy to see you."

Marla kissed the top of the girl's head. "Me too. You speak English very well. Show me what you've been doing."

Kata released Marla and rushed to the kitchen. "I clean all your dishes and glasses and the shelves they sit on. The counters, the table, the chairs, the floor. I clean it all."

"Yes, I see. And vacuum too? I forgot I had that."

Kata latched onto Marla's hand and led her to the bedroom. "I wash the sheets, clean the windows, and the bathroom." She scrunched her nose. "Messy bathroom, but I clean everything on the counter."

"Everything?" Marla entered. The recently oiled marble countertops re-emphasized the golden flakes glittering between a meld of black and gray stone. Brass knobs on creamy white cabinets buffed to a shine. Her hairbrush, sprays, hand mirror, makeup — everything missing. "Where did you put my stuff?"

Kata opened the drawers, revealing everything in perfect order. She opened the shower glass door. "I clean all spots off glass and floor too."

"Have you been doing this since I left?"

"I sing and dance and clean all day and all night."

Marla bent down on one knee in front of Kata. "Thank you, but you shouldn't have done this. You were supposed to rest and get back your strength."

"I want to repay you for taking me out of jail." She hugged Marla's neck. "You saved my life."

Marla motioned toward the barn. "And what about the animals? I asked you to stay in the house."

"I waited until just before the sun came up this morning and then gave the horses hay and fed the chickens. I see no one outside."

Marla remembered the broken fence. A deer jumping the fence and didn't clear it? She took Kata's hand. "Come on, let's have a late breakfast." She smiled back at Kata. "I may have a new ranch hand."

"I would like that very much."

The bacon sizzled and popped in the cast iron skillet. Marla used her right hand to fork each piece and gently placed them on paper towels to soak up the grease.

On the opposite side of the kitchen island, Kata smiled while leaning on her elbows with her head resting in her palms. "What happened to your arm?"

"Nothing. Would you like a glass of orange juice?" Marla asked.

Kata sat up. "I have not had that in many months."

"Did you not look in the fridge after I left?"

Kata shook her head. "No, no. There may be something personal inside there. I would not look."

Marla snickered, *but you'll clean the bathroom*. "You may open it anytime and eat or drink anything."

Marla turned, opened the door, removed a quart bottle of juice, poured a glassful, and handed it to Kata. She downed it all at once. Marla couldn't keep from chuckling. "More?"

Kata nodded and smiled back.

The grease sizzled louder when Marla placed the eggs in the skillet.

After they ate and the little girl washed the dishes, a message pinged on Marla's phone. The name said UNKNOWN. Her finger hovered over the message before pressing the open button.

AGENT ADAMS, I AM GLAD YOU ARE DO-ING WELL AFTER ALL YOU WENT THROUGH. DOGS, FIRE, FLASH FLOOD. PLEASE ACCEPT MY APOLOGY FOR AGENT WALES BEING SHOT. IT SEEMS MY BULLETS DON'T KILL DEA AGENTS. YOUR NEW FRIEND BELONGS TO ME. I WANT HER BACK.

Did Bird find her phone number on one of those reverse number websites? And how did he find out so quickly about last night?

Her phone dinged. Breaking News in San Antonio. Two DEA agents survive a harrowing night fighting a Mexican drug cartel and wild dogs.

"Geez. The firemen? Hospital personnel? Police? Who can't keep their mouth shut?" Marla trudged out to her truck, returned with the laptop, and sat on the couch. Typing in the DEA work site, she entered her eighteen digit password and retrieved cartel arrest photos. "Kata, come here, please."

The young girl came out of the kitchen smiling and wiping her hands on a dishtowel. "Si."

Marla turned the laptop screen toward Kata. "These are called mugshots, and I want you to look very carefully at these photos and tell me if any are Torres-Hernandez."

Kata's smile disappeared.

Marla patted the couch. "Come sit."

Kata sat on the couch with her knees touching each other and toes pointed in. The tips of her fingers covered her mouth while flipping through the photos, hoping never to see his face.

Marla left the girl to review the photos by herself while she returned to the kitchen and called the DEA office.

"Drug Enforcement Agency. How may I direct your call?"

"ASAC Borland's office, please."

"Who may I say is calling?"

Marla turned toward the back door and away from Kata's ears. "Special Agent Marla Adams."

"Hold, please."

Elevator music from the eighties, with too much tenor and no bass, tinged Marla's phone. She held it away from her ear and made a mental note to contact IT to change it.

Could I have done anything different to keep Quinton from being shot? It was mayhem; the creek, an ambush, a man killed, rabid animals, and a wildfire.

The music stopped.

"Adams, why are you calling?" Borland asked. "You are officially on medical leave."

Marla cleared her throat. "Yes, sir. Not sure of the protocol for completing my report. Do I send it in by email or drop a hard copy off at the front desk, and someone delivers it to you?"

"Encrypted email. I spoke to Agent Wales. He said you did an excellent job out there. He also said you shot another man."

Her neck muscles tightened. "Yes, sir."

"Is every report from you going to involve a shooting?"

"No, sir. I hope this will be the last."

Kata screamed in the living room. She screamed again. Marla dropped her phone on the table, drew her weapon, and ran out of the kitchen. Kata stood with her feet antsy on the couch.

"Stop screaming. What's wrong?"

Kata pointed at the floor, still screaming.

Marla aimed her pistol at the floor and pushed the coffee table to her side. A snake, about a half-foot long, wiggled along the baseboard. Marla holstered her weapon. She gently placed the toe of her boot on top of the snake's head and picked it up by the tail.

"It's okay. Just a hognose snake. They don't bite people." She carried it outside and flung it into the bushes. Upon returning, she asked, "Recognize anyone?"

Kata slumped back on the couch. "No."

"Oh, crap," Marla said. "Borland." She rushed back to the kitchen and picked up her phone. "Hello? Sir? Are you there?"

"Sounds like you have a child screaming."

Marla rubbed her hand across her face. "A small harmless snake. I pitched it outside."

"Your file shows you have no children."

"No, sir. I mean, yes, sir. I, uh, I don't have any children yet."

"Friends at the house?"

"Um, right." Marla glanced back at the girl. "Someone who recently moved to Hildebrandt."

"Don't forget, you're on medical leave until cleared."

"Yes, sir. I called to ask how I go about getting medical clearance."

"Call the clinic for an appointment and send the paperwork when released."

"Yes, sir. A doctor's appointment would take a few days. Didn't know if you could help in, you know, a little help to get in sooner."

"Adams? That's up to the doctor. Call and take the first one they have."

Chapter 30

After ensuring all the doors locked and Kata safe inside, Marla put the chickens in the coop. The horses needed a run, which she needed as much as they did. Blackie pranced his front legs around, ready to go. Tightening the saddle on Daisy, her hand brushed over the image of a heart burned on the leather. She remembered the burning odor as Crosby held the brand against the leather fender days after they married.

The thought nagged her. Should she leave the doctor alone with Crosby? But squeezing three in the trailer quickly became intense, and she'd told no one the location. Her hopes skyrocketed when Crosby moved. She wanted to be there constantly, but she needed to give the doctor space to work. After mounting Daisy and grasping Blackie's reins, they headed for the creek.

Water trickled over rocks, and doves cooed in trees. Marla dismounted and let the two horses drink from the creek. She chuckled when they were as close as new lovers, tails intermingling like her and Crosby's fingers once did.

An eleven-foot-wide oak tree with a magnificently formed crown stood near the water. She ran her fingers over a heart brand burned into the trunk chest high. Marla smiled, remembering Crosby branded their house, barn, chicken coop, and gate. Anything he could brand, he did.

She twisted her hair into a bun and clasped it with a hair band. Bending down on her haunches, she gazed into the water and remembered the two laughing and skinny-dipping prior to her departure for Quantico. "You must come through this, Crosby Adams.

Leaving me behind is not part of our plan. We have kids to raise, a life to live." She folded her hands in front of her and prayed to God for Crosby's life.

On the opposite side of the creek, Marla caught a glimpse of a deer poking its head around the tree and nibbling on acorns. It froze and stared at her for a moment before dashing off.

A heavy weight captured her body. She didn't sleep the night before, fighting for Quinton Wales' life. Her life too. Everything would have gone to shit if she died out there. Would the English doctor continue his work or pack up and leave? With no one to speak for his medical license application, why stay? He would leave Crosby to die in the trailer, found days, weeks, even months later. And the girl, Kata, ICE would take her back to Mexico, and the Los Zetas Cartel would kill her.

She sat on the ground and made a phone call. "Is he doing fine?"

"Yes," McCollum said.

"A little more information, doctor," Marla replied.

"Bollocks, woman." He licked his fingertip and wiped the small amount of cocaine on the table. "He's resting." The alarm rang. "Time for another dose. I must go." He disconnected the call and rubbed the powder over his gums.

She decided against calling him back. With the reins in her hand, the two horses strolled behind her along the creek bank. A turtle crawled from the mud and disappeared underwater. A willow tree's branches arched in flawless fashion with fallen leaves swirling in the water.

Time got away from her, and twilight inched toward the sky. She mounted Daisy and flipped Blackie's reins over his neck. She didn't need to hold them. The horse knew where to go, and they headed back toward the house.

After putting the horses in their stalls and ensuring they had hay for the night, she returned to the house, locked the doors, and closed the curtains. Kata stood in the living room wearing Crosby's Dallas Cowboys t-shirt hanging below her knees. Kata gave one of those sad smiles. "When I cleaned the bedroom, I found this lying on the chair. Is it okay for me to wear?"

"Yes, of course. I thought no one could wear it better than my husband, but I like what I see."

Kata dashed toward Marla and hugged her again. "Thank you for saving my life." She released Marla, grasped her hand, and led her to the kitchen table. "I made you dinner." A glass of orange juice sat beside a small plate with a peanut butter sandwich and potato chips.

Marla smiled and bowed to her. "Thank you." They both sat at the table. Marla took a bite and remembered she had forgotten to throw the stale bread away after breakfast that morning. She had worse. "Mmm."

Kata's brow furrowed. "What does that mean?"

Marla swallowed the bite before she took a drink of juice. "It means this is wonderful. Thank you for the lovely food and for thinking of me."

Kata scooted her chair closer to the table. "Where is your husband?"

Marla put the sandwich on the plate. "He is...he has been sick, and a doctor is helping him."

"Is he in the hospital?"

"Something like that."

She laid her hand on top of Kata's. "Tomorrow, you have one job. No cleaning. You sit in front of the computer and look at photos all day. If you recognize anyone, then tap the mouse on the photo. I can look at the ones you pick out when I return tomorrow afternoon. Agreed?"

"Yes, agreed." Kata smiled. "May I have juice tomorrow?"

"Of course." Marla laughed and wrapped her arm around the teenager. "You can have anything you want in the refrigerator."

They watched a rom-com movie on television Kata had not seen it before. Marla had to remember the girl was sixteen, even though her height was that of a thirteen or fourteen-year-old, and she acted much younger than her age. Malnourished and inexperienced, Marla couldn't imagine this girl in a life of forced sex.

With the television off and the kitchen clean, Marla tucked the girl on Crosby's side of the bed and turned out the lights. Returning to the couch, she spun the laptop around and flipped through the mugshots while rubbing her temples, trying to remember what the man looked like with the pistol at the stockyard. Could it have been Bird? Torres-Hernandez?

After a while, all the photos became a blur. She closed the laptop and called the doctor. It rang three times before he answered.

"Hello."

"It's Marla."

"I see your name on my screen. I'm busy. What do you want?"

"I think I should be there."

"No. There is not enough room for you here. I hardly have enough room for myself."

"Put the phone next to Crosby's ear. I want to tell him goodnight."

After dropping the phone at the foot of the bed, he returned to the countertop. He had a few more minutes before the centrifuge would ding, so he straightened a row of coke, bent down, and sniffed it. After rubbing his nose clean, he picked up the phone. "I have work to do. Come by in the morning—bring me food." He disconnected the call.

Marla wondered if the stress had gotten to him. Something bothered him; therefore, something bothered her. What bothered her? Take a number. A soon-to-be woman needed her, a near-death husband needed her, the DEA needed her, and Bird needed to die. At first morning light, she will head back to the trailer.

She eased the bedroom door open and gazed at Kata sleeping. Creeping past the bed, Marla closed the bathroom door behind her. She showered every night before climbing into bed with Crosby but couldn't stop the habit. After drying off and slipping on her cotton pajamas, she turned off the light switch and opened the door. Kata hadn't moved. Marla sat on the bed but couldn't force herself to lie down. Not yet. She tiptoed toward the bedroom door but paused at Crosby's closet. Her fingertips gently touched his doorknob. After glancing at the girl sleeping soundly, she turned the knob and entered the closet. His cologne hung in the air. A pair of work boots lay on their sides under a clothes pole. Three pairs of blue jeans, white and blue dress shirts, and a black belt hung from a hook. She sat on the floor and pulled her knees to her face. His scent drifted through her mind.

Kata muttered in her sleep. She called out, "Help! No. Don't."

Marla looked out of the closet. The girl rolled back and forth under the covers, crying. Marla stepped out, sat on the bed, and swept the hair off the sleeping girl's face.

Kata awoke and tugged on the sheet before wrapping her arms around her savior's neck. "What happened?"

Marla held the girl close to her. "You had a bad dream. Everything will be fine. Go back to sleep."

"Please come to bed with me. I am so scared."

Marla moved around to the other side of the bed and climbed under the covers. She looked at the girl wiping tears away. "Try to go back to sleep. Tomorrow will be a good day." Marla laid down and prayed with pain and sorrow inside her heart. She buried her face in her pillow and closed her eyes. Her last waking thoughts wandered to Crosby's smile, Hildebrandt as a happy town, and the multi-faced man who shot her husband.

✦

The alarm blared. Marla slapped the top of the clock, but it continued to cry out. The sky behind sheer curtains was black. Inside the bathroom, lights flickered. She hit the alarm again, but it continued blaring. She sat up, half-asleep, and softly laid her hand on the sleeping child like a mother would. The sound didn't come from the clock. It was the fire alarm. Marla threw the covers off them and yelled, "Kata, get up!"

The girl jumped up and grasped Marla's hand. "What is happening?"

"Lie down on the floor!" Marla lunged out of bed and headed for the window, which had always been the designated emergency exit. Heat poured from the bathroom, with flames crawling across the ceiling. Smoke hovered above them. Wood creaked. Unlocking the window, she flung it open. Marla dove to the floor as the fire spewed its flames toward the open air. Flames caught the bottom of her pajama leg.

"We are going to die!" Kata slapped Marla's leg until the fire was out.

From the bathroom ceiling, a beam cracked with a concussive crash into the glass shower door. Water sprayed on the floor from the broken showerhead.

Kata latched onto Marla. "Please do something."

"Stay low and follow me," Marla said.

The two crawled to the bedroom door, and Marla touched the knob; warm, not hot. Smoke penetrated through the door gap. Kata couldn't stop coughing. Marla cracked the door open, and the alarm in the hallway screamed louder. Yellow flames rolled over the couch and clawed up the curtains. She opened the door wider and looked around the corner toward the kitchen. The back door had not caught fire. Smoke clogged the view through the windows.

Marla closed the bedroom door, ripped the sheet off the bed, and wadded it around her arm. She choked on hot air and black smoke. Fighting to the bathroom, she threw the sheet on the floor and soaked it in the water. Kata stood inches from Marla, crying and begging the fire to stop. Flames crawl over walls and ceiling.

When the house groaned, she knew the conclusion. "Come on. We have to get out of the house!" She flung the wet sheet over their heads, but Kata dropped to her knees.

"No. I can't," the girl cried. "I'm too scared."

Marla didn't answer. She wrapped her arm around the girl's waist, lifted her off her feet, and charged out of the bedroom. Flames rolled over kitchen cupboards. Swirling hot wind shoved them back and forth. Marla felt immense heat on her back as she kicked the back door open, slamming it against the house. Fire roared over their heads as they ran outside and rolled on the grass. They inhaled cold, clean air into their lungs.

The house moaned death. Glasses and plates shattered as they slid off the cupboards. When a beam thudded to the floor and sparks spewed out the back door, they crawled further away.

Marla heard banging in the barn. She ran around the corner of the burning house—Daisy and Blackie were inside the barn with flames charging up the side. She turned toward Kata on the ground. "Stay here." She rushed toward the building ablaze and flung the doors open, revealing a heavy smoke hanging low. She charged into the inferno, covering her mouth and nose with her elbow. Burning flecks of hay landed on her.

The horses kicked their stalls, trying to escape.

"Daisy, I'm here."

Marla unlatched the locks and swung the gates wide open, but the horses didn't run away. They stayed. The hay inside Daisy's stall caught fire. Marla squeezed into the stall, and the nervous horse kicked.

"Come on, girl. You got to go. She pitched a wool blanket over the horse's eyes and slapped her on the haunches as hard as she could. Daisy slammed Marla against the wall. Marla pushed back against Daisy. The horse snorted and swung its head around, hitting Marla in the chest.

"Damn it, Daisy. Get out of here. Go."

Marla had never hit her horse, but she raised her fist and punched as hard as possible against the horse's shoulder. Daisy vaulted from the stall but suddenly stopped inside the barn. The blanket slid off the head and down the neck. Blackie stood beside Daisy. Marla knew better than to get behind a scared horse. Daisy had already kicked several times in fear. She put the blanket back over Daisy's eyes again and grabbed the broom leaning against the stall, shooting pain through her injured left arm. She slapped the horse on the leg. "Git, damn it. Git." The horses charged out past the doors into the open field.

A wooden slat from the roof broke free and slammed against the horse stall. The barn creaked and moaned. Another burning board fell from the ceiling. With her hands over her head, Marla ran out the door and back toward the burning house and Kata. Flames engulfed the chicken coop.

Yelling as loud as she could, "Kata? Where are you? Kata?"

Marla heard a scream.

"Kata? Where are you?" She turned full circle. "Kata?"

Burning buildings surrounded Marla, with black smoke rising straight into the sky. Screams mixed in with the roaring fires. Marla turned back and watched the fire overtake the barn. Kata's cries came from inside.

"No. No." Marla ran to the water hose they used to fill the horse trough. Its feeble spray did nothing.

The little voice cried out, "Help me! Help. Please stop. No. No. It's burning." Kata screamed when a burning wall collapsed. Marla raised her arms to shield her face from the heat and flames. The other walls collapsed, and the roof fell on top. The barn turned into a fire-breathing monster, and Kata's voice stopped.

Chapter 31

A cruel morning sun woke the world. Capitulating lines of black smoke rose from the smoldering masses. A single blackened stanchion stood in defiance to the rest of the gutted sanctuary. Marla had nothing. Inside, her wedding pictures and dress, the china and silverware they picked out, everything Crosby owned, and her gun and badge were gone. She had one thing the fire didn't steal. Her truck, which she parked far enough from the house, never caught fire.

Marla paced toward Fire Chief Verdon. "Don, may I borrow your phone?"

As if that was all he could give to comfort her. "Sure." He handed it to her. "Use it as long as you need."

She turned away and called Dr. McCollum.

"Hello?"

"Don't have time for chitchat," Marla said. "Are the two of you safe?"

"Safe?" The doctor gazed out the small window of the trailer. "Yes. Why?"

The barn ashes smoldered as firehoses drowned any last hope of finding Kata alive. Daisy and Blackie cantered back to the property, keeping their distance like anxious onlookers.

"Good. I'll call back in a little while." Marla handed the phone back to the Chief.

Verdon adjusted his hat. "I'm very sorry, Marla." He glanced at what once existed as a home. "You know this couldn't be anything besides arson."

Marla's shoulders hunched forward. Black soot covered her hair, face, and clothes. She squeezed a Mylar emergency blanket tighter around her while scraping the soles of borrowed Crocs over dirt. "Right."

"And you know there is no chance of finding the girl alive."

She gazed over the collapsed barn. "Yes, I know." Scorched wood, plastic, and furniture competed with the stench of burned chickens and feathers. "The girl had her entire life in before her. Young, vibrant. She seemed happy yesterday."

"I'm going to cordon the house, barn, and chicken coop."

A sheriff's vehicle rode over the cattle guard and stopped near them. Deputy Jeffrey Keene stepped out and walked to Marla with his arms out. She wrapped her arms around him and buried her face in his shoulder.

"My God, Marla. This son of a bitch is going to hang for this. I promise we will find him."

Marla stepped back and threw a sad smile at him. "I know you will. Not just for me; the girl." Marla's words were barely audible. "Kata."

Jeffrey gazed around the perimeter of festering smoke. "The girl you brought home from the trailer. Where is she?"

"In," Marla turned away from the smoldering pile of burned wood, "the barn. She's dead."

Chief Verdon asked, "Deputy, would you surround the areas with yellow crime tape? When we give clearance that the fire is out, you can retrieve the girl's body."

"Yes, of course," Jeffrey said. "We will close the entire ranch and check every inch for evidence." He stared into Marla's eyes. "I promise you; we'll find who did this."

She wiped her eyes with the cuff of her pajamas. "I know you will."

Jeffrey looked away for a moment before returning to Marla. "Two deputies called in and reported a section of fence knocked down about a quarter mile from here. They found multiple footprints going toward the house."

"I saw the damaged fence," Marla said, "but I didn't investigate it as well as I should. As a police officer for years, I should have checked it out. Basic 101. A rookie mistake. I might have found these people, arrested them, saved my house and barn... and the girl's life. My fault for all this."

"You can't beat yourself up for this, Marla," Verdon said. "No way to know. We're glad you and Crosby weren't hurt."

"Yeah, sure. I'm safe."

"Where is Crosby?" Verdon asked.

She sniffed a few times. "He's safe."

Deputy Keene walked toward the barn.

"Come with me." The Chief motioned her toward the rear of the house. "Let me show you something."

They both paced around her truck to the back corner. Chief Verdon held a long metal bar with a hook and stroked a six-foot line of burned grass. "Someone poured an accelerant to start the fire." He chipped a few pieces of charred wood off the corner of the house. "See this? It's darker; burned heavier. This is one corner where the fire started."

"One corner?"

"The same setup at all four corners. Someone wanted you dead, and you're lucky to be alive."

"Right. I'm a lucky girl." For the first time since she arrived back in Texas, Crosby had escaped her thoughts. While examining the remnants of the blackened house, her eyes itched from soot and smoke. "What about the barn and chicken coop?"

"Same thing. An accelerant. Someone sent a message." The Chief adjusted his fire helmet again.

"I believe it." Marla remembered the tough calluses of Crosby's hand in her palm, his soft listless lips touching hers as she knelt over the bed and kissed him. Only a few months ago, they played silly games with each other, laughed, and tangled under the sheets. His firm hands held her, caressed her; she wanted it all back.

"I've lost everything." Marla wiped her eyes. "A young girl is dead. It was stupid of me to bring her here. If I had left her at the detention center, the girl would be eating breakfast," she turned toward the barn, "not buried under ash and blackened wood."

She rubbed her fingertips over her closed eyes. "Is there anything else you need?" Marla asked. "I should go soon."

"You know, you could come to the fire station and get a hot shower. I'll have someone send some clean clothes for you to change into," the Chief replied.

She squeezed his forearm. "Thanks, and then I have to check on Crosby."

❖

Marla trudged to her truck and started the engine before leaning across and opening her glove box. She removed a 9mm pistol in a waistband holster and placed it in the console between the seats. The next stop before the phone store had to be a shower and clean clothes at the fire station, then lots of caffeine.

Two hours later, Marla turned into the coffee shop. Her dually pickup back tires barely squeezed into the drive-thru. After lowering her window, she heard the disembodied voice call out from the backlit menu.

"How may I help you?"

"Coffee." She thought of Crosby. "Black, strong. Yesterday's coffee."

"Our coffee is always freshly brewed. Small, medium, or large?"

"Large, please."

When she stopped at the window to pay, a young girl smiled and said, "That will be three dollars and twenty-four cents."

Marla thought of Kata never reaching that age, never having a smile again. She opened her console, fished for a ten-dollar bill under the pistol, and handed it to the young girl. Near the cash register, a clear plastic container with coins and a few dollars inside had a picture of the high school band raising money for a trip. When the girl held the change out, Marla said, "Give it to the band, please."

The cell phone store became the next stop, which took longer than expected. After signing all the paperwork and denying all the extras and extended warranties, Marla opened the glass front door while holding her new phone. Before she reached her truck, the phone dinged.

A NEW PHONE? DID YOU LEAVE THE LAST ONE AT HOME? I TOLD YOU SHE WAS MINE AND YOU LET HER DIE. I HAVE IMMENSE RESPECT FOR YOU AND YOUR HUSBAND. YOU HAVE SURVIVED A FIRE AND HE WITH A GUNSHOT TO HIS HEAD. I WON'T MAKE THOSE MISTAKES AGAIN.

How in the hell did he know this quick? She spun back toward the store. The employee who helped her stared through the window, then turned away.

Rushing back to her truck, she locked the doors before calling Quinton. She gripped the pistol in the console when a car crept behind her.

"Wales here."

"It's Marla." She should tell him about the text, but that would put her further down the rabbit hole.

"You sound shaken."

"Someone lit my house and barn last night. Burned everything."

"Geez, sorry. What can I do to help? Just ask. Anything. Oh, wait, Jesus, what about the girl?"

Marla glanced down, then out her side window before answering, "She died in the fire."

"Do you have the police there, now, investigating?"

A motorcycle stopped beside her in the next parking spot. A fully enclosed black helmet turned toward her. She jerked out the pistol. "Damn it." The rider lifted his helmet off his head and walked toward another store.

She squeezed her eyes shut. "God, help me."

"What?" Quinton asked.

"Nothing."

"They'll find the arsonist."

"Fire Chief has been there the entire time. Sheriff's department is there now, looking around." Marla shifted in the seat of her truck. "I know who did this, and I want that bastard. He's taken everything from me. Everything!" She pounded her hand against the steering wheel. "I'm going to make sure that bird-shit asshole knows, exactly, you hear me, damn it...exactly what he has done."

Quinton stalled for a response. "I'm here for whatever you need. Just tell me—" The call disconnected. He looked at his phone. "I should call Borland. She's on edge."

Marla called Fire Chief Verdon. "Is the fire out? I want to come by and check on the body...Kata's body. I should, I mean, someone should take her to the funeral home."

"Glad you called, Marla. Come on back out here. Deputy Keene has some information about the girl."

"What about her?"

"I shouldn't say over the phone. Hurry on back and see for yourself."

Five minutes later, Marla turned hard, and the truck bounced over the cattle guard. She slammed on the brakes and jumped out, leaving the motor running and the door open. More sheriff's vehicles and a single ambulance surrounded the remnants of the barn.

Two men wearing hazmat suits stood amidst the debris. Jeffrey positioned himself in front of Marla.

"What?" she asked. "Why are there more people here?"

A blackened, charred body lay against a partially burned post.

"We found her under the wood and ash."

"Okay. Yeah, the girl died in a fire. She ran in to help me and couldn't find a way to get out. You don't need to tell me she died in the fire." She pushed against Jeffrey's chest. "What is going on? Why are these people here?"

"Marla." Jeffrey clamped onto her shoulders and stared into her eyes. "Someone tied the girl to a post with an extension cord, and there's a zip-tie melted around her wrists."

Her thoughts shot out in different directions. *The fire, horses, the girl, she just wanted to help. She ran toward danger. What kind of teenage girl does that? Kata ran in to help. Why her, or had someone been waiting for me?*

"When Kata called out to me," Marla said. "I remember she said, 'Please stop.' I thought she yelled at the fire. Scared, helpless, trapped. She yelled at someone to stop, and I'm an idiot for not thinking that."

"Marla," Jeffrey said. "There was too much going on. You can't blame yourself."

"She said, 'Please stop.' I ignored her call for help. She said stop because someone tied her to a post. Someone murdered her."

Marla rubbed her forehead, visualizing Bird standing before her. Her scalp tingled, heartbeat pounded, breaths increased. The sensation of her pistol rising out of the holster, aiming, firing, and watching him fall would be gratifying. Do the ends justify the means? She glanced at the weapon in her hand and didn't recall drawing it from the holster. Did she? People on trial say they don't remember killing someone. She didn't remember drawing her gun.

After holstering the gun, she went to her pickup and called Dr. McCollum again.

"What?"

Her fist tightened. *I'm about done with your attitude.* "How is Crosby?"

He drummed the table with his pen. "Why did you ask earlier if I was safe?"

"I'm concerned about you." She slid back against the seat. "Is it all right if I worry about the two of you? And you, with a stranger showing up and robbing you. Hiding Crosby. A lot is going on," Marla said.

"Why are you hiding the patient?" He quipped back while still tapping the table. "And who is this bloody bird person you mentioned before?"

Her voice rose an octave and a dozen decibels higher. "I'm hiding him because I have a crazy-ass doctor with no license to practice medicine sticking unknown things in my husband's brain." She heard a repetitious sound. "What are you doing?"

He stopped tapping the table. "Do you have my package?"

Marla furrowed her brow. "What are you talking about?"

"I had a friend send an overnight package to your DEA office address. Pick it up and bring it with my breakfast."

"The package we talked about where Crosby can speak to me?"

"Sodding hell, woman. Yes."

Marla shifted the transmission to drive. "I'll be there within the hour." She arrived at the DEA office wearing a new button-down cotton blouse, blue jeans, athletic shoes, and a pistol holstered to her belt. She entered through the front door and aimed for the desk where the same two security guards, Michael and Jason, sat every day.

Michael asked as Marla approached. "Are you going upstairs?"

"No," she snapped back.

"Good. Borland told us we can't let you past the desk."

"I'll go upstairs if I damn well want to go upstairs. Do you think you can stop me?"

Michael shifted in his chair. "I'd have to try."

Marla shook her head in disgust. "Sorry." She patted the countertop. "I'm here to pick up a package."

Jason asked, "What's with the clothes? Not your normal DEA attire."

"Had a fire at my house last night, and it burned all my clothes, everything."

"So, you lost your ID badge?" Jason asked. "We couldn't let you up there without your ID."

"Don't push me. You won't like the result."

"Agent Adams," Michael said, "I'm sorry for what happened, but we told you before that this is not a place to send personal packages."

"Not personal, business. It concerns...investigation stuff."

Michael reached down close to his feet and placed a small cardboard box on the countertop. "Glad it's not personal. I would be worried if it were."

"Why?" Marla scooted the box closer to her.

"Because whoever sent it to you misspelled your name," Michael said.

Chapter 32

Marla faintly sang the words to George Strait's "Amarillo By Morning" as it played on her pickup's radio. Dr. McCollum's package sat in the front passenger's seat. A joyous disc jockey announced he was halfway through his run of singers named George. When "He Stopped Loving Her Today" by George Jones came on, she immediately switched the radio off. Edging off the road, she turned onto the dirt trail before stopping behind the metal shed. Closing her door and leaving the window down, she squinted at the mid-morning sun blazing down on her head. Feeling slightly cooler after entering the shade of the shed, she glanced over the structure for any new bullet holes before opening the trailer door.

The doctor sat at the small table, leaning forward with one leg tightly crossed over the other as he twirled the end of his mustache. He still hadn't shaved. "Did you bring me breakfast?"

"You have a shower and a sink in the front compartment. Use it to shave." Marla placed the food sack and the overnight package on the table, never slowing before stopping beside Crosby.

Dr. McCollum opened the sack and looked inside with only one item. "Did you eat?" He unwrapped an egg and cheese breakfast sandwich.

"I had coffee."

"Brilliant." He took a bite.

"How's he doing?" Marla asked.

With a mouthful of food, he said, "See for yourself."

She interlocked her fingers between Crosby's and felt him light-ly squeeze hers. His biceps muscle tightened, gently pulling her hand closer to him.

"Amazing. This is absolutely amazing." Still holding Crosby's hand, she turned back toward the doctor. "I need him to talk about the shooter. You know, confirmation of Torres-Hernandez, and what he looks like. When can that happen?"

The doctor swallowed his last bite, wadded the paper into a ball, and dropped it close to the empty sack. "Told you before, I can fill the brain with new tissue, but coordinated actions like talking could be weeks or months." He leaned back in the chair and crossed his legs again. "But you brought something that might help."

She nodded at the package on the table. "Is that what you need to have Crosby talk?"

The doctor cleared his throat and sat up. "This computer tablet and program app are exactly what I need."

"An app?" she asked. "Like Donkey Kong or Minecraft on someone's phone?"

"It's a bloody lot more than something you buy for ninety-nine cents. It's a program I developed with another person. We started working on this for stroke victims who could not speak."

Still holding Crosby's hand, she said, "Go on."

"I insert a probe into a patient's brain and—"

"No." Marla waved her hand in the air. "No more things stuck in his head."

"Understand—no extra incisions. I insert a narrower probe inside the tube already in the patient's head and pull it out when I need to do a stem cell injection. When finished, I place it back down the tube."

"How can he talk without speaking?"

"It's like an electroencephalogram, an EEG. You've seen pic-tures of people with wires stuck to their scalp?"

Marla nodded. "Sure, on weird-ass Halloween horror movies. Frankenstein lab with gigantic machines. Do you need lightning from the top of a castle?"

"Good God, no, you twit. You Yanks are worse than the Bloody French."

She held her hand up in acceptance. "Sorry."

"It identifies electrical brain waves, transmits the information to the computer tablet via Bluetooth, and changes patient's thoughts to spoken words and pictures."

"Sounds like crazy sci-fi baloney."

"You doubt me?"

She tried to look at his eyes but couldn't see clearly through the thick, colored lenses. "When did you last use this thing?"

"We performed a test three months ago in London."

"Who is 'we'?"

"Dr. Hugo Wilborn developed the test, the procedure."

"With a survivor or one that died?"

"It's not an exact science. It's, um, experimental. Each human is unique."

"Where is Dr. Hugo Wilborn?"

"That's a bit of a tricky question. Indisposed for a while."

Marla bunched her brow at him. "For a while? Does that mean incarceration?"

"We originally developed this for a research center in London, but when they didn't treat us well, my associate threw a virus into their computer system and demanded reparations."

"You mean he tried extortion? How much?"

His finger twisted the end of his mustache. "Forty million pounds...of which I did not have any knowledge, and I had been cleared of any wrongdoing."

Marla exhaled loudly. "How will this help if this person is not here?"

"We worked on our subjects together, and I know how to use it."

"Are there more parts to this gadget?"

"No." He tore the package open and emptied a small computer tablet and a metal probe inside a sterilized bag on the table. "Brilliant. Nothing broke."

"Fine. Great. Hook him up, and let's get talking."

Dr. McCollum shook his head. "Not quite that easy. The stem cells may have grown the patient's brain to almost normal size, but it must develop well enough to produce thoughts and translate to words."

Marla moved out of the way. "So, how long?"

The doctor picked up the computer tablet. "I'm not sure if his brain has recovered well enough. The patient may need another injection or two." He glanced at the timer. "Fifty-two minutes until the next dose is due."

Marla wanted to hear Crosby tell her what happened; the sooner, the better. "There's no more risk in doing it now, is there? If nothing happens, then nothing happens. What if he says a word or we see a picture on the tablet? Why wait?"

"I don't want you to feel an ocean of despair when he doesn't speak to you."

"I can swim just fine. Hook him up."

He opened the tablet and placed it on the counter. The screen whitened. "This is too soon. The patient won't talk." He put on gloves, ripped the top off the sterilized bag, and gently lowered the five-inch probe inside the tube.

Marla's hair on the back of her neck rose as metal scraped against metal. "That's it?" she asked.

"No. I must adjust the probe to the correct angle and connect it to the tablet." He pressed a few keys, and the machine beeped three times with a horizontal black line stretching across the screen from one end to the other. After connecting the Bluetooth, he turned the probe slightly left, producing high-pitched feedback. Turning it slightly to the right, the sounds lowered an octave, then popped and crackled like an old-time radio searching for a station. He stopped when all the noise ended and nodded his success. Slipping the gloves off, he told Marla, "Kneel beside him and hold his hand."

A muffled sound came from the tablet's speakers when she grazed Crosby's palm. The black line wavered slightly. Marla and Dr. McCollum looked at the screen and then at each other.

"Is that him?" Marla asked.

Short repetitious hums like monks chanting came from the tablet. The sounds repeated quicker, and the line wavered higher when she squeezed Crosby's hand.

"My Love? Are you trying to talk to me? I'm here. You can talk to me." The pads of his fingertips pushed against her hand. His breathing deepened. She listened to the monitor above his head beep faster as his pulse increased. Her heart desperately wanted him to open his eyes.

"I think I see his upper lip move," Marla said. "Yes. Look. His cheek moved." The tablet screen changed to a grainy gray, and the sounds stopped. "Are you sending me a picture?" Marla skimmed the screen before turning back to Crosby. "A picture of Torres-Hernandez? Is that what you want me to see?"

The speaker moaned again. The black line returned and quivered on the tablet screen. Marla kissed the back of Crosby's hand. "I love you." The sound changed to a low octave hum, and a sound like an 'M' became more prevalent, clearer. "Are you trying to say my name?" She stared at Crosby's mouth, expecting him to speak. His fingers tightened between hers. His breathing moved faster, shallower, like he was out of breath. The hum from the screen increased. Crosby's eyes moved under his lids. "You can do it. Talk to me," she said. His eyes moved quicker, side to side. His cheek muscles tightened, lips narrowing into a straight line.

The heart rate alarm blared on the wall monitor, and the speaker screeched a long, high note. Marla winced with Crosby's forceful grip. She tried to pull away. His wrists and elbows flexed; seconds later, his hands went limp. The alarm stopped. The tablet silenced, and the line disappeared.

Marla pulled her hand away. He had never squeezed her that hard before. She turned toward the doctor. "Another seizure?"

"It's his first attempt at real interaction, his brain trying to be more active. The stimulation might have caused a small seizure."

"What's different this time?"

"Humans. You can't trust them to do anything reliable."

"Can you stop all these seizures?"

He scoffed as he twirled his mustache again. "In a hospital with medications, I could, but I'm not, am I? You have me hiding amid a wheat field."

She stood and nudged close to his personal space. "I have you here to save my husband; when that happens, you could gain national attention. Saving a DEA agent with a gunshot wound to his head would bode well for you."

"Only if it was a bloody success. What if—"

"No." Marla stared into the doctor's eyeglasses. "There will be no talk of anything else besides success."

He averted his gaze and sat at the small table. "Because it would not bode well for me if not successful?" His eyes skimmed across the narrow walls. "Would you place me in a situation worse than where I am now?"

Marla sat across from him and leaned in. "There is a reason you are here in this place, this wheat field. Average men are not thousands of miles from home seeking refuge."

"I am not average."

She leaned against the back of the chair and crossed her arms. "And that is why you are here. Make the best of it. Here is your chance to become famous. That's really what you want, isn't it?"

"Indeed." With a conviction in his voice, he said, "The world needs my help." The timer dinged. "Brilliant. Step aside. I must administer another injection into the patient."

"How long until he can say words, sentences? I think he was trying to say my name."

The doctor opened the small refrigerator and removed the plastic container holding the stem cells. "Bloody hell."

She leaned around him to see what had happened. "What?"

He held the cap in one hand and the container in the other. "It must have fallen over with the cap loose. All the stem cells leaked out."

"Okay. Okay." Marla rubbed her forehead. "Just, you know, just do what you did before and take some more from his bone."

"I did that once, but the second time won't be the same with enhanced cells."

"What will that do?"

"I'm not sure." He pitched the cap and container into the wastebasket. "I've already used the protein extract, the catalyst, and ultraviolet light on the stem cells inside his body."

"Well, take more like you did once before."

"You don't understand. All the stem cells I inject into the brain don't stay there. A small amount will be absorbed into the circulation." Dr. McCollum whisked his hands above Crosby's body. "Through his entire body. Even the cells in his hip bone that I remove. The second set of cells may do more than the first."

"More? That would be good, right?"

"I," he exhaled, "I don't know." He bent down and cleaned the bloody solution inside the refrigerator before standing again. "I have no choice." Staring at Crosby lying on the bed, he said, "This patient has no chance of survival without stem cells. I must get more."

Chapter 33

Marla rolled Crosby onto his side. She had done this once before and felt less anxious the second time, but she turned her head away when the doctor pushed the big bore needle into Crosby's skin. That should hurt.

The doctor aspirated a mass of bone marrow slush from the iliac crest, part of the hip bone. His concentration wavered, the patient out of focus. The devil inside his own brain called for more cocaine, sniffing and wanting the feel of the powder in his nose. His throat tightened, and he coughed once.

After pulling the needle out, he pressed on the puncture wound and motioned toward Marla. "Push here for a minute, then place the bandage on it." He injected equal amounts into two 50ml conical tubes.

"Different this time?" Marla asked. "Two tubes, not one?"

"Blimey. Quiet. I'm concentrating." After placing the two tubes in the centrifuge and pushing the high-speed button, he said. "Two, in case one spills again."

Marla watched the doctor in silence. His smooth technique, hands gliding over the equipment like an experienced surgeon. She caught a glimmer of sweat on his forehead, even though the temperature inside the trailer hung at 72 degrees.

The centrifuge bell dinged, and the motor slowed to a stop. He transferred the cells into two smaller plastic vials. Checking the caps to ensure they fit snug, he unscrewed it, then screwed it back on, repeating it twice more before placing one into the refrigerator.

With his back toward Marla, he hid his technique from her in case she wanted to steal his secrets. After transferring two milliliters of the stem cells into a glass test tube, he added two drops of his protein extract and one drop of his catalyst before placing it back into the centrifuge. After he closed the lid and pushed the slow spin button, the rotor spun with the ultraviolet light shining inside. His fingertips tingled. Lack of cocaine or tight gloves? He snapped off his gloves, but the prickling continued. From his peripheral vision, he watched her. Was she going to steal his cocaine?

He entered Marla's personal space and stood a full head taller than her, staring down at her. "I want you to write a letter to the Louisiana Medical Board."

She patted his forearm. "In due time, Doctor. You have done an excellent job, but I wouldn't call this a success story quite yet."

"I must have the letter. You need to write one now."

"Listen, bud," her eye twitched, "here's the deal, heal my husband, and after that, I write the letter." She felt the lies getting easier; this time, they sounded more truthful and promising.

He fixated on his patient. "Four or five more injections. When the patient speaks and tells you what you want to know about this person you are finding, will you write my letter?"

Marla gently grasped his shoulder. She wondered what he would do when he found out the letter constituted an unknown person to the medical board. "I could see that happening. Do you think four more and he is talking?"

"Yes. I could have him drinking through a straw by tomorrow. Once he gets nutrition and fluids into his stomach, everything works better. Why don't you go to a store and get him some protein drinks?" He thought to himself, *and buy me drugs?*

Feeling the inside of the trailer enclosing on him, the call for cocaine became stronger. His hand pressed against the vial inside his pocket.

The centrifuge bell dinged again and the motor decelerated. "It's too crowded in here. I have work to do, and you are in my way. Go out and shut the door behind you."

Marla stared at the sweat beads above the doctor's eyebrow. She stared at the thick glasses and wondered what an almost blind man's eyes looked like. What made him so anxious about the second batch of stem cells? Her tongue clicked. "All right." She kissed Crosby's forehead. "I'll leave, but just long enough to get those drinks. I can be back in thirty minutes."

Dr. McCollum's skin itched; nerves ricocheted. His tongue rubbed his gums and teeth, searching for a grain of cocaine. His hand felt the small vial in his pocket. "Leave, now. I have work to do."

Marla stood. "All right. I'm going."

A high-frequency screech came out of the tablet speaker. Crosby's body twitched. They both turned toward the bed.

Marla looked at the doctor. "He's yelling?"

In a second, Crosby's arms and legs stiffened. His fists clamped tight, and his head turned as far to the left as she had ever seen him do.

"Bollocks. Another seizure." Dr. McCollum grabbed Crosby's head, trying to hold the probe and tube in place. "Don't let him fall off the bed."

Marla laid her arms over Crosby's legs and leaned over him. She felt his body jerk. And just as quickly, the seizure stopped. His body relaxed. When he took a deep breath, she did too.

Marla turned and shoved the doctor against the wall. "You said he would be better. Why is he still having seizures?"

"Because he has a brain injury." He looked at Crosby's head. "Bloody hell." He bent down onto his knees and looked under the bed.

Marla knelt and scanned the floor. "What are you looking for?"

"The tube fell out of the patient's brain." He reached under the bed and behind the frame wheel. His fingers rolled the tube toward him and grasped it in his hand. "It's dirty. I can't replace this inside the brain without sterilizing it." Digging through his medical bag, he pushed the bent spoon and disposable lighter to the side and removed a small bottle of ethyl alcohol. "I could soak the tube in this." He wiggled the bottle back and forth. "No. There is not enough alcohol."

"Will alcohol burn?" Marla asked.

He gazed at the bottle and then at her. "You mean to light the alcohol? It wouldn't burn hot enough. Need something else."

"How about gasoline? Outside, near the generator, is a plastic five-gallon gas can. Do you have a lighter?"

"In my medical bag, but that's too dangerous," he said. "We could burn this trailer down. Besides, who is holding a tube with burning petrol?"

Marla remembered the house and barn burned out of control. The heat felt like what hell would be, and Kata died. "Hold on." She ran out to her truck. A minute later, she yelled, "Hey, Doc. Come outside."

McCollum stepped out.

Marla held pliers in one hand and the gasoline can in the other. "How about this? I hold it with pliers, and you drop the tube inside, fill it with gas, and light it."

"That's bonkers. The pliers would break the glass. We need something softer or smoother against the glass."

Marla looked down at her hand and rubbed her ring finger. "Something smooth?" She slowly twisted her wedding ring. "I have never taken this off since my wedding day." She slipped the ring past her knuckle and stopped. Sniffing, she rubbed her nose on her sleeve. Turning the ring, she felt the smoothness of the gold against her skin. Like her finger had a mind of its own, it flexed, not letting the ring move forward.

She promised Crosby never to take it off, but this was for him. He would understand. Would he? She remembered the touch of her white lace veil against her cheek and the smell of Crosby's cologne as they vowed a lifetime of love to each other. The muscles in her hand relaxed. Her finger straightened, allowing her to remove a promise to her husband. She stared at the simple roundness of the yellow gold, then slid the test tube inside the ring. "Something smooth against the glass." She clasped the pliers around her ring. "All right. Do it. Burn it."

He rinsed the stainless steel tube in the small sink, dropped it in the test tube, and filled it with gasoline. "I am not sure what will happen when I light the petrol. I have never lit a test tube full of flammable liquid."

"Time to find out." Marla held the apparatus out as far as she could.

"You must not drop this."

"Light it up, doctor. My husband needs another dose of those cells."

Outside the trailer, Dr. McCollum's hand tremored. He wavered the disposable lighter near the test tube. "Are you ready?"

Marla remembered the fire extinguisher in her truck. She should have gotten it in case all this went wrong. Covering her face with her elbow while holding the pliers with her other arm out straight felt wrong. Never mind. She nodded at the doctor. "Do it."

When he flicked the wheel on the lighter, sparks shot out. He did it again with sparks shooting out into the air. "It won't light. I need a new one."

"Give me that." She took it from his hand and knocked the top of the lighter against her thigh five times. "Now try it."

He held the lighter over the test tube and flicked the wheel again. A red flame shot in the air. Heat surrounded her hand and forearm. She didn't dare let go. After the flame burned for a minute and withered away, she couldn't help but touch the hot glass. Returning to the trailer, she relaxed the grip of the pliers and laid the test tube on the countertop. The metal tube was blackened from the gasoline, like the color of burnt wood where her house once stood.

Her ring had a single scratched line on the gold. She and Crosby would laugh about it one day.

The doctor slipped on surgical gloves and touched the glass. It had cooled enough to slide the metal tube out. He cleaned it with the small amount of alcohol left in the bottle. "Done," he said.

Marla slipped her ring back on, promising herself it would never come off again. She smiled at Crosby and said, "That kinda scared me. All set and ready. The doctor can replace the metal tube in your brain, and then we start again. Keep going."

"Get out!" He whisked his hands through the air. "Get out while I try to fix this mess. Go. Now. Get his protein drinks."

Marla stood. "He needs me here with him."

"No. I must replace the tube as quickly as possible. Go." He swished his hands toward the door. "Out, now." He watched her move toward the trailer door. *Hurry up. I need a bloody fix.*

"Fine. Drinks and clothes. He needs clean clothes."

"Out. Out." He turned away from her and heard the door close. His gloves snapped off his hands, then anxiously retrieved the vial from his pocket and tapped a line in the crook of his hand. The powder shot up his nose with instant clarity entering his head.

Chapter 34

Bird stood near Mrs. Parrilla in the kitchen of La Zapata restaurant. Plates crashed on the floor as her husband unloaded the dishwasher. Bird placed his heavy hand on the woman's shoulder, forcing her to her knees. "Who killed Benito?"

"I promise, I never saw him before. He was different."

"What do you mean?" Bird stepped to Mr. Parrilla at the dishwasher. "This is your husband, no?"

The man stuttered and stumbled over his words. "Please, please, Señor Torres-Hernandez, sir. She knows nothing."

"Nothing? She saw something." Bird grasped the man's shirt and shoved him backward inside the storage room. "Someone killed my Benito, and she saw it. There is blood on the floor and the wall. She watched him die. She should watch you die."

"No, please," Mrs. Parrilla cried out. "He was different."

Bird pushed her husband against the shelves. Canned tomatoes and beans crashed to the floor. "You already said that." He grabbed the old man's collar and pushed him to the corner against the bloodied wall, then drew the .22 caliber pistol with the suppressor from inside his jacket and pointed it at the man's head. "How do I know you didn't kill him?"

The woman clasped onto Bird's hand and knelt at his feet. "We make food. We no kill him. Mister Bird, please, don't hurt my marido."

He swung the barrel toward her. "Tell me what he looked like. Mexican?"

"No. White, very white, and talked funny. I never heard no one talk that way." She kissed his hand. "Please, Mister Bird."

He thought for a moment and then smiled. *The Englishman is helping that DEA woman likes the snow.* He shoved the kneeling woman onto her back and pistol-whipped the old man across the face. "You can live." Bird charged out of the storage room and into the alley.

Arturo started the engine when he noticed his boss leaving from the restaurant's back entrance. After Bird climbed in, they drove away.

Arturo turned at the intersection. "Was it the Sinaloa Cartel?"

"No. An Englishman. Ask around the neighborhood. Did this guy drive here, or did someone bring him? I'll put up a five hundred dollar bounty to whoever provides what I want."

"I'll spread the word."

"We have another delivery tonight. Contact Rafael."

"You sure you want to keep doing this?" Arturo asked. "It's dangerous crossing the line."

"A few more months, then you and I can hide out on our little Pacific Island, drink all day, and fuck every girl we see."

✦

A sliver of moonlight traced through the night. Stars speckled a million miles away. Three semi-tractor trailers at the Schmidt & Schmidt Slaughterhouse had backed up to the unloading docks and let their diesel engines idle. A single overhead streetlight shined down near the trucks. Cattle mooed and bellowed as they hoofed down the chute into pens. Light winds pushed the odor of feces and fear.

With headlights off, a minivan veered off the road to the lot and eased to a stop in front of the three semi-trucks. Bird climbed out from the driver's side and slid the side door open. Two men carrying AK-47s rushed out and headed for the back of the holding pens, sweeping their flashlights and checking for intruders.

Bird motioned toward the three drivers with his arms and hands like a police officer at an intersection. "Vamanos." The drivers tracked to the back of their trailers, climbed inside, and a minute later, each came out with a metal briefcase and placed them near the slaughterhouse front door.

The lock snapped open, and the door swung wide. A man wearing a blood-splattered long apron took three steps outside, holding four identical cases, two in each hand, placing them on the ground, grabbing the other three cases, and returning inside before securing the entrance. Each driver took a case and disappeared inside their trailers. Bird grabbed the fourth case and placed it inside the minivan. The two armed men returned from the holding pens, entered the side of the minivan, then slid the door closed.

The three drivers climbed into their cabs, the transmissions shifted into gear, and the vehicles drove away. It appeared as a smooth, practiced routine.

DEA Special Agent Quinton Wales sat in his black Tahoe across the road at the farm implement building hidden behind large equipment. His night vision camera clicked, taking pictures of the men and the license plates on the trailers. The engines roared and transmissions shifted as the trucks headed south for the border.

Quinton focused back on the minivan, took pictures of Bird talking on the phone while sitting in the driver's seat, then checked the images on the camera screen. They were slightly out of focus.

Two headlights approached from the road to the left, and a dark blue Ford Expedition eased alongside Bird's minivan, driver window to driver window. Quinton couldn't tell what was happening, so he climbed out of his Tahoe and eased around a large tractor until he could see between the two vehicles.

Through the camera lens, he watched a man sitting in the driver's seat with tattoos on his bald head and a Fu-Manchu mustache hanging below his jawline, talking to Bird. Quinton recognized the man, Rafael Villegas, a mid-level Sinaloa Cartel man. Bird was tapping two cartels.

The minivan's side door slid open again, and a man pushed two girls out with their hands tied behind their backs and mouths covered. Rafael opened his back door and shoved them inside the Expedition before slamming the door closed. Bird held the metal case out of his window, and Rafael took it. Seconds later, they drove away in opposite directions.

Quinton scoffed. "What'll you know? The infamous high-ranking Los Zetas officer, Bird himself, Alejandro Torres-Hernandez, the slimiest of the slime, is skimming off the Los Zetas Cartel. When they find out, you can never go back. Both cartels will want you dead." He returned to his Tahoe before running through the images on the camera.

◆

The next morning, the word spread throughout the San Antonio downtown neighborhood about a five hundred dollar reward for information about the man who killed Benito. Nothing like a thousand people calling the police for a reward. If you lied to Bird, you died.

A Hispanic man wore a black t-shirt with an image of Mexican singer Vicente Fernández, jeans never washed, and worn boots never cleaned. With his knee bent, he leaned the sole of his boot against the restaurant while peeling dirt from under his fingernails with a hunting knife. A twelve-year-old girl prancing toward him wearing a strawberry print dress, white eyelet lace ankle socks, and black flats caught his eye. Her curled brown hair bounced with each step. She strolled along the sidewalk and stopped right in front of him before she tilted her head. "I know what happened."

"Yeah? Bet your life on it, niñita?"

She placed her hand on her hip while holding rolled-up papers in the other. "I want the five hundred."

He dragged the knife blade across his jeans. "Tell you what. Go inside and sit at the back booth, and someone will come along and hear your story.

"It's not a story. It's what I saw."

"Mm-hmm." He glanced over at the thin girl. "Tell the people inside you can have anything you want to eat. On the house."

"I don't want anything to eat. I want a Pepsi. In a glass. With ice."

The man nodded and slipped the knife into the sheath attached to his belt. "I believe they can do that for you."

Thirty-five minutes and two empty glasses later, Bird entered the restaurant wearing a white, wide-brim hat, a pink pastel jacket, and oversized mirrored sunglasses. He pointed at the waitress while turning toward the girl sitting in the booth. "Pepsi, no two—with ice." He sat across from her, slipped the glasses off, and studied her; normal breathing, not fidgety, no smile, no frown—flat-faced. "Do you know who I am?"

She stared into his eyes and then at the sunglasses in his hand. "You're the one they call Bird."

"You have something for me?"

She reached across the table and lightly rubbed the frames.

"This? You want this? And a Pepsi? And five hundred dollars?" He let go of the glasses, and she slipped them on. The large dark lenses covered most of her face.

A server placed two glasses with straws on the table. The girl slurped hers down while staring at Bird before putting it back on the table. "I'm an artist. I draw pictures. A car turned into the alley and stopped. Not straight, kinda sideways."

"How did you happen to be at the right place at the right time?"

"I like to sit on the park bench across the street and feed the pigeons." She placed a drawing of the car from her lap on the table. "Benito opened the car door, and I saw him dripping blood. He wobbled down the alley and banged on the restaurant's back door. Mrs. Parrilla opened it and let him in." She placed another drawing with the car door open and a man and a woman standing at the back door. "I stayed to see what would happen. Something always happens when blood is spilled."

Bird studied each drawing. "These are exceptionally good. You may be famous someday if you make it out of here alive."

The girl sucked on the straw until it gurgled at the bottom of the glass. "Another car stopped behind Benito's." She placed another drawing in front of Bird. "A man got out of a gray car, then it sped away." She laid the last sketch on the table, showing a tall, thin man with curly hair and a large mustache standing next to a car with the license plate number on the back bumper.

"Are you sure this is the correct number?" Bird asked.

She nodded. "The tall man went to Benito's car and looked inside before he banged on the restaurant's back door. I heard a gunshot a minute later, and the tall man ran away." Her lips smiled under the sunglasses. "Five hundred, please."

◆

On the east side of San Antonio, a black SUV stopped at an intersection with a gray Prius easing in behind it. Another black SUV stopped on the left side of the Prius with side mirrors almost touching each other. The Prius driver threw his hands up and yelled with his windows still up. In the rearview mirror, he watched another black SUV grille get too close. The driver yelled again when it bumped into the back of his car. A metallic tap on the front passenger window startled him. A stranger held a revolver close to his chest and pointed to unlock the door.

"I don't have any money. Nobody pays me. I promise it's all online." He saw the gun pointed at him. The locks clicked open.

Arturo entered the car and shut the door. The SUV in front drove away. "Roberto, turn right and go straight until I tell you to stop." Snapping the phone attached to a plastic stand off the dashboard, Arturo placed it in his shirt pocket.

"Hey. That's mine. And how do you know my name?"

Arturo pointed the revolver at Roberto. "Drive."

"You can have the car." He tried to open his door, but it hit the SUV to his left, keeping him from escaping. "Please, don't hurt me."

"Shut up and drive."

Roberto turned right at the intersection.

"Yesterday, you picked up a man with a funny accent."

"I didn't do anything. Please get out of my car."

Arturo slapped the side of Roberto's head. "Listen to me."

"Okay, fine. Don't hit me anymore."

"You drove a man to La Zapata, right?"

Roberto thought for a moment as his knuckles whitened on the steering wheel. "Yes. He said something about London and wanted to go downtown."

"Where did you pick him up?"

Roberto floored the accelerator. "You're going to kill me. I know it."

Arturo pushed the barrel against Roberto's neck. "Slow the fuck down."

"No." Tears rolled down his cheeks. "No. I die," he turned the steering wheel back and forth, wheeling the car in wide swaths, "we both die."

"Stop the car, or I'll blow a hole in your head." Arturo grabbed the wheel.

Roberto tried pulling Arturo's fingers off the wheel. "Let go. Get out of my car." He hit his fist on Arturo's hand. "Let go."

The gun fired. Blood splattered the side window, and Roberto slumped forward. The car slowed as the front tires bumped over the sidewalk curb a block later and stopped.

◆

From outside the fourth-floor patio at Bird's condo, he looked down and watched Arturo exiting from a tan minivan and walking past the entry gate. Moments later, Bird met him in the lobby. "Do you have it?"

"Yes."

They sat at a small table next to the swimming pool, and Arturo withdrew the phone from his shirt pocket.

"Any problems?"

"No fingerprints and no witnesses." Arturo turned on the phone. "I went into settings and locations. It looks like he drove to a place outside of town twenty-three minutes before Benito died. Must be the one who killed him."

Bird took the phone. "Good man. Go over to the restaurant and get a beer and something to eat. Tell them it's on me. After that, check out this place and call me."

Bird gazed at the list of recent calls, then touched redial.

Dr. McCollum's phone rang. He turned toward the table and glanced at the Uber driver's name on the screen. He touched the red X. A few seconds later, it rang again. *Why would this wanker call me?* He picked up the phone. "Hello?"

"I'm glad you answered," Bird said. "You left something in my car."

The doctor patted his wallet in his back pocket. "What would that be?"

"Your life."

"What?" He rechecked the screen. "This doesn't sound like the Uber driver."

"You're right. I have his phone, and you killed Benito."

McCollum plopped down on the seat at the table. "I...I don't know what the bloody hell you're talking about. I'm hanging up."

"Not wise, doctor," Bird said. "You are a doctor, right? And you like cocaine."

"Don't know what you're talking about. I'm hanging up."

"Want more? I can pass on you killing Benito. He must have done something stupid to let a lanky English doctor take him down. I'll let you live, and you can have all the coke you can snort up that limey nose."

"What do you want?"

"You can have it all if you give me the DEA agent."

McCollum crossed his legs and leaned forward. "What?"

"Is the DEA agent with you?"

He spun around and gazed at his patient while his hand patted the vial in his pants pocket. *I can slow down, and the cocaine could last me another day or two. Push that wanker woman for the medical board letter and get the bloody hell out of this place.* "No. I don't need your drugs."

"He's with you right now, isn't he?"

"You don't know where the patient is," he stopped before he said anything else, "and you don't know where I am."

"You want me to come to you?" Bird asked. "Your choice, all the coke you can manage or two bullets in your head."

Chapter 35

Three livestock trucks bore down the highway. Arturo's car shook from the turbulence as they passed him. He smirked. "Money."

The sun bled into the dimming horizon. A half mile ahead, a gray dually pickup truck drove the speed limit. He flicked a cigarette out the window as he watched it slow down, then eased off the road and turned toward a large farm equipment shed. Tires ground against gravel as he slowed. When the pickup stopped, he jogged up the dirt trail and hid behind large cactus plants. A small gasoline generator hummed near an extended trailer.

Bird told him about the wife, another DEA agent. She was his primary threat. After taking her out, the Englishman and the other DEA agent inside should be an easy kill.

Marla exited her truck with sacks of clothes and protein drinks.

Arturo flinched when something moved in a bush behind him.

She dropped the sacks and drew her weapon before they hit the ground. Easing around the mass of cactus, she found an armadillo curled into a ball. She heard the doctor's voice inside the trailer. Was he talking to someone inside? She rushed to the door, swung it open, and entered with her gun pointed inside.

Dr. McCollum turned toward the door. "Are you a bloody nutter?" He stood beside Crosby. "Put that thing away."

She holstered her weapon. "Outside the trailer, I heard you talking to someone."

"Me?" He had to think of a reason other than being on the phone. "No one. Myself. I talk to myself when I…never mind. Stop winding me up."

"And speaking of that, it has been three days. You promised Crosby would be sitting and talking. He's neither."

"It's medicine. Every patient is different, and this patient is not responding as fast as he should."

"So, it's Crosby's fault?"

"The procedure became quite difficult. Replacing the tube inside the patient's brain is extremely complicated. No other doctor knows how to do what I do."

Marla hated when he said 'patient.' It was Crosby, not an unknown body. She cringed at the tube angling out of his head like a straw in a glass. "How much more?"

"A day. Where's the bloody protein?"

Marla sighed. "Okay, so it took longer than I thought. The first place I went to had no protein drinks. Went to another, and they only had two. Went to another and found four more and then bought some clothes for Crosby. What are you doing?"

"The patient is asleep, so I am wiping the last of the blood off his face. The wound still oozes."

Arturo glanced through the side window of the pickup and saw paperwork with the DEA letterhead on the passenger seat. He fished for his phone to call Bird. He had to get the okay for the killing.

"I left our food in the truck and Crosby's clothes and protein drinks outside. Be right back."

When Marla opened the trailer door, Arturo dropped to the ground and caught a glimpse of a tall man standing inside and another lying on a bed. He ended the call before it rang.

She opened the back door of her truck and grabbed two plastic sacks. Closing the door, she felt something odd. Edging her right hand near her weapon, she skirted around the back side of the cactus again. The armadillo had left. From under the truck, Arturo pointed his gun at her boots. Marla turned when two cars drove down the road. The sound of helicopter blades fluttered above her. *Transport to the hospital? A head wound?* After reaching for the sacks on the ground, she headed toward the trailer again.

Closing the door behind her, Marla placed the sacks on the table. "Before we eat, I'm changing him."

The doctor snapped off the gloves and dropped them into the wastebasket. He squeezed his eyes shut while adjusting his glasses. The monitor on the wall beeped a high-pitched sound.

Marla pointed at the blood pressure reading of 186/95. "Is that important?"

The repetitive beep continued every three seconds.

"It's the tube. It's stimulating an area in the brain and causing the blood pressure to elevate." Struggling with his coke-infused concentration, he slipped another pair of gloves on and slowly turned the tube. The pressure decreased, and the beeping stopped.

"What happened?" Marla asked.

"His brain is growing. I had to pull the tube out a few millimeters." He furrowed his brow. "Something wrong?"

Marla opened the camera app on her phone. Even with no movement outside the trailer, she became concerned. "Not sure." Marla closed the app. "It's time we move to another spot."

The doctor shook his head. "No, no. We can't move the patient. It's too dangerous."

Arturo hustled to his car and called Bird. "Found all three of them, the doc and the two DEA agents. They're out on the edge of town."

Bird asked, "What can you tell me about the one I shot?"

"Inside an air-conditioned trailer, flat on a bed."

"Excellent."

"Want me to kill them?"

"I heard the woman was good with a gun," Bird said. "Need a better ambush, so hustle back to town. We have work to do."

Inside the trailer, Marla's phone rang. "Agent Adams."

Borland said, "A murder occurred downtown at the La Zapata Restaurant. We found cocaine spread across the alley, and a twenty-two-year-old Los Zetas member that goes by Benito is dead. The victim's fingerprints match a few on the burned van. He must be one of Bird's men. Witnesses said a tall Caucasian man with a funny accent killed him. Maybe British."

Marla exited the trailer and gently pushed the door closed behind her. "Want me to investigate this?"

"Adams, I don't normally interject myself into agents' personal lives, but is the doctor that helped you take Crosby out of the hospital tall?"

She anxiously rubbed her chin and neck. "Tall, sir? I guess that's all relative. Probably not to an NBA player."

Borland snapped back, "Adams? Is he taller than you?"

"Could be. Not for sure. He's not in front of me, so not a hundred percent sure."

"Does this doctor have an accent?"

"Well, he lives in Louisiana, so I guess that could be an accent of sorts."

"Bring him in for questioning."

"Shouldn't we leave this to the San Antonio police? We don't want to step on anyone's toes."

"Don't worry about what we should do. I want to talk to him."

She leaned her hand against the trailer. "Yes, sir. I'll do that." Without replying, Borland disconnected the call. She slid her phone into her back pocket. "Son of a bitch."

She swung the door wide open. "Dr. McCollum?" She slammed the door behind her. "Did you leave Crosby here, alone, and go downtown?"

His eyes widened. "What? I have no idea what you are inferring?" He pretended to adjust the monitor on the wall. "His vital signs are—"

She clamped onto his wrist. "Did you leave the trailer yesterday, travel to La Zapata Restaurant, and kill a man inside that business?" Glancing back to the door as if she could see outside, she asked, "Is that why there's a bullet hole?"

"Pfft." He tried to pull her hand off his wrist. "If you think I killed a man, then arrest me. Take me in. Lock me up. But if you do, without me here, your husband will be dead tomorrow."

Marla's grip tightened. "Give me your phone."

"Why would I do that?"

She turned his arm, and he dropped to his knees. "Okay, sorry." He held his phone up to her.

"If Crosby dies, you have no leverage. I'll throw you in jail with men who would love to know you killed a Los Zetas member." She took his phone and released his arm. "You're in the middle of Texas. No car," she held his phone in front of his face, "no phone, and no place to hide. Get all this working, so Crosby can get better. Now!" She took the SIM card from the doctor's phone and put it in her pocket.

"What will you do with me once I save your husband's life? Have me killed? I should have known better. Bloody well should have told you no when you begged for my help. Arrogant Yanks have no gratitude."

She sat on her haunches and held Crosby's hand. "I must catch a man who shot a DEA agent, my husband. And you promised to heal him."

The tablet speaker crackled and hissed, with the screen randomly flickering a million gray dots.

A robotic voice whispered, "Marla."

Her head shot up. "Did you hear that?"

The voice repeated, "Marla."

She clasped her hands around Crosby's hand. "Yes. Yes. I'm here."

The voice looped a word. "L-L-L-L."

"Yes," she said. "That's right. Mar—La. La. Marla. You can say it."

"L-L-LO-LOVE Y-Y-Y-YOU."

"Oh, Crosby. I love you too." Her lips strained into an enormous smile. "We'll be talking in no time."

"B-Bird shshshshshsh-shot…"

Dr. McCollum stared at the gray dots moving on the screen. The image improved. A picture better than any police drawing, an image straight from his patient's brain. Might as well have a camera take a photo of Bird and insert it inside the tablet. The DEA could find a man with a perfect picture spread across the nation. The doctor's fingers twirled his mustache as the need for cocaine rose. More cocaine. He could have all the cocaine he wanted, for life, forever, if he did what Bird wanted. Second thoughts entered his mind. What about the Hippocratic Oath? Do no harm. He shouldn't have talked to Bird; he should have hung up.

An hour later, Crosby's improvements escalated. The tip of his tongue licked a line between his lips. The robotic voice became less mechanical but still struggled with words.

"See? I told you he would speak in three days. You doubted me."

"I apologize, doctor. This is more than I ever truly expected."

"Ddddruuugs." Crosby's pulse jumped past 120. The monitor beeped once, then stopped when the pulse dropped below 100.

"Yes," Marla said. "Drugs. Where?"

The monitor beeped again, declaring a racing heart rate. Mc-Collum stared at the probe. He wondered if Bird came now, would he kill the two DEA agents? Would Bird kill him or hand him a bag of coke?

Crosby's breaths slowed. The machine-driven voice called out, "O-o osh-osh-occan."

"Ocean?" Marla asked. "The ocean? Do you mean the Gulf? Drugs coming across the border from the Gulf? Boats?"

Crosby moved his head slightly. He bent his elbow and brought their clasped hands to his lips. His eyelids slowly opened, eyes staring at the ceiling. "A-a-acean."

"Did you see that?" Marla looked at the doctor. "He's moving more. His eyes opened." She turned back. "Crosby, what does that mean?"

Chapter 36

ASAC Ronald Borland flipped through the contacts on his phone.

Quinton sat at his kitchen table when his phone rang. "Agent Wales here."

"This is Borland."

"Yes, sir. What can I do for you?"

Borland tapped a key on his computer while reviewing information on Dr. Reginald McCollum. "Do you know where Adams is hiding her husband?"

"No, sir. She's tight-lipped about the whole enchilada."

Borland clicked on an image of the Englishman. "Find out."

"Why do you want to know, sir?"

"A tall, lanky Caucasian male with a possible British accent was reported at the scene of a murder in downtown San Antonio. Cocaine was all over the alley and street. The doctor helping Agent Adams' husband fits the description. I asked her to bring him in for questioning, but she didn't seem too enthusiastic. I don't think placing an official tail on one of my agents is smart. Not sure if that would fly past the HR scrutiny."

"You want me to call her and meet somewhere?" Quinton asked. "I could follow her afterward, and possibly lead me to where she has him hidden."

"Sounds okay, except it can't be you. She could easily pick out your government-issued Tahoe behind her. Do you have someone else?"

"I'll take care of it." Quinton terminated the call.

Quinton scooted his chair back and entered the living room, where he opened a book with pages cut out of the center and a burner phone sitting inside. He removed it and made a call. "A quick favor. I need a motorcyclist on a quiet bike down the street from my house and a five or six-year-old car, not an SUV, with two men at the far end of the block. Have them here in five minutes. They are going to follow a dually pickup truck…Yeah, that's what I said, a pickup with four wheels on the back."

Someone spoke on the other end.

"No," Quinton said. "Need a motorcycle to follow the truck. Find someone, anyone, here in five, put him on a bike, and get him here ASAP." He disconnected and called Marla on his work phone.

Marla's phone rang. She answered, "Agent Adams."

"Checking on my favorite newbie," Quinton said.

She smiled. "All good. How's the leg?"

"Dancing around the house like Fred Astaire with a cane. I thought you should know I have additional information on Torres-Hernandez."

"Did Bird surrender?" she asked.

The doctor perked his ears at her conversation while counting the number of packaged syringes he had left.

Quinton chuckled. "I wish. More about that kid killed at the downtown restaurant with a possible connection to Bird."

"If this is about the shooter," Marla glanced at the doctor, "that should go to the local PD."

Leaning against the back of the kitchen chair, Quinton drew his pistol from his holster. It clunked on the tabletop. "Can you come by my house?"

Marla covered the face of the phone with her hand and whispered to the doctor, "How long will he sleep?"

"Two-three hours. Maybe more."

She removed her hand from the phone. "Sure. Now?"

"I'll text you my address."

McCollum held his empty hand out to her.

"What?" she asked.

"You're leaving, and you have my SIM card. What if I must call you or you call me? How would that occur?"

Cringing at his beamy smile, she dug into her pocket and handed it to him.

⁂

A sunset lingered, bouncing a prism of colors under the clouds. Marla's pickup truck turned into Quinton's driveway. He looked at his watch. "Eleven minutes. She's close." He opened the front door and waved. She held her hand out while stepping onto the porch. Quinton switched the cane from his right to his left hand and shook her hand. "Come in." He closed the door and directed her to his living room, then ambled to the kitchen with a clunk of the cane and a slower second step. He called out, "Coffee, water, beer?"

"Water's fine."

Quinton returned, water glass in hand, and caught her looking at pictures hanging on the wall. "Here you go."

She turned and took the glass. "Family?"

"Most are vacations with friends from a bygone era. Fishing, skiing." He waved the cane like a ski pole. "Guess I won't be doing that anymore."

She sipped the water. "When are you coming back to work?"

"They said two weeks, but I'm ready now."

She sat on the couch and placed the glass on a coaster. "What's going on with the case?"

He sat in a high-backed leather chair across from her and laid the cane over his lap. "We learned the victim's name. He was a mule, slash, dealer."

"I figured that part. What else?"

"He dealt Mexican cocaine. Forensics detected it scattered over the body, down the alley, and the sidewalk."

"Right." She picked the glass up again and sipped more water. "Either a deal gone bad or another cartel member ambushed him."

"Witnesses said the shooter was Caucasian, not Hispanic. Rules out a cartel hit."

"Any prints?"

"Nothing except people working at the restaurant and the vic."

She put the glass on the coffee table again. "What can I do to help?"

"Just keep your eyes and ears open."

Marla's phone rang. "Hello?"

Dr. McCollum said, "Get back here. The patient's in trouble."

Marla jumped out of her chair. "I have to go." She opened the front door, revealing a row of streetlights across the road illuminating an off-white glow in the darkness.

"A lead?" Quinton asked. His cane clunked behind her.

"I'll call you tomorrow."

She rushed to her truck and started the engine. Headlights glared into Quinton's eyes. Her truck charged down the street. Seconds later, a motorcycle gave chase without the benefit of a headlight. A dirty green, 2015 Toyota Camry with two men followed.

Quinton called Borland. "Something happened. Adams left in a hurry, but I have a tail on her."

Chapter 37

Marla turned left at an intersection and checked her rearview mirror. A motorcycle with the headlight turned off, followed her. Half a block later, she changed lanes and sped past two slower cars. The motorcycle stayed behind the vehicles. She slowed to a stop at the red light at the next intersection. A black Tesla beside her to the right. Through the rearview mirror, she focused on the cars behind her—no motorcycle in sight. The light turned green, and the Tesla drove through the intersection as quietly as a bicycle. Marla stood still and kept her foot on the brake. The car behind her honked. She didn't move until the light turned yellow and then floored the accelerator as the light changed to red. The motorcycle never moved.

Marla exhaled and merged onto Highway 281. Nervous about the motorcycle, she continued to glance at her mirrors. No cycle in sight. Blending into the traffic and shifting lanes for several miles, she exited with two other cars following. She could turn right onto the farm-to-market road and head toward the trailer or go left and cross the overpass. The first car behind her sped through the intersection. The second vehicle, a green Toyota Camry, turned and followed. Marla turned left again and merged back onto the highway, going in the opposite direction. The Toyota did the same, staying two cars back. When she slowed to forty, the two vehicles behind her changed lanes, but the Camry stayed behind her. She sped up. So did the car.

Moving from the inside to the middle lane in front of an Amazon delivery van, she lost sight of the green car in her rearview mirror. She glanced at the road sign stating exit 42 one mile ahead and switched to the outside lane. The van which was behind her sped up and passed.

The green car closed in with a commercial bobtail truck behind the Toyota.

"Let's see how you manage this, whoever you are."

Marla slammed on her brakes. The Toyota's tires skidded. The commercial truck smashed into the back of the Camry before she sped up and exited the highway.

Moments later, she turned onto the dirt trail and stopped near the trailer door. She entered with a loud, repetitive dinging of the monitor alarm dominating the trailer. The doctor leaned over Crosby, pressing a stethoscope against his chest. She focused on the screen showing a blood pressure of 188/112 and a pulse racing toward 130. "What's happening?" The tablet on the counter showed an out-of-focus picture of a man with a gun between two livestock trailers.

"I can't get his pressure and pulse down."

The speaker on the tablet moaned. "Back hurts."

Marla knelt next to Crosby. "Tell me what to do."

Dr. McCollum closed the tablet. "Why are you asking him? He doesn't know piddly what to do. I've seen this, and I'm the one who knows what needs to be done."

She covered her ears from the constant dinging of the alarm. "Can you mute that thing?"

He pushed a button on the monitor above Crosby's bed, and the alarm went silent. "I need an EKG machine, X-rays, and meds." He turned toward Marla. "I fear for his life. We must take him to the hospital."

"We can't take him there. They'll take the probe out. All this for nothing."

"I will never get a license if I have a death in this country."

Marla stood inches from the doctor's face. "You don't care about my husband. All you care about is your grandiose illusions."

"We must go now." The doctor ripped the blood pressure cuff off Crosby's arm. "He will die if he stays here."

"Wait. Let me think." She bounced the heel of her boot on the floor several times.

"We must go," he said. "His blood pressure is too high."

"Shut up and let me think." She kissed Crosby on his forehead. "It's not a hospital, but I can take you where there are all those things you need."

"No, the hospital."

"No. They'll turn him into a vegetable, or Bird will find him and kill him. Get Crosby ready for the road." Marla stepped out and backed her truck to the trailer hitch. After connecting the hitch to the truck, she asked, "Is he ready?"

The doctor raised his hands. "Almost. Where is this place?"

"My hometown. Dr. Sanborn's office in Hildebrandt."

Thirty minutes later, Marla's truck and trailer turned into a long parking lot with a row of retail stores and a stand-alone medical clinic. She stopped near the back door.

"Dear God, I pray for Crosby to be better."

She opened the back doors of the trailer and slid the ramp out. "Are you ready?" Dr. McCollum unlocked the wheel brakes on the bed. "We wheel his bed out and through the clinic's back door."

She briefly scanned the tablet with a picture, out of focus but looking closer to one of the four sketches of Torres-Hernandez. "You're doing fine, my love."

"Doing my best," Crosby said through the tablet speaker.

"Sorry to interrupt the two of you, but do you have a key to this facility?"

"No," Marla said.

"What we're doing is illegal. I will not get a medical license if I'm arrested for breaking and entering."

"Shut up about your stupid license."

They stopped near the back door.

"Dr. Sanborn will forgive me. He's my doctor."

McCollum wiggled the door handle and shrugged his shoulders. "Brilliant. It's locked."

Marla drew her pistol out of her holster.

"Wait. What are you going to do? Shoot the door lock like they do in movies?"

"No." She hit the window near the back door with the butt of her pistol. Glass shattered inside.

"You twit. The alarm will go off."

"Don't worry. I know Dr. Sanborn disconnected his alarm last year after he kept forgetting his passcode." Marla climbed through the broken window and disappeared inside. The back door opened a few seconds later. She flipped the light switch on, and long fluorescent bulbs flickered above their heads, revealing a long hallway with a white linoleum floor and bland, cream-colored walls.

"I'll never get a license."

She opened the door as wide as it would go and used the rubber doorstop to keep it open. The two pushed the bed down the hall.

"Second door on the right is radiology. An X-ray machine and an ultrasound are in there. You know how to use all those?"

"Yes, of course. What about blood tests?"

"He has his lab in another room. He does it all in the clinic."

They moved Crosby to the X-ray table, and Marla gently laid the sheet over him before she kissed his forehead. He smiled.

"I'll be in the hall while the doctor takes pictures."

Closing the heavy radiology door behind her, she leaned against the wall and slid down, feeling the empty hush of the building. A milky haze filled her head. *What in God's name am I doing?* She pushed back up the wall, wandered into the lobby, and then sat in a chair. It would be doubtful she could escape being relieved of duty. More than likely, jail time for breaking and entering, hiding a potential fugitive, taking medical equipment and drugs under false pretense, and whatever else the district attorney could muster up.

Outside, tires hissed on asphalt. Headlights cut through the black night. Cars filled with people rushing to fix their own problems.

The X-ray door opening stirred her back to reality. Footsteps echoed down the hallway. The lab machines kicked on.

Marla rolled her wedding band around her finger. She half-smiled, remembering the San Antonio Rodeo, where several small town police officers rode their horses in the arena. Crosby proposed to her that night, four years ago, but now it feels like decades.

The heavy door slamming shut startled her. The wall clock in the lobby showed past midnight. Her eyelids became heavy; thoughts drifted with her and Crosby riding their horses side-by-side near the creek on their three hundred acres of ranch land.

Dr. McCollum called out, "Need help."

Twenty minutes had passed. She rushed around to the room and found the doctor standing close to the X-ray table observing films of a chest, abdomen, and skull hanging on a light box on the wall.

"Are you finished?" Marla asked.

"Yes. Let's get him off this hard table and back on the bed."

They grasped the corners of the sheet under Crosby and swung him onto the bed.

The doctor held a blister pack in his hand. "I found blood pressure pills in the sample closet. These should bring the pressure down."

"He can't swallow a pill."

"I'll crush this with a tongue depressor, put the broken pieces on the back of his tongue, and give him some water. He'll get it down."

After watching the ease of how Dr. McCollum performed, she leaned over and kissed Crosby's lips before turning back toward the doctor. "Talk to me. Tell me what is going on."

He plucked the chest X-ray film off the light box, studied it intently, then laid it on Crosby before flipping through the EKG pages.

"I've only had one cock-up like this."

"What?"

"A cock-up." He contorted his hands in the air, trying to find the right word. "A problem, a screw-up."

The lab machine clattered like a fast typewriter. "Took long enough." He hurried to the other room.

She followed. "What? Tell me!"

"Blimey. I knew this could…" Dr. McCollum raced back into the radiology room and stared at the skull X-ray film on the light box. "I should never have used a second lot of stem cells."

"Don't understand what you are trying to say."

He pointed at the side view of the skull. "See these white dots? They're metal from my catalyst stippled throughout his brain."

"I've seen X-rays of shrapnel before. Looks sort of the same, but lots smaller."

"The metal precipitated out of the solution and clumped, but I never took the time to X-ray a skull after using a second lot of stem cells; enhanced cells."

"Thought you said you had never done this before."

"Only with animals. Never a human."

"So, what does it mean?"

"Could be why he increased having seizures. The metal can be an irritant, like using a scrub brush on brain tissue. But this is not the worst of it." He grabbed the chest X-ray from the table and placed it back on the light box. "See here?" He pointed at the film. "This is his heart."

"Right," Marla said, "big white thing, middle of the chest."

"It's almost twice the normal size." He pointed at the abdomen X-ray. "The kidneys are twice the size they should be, and white dots are scattered throughout." He held the lab results up in the air. "He's made too much blood. It's like he's pumping sludge in his veins. It's a bloody mess."

"All this from the stem cells?" Marla asked.

"Right. The cells are supposed to work in a localized area, growing only where the stem cells are in contact with tissue, but I worried this would happen." He held his hands up, yielding to the obvious. "The second set of stem cells, the enhanced stem cells, made everything grow. Every organ in his body."

Marla dropped her hand on the doctor's forearm. "What do you need to do?"

He pitched the lab results and X-ray films on top of Crosby. "His heart is pumping too hard, kidneys shutting down. I shouldn't give him another injection. What he needs are transplants. He needs a new heart and kidneys." *A new brain*, he thought.

And then it hit him hard. Bird planned to come to the shed that night to kill his patient. *I'm supposed to save lives. Convincing the wanker to leave the cocaine with me and leave them alone should be easy enough. I'm intelligent—a doctor. I talk to people every day.*

He gathered the X-rays and paperwork. "We should return to where we were, and I will think about how to fix this."

Marla paced in the hallway and then stopped. "Should we take him back to the hospital?"

"No." The doctor waved his hands at her. "No. There is no telling what they will do to him." He turned away from her and grumbled to himself, "To me. I don't have a medical license in this state."

"Come on, let's go. I have a better idea."

With Crosby's bed pushed outside the clinic, Marla kicked the rubber stopper under the back door away and stared down the hallway. The rooms were dark, and the lab and X-ray machines were off. She flipped the hallway light switch off as the door slowly closed and latched.

"We have to go." He hurriedly pushed the bed toward the trailer, knowing Bird waited for them. "We must return to the same place and let me think about what I can do."

The wheels under the bed rumbled over the asphalt. Marla opened the trailer back doors, and they pushed the bed up the ramp. After locking the bed in place and Crosby comfortable, she closed the doors before telling the doctor, "Stay by the truck. I'm running across the street to Walmart. I'll be back in ten minutes."

Chapter 38

With the back and side trailer doors closed and the patient's bed locked inside, Dr. McCollum eased around the trailer, glanced inside the pickup cab, and then back toward Marla running across the street. "Where is the shed from here?" He opened the driver's door, and the inside light lit up. "I've made a cock-up of everything. If she won't give me a reference letter, what am I getting out of this?" He slid into the driver's side of the front seat and stared at the massive dashboard three times larger than his vehicle in London.

The doctor turned the steering wheel slightly and it clicked. "Bollocks, it's locked." He found the start button on the dash and when he pushed it, 'Key Not Detected' flashed on the screen. "Sodding hell!" He pushed the button again, and it dinged. "I must tell Bird where we are. He could come here. I should call and tell him we're at a medical clinic in some small town. How many could there be? I could leave Texas with a bag of cocaine. No, a suitcase full. Hide from these nutters and work on my research every day. I'll be famous."

"Who are you talking to?" Marla looked for anyone inside. "And what are you doing in the truck?"

He slid out of the seat and closed the door. "Nothing. Absolutely nothing."

❖

Headlights darkened from two minivans before turning off the road toward the metal shed where Arturo had found the trailer. A Ford

F-350 pickup truck with a trailer hitch followed close behind. The minivans stopped, and the side doors slid open. Four men carrying AK-47s rushed toward the shed. Moments later, one man returned from the building and waved his gun above his head. Bird lowered the passenger window of the pickup truck.

The man called out in Spanish, "Nothing there."

Bird slapped the dashboard before turning to Arturo in the driver's seat. "The doctor lied to me. He'll pay for that." He turned back to the man near the shed. "Is there anything inside which shows a trailer was there?"

"Tire tracks with a broken camera on the ground. And there's an orange extension cord connected to a generator."

"A generator?" Bird nodded. "For lights and air conditioning. Leave the camera, take the generator and electric cord, and put them in the pickup bed. I'll make them sweat." He motioned to the other minivan driver. "Park a hundred yards down the road. If they return, call me."

✦

Marla pitched a plastic sack in the front seat of the truck. "We need to go. The security guard at Walmart had a police radio on his belt, and I heard the dispatcher ask for a drive-by of this clinic."

Dr. McCollum swung open the side door, entered the trailer, and sat in the chair beside the bed, resting his elbows on his thighs. *I'm feckless. How am I getting a license with a police record?*

"Ready?" Marla asked.

He mumbled, "I'm a bloody bag o' shit, I am."

She closed the side door. After starting the engine, she eased past the clinic to the far end of the parking lot. A police car eased around the clinic and stopped near the broken window.

"That didn't take long." She stopped and killed the engine.

A minute later, two more police cars with emergency lights flashing stopped on each side of the clinic. Marla called the doctor on the two-way radio. "Looks like we're stuck here for a while."

"Why?"

"Police are at the clinic. They'll check it and probably call Dr. Sanborn to come down and see what was stolen."

"We didn't steal anything."

"They don't know that. Driving out may get us noticed, so we'll sit and wait. Lie down on the floor and take a nap. I'll call you when it's safe to leave."

He tapped a small line of white powder onto the crook of his hand and snorted it up his nose. He shook his head in despair. "There's nothing else I can do." He glanced at his wristwatch. "Bird is supposed to be at the shed tonight, and I've buggered up this whole thing." His palms rubbed his days-old beard. "Maybe he hasn't been there yet. If this crazed woman hurries, we could get there before he does."

He called Marla back on the radio. "Hurry up, woman. Go straightaway to the shed."

"Don't have a good feeling about that place anymore. When it's safe to leave, we're going to a new location."

He stood and ran his fingers through his hair. "No. No, we can't."

"Why not?"

"I might need to give him more medicine, and going somewhere else will take too long."

"Thought you said no more stem cells?"

He grabbed the rail on the bed. "Right. No. I mean the blood pressure medicine. He may need more, and you must help me. You can't help if we are going somewhere else."

"I have the perfect place, in the middle of a crowd, where no one will see us."

The doctor's phone dinged with a message. *You lied to me.* He sat back in the chair and rubbed the heel of his hand up and down his nose. He couldn't stop his left leg from bouncing.

After clearing his throat, he tapped the phone number from the text. Before Bird said anything, Dr. McCollum blurted, "I'm not ready to die. I have too much to give to humanity. I can save—"

Bird cut him off. "You will pay for lying to me."

"I didn't. I was expecting you. Promise. It was an...an emergency. The patient's blood pressure rose to critical levels. Why didn't you come sooner? It's your fault, not mine. Your fault."

"I'm here now, and you are not."

"We had to take him somewhere. For his blood pressure."

"A hospital?" Bird asked. "Which one? What room number?"

Marla called on the radio. "Dr. McCollum?"

He declined to answer and kept talking to Bird. "No, a clinic. We broke in and used their equipment and meds. I will have her return as soon as possible. Do I still get the stuff? I deserve what you promised me."

Bird waited a few seconds before he answered. "Only if you tell me where you are right now."

"In a small town. I don't know the name, but you can't come. There are police nearby."

"Which town?"

"I told you I don't know where I am. I'll tell you as soon as I can." He heard the phone disconnect. "Bollocks."

He called Marla on the radio. "What is the name of this town? I must be informed of where I am."

"Why must you... never mind. I'll tell you later. And why didn't you answer when I called a minute ago?"

"I was, uh, don't, I," he grabbed the stethoscope, "checking the patient's blood pressure."

"What was it?"

"Don't worry, it was good."

"Okay, lie down and rest. I'll call you when we are ready to leave."

An hour later, the starting of the truck engine woke McCollum. The a/c kicked on and circulated stagnant air. Marla called on the radio, "We're clear, so heading out. How is Crosby?"

He sat up and glanced at his patient. The engine revved, and he felt the trailer move forward. Grabbing the bed rail, he sat in the chair. "We should return to the shed."

"No. Sit back and wait. How is Crosby?"

Dr. McCollum repeatedly twirled the end of his mustache. "He's asleep."

"Sit back and relax. We'll be there in fifteen or twenty minutes."

"Where? Tell me where? Where are we going?"

The heart rate monitor beeped steadily, and the blood pressure was stable. Everything was stable, against Bird's wishes. *Should I allow this man to kill my patient? Telling him would be the same as me doing it. No, I bloody can't. Ethics. I must abide by medical ethics. But save who, him or the world? Bird would understand. I'm a doctor. Would I get the cocaine?* It was too dark to see anything out the trailer's side window. He leaned toward the door and thought if he opened it, there could be a landmark or a building he would recognize. The trailer wheel hit a pothole, and he bounced against the wall. Another pothole dropped him to the floor. The trailer slowed, then sped up. He called Marla back. "You're bouncing me all over inside here."

"Sorry about all the potholes. I didn't see them until I was on top of them. We have a smooth road ahead. Crosby good?"

"How much longer?"

"About ten minutes. When I stop, stay quiet."

"Why? Where are you taking me?"

He felt the trailer turn before stopping. The truck door opened, then closed. Voices outside yelled. If he cracked the door, he might see something recognizable. Something he could tell Bird.

Reaching into his pocket for the vial of cocaine, he realized it was almost empty. *Hold it. Save it for later.* He twisted the cap off. *Just smell it, that's all. That would be enough to get past whatever was coming tonight.* Saliva built inside his mouth. His tongue scraped the top of his palate. *Just a tiny amount. Not all of it. Tap a sprinkle on the webbing between my thumb and finger and just smell it. That's all, smell it and put it back in the vial.*

His nose almost touched the powder, smelling every granule. He couldn't stop. A quick sniff and it was gone. His body shivered. More. He wanted more. It was like half a beer, half a shot of whiskey, sex without... Not enough. It was the only thing that gave him pleasure, made him happy, and kept him alive.

He didn't remember snorting the rest. He flicked the side of the vial and stared at the emptiness. There was no more, but Bird had more, lots more. He slapped his face several times, then vigorously rubbed his whiskers and mustache. He could stop if he wanted, but why? It allowed him to concentrate, focus on what needed to be done, and he could have all he wanted, forever and ever, with a touch of the number on his phone. Tell Bird where they were, and he could get what he wanted, except he didn't know where he was. "Where the bloody hell am I?"

Voices yelled outside again. Who was it? He dropped to the floor and scooted against the wall, away from the door. Was it Bird? His men? Bird would give him the coke. He promised.

The doctor scratched his forearms with his fingernails and then his legs and ankles. He had to stop before she came back inside. He should get up and wash his face. Clear his head.

Someone or something pushed on the side of the trailer and made it wobble. Were they trying to topple the trailer? He envisioned a spray of bullets ripping a line in the wall—dead in a second. No more cocaine. He crawled under the bed and covered his ears.

Marla came out of an office with papers in hand. To her left, bright lights lit a large, square grassy area. Teenagers played tag football. Five yards away, a kid threw a ball high in the air. A boy ran, ready for the touchdown. The ball arched downward. She caught him from falling when he bounced against her truck. The trailer wobbled.

"Sorry, Miss. My brother always throws it too far."

Marla glanced at her watch. It was four in the morning. "Kind of late, or early to be out here."

"Our parents don't care, and the owner keeps the lights on all night."

Marla knocked on the trailer door and opened it. "I've signed us up for a week...what are you doing?"

Curled under the bed, he stared behind her at a bright-white sign twenty feet above the ground, RV PARK.

Marla entered the trailer and closed the door behind her. "I said, what are you doing under the bed?" She grabbed his leg and pulled.

He rolled to his hands and knees, grabbed the bed rail, and stood. "Nothing. I'm doing nothing. That noise outside is bothersome. I was trying to protect the patient." He stumbled toward the counter and pitched his glasses near the small sink before turning the faucet on and splashing water on his face. "This place is not safe. We should go back."

"Look at me." It was the first time Marla had seen him without wearing his eyeglasses. She stared at his dilated eyes, the twitches of his facial muscles, and the redness of his nose. "Damn." She shook her head. "Right in front of me. I never noticed, and all the signs were right there. You're high. Which is it? Cocaine? Meth? Ritalin?"

He sat at the table and looked down. "Leave me alone. I don't know what you are talking about."

"Where are you getting drugs?" She latched onto his collar and yanked him off balance. "Who? Tell me who?"

"I brought it with me. Everything. All of it. I brought it in my medical bag."

"No. Customs would have picked it up at the airport." Marla grabbed his bag off the table and turned it upside down. All the contents fell out between Crosby's legs. There it was. A bent spoon. She thought nothing about the oddity of a doctor who didn't smoke having a disposable lighter to light the gasoline. She felt like an idiot.

"Where is it? The rest of it?"

"It's gone. All of it." He grabbed the empty glass vial from his pocket and threw it against the wall. "See? All gone."

Chapter 39

Marla drove the pickup and trailer to a concrete pad at the outer edge of the RV Park. Scrub brush and trees lining a chain link fence. She plugged electricity into the trailer and opened the Walmart sack. "I'm watching you, bub. In fact," she removed two plastic-sealed packages from the sack, "I'm going to watch your every move with these two Bluetooth cameras."

After hanging the first one outside the trailer, Marla loaded it to her phone, and the screen showed a row of RVs parked like houses on a suburban block. She turned the camera toward the entrance gate and the main building.

Dr. McCollum started walking toward the grassy area.

"Where do you think you're going?"

"Out there," he said. "Just to stretch and move around."

"Nope." She fluttered her fingers back at him. "Get your cocaine ass inside. You have work to do."

"Am I a prisoner?"

"Call it what you want. Back inside."

McCollum re-entered the trailer with Marla behind him. She hung the second camera in the corner with a wide lens enveloping the entire trailer. He pretended to ignore her while plugging in the tablet and sliding the probe down the tube inside Crosby's brain.

"I put this camera here to watch your every move. I'll deal with your B.S. after you figure out how to save my husband. And by God, if you screw this up, I'll..."

She leaned toward Crosby. "My love. Sorry about all the confusion and moving you around like this. We're going to get you well." She reached for his hand and touched his fingertips to her cheek. "We'll have you talking all day long in no time."

The doctor's head buzzed. His tongue searched his teeth and gums for more cocaine. He concentrated on a single thought, taking the blood pressure. His hands ripped the Velcro apart on the bp cuff. The sound threw shivers down his back. He wrapped it around Crosby's arm and pumped the cuff up before slowly releasing the pressure while listening with the stethoscope.

"How high is it?" Marla asked.

He had already forgotten. "It's better." His hands trembled while holding the pulse oximeter. It was the size of a matchbox. Aiming the pulse oximeter toward Crosby's finger, he missed. The light bulb in the gooseneck lamp on the counter felt hot to the back of his head. Sweat dripped down his neck. Grasping the hand, he tried again, finally clamping it on the fingertip. The monitor lit up; BP 206/116, pulse 114, oxygen 98%.

"The pressure is too high." Marla pushed the doctor's shoulder. "You said it was better."

He reached for the blood pressure medicine bottle but knocked it on its side. The pills spilled on the counter.

"How much have you been taking?" She gathered the pills with the edge of her hand and placed them back inside the bottle.

He avoided her gaze. "I'm fine. Don't worry about me." He gestured with his hand. "Give me one of those."

She dropped a pill into his palm and noticed the tremble.

He continued to look away from her. "I'm fine." He placed the pill on the counter. "I need something to crush the pill."

Marla drew her pistol from her holster. "How about this?"

"No." He held his hands up. "Don't be a bloody prat. Look, I stopped. I can still help your husband."

She pushed the bottom of the handle against the pill and cracked it. "That enough?"

Closing his eyes for a second before saying anything. "Yes." Pinching the broken pill between his fingertips, he rubbed the medicine on

Crosby's teeth and gums as he felt like one of Pavlov's dogs, salivating for the taste of coke on his own gums.

"Shouldn't you be wearing gloves?"

He stopped. "I...I ...washed my hands."

"When?"

He snapped back, "Stop winding me up." He grabbed the hand gel dispenser bottle. "Look. I'm washing."

Marla leaned into the doctor's face. "What are you thinking? A doctor who wants a medical license, and you're high?"

He squirted a dab of gel on his hands again and rubbed them too long. "I'm alone, in bloody Texas, around a bunch of bloody bastards. You kidnapped this person, and you want miracles. Yeah, I'm using a little cocaine to help get by. So what? Are you going to arrest me? Send me to jail? Or maybe a reprieve, amnesty? How about a pardon for saving your husband?" He leaned in toward Marla. "Remember who's shot in the head, and who's the only person in this world that can save him?"

She clasped her hand onto the front of his shirt. "Are you hiding any drugs?"

"It's gone. I told you. All of it." He slapped her hand away. *But I want more.*

Things fell into place. She understood. It was the doctor who killed the kid in the restaurant. Borland was looking for him; she lied and now became an accomplice.

"Move. I need to take care of the patient." He adjusted the probe before opening the tablet wider. From hours ago, the grainy mess on the screen had progressed to an almost completed face and gun. He wondered which was best, a dead patient or Bird dead? A medical license or a bag of Utopia?

Marla had to turn this drug-addicted doctor in before Borland found him; found them. Her career, her life with Crosby, would be over. But this man was the only person able to save Crosby, and he couldn't do it if in jail. "Turn the speaker on."

Crosby turned his head toward her, and his gravelly voice called out. "Marla."

She spun around. "You're speaking? This is unbelievable. Yes, Crosby. I'm here."

"Bbbird."

"Bird? Say what he did."

"Ssshot." He cleared his throat. "Me."

She clasped her fingers between his. "That is enough to arrest him, but I need a clearer image of his face to send to Borland." She glanced at the tablet. "Keep working on the picture."

"Mex." Crosby's eyes squinted shut, and his head jerked. The probe moved, and the tablet squealed. The doctor adjusted the probe slightly.

"Mex," Crosby said.

"Mexican cocaine? Heroin?" Marla asked.

He squeezed his eyes tight.

"Do you know how it is sent across the border?"

He nodded again.

"How?" Marla asked.

"Bbbb."

"B?"

He shook his head. "Bl...bl."

"Blood?"

He furrowed his brow and took several breaths. "O."

"Do you mean Blood?"

Crosby frowned.

"Red like blood?"

Crosby blinked twice.

"Twice means no. Come on. Stay with me. You can do it."

He opened his mouth and stuck the tip of his tongue behind his upper front teeth. "La." He stopped and exhaled. "Lil."

"Lil? I don't understand."

"Eeee."

"Bloody?"

Crosby's eyes closed and stopped.

"I think he fell asleep," Dr. McCollum said.

Marla laid Crosby's hand on his chest. "Long day, long night for him. He needs rest. What about the blood pressure and all his organs?"

The doctor pointed at the monitor. "BP 162/84." He beat his chest like a miniature King Kong. "I am your only hope."

Crosby mumbled, "Not alone."

Marla leaned over Crosby. "Yes. We're not alone. We are at an RV park mixed in between metal houses on wheels."

"Bird... not...alone."

"Someone was with him?" She felt his hand loosen. "Stay with me. Who was with him?"

Crosby's eyes closed again.

Marla's phone buzzed. She released Crosby's hand before rubbing her palm over her eye. She glanced at the screen; it was Bird.

I'M DEEPLY DISTRAUGHT YOU MOVED. STILL IN THE DARK GRAY TRUCK PULLING A LONG WHITE HORSE TRAILER? I HAVE EYES EVERYWHERE. SLEEP WELL. I'M SURE WE WILL MEET VERY SOON.

She jumped to her feet and drew her pistol when two hard knocks came against the door. The doctor back-peddled as far away from the door as possible, squatting next to the head of the bed. She held her finger against her lips and whispered a hush toward the doctor.

Two more knocks on the door. A voice called out, "Mrs. Adams? It's Ms. Howard from the front office. You dropped your receipt."

Marla lowered her head and raised a slow smile. Hiding the pistol behind her back, she opened the door to an elderly woman holding a piece of paper toward her. "You dropped this outside the front door.

"Thank you. I must have done that when I spoke to the boys throwing the football. Thank you."

"I'm so sorry you had to deal with them. Those boys and their families travel together and are out there every night playing, but don't worry, they leave in two days. On their way to Florida, I think. I can't remember if they said Orlando or Miami." The woman waved and turned away.

"By the way," Marla said, "if anyone, man or woman, anyone—my ex-husband, asks about me, my name, description of my rig, or just anything, you have my cell phone number, please call me immediately."

"I understand, sweetie. I had one of those ex-husbands. He's in jail now, so I don't have to worry about him no more."

Marla waved with the receipt in her hand. "See you tomorrow."

Dr. McCollum caught Marla frowning at him. "What?" he asked.

"Get off the floor." She holstered her pistol. "Are you sure you can't put more stem cells down the tube?" Marla glanced at Crosby and then at the doctor. "Someone wants to kill my husband, so you must get him well."

Chapter 40

Seven in the morning came too soon. Marla sat across from the doctor inside the RV Park dining area with a wall separating them from the lobby. Other people sat at tables eating their continental breakfasts. Her phone sat on the table, showing a split screen of Crosby sleeping on the bed and the other half with the gated entrance.

She scooped the last mini wheat with a flimsy white plastic spoon and ate it. "I've thought about it. If I sent Crosby back to the hospital, he would need round-the-clock protection, and I need confirmation of that before I take him there."

Dr. McCollum spread butter on his toast. "You can't stay here forever."

She glanced up. "Not forever. I need you to heal Crosby so he can finish the picture of Bird. Even better if he can give testimony."

She sipped her coffee from a disposable cup. On her phone screen, a black Tahoe crept past the entrance gate and stopped.

"Our morning just went to hell," she said.

The doctor bit into his toast. "What?"

A football bounced off the front quarter panel of the black Tahoe. The same boy from yesterday picked it up from the ground and waved at the driver. On her phone, Marla watched the driver's door open and the end of a cane hitting the ground. She touched the gun and holster under her untucked shirt. The front entrance door opened, followed by a rhythmic cadence on the floor; clomp, step, clomp, step.

Mrs. Howard said, "Good morning. Checking in?"

Quinton showed his badge to her. "Are you the manager?"

"Owner."

"I'm looking for a woman. Her name is Marla Adams. Has she checked in? She's about five-eight with shoulder-length darkish blond hair." Quinton slid a photo across the countertop.

"No one here like that." Mrs. Howard pushed the photo back toward the man.

Marla whispered to Dr. McCollum, "Stay here and don't move." She pushed her chair back and tiptoed to the women's bathroom.

"Mind if I look around?" Quinton said.

"Yes, I do," Mrs. Howard said.

Quinton turned and glimpsed inside the dining area where two families sat at separate tables, and a single person was facing away from him.

"Hey!" Mrs. Howard yelled.

Quinton turned back toward her.

"This is a legitimate place of business, with children and families here. See that American flag on the pole? That means this is private property, and you can't just wander around here like a Nazi SS Trooper. You have a warrant on you?"

"No, ma'am. Hoping for some cooperation," Quinton said.

"I can have my attorney here in two minutes. How about you cooperate with him? Go on, outside with you. And back that vehicle of yours out of here, or I'll call the police. I don't want you driving on my property."

Inside the bathroom, Marla stared at her phone again and zoomed the trailer camera in on the Tahoe. Quinton limped to the driver's door and climbed in with the help of his cane before the vehicle backed out onto the street.

She opened the bathroom door and saw the doctor sitting at the table, head down, thumbs rapidly tapping the table. She waved at him to follow, then turned the corner and stopped at the desk. "Thank you for what you did."

"You didn't tell me your ex is a federal officer."

"No, sorry, I didn't. Now you understand why I'm scared," Marla said.

Mrs. Howard glanced at McCollum and then at Marla. "New boyfriend?"

"No. Brother. My older brother."

"I don't want any trouble here. This is a respectable place. You should leave today. I'll cancel your payment and return it to your card."

"No, you keep the money. But may I ask, because of this, I want to go to town and file a restraining order against the man, fill my tank, and buy groceries before we head out of town. You can't drag a trailer around all those places. We could leave later this afternoon. I'm sure he won't come back."

"All right. And good luck to you, sweetie."

They left the building and headed straight for the trailer. The doctor turned toward her. "You can lie like the best of them."

"Shut up. All this is your fault."

"What?"

"Your cocaine. It's going to get us killed or thrown in jail."

"Does the patient know about your house burning down?"

"Shut up." *Stop calling him the patient.* "No. It would break his heart."

"Who was that guy in the office?"

"DEA. My partner was shot in the leg and was supposed to be on medical leave, unless not anymore. My boss could have him looking for me. Hunt me down like a criminal."

"Why does he care where you are?"

"Two reasons, and you're directly related to both. Borland wants you to come in and talk about the shooting in the restaurant."

He marched straight ahead. "I have nothing to say about that."

"Second, I'm not at work, not in the office. It hasn't even been a week since I started this assignment, and I've gone AWOL."

Marla opened the trailer door. Crosby lay still, asleep, with the monitor beeping with each pulse. The tablet had more on the screen.

The facial outline was complete, with darkened round spots for eyes and two lines for a nose, the mouth almost finished.

"I need to find out why Quinton was here and where this son of a bitch Bird is hiding, or I'm just flat-assed shit out of luck." She punched the doctor twice in the chest with her finger. "You stay right here with Crosby and fix this mess, or your life isn't worth a plane ride back to London where Scotland Yard is waiting."

"I could consider one more injection."

"He's going to survive this, isn't he?"

"Survive?" He looked at Crosby. "Not sure. With the size of his heart and kidneys, he needs organ transplants or dialysis."

The tablet continued with the picture. The grainy dots moved like a magnet, dragging them to the correct spot.

She patted her holster. "I have more work that needs to be done. I'll be back in a few hours." She pointed at the camera in the corner and her phone. "Don't you leave this trailer. I'm watching you."

Crosby turned his head and said, "Azul."

Chapter 41

Marla stopped outside the gate to the DEA office and used her keycard. It didn't work. She slid it inside the gray box again. Nothing. She hit the steering wheel with her palm. "Great. My card doesn't work. I'm probably sacked." She stuck the card back in. Nothing. "Damn, you stupid ass. Come on, damn it."

A knock on the back window startled her.

"What are you doing, newbie?" another Special Agent asked. "Have you gone nuts?" He took the card from her and flipped it over. "The strip goes down." He slid the card into the box, and the gate opened.

She cleared her throat and pushed the hair off her face. "Thanks. I knew that. I just, well, thanks." She entered and parked in the back row, and the other agent parked nearby.

"Come on, newbie," he called out. "Time to go to work."

She waited in her car until he went inside. When she pulled open the glass front door, she gazed at the DEA sign and couldn't imagine ever being tired of seeing it on the wall. The two security men behind the desk smiled. She showed her badge and signed in.

Jason smiled. "Look. No packages for you this morning."

Michael shoved Jason's shoulder. "It's early. FedEx comes several times a day. Check back with us before you leave." They both laughed.

"Thanks, guys." She pretended to smell over the counter. "Should I bring a drug dog over here? He wouldn't smell anything on you, would he?"

"Just joking with you," Michael said. "Oh, by the way, Borland left a message. He wants to see you."

After leaving the elevator, Marla entered Borland's office, immediately noticing Suzie's purple hair had changed to blonde with black tips. *When did she do that?*

She sat behind the desk, on the phone, smiled, and spun the earpiece of her tortoise shell eyeglasses between her fingertips. Sunlight flickered across every ring on her hand. "Yes, sir. She's just arrived. I'll send her in."

"Is he in a good mood?" Marla asked.

Her fingertips dabbed the black tips of her hair, ensuring each monochrome-dyed hair was in place. "I've only been here a few months, but when you get to know him, you'll find his needle on the mood scale moves just a hair on each side of neutral."

"Not lately with me." Marla knocked twice on the door before entering. "Good morning, sir."

"Come in, Adams. Sit."

Her throat tightened. This was reminiscent of when she faced him after shooting Bird's brother. She drew in a deep breath and sat.

Borland gathered papers on his desk and moved them to the side. "Where are you in the trafficking case?" He leaned back in his chair. "I like to stay abreast with each case in my district. Daily reports on my desk are the usual. You've missed some." He unfolded his arms. "I understand, Special Agent Crosby Adams and you are going through challenging times. I have discussed this entire situation—"

"Situation, sir?"

"Yes. Situation. This whole mess of a situation. HR wants to classify your husband as unable to return to work and you as an immediate family provider."

"I don't understand what that means."

"Both of you would be off the force. Compensated, of course, but gone."

Marla shuffled in the chair. "Crosby will return to work sooner than you expect."

"I expect him to never return to work."

"A few more weeks." Marla clamped harder on the chair arms. "That is all I need to prove Crosby's abilities to heal. He will return, sir."

"And where are you while he is miraculously recovering from this necrotic mess?"

"Here...and there. Both places. I can be at both places."

"You can take your choice, work the case, or take family leave. I need a full-time agent on this."

"Understand, sir, and I want to continue working. I have new information."

"That is where you take the time and send me a daily report. New info is inserted in the daily report."

"Yes, sir. I will, but while I am here, I have more info on The Blue Lily."

"This info came from whom?"

Marla shifted in her chair. "Another agent gave that intel to me."

He leaned forward and put his clasped hands on his desk. "And which agent is that?"

"Special Agent Adams, sir."

"As in your husband?"

"Yes, sir."

Borland stared at her for a few seconds. "Isn't he unconscious, half his brain gone, flat on his...I'm not asking any more questions. I'm done with you. I'll have Wales check it out."

"Is Quinton, excuse me, Special Agent Wales, back on the case?"

"Interesting that you should ask. Have you seen him?"

She shouldn't lie to her boss. Not a clever way to start a long term relationship if it actually will last that long. But did Borland put Quinton on a search for the doctor?

Marla kept her knees tight and crossed her ankles. "I believe a connection exists between Bird, The Blue Lily, drugs, and trafficking. Not sure how yet, but something." *How's that for redirection?* "May I head back, sir?"

"Special Agent Wales is your trainer. You stay with him."

Finally, the question she came here for. "Is he able to return to work?"

"We are desperately short-handed." He gathered papers on his desk. "That is why you are here. You requested this office, and against my advice not to have husband-wife employees in the same office to work here, there was a void to fill. I need every agent working in my office, so medical has released Wales to short distance walking with a cane for three weeks. Other than that, he can do anything."

She decided she could watch Quinton better if he were with her. "I would appreciate his expertise and knowledge and continuing to collaborate with him. That would be ideal. I could pick him up today and dive back into the investigation." She stood and aimed toward the door, not wanting Borland to ask more questions about Dr. McCollum. "I'll call him. Thank you."

Marla parked her pickup truck in front of Quinton's house with no vehicle in the driveway. She called him.

Quinton answered. "Wales, here."

"Borland asked me to double down with you on the trafficking case. Tell me where you are, and I'll pick you up?"

"You're right about Borland. He's up my ass about this Bird case, moving it to priority one." Quinton drove through the fourth Walmart parking lot, hoping to catch her truck and trailer hiding in plain sight between semi-trucks. "Meet me at my house in ten minutes." He turned out of the parking lot and floored the accelerator.

Marla sat on the porch steps with her phone in hand. The live shot of Dr. McCollum performing another injection made the hair on her neck stand up. She stuffed the phone into her pocket when Quinton arrived. The tip of the cane clacking on the concrete drive burned into her memory. He walked toward her with a minimal limp.

After standing and adjusting the holster on her belt, she smiled. "You're looking good, rested, or is it because you're full of painkillers?"

He thumped the cane against the wooden railing beside the porch steps. "A bit of both. Come inside."

He plopped down in the overstuffed chair in the living room. "We know Bird is working two cartels, Los Zetas and Sinaloa. If we leak that, he'd be a dead bird."

She sat on the couch. *If Bird dies, I could quit looking over my shoulder every second, but that wouldn't help anyone else. Where is the tunnel Kata went through?* "No, we need him alive. If he dies, the cartel just keeps plodding along with the drugs and trafficking."

Quinton bumped his cane on the floor. "If you kill a general, it disrupts the flow, the action. That's what we need. Disrupt it long enough, and the trafficking could stop."

"He's no general. He's more like a captain, and captains die all the time in war. They stick another shmuck in his place the next day and move on. We need him arrested, alive, flip him, and tell us how Los Zetas works."

"You want to flip him? Continue to have the man who shot your husband out on the streets?"

"If it saves hundreds of lives, and slows the sex trade, then yes."

"All right. You have an idea how to capture him?"

"Maybe," Marla said, "Schmidt&Schmidt Slaughterhouse. As I said, it's open from 7 a.m. to 9 p.m., but few cattle are in the pens. Have you noticed that?"

"No. I'm not a rancher," Quinton said.

"Busy slaughterhouses have full pens," Marla said. "Feed and water the cattle a day or two and get the weight up before turning them into steaks. They should run hundreds, if not thousands of cattle a week. That is twenty-five to thirty full livestock trailers a week. Kata said she was with six other girls. Is Bird bringing thirty trailers from Mexico with girls every week?"

"I don't think pulling over a livestock trailer is smart. If we find nothing, we alert Torres-Hernandez, and he will disappear again like the proverbial bird he is so named."

Marla looked at the cane and then at Quinton. "Wish you didn't need that."

"Wish I didn't, either."

"Right." Marla leaned back on the couch. "There is something that's not adding up."

"What are you getting at?" Quinton asked.

"Kata said the truck drivers drop off their load of girls at a place with a white fence. That is not what the Schmidt & Schmidt slaughterhouse looks like. The trucks stay at the slaughterhouse too long. Drivers should unload and go, but they stay. Why? Is there a secondary place between San Antonio and the Mexican border? A place to switch products, girls, drugs, whatever else the cartel deals in?"

Quinton leaned against his cane. "Nice deduction, but you haven't said what you want to do."

"I don't know yet. I'm not sure which happened with Kata. Did she get dropped off at the white fence because something went wrong or because all went right?"

"Do you think there is more than one place they drop off the girls?"

"I don't know." Marla leaned forward, resting her elbows on her knees. "I'm close friends with the nephew of the Bexar County Sheriff."

"A friend of a friend?" Quinton asked. "Borland and Sheriff Johnson have butted heads for a long time."

"He owes me a big favor, and I've been sitting on it for a while," Marla said. Quinton held his hand up in wonder. Marla scooted up on the couch. "I introduced Jeffrey Keene to a Hildebrandt girl he wanted to meet."

"So, he moves on after a roll in the hay, and you think he remembers this?"

"Not quite. They married, so I have a connection to the sheriff's office."

Quinton leaned forward in his chair. "So that is why the picture of you and the girls hit the media by the next morning. Deputy Keene sent it all in."

Chapter 42

Across the road from Schmidt & Schmidt, Quinton's Tahoe hid behind a combine harvester in the farm implement parking lot. Through their cameras with long-distance lenses, Quinton and Marla watched three drivers shuffle between their empty semi-trucks aligned like dominoes at the unloading ramps. A driver leaned against the front chrome bumper, removed his cap, and wiped his forehead with his sleeve.

"Those three guys are pacing between the trucks." Quinton's camera clicked. "What's the reason for them being nervous?"

"Right. Like someone standing in front of a cashier and thinking about robbing it." Marla's camera clicked several times. "Are they waiting on something or someone? Drugs? Girls?"

A dark blue Ford Expedition made its way into the lot and stopped near the trucks. "There's your answer." Quinton's camera clicked several times. It was the same blue automobile he noticed when he was by himself a few days ago. "I'll take the SUV, and you concentrate on the drivers and trailers."

With the vehicle's front window down, Quinton studied the man behind the steering wheel with tattoos covering his bald head and a Fu-Manchu mustache. His camera clicked more. The driver flicked a cigarette butt to the ground. "I recognize this guy. The driver is Rafael Villegas, and he's with the Sinaloa Cartel."

Marla lowered her camera. "Bird double crossing Los Zetas? Balls of steel."

Quinton caught Marla glancing at her wristwatch. "Am I keeping you from something?"

"Why would you say that?" She took more pictures. "I've got all three drivers climbing into the back of their trailers. Wait, they're coming back out with each carrying a metal case about the size of an overnight bag. Got to be drugs or money." Marla snapped more photos. "Is Bird in the passenger seat? We could grab him here."

"Hard to tell. I can't see inside the vehicle very well," Quinton said.

"We have action at the truck on the left," Marla said. "Passenger door opening, and a girl climbing out of the cab?" She took more pictures. "Hold on. That's not a minor. She looks older, mid-to-late twenties."

"Villegas is smiling at the woman," Quinton said. "This should be interesting."

A woman in a paisley blouse with most buttons undone, a short red skirt, and blue high heels pranced from the truck cab toward the Expedition. She rubbed Rafael's bald head before climbing into the back seat behind him.

"Hooker?" Quinton asked.

"Looks like it." Marla turned her attention back toward the drivers. "Hold on. Something new. Two men emerged from the front doors wearing bloody aprons and holding identical metal cases in each hand. That's four cases. The drivers are exchanging cases with the bloody apron guys. One driver took two cases." Her camera clicked more. "Who's buying and who's selling?"

Quinton caught Marla glancing at her watch again. "You got someplace to be, Agent Adams?"

She shook her head. "No." She raised the camera to her eye. "Two drivers, each with a case, are heading to the backend of their trailers. They're climbing in, but the third driver didn't go to the trailer. Instead, he went to the SUV."

"Concentrate on the two drivers in the trailers," Quinton said. "I got the third holding two cases. He's pulling the Expedition's liftgate up, pitching one of his cases in the rear, and keeping one. It looks like Sinaloa gets twenty-five percent of the take."

Villegas opened his door, jumped out, and shoved the driver against the side of the vehicle. The guy dropped his case.

Quinton turned toward Marla. "For some odd reason, baldy-boy is giving the truck driver a hard time." The side window lowered. "Uh, oh." He laughed. "The hooker stuck her arm out and wrapped it around the driver's neck. Rafael punched the guy in the stomach and chest. The hooker released her hold, and the guy dropped to the ground." Quinton's camera clicked several more times. "The truck driver is on his hands and knees with one hand up. Looks like he's saying something."

"Can you read lips?" Marla took more pictures of the trailers.

"No, but the driver pushed his case under the vehicle so Villegas can't reach it."

"I lost the two drivers," Marla said. "I don't see any movement inside the trailers."

"Something spooked them," Quinton said. "Villegas rushed back into the driver's seat and slammed the door shut."

The back tires spun, and the vehicle shot down the road with the liftgate still up. The case slid out the back and bounced on the ground.

Quinton laughed. "He forgot to close the liftgate and lost his take."

"Found the two drivers. They looked spooked, too. Both jumped out of their trailer and ran around to the cab of their trucks. The third guy gets up off the ground and grabs both cases."

"With all these pictures, I hope I caught their faces," Quinton said.

"Me too."

Emergency lights flashed as four sheriff's department vehicles charged into the parking area and blocked the tractor-trailers.

Deputy Keene opened his door and called out from a bullhorn, "Drop to your knees. Hands on your head. You're under arrest."

The deputies jumped out of their vehicles and rushed to the trucks. The drivers raised their hands while yelling profanities in Spanish as the deputies slapped handcuffs on them and led them away.

Quinton lowered his camera. "Deputies?"

"Mm, hmm."

Quinton stared at Marla. "Why?"

Marla placed her camera on top of the dashboard. "Told you he owed me a favor."

Other deputy vehicles arrived, and the officers surrounded the slaughterhouse.

"Tell me Borland knows about this," Quinton said.

"Not sure what you mean." Marla opened her door.

"Did you tell Borland?"

"No. Why should I? Do you ask permission for everything you do?"

"Yes! That's how it works with Borland. The DEA collaborates with other agencies. We don't go Jason Bourne."

"I am collaborating."

"Borland wants it official. Not done on the sly." Quinton started the engine.

Marla grasped the steering wheel. "What are you doing?"

"Going after Bird."

Marla thought for a moment. "We don't know for sure if Bird was in the vehicle. By now, it's a mile or more away. Bird loses if we interrogate the drivers and find drugs and the girls. The operation is a bust. Where would he go? Los Zetas or Sinaloa? Either way, they would kill him if we broke the trafficking ring. We need to find where they're hiding the girls."

"You want to let Bird go?" Quinton asked. "Borland's not going to like that one little bit."

"Fine. You tell him I set up this bust with the sheriff's department."

Marla hopped out of the Tahoe and paced across the road toward the trucks. Quinton followed while limping his way across the street.

With her flashlight in hand, Marla stopped beside Deputy Keene. "Thanks, Jeffrey. I couldn't have done this without you."

"Looks good so far," Keene said. "Something should be inside the cases on the ground. The Sheriff will be excited."

Marla pointed at the two metal cases. "Those came from inside the slaughterhouse," Marla said.

"Inside? Excellent. We'll open these bad boys and find what is so important."

She grasped Jeffrey's arm. "We saw two drivers take the same kind of case and went inside their trailers."

"This is turning out better and better," Jeffrey said.

Marla smiled. "I have a witness who says underaged girls are being transported in the doghouse. There might be some up there."

Slipping two blue gloves out of her back pocket, she slid them on before climbing inside a trailer and yelled in Spanish, "Anybody in there? Come on out. The police are here." While dodging cow dung, she hit the sides of the trailer with her flashlight. The clanging of metal bounced off the walls. "You're safe. You can come out." Nobody answered her. She climbed to the upper level and turned toward the doghouse. The door was closed. "You're safe. Police are here." She opened the door, revealing nothing. "Rats."

A deputy climbed on top of the middle truck and jumped onto the trailer roof. He aimed his flashlight inside and yelled, "Got something!"

Marla rushed out of the trailer she was in and ran around to the middle truck. "Someone inside?"

"No," he hit his heel against a flat steel plate, "but I got something on the trailer roof that's not original equipment."

Chapter 43

Marla climbed on top of the truck and then the trailer. "What is it?"

"Look at this." The deputy knelt and hit a steel plate welded to the roof with the end of his flashlight.

"Hey," another deputy called from under them, inside the trailer. "I see a box welded to the ceiling, the roof, or whatever you call the top," he hit it with his flashlight, "and it's locked."

"Hot Damn," Marla yelled down to Jeffrey. "We need a crowbar." Jumping off the trailer to the roof of the tractor cab, she slid off the hood to the ground.

Jeffrey opened his trunk and returned with the tool. Marla grabbed it and then eyed Quinton and his cane. "I'll let you know what we find."

Climbing onto the upper level of the trailer and running to the nose where the deputy waited, she saw a closed metal lock box hanging from the roof.

"That thing is welded on all four sides to the ceiling." The deputy flicked the padlock.

She handed the crowbar to him. "You do it. You're taller."

"Looks like it's sealed tight," the deputy said.

Marla scanned the inside of the trailer. "Between the cattle odor, cow feces, and piss, and thirteen feet in the air, you think it would be tough for a drug dog to smell anything this high up?"

The deputy shoved the flat end of the crowbar between the shackle and the lock body. After a few attempts, it broke. "You ready?"

Marla nodded. "You bet."

He extracted a metal case and handed it to her.

She placed it on the floor and snapped open the latches, revealing a package wrapped in bubble wrap. "Hot damn! Hot damn!" Marla couldn't stop smiling. "Money or drugs? Which is it?"

"Let's find out." The deputy opened his pocket knife and slid the blade through the bubble wrap.

They both said, "Wow!"

"What's in there?" Quinton yelled.

"Money. Stacks of hundred dollar bills." She carried the case to the rear of the trailer and then flung a single stack of cash toward Quinton. He caught it with one hand.

"No girls or drugs. Just money," Quinton said. "You got nothing a lawyer can't cover, Marla. We can't get much traction out of this."

Jeffrey called out, "How many stacks?"

Marla slipped her gloves off. "I count ninety-nine plus the one Quinton has. That should be a million dollars."

"Nothing," Quinton said. "Money means nothing."

"Congrats, Marla. You did well." Jeffrey held both cases from the ground and put them on his vehicle's hood. He opened one, revealing a package just like the other.

"See? I told you," Quinton said. "Taking a few million dollars from the cartel means nothing to them."

Jeffrey spun the second one around. "This is the one you said fell out of the Expedition." He snapped it open and raised the lid. "Look what I have." He held out a plastic-wrapped package of brown powder. "Looks like Mexican heroin. We have money and drugs."

Sheriff Johnson's vehicle stopped a few feet from the action. After opening the door, he put his cowboy hat on and strolled to the trailer.

"Hi, Sheriff," Marla said. "We found a butt-load of cash and drugs."

Jeffrey said, "Marla pulled out a case with a hundred stacks of hundred dollar bills. That's a million dollars. With three cases, we're talking three million. Look at this one. Two bricks of brown powder."

The Sheriff smiled. "Nice going, Adams. It may not be the girls you are hunting for, but you hurt the cartel. I've already called out a BOLO for a blue Ford Expedition."

"Thank you, sir."

"Does Borland know you invited us?"

"No, sir. I didn't ask him. He would want the Organized Crime Drug Enforcement Task Force involved. I decided this needed to go down today, not in a week or two after bickering about who leads the raid."

The sheriff adjusted his hat on his head. "Borland and I have different opinions about things. He's a good man, but he wants things done at the speed of a snail. Check, re-check, re-check the re-check. I'm glad you and Jeffrey know each other. You can call me anytime."

"Thank you, sir."

The Sheriff pointed to Jeffrey. "All right, enough chit-chat. The cash and drugs we found provide enough evidence for an internal search. Shut this facility down and arrest every person on the grounds. Let's go."

Sheriff Johnson and two deputies rummaged through the front office.

Johnson tried to stretch his too-tight gloves. "Remind me to send a request to buy extra-large gloves." He opened a desk drawer and found a pint bottle of Jack Daniels. "It's always five o'clock in the manager's office." He opened the bottom drawer. "Well, looky here." He slid a pen through the trigger guard of a 9mm pistol, lifted it in the air, and dropped it into an evidence bag.

"Sheriff?" A deputy also wrestled with his gloves. "My Spanish is not great, but it looks like all these papers are from one Mexican business."

Johnson turned around and glanced through them. "You're right; everything's from the 612 Ranch."

"Never heard of it. Have you?"

"Nope," the sheriff said.

The other deputy rattled an eight-by-twelve-inch security box from inside a metal filing cabinet. "Got something."

Johnson chuckled when he lifted a string tied to the handle and the other end attached to a small key. "Security is not too secure." He opened the box and found a handful of passports with work visas inside. "Looks like the manager held all the workers captive." He dropped them back inside the box. "Match each one to the detainees."

Marla rushed into the office. "You are not going to believe what we found."

"Yeah? What?" Sheriff Johnson asked.

She waved her arm forward. "Come follow me." She trotted through the lobby into the processing section. The Sheriff and the two deputies followed past a row of cattle carcasses hanging on hooks and a dozen men sitting on the floor with wrists handcuffed behind their backs.

Marla stopped at the room named White Viscera, where the internal organs were held. She knocked twice on the door frame for good luck. Quinton stood by piles of stomachs lying on a stainless steel table.

Johnson tried to catch his breath when he stepped inside the room. "Hold on. I'm not as young as I used to be."

Marla pointed toward a row of 55-gallon plastic drums with locking lids lined against the building. "Look at all these drums."

"What's inside?" Johnson asked.

One drum was open, with the lid lying against it. "Take a look," Marla said.

The sheriff leaned over the drum and picked up a 3.5 by 1.5 inch capsule. "Those are big livestock capsules. Explain."

Marla reached into the drum and plucked one out. "These are hard plastic. Real livestock capsules are soft and thin and dissolve in the stomach in a few minutes." She knocked it on the rim of the drum. "These never would." Twisting the ends apart and opening a capsule, she poured the brown powder over other capsules inside the drum.

"It has to be the same heroin we found in the case out in the parking lot."

"And then we have this." Quinton stood at the table with a hook and a long knife and sliced open an animal's stomach, releasing capsules over the steel table. "At least twenty more stomachs are waiting to be cut open."

The sheriff pushed one closed drum and heard capsules clatter inside. He reached into the open drum and pulled another one out. "Twenty head in each trailer, times three?" He dropped it into the drum. "That's a lot of heroin. Check the rest of the building."

Marla stared at the restroom door with the placard of a stick figure in a dress. With her pistol in one hand, she pushed the door open. "DEA. Anybody in here?" She shoved each stall door open and found nobody hiding, but it stopped her cold when she pulled open the door marked for the disabled. Marla squatted down and stared at a naked teenage girl lying sideways between the toilet and the wall with pale white skin and eyes staring into nothing. Her arms taped behind her, and a bullet hole in the center of her chest. There was a pile of women's clothes in the corner, enough for twenty women. "The bastards stripped the girls." Marla laid a blouse over the girl's face. "I'm sorry."

◆

Deputy Suggs shoved a large key inside the jail cell lock and turned it. He motioned Marcelino Garcia, a prisoner with wrists cuffed behind his back, to walk down the Bexar County Detention Center hallway. A clang echoed through the whitewashed cinder block hall when Suggs slammed the cell door shut. His hand grasped Garcia's arm and led him to the interrogation room where the door stood open with three chairs on one side of a metal table and one on the other. The deputy switched the cuffs from behind Garcia to the front, then locked them to a metal ring bolted onto the table.

It startled Garcia when the door clanged shut, leaving him alone with the air conditioning blowing cold and hard. After fifteen minutes, goosebumps rose and skin shivered. He propped his forearms on the tabletop and tugged the handcuffs against the ring.

Marla, Quinton, and Jeffrey entered the room and sat on the opposite side of the table. Another deputy, about twice the size of anyone, followed in and stood behind Garcia.

Quinton went right into the questions. He spoke in Spanish. "Where is Alejandro Torres-Hernandez?"

Garcia sat motionless. "Who?"

"Tell me about the men inside the blue SUV. You owe them nothing. I saw Rafael Villegas beat the shit out of you."

"Then you saw him take off before the cops came." Garcia sat upright. "How do I know where he went? Maybe back to Mexico."

"You're right," Quinton said. "I watched them leave. Villegas and Torres-Hernandez are playing Los Zetas and Sinaloa against each other. Are you playing both sides, too?"

Garcia looked down. "I don't know what you're talking about."

"Once you leave this place," Quinton leaned toward Garcia, "it might accidentally get leaked you are taking money from both sides."

"No. Don't do that. I'll be dead by tomorrow."

Quinton asked, "How often do you drive to the slaughterhouse?"

Garcia wiggled in his chair. "Every day."

Marla jumped in, knowing the answer to her questions. "Why didn't you leave after unloading the cattle? No reason for you to hang around unless someone was coming. And the case you put in the rear of the Expedition, was it heroin or money?"

"No comment. I mean, it's not mine. I didn't look inside the case."

"Your truck was the first in line," Quinton said. "I think that makes you the leader. Everyone gets five years in prison as a mule, but you, as the ringleader, set this up. You'll get twenty."

"I'm no leader. My truck was last, not first."

"Last?" Jeffrey snickered. "Sort of like a cleanup hitter, ensuring everyone gets to home plate. Is the slaughterhouse home plate? We found enough heroin to put you away for a long time." Jeffrey clapped his hands once. "Just like that. You're in prison, never to see your family again. Your business is shut down."

"It's not my business."

Jeffrey pointed at Garcia. "State Troopers are stopping every livestock trailer coming from Laredo. How many drivers will pick you out in a lineup and say you are the ringleader so that they get a lighter sentence?" He leaned back in his chair. "With good info, they may just get deported with no jail time while you get more years added on."

"I told you, I'm just a driver. Don't know nothing about drugs or money or anything, man. I drive cattle from Laredo to San Antonio, and that is all I do."

"Tell us everything," Jeffrey said. "You help us, and we'll help you."

Marla decided to play the good cop. "We could tell the district attorney you helped. That could mean a lighter sentence. Possibly no jail time?"

"I'm tired," Garcia said, "I want some sleep." He leaned back as far as he could in the chair while the handcuffs stayed hooked to the ring in the center of the table. "I want a lawyer."

Marla smiled while she folded her arms. "That's the magic request here in the US of A. Now we must stop. Okay, we can let you sleep until a lawyer comes." She patted Jeffrey's shoulder. "The deputy will take you back to a cell."

"We have a problem," Jeffrey said. "We're holding everyone that was working in the slaughterhouse. The cells are full except the one with two men from the Sinaloa Cartel. They've been in there for a week and getting pretty irritated about why no one has come to help them. You being a Los Zetas, I'm sure it'll be okay."

Garcia stood with his hands still cuffed to the metal ring. "No, you can't. I want to go back to the cell I was in."

The deputy shoved him back into the chair.

Jeffrey said, "Sorry, that cell is full."

Quinton, Marla, and Jeffrey stood. "I'm done with this guy," Jeffrey said. "Lock him up for the night. We'll check on him tomorrow."

"Wait," Garcia said. "I don't believe you. What two Sinaloas?"

Jeffrey said in Spanish, "You know them, Ice Pick and Bo. Ice Pick? He's bad. The name fits. But Bo? There's a reason they call him that." Jeffrey held out his arms and motioned like he wrapped them around an imaginary person. "He squeezes people until they stop breathing. I've heard he doesn't stop until he hears ribs breaking." He motioned for Garcia to stand. "Come on. I don't have all day."

"Okay, okay. I'll talk if you don't put me in with those shitholes."

After an hour, Marcelino Garcia spilled his life like water through a sieve; trucks hauling cattle stuffed with drugs and Mexican girls to Texas, returning with money to Mexico, murdered mules and drivers, and Torres-Hernandez as the leader.

But Torres-Hernandez earned his namesake again. The Bird flew off and disappeared.

Chapter 44

Suzie Moore sat at her kitchen table and bit half a small cracker before sipping wine from her glass. The app on Quinton's phone had worked perfectly. She transcribed everything on her laptop keyboard while listening to the entire scene inside the sheriff's interrogation room. After completing tonight's pages, she sent the attachment and the audio recording to her literary agent. What started as a two-page article for a magazine had turned into a potential novel. Her agent returned a reply within a minute, telling her it was reading well, but reminded her that dealing with a Mexican cartel, sex trafficking, drugs, money laundering, and potentially dirty law enforcement was headline news and dangerous. Suzie smiled and poured more wine into her glass.

Her doorbell rang. On her phone, via the camera app, Quinton stood outside the front door. After closing her laptop, she slipped her high heels back on and straightened her dress before fluffing her hair. She called out, "Door's open."

Suzie met Quinton in the entryway, and they wrapped their arms around each other and kissed.

"I am so glad you came over," Suzie said.

"Well, I was hoping you weren't tired of me after last night." With the help of his cane, Quinton moved to the couch and sat.

Suzie squeezed as close as she could to him and snuggled against his arm. "Never."

"I didn't have time to eat," Quinton said. "Busy with all that is going on. How about we get a late bite?"

"That would be wonderful. You wouldn't mind being seen in public with me and my new hair color?" She spun her finger through her blonde hair with black tips.

He smiled at her. "I like the colors."

She pecked him on the lips. "I need to freshen up a bit." Suzie pranced around the coffee table. "I won't be long," she called out as she entered her bedroom.

"Take all the time you need. No hurry." *Why the hell are you at the DEA?*

When Quinton heard the bathroom door close, he went to her laptop. She was hasty last night. When he asked her to do a Google search, he watched from behind her as she keyed her password. He opened her computer and typed the password. Her email popped up with a literary agency. "Oh, shit. Not good." He slipped a thumb drive in the slot and downloaded her emails.

When Suzie opened the bathroom door, Quinton yanked the thumb drive out and slipped it into his pocket.

Glancing across the empty living room, she called out, "Quinton? Where are you?" Her laptop was open. She couldn't remember if she had closed it before answering the door. She touched a key, and the screen lit with the password box empty.

Quinton came out of the kitchen with a glass of water. "Are you ready?"

"No cane?"

He forgot he left the cane on the couch when he hurried to check her laptop. "Getting better."

Suzie smiled and closed the laptop before wrapping her arms around his neck. "Yes. I'm famished. How about Mexican?"

The mariachi band finished playing for them at their table. Quinton drank the last of his beer while Suzie sucked on the straw in her frozen margarita. He reached for her hand on the table.

"Thanks for letting me look at the Adams' file."

"You're welcome, but that was dangerous." Suzie feigned nervousness. "I could have been fired for leaving that on my desk."

He interlocked his finger with hers. "You're right, and I'm feeling close to you. After, well, after my wife died, I haven't thought much about anything good, but you have brought something new into my life."

Suzie clinched their hands tighter, lifted them to her lips, and kissed his hand. "I like you too."

"How about we go away for a few days?" He grazed his fingertip over her hand. "I have a place in Cozumel. The view of the water is beautiful."

"Cozumel? How?"

"I have a small plane. We could be there in two hours."

She laughed. "How can you afford a plane?"

He shrugged. "I have a life outside the DEA."

My agent will go crazy; DEA employees spying on each other, buying planes, cartels, drugs? I'm going to sell a million copies, but am I going too far?

Suzie dropped the straw on the table and finished the rest of her drink. "Sounds fun."

◆

A row of streetlights spotted patches of brightness along Bird's street. From inside the blue Expedition, Bird stared straight ahead as they passed his underground garage. Rafael didn't know where Bird lived. Across the street, a tattoo parlor had a flashing neon sign declaring, OPEN 24 HOURS A DAY. "Stop here and let me out."

"Who's inside?"

"A friend." Bird took a risk being so close to his condominium. "I'm ready for another tat."

The vehicle stopped. Rafael frowned as he tilted his head slightly to the side. "You owe me two kilos of heroin."

Bird straightened his black jacket with gold threading and a canary yellow tie. "You're a fucking idiot for leaving the backend up when you drove off."

Rafael clutched a handful of Bird's hair and yanked his head back. "My men have your son. I say the word, and he's dead. You get me what I want in two days, or I kill that little shit." He released Bird's hair. "Get out."

Bird opened the door, climbed out, and kicked the door closed. His hand reached for the pistol stuffed behind the small of his back.

"Do it. I dare you." Rafael laughed. "Pull it out. The bitch in the back seat has a pistol aimed at your head."

Bird held his hands out in front of him.

"Two kilos," Rafael said, "or your family shrinks by one."

Bird watched the red taillights disappear before calling Arturo on his phone. "I'm ready." Moments later, the tan minivan stopped close to Bird, and the driver's window lowered. He placed his hands on the roof. "Where is the doctor?"

Arturo said, "Bluebird RV Park, half a mile off 410."

"Are you sure that English shit is there?"

"I have a maintenance man working at the place. He said a woman and a tall guy with a funny accent parked there. The woman unhitched the trailer, then left in the pickup."

"All right. I need to go up to my place and get a bag."

"You want to come with us or meet us there?" Arturo asked.

"With you. Wait here."

Bird stood at his front door and checked for the torn piece of paper at the hinge. It was still there. After opening the door, he turned the alarm off and froze. He listened as he slid his pistol out. Hairs on the back of his neck stood on end as he made his way down the hallway. Curtains fluttered against the wind; the plate-glass window had been shattered, mannequins broken into pieces, and his priceless Frida Kahlo painting slashed. In the living area, on the floor, the photo of his son had a pencil stuck through an eye. Someone ripped the hinged cabinet from the wall, and the safe door stood open with the cash gone.

Bird entered the kitchen and opened the dishwasher filled with dirty dishes and glasses. He reached into the back and removed a plastic container with a bag of cocaine inside, then left.

He crossed the street and sat in the passenger seat of the minivan. "After this, we kill Villegas."

The vehicle zigzagged between cars on Loop 410. It took twenty minutes to reach the exit to the frontage road. The minivan pulled to the shoulder of the road and stopped before reaching the RV Park entrance.

◆

The doctor sat in the chair inside the trailer and watched the tablet screen. Crosby's mind slowly filled in Bird's face with an unknown image behind him. McCollum's eyes and nose itched, and the need for another line grew. He stood and paced three steps at a time. The camera in the corner caught his eye. *Did it move? It's not supposed to.* He shook it off as needing more coke. The lens stared at him. *Is she watching? Staring? Forget that twit. I'm out.*

When he opened the door, the afternoon sun glared in his face. He walked around the trailer; even in daylight, the campsite bore lights brighter than a Friday night high school football field. Children played catch and chased each other on the freshly cut grass. Several more RVs had occupied empty spaces since yesterday. "Somebody out there must be carrying dope. These idiots drive all day and get bored. They listen to whoever else is inside their RV for hours. Someone must have some coke. It's the only bloody answer to all this gobshite." He power-walked to the closest RV, where a man sat in a lawn chair wearing a green cap with an image of a tractor on the front. He held a ceramic coffee cup with steam rising from the inside.

McCollum waved. "Nice day."

The man stood. "It is. Coffee?"

"No, thanks. Have anything else?"

"Water, maybe some iced tea from lunchtime. Might be too old."

"I was thinking something stronger."

"Stronger? You mean like a beer? No, sorry. The wife and I don't drink."

"Hmm. Well, I was getting some fresh air. I'll see you later."

The man sat back down in his lawn chair and waved. "See ya."

The doctor passed two more RVs before he saw someone else outside. A burly man wearing a red and black plaid shirt had an open toolbox and a portable flood light next to him. The front wheel was jacked up, and he had his hands and arms behind the tire. An open can of Lone Star beer sat on a small table.

He tried to soften his British accent. "Need any help?"

The man turned around with a wrench in his hand and smiled. "Nah, got this. Leaky brake line." He went back to his work.

"Never heard of that beer. What is it?"

The man stopped again. "Never heard of Lone Star? You're not from around these parts, are ya? Want one? In the fridge inside. Go ahead and get one."

McCollum patted his stomach. "Never liked beer. All the carbonation gives me gas. Got anything stronger?"

"Stronger? Like whiskey? No. The wife told me I had to quit."

"Do you smoke?"

"Smoke? No. Oh, you mean like..." Pantomiming smoking a marijuana joint to his lips. "You mean weed? Oh, man. Long time ago. Haven't touched it in years."

The doctor froze when a minivan pulled past the entrance and turned toward his trailer. "Christ." He texted Marla, HELP.

McCollum peered around the corner of the disabled RV as the minivan eased along the narrow strip of black asphalt. When it stopped, the passenger door opened, and a man stood while glancing around the area.

McCollum leaned against the RV.

"You still here?" The man took a swig of his Lone Star. "Told you, got no weed, so shoo. Go on, get."

The doctor's phone rang. He stared at the screen with ROBERT, the Uber driver's name, on it. It rang again. When he tapped the green button, his voice trembled with a single word. "Hello."

"I knew you would be nice enough to answer," Bird said. "Come out from where you are. There is no need to hide from me."

Chapter 45

The deputy led Marcelino Garcia out of the interrogation room with handcuffed wrists behind his back. Marla's phone vibrated in her back pocket with a message of one word: HELP. She pushed the doctor's number on her phone. It rang four times before a voice told her to leave a message. "Cheez," she said.

Behind her, Quinton's cane clunked rhythmically, "What's up?"

"I might have some trouble." She slipped the phone into her back pocket. "Have to go."

"Let me help."

She turned and saw Quinton leaning on his cane. Her lips tightened, then she spoke, "I have to hurry." She jogged down the hall and out the front door.

⁜

"Hey, Doc," Arturo and another man stood between RVs. "We've been looking for you."

"Good," the RV owner said. "You found some playmates. Go get high somewhere else."

Arturo smiled and motioned with his hand. "Yeah, come with us."

"I don't know these people," McCollum told the RV owner.

"And I don't know you." He waved a large wrench in the air. "You and your buds best be moving on."

Arturo grabbed the doctor's wrist. "Let's go to your trailer and talk more."

"You can't do this."

They walked away from the RV as Arturo said, "Which way?"

"No, I won't tell you."

"You want me to kill you right here? Won't take but a second, right here between these little snot-nosed kids."

The other man clamped onto the doctor's wrists and pushed him forward. McCollum looked behind him and saw the minivan following. He tried to slow his footing, but the men kept pushing.

"Take your hands off me, you bloody wanker." He dug his heels into the ground. "You can't make me do this."

Arturo laughed. "You are an arrogant piece of shit."

"I said, take your hands off me." *Will Bird keep his promise and give me my cocaine? Everything will be fine.* He glanced side-to-side, needing a diversion. *I'll step on the wanker's foot and run inside the trailer and lock it.* He nodded toward the opposite side of the park. "That way."

Marla drove through San Antonio streets with lights and sirens blaring, dodging cars and trucks. Merging onto I-10, where everyone's speed was 10 or 100, Marla did a double take when passing an empty livestock truck. She held her phone head high, glancing at the outside camera, watching a tan minivan stop near her trailer. "I'm coming, doc."

Now. Step on his foot and run. He slammed his foot on the ground, missing Arturo's boot.

Arturo hit him in the stomach. "What the fuck are you trying to do?"

The minivan rolled near the two men pushing the doctor. The driver's window lowered. "I'm disappointed in you," Bird said. "You never called me. How could I ever trust you again?"

The doctor raised his chin. "I've been waiting for Mrs. Adams to be here and away from others." He tried to wiggle away. "I'm trying to be cautious with all these people. You don't want to do anything with witnesses and all."

Bird nodded. "Well, thank you for your concern."

"Right." McCollum tried to pull his arms away from the men's grip. "I'm trying to protect you."

"And I'm still willing to trade you the coke for the man." Bird patted the driver's door twice. "Which one, Doctor?"

The doctor capitulated and turned toward the trailer. "This one."

Marla changed lanes, then glanced at her phone. A man stepped out of the minivan whose face was the same as what Crosby's mind produced on the tablet. "Oh, shit."

Bird walked around the trailer and opened the side door. A small round table and two chairs sat inside near the door entrance. He glared at the DEA agent he shot in the head lying on a hospital bed with his head shaved. He was surprised that most of the facial swelling had dissipated. A wall monitor above the bed beeped every second.

Marla switched to the camera inside the trailer. Traffic piled up in all lanes, ignoring her emergency lights. She veered off the asphalt and wavered through the soft grassy median.

"Come inside, Doctor," Bird said.

After the two men shoved McCollum past the doorway, he straightened his shirt and collar like he had a coat and tie. "I present to you, Crosby Adams. We agreed on cocaine for the exchange."

"We did, but you did not hold up your end."

"I certainly did, and you are here as proof." He cleared his throat. "I may not have called you, but you would not be here if not for me."

"You're right. You did not call."

"I waved my hands and got your men's attention as soon as you entered the facility."

"Waved?" Bird asked. "I must have misjudged you. I thought you were hiding between the RVs."

After pushing a few items around the countertop, McCollum closed the tablet with the images on the screen. "I did not want the caravan owner to get hurt, so I waited."

"What's a caravan," Arturo asked.

"One of those things out there, you ninny."

Bird leaned over Crosby. "What is that stuck in his head?" He jerked the stainless steel tube out and pitched it behind him.

Marla watched Bird throw the lifeline to Crosby's brain on the floor. "God damn you! Leave my husband alone." She swerved off the median and zigzagged between cars to the 410 Exit.

Crosby opened his eyes and said, "Bird."

Bird smiled and looked directly into Crosby's eyes. "Two bullets in the head are better than one in hand. Don't you think?" Bird chuckled. "I'm hilarious. You can't be a man with half a brain shot out of your head." His finger tapped Crosby's forehead. "And you won't live with this new shit in your head."

Crosby swung his fist slowly toward Bird. He dodged it with ease.

Dr. McCollum interrupted Bird. "Let me tell you about my special procedure. I dispense medication down the tube, and it heals the brain."

"Your stem cell treatment?"

The doctor's eyes lit up. "Yes. Do you have knowledge of stem cells?"

"I am an educated man with two degrees."

He gave his one-minute story on his ten years of work. "I have developed a new technique using a protein catalyst and mixing with stem cells, injecting the solution into the brain not once but many times, therefore stimulating rapid repair and producing new tissue in not months but days, if not hours. I could heal your men when they are shot." He stopped, then asked, "Where did you acquire your doctorate?"

Bird shook his head. "Master's at Vienna."

"A Master's? Well, that's a start."

"You look down on people who do not have a doctorate?"

"No, of course not. We need all types of people. Some take the time to, well, continue education and increase their intellect."

"Interesting. Are most doctorates addicted to cocaine?" Bird pointed to Arturo, and he placed a plastic bag of white powder on the round table.

McCollum sniffed and swallowed; saliva built in his mouth. His tongue could taste the sweet bitterness, the feel of fine powder, the incredible, fantastic burn in his nose. Focusing on the bag, he forgot about Crosby, Bird, or the other two men in the trailer. He opened the top of the bag, dipped his pinkie into the powder, and sniffed it into his nose. The world disappeared, and euphoria enraptured his mind.

A sharp pain hit his side. His breath shortened, vision blurred. Another pain hit him again. The muscles between his ribs spasmed. He reached for the pain, and blood covered his hand. Knees buckled. His glasses clattered to the floor when a hand slapped him across the side of his head. He struggled for a shallow breath when another sharp pain hit him, this time in his back. He rolled to his side into a puddle of his own blood. The lights dimmed. "My...my...work."

Bird leaned over McCollum. "Some people want a last meal. You? You wanted a last hit." He pulled the knife out from the doctor's back and closed the top of the plastic bag full of cocaine. "So much for being a smart-ass, think you know it all, druggie."

Marla's truck swerved into the RV Park and roared toward her trailer. Her siren screamed as red and blue lights flashed from the grille. Parked outside her trailer was a tan minivan like the ones at the Schmidt & Schmidt Slaughterhouse. She positioned her truck as a barricade and aimed her pistol at the trailer. "DEA. Come out with your hands up."

No one responded.

"Drop your weapons and come out."

No response.

On her phone screen, she watched three men standing inside with Crosby lying in bed and McCollum motionless on the floor.

"Last chance. I know there are three of you in there."

Bird said, "Javi, go out there and get rid of her."

Watching the screen on her phone, a man wielding a gun swung the door open. She sprinted past her truck to the rear of the minivan.

Javi fired at her pickup, shattering a side window. Marla spun around and fired twice, dropping him to the ground.

Marla knew the doctor was on the floor and Crosby in the bed. She fired four times, head high into the trailer.

Bird and Arturo dropped to their knees. Another bullet hit the wall. When the two crawled outside, Bird shot his pistol in the air. Marla ducked and then aimed at the trailer again. Arturo snuck around to the front of the minivan.

Something flickered in her periphery. She heard a gunshot and felt her pistol jump out of her hand. Another bullet banged against the side of her truck. She dropped to her knees and crawled away while Bird and Arturo jumped the fence and disappeared through the brush.

Half of Marla's right little finger was gone. When she touched the bloody nub, shooting stars filled her eyes.

Crosby flashed in her mind. She picked up her pistol with her left hand and ran inside the trailer. The doctor lay on his side with multiple stab wounds and a pool of blood surrounding him. She checked for a pulse; nothing. Broken and scattered equipment covered the floor. Crosby was on the bed with the stainless steel tube missing from his scalp. She reached for the tablet on the floor and opened it. Crosby had finished his drawing, revealing a clear picture of Bird holding a gun against Crosby's head with another man behind Bird. She snapped a photo with her phone.

Her phone dinged. Marla closed her eyes and shook her head. "You disgusting shit." She closed the tablet and laid it on the bed alongside Crosby. She knew who had sent the message.

DEAR MARLA. I HOPE IT IS ACCEPTABLE TO CALL YOU BY YOUR FIRST NAME. IT SEEMS AS THOUGH WE HAVE COME TO UNDERSTAND EACH OTHER SO WELL. I HAVE SEEN YOUR HUSBAND TWICE AND HE HAS DONE SOME-THING NOBODY HAS EVER DONE BEFORE. HE LIVED.

Marla bent over Crosby and kissed him on the lips. She sat on the floor beside the bed and somberly watched the videos on her phone of two men holding onto McCollum, pushing him inside the trailer, and Bird stabbing him.

Why was I hanging around at the sheriff's department? I didn't need to be there. I should have been here. She reached behind her and caressed the sheet covering Crosby's legs. Clearing her throat, she glanced at the body on the floor. "I was playing the wrong game. Now, how is this going to end? Bird disappears again?"

The bed rails rattled against the wall. The bed shook. Marla spun around and helplessly laid her arms across Crosby's body while watching him spasm and jerk. Dr. McCollum told her to let him finish his seizure.

Sirens screamed outside the trailer, and tires screeched on the pave-ment. Multiple car doors opened and closed before a voice from outside yelled, "Police! Come out with your hands up."

Blood dripped from her nub onto the floor. "Well, hell. I just said that a few minutes ago." When Crosby stopped his seizure, she climbed into the bed and lay beside him. "I won't leave."

A person yelled through a bullhorn, "Step outside with your hands raised."

Three officers rushed through the doorway, yanked Marla off the bed, and shoved her down on her stomach.

"I am DEA Special Agent Adams."

An officer stepped to the bed and used his rifle barrel to push against Crosby.

Marla swung her arm around and grabbed the officer's boot. "Leave him alone. He's sick."

An officer grabbed her hand and pulled it back behind her. She felt the metal snaps of handcuffs over her wrists. Her bloody finger throbbed.

"Be careful with my husband. He's sick."

They lifted her by her shoulders, led her out of the trailer, and stuffed her in the backseat of a police vehicle.

A police officer asked, "What do you know about a body stabbed multiple times inside the trailer and another outside with a gunshot wound to the chest."

Marla read the nametag on the officer's shirt. "Listen, Williams, I didn't kill the doctor. Bird, Torres-Hernandez did. I have proof. Rock-solid proof." She motioned to the blood around the handcuffs. "I need medical attention. I'm wounded."

Officer Williams motioned for an EMT. "What do you mean you have proof?"

While the EMT wrapped gauze around what was left of her finger, Williams asked again, "What proof?"

"The trailer has two cameras, one outside, one inside. Everything is recorded on my phone." She jerked her finger away from the EMT. "Hey, take it easy. That hurts."

"Do you have that on you?"

"In my back pocket." She leaned forward. "Look for yourself."

He watched the videos before dropping the phone into her lap. "Okay, good enough for me." When he uncuffed her, Marla rubbed her wrists. "You must go from here to the station and talk to Detective Barnes. Understand?"

"Sure. Barnes." *With two more people dead, I damn sure don't want to talk to Borland.*

Chapter 46

Instead of going to the police station, Marla drove to the Bexar County Community Medical Center Emergency Department entrance. After parking her truck in a Physician's Only parking spot, she slid a DEA business placard on the dash and grabbed a plastic bag from the passenger seat. The double glass doors opened with a blast of cold escaping into the hot San Antone air. She charged like a guided missile through the emergency department and ran into a hospital attendant pushing Crosby's gurney into the hallway toward the elevators.

"What's going on?" Marla asked.

The attendant said, "Fastest transfer I've seen in a while. He's heading to the ICU."

Marla followed to the elevator, pushed the up button, and waited while the numbers above the elevator lit up. 4, 3, 2, 3, 2. "It's too frickin' slow." She pushed the button a dozen more times.

"Doesn't help," the attendant said.

"Helps me," Marla replied. She pushed it again as electric pains shot through her injured hand.

The bell dinged and the doors opened. Marla followed the attendant and the bed into the elevator. Her phone rang as the door snapped shut behind her.

"Adams, here."

"How is he?" Borland asked.

"Not sure, but we're back in the hospital. How did you know?"

"Officer Williams called me to confirm your employment. Why are you not going to the SAPD to give your report?"

"I'm busy with my husband."

"Where is he?"

"ICU. It's dangerous for him to be here. Don't tell anyone."

"Be here at my office at eight o'clock sharp."

When the doors opened, she heard a steady buzz. "Got to go, sir." The smell of floor cleaner and wax penetrated the air, with an elderly man buffing the lobby floor. The attendant pushed Crosby's gurney out of the elevator and headed into the ICU. After a quick transfer to the bed, the nurse connected the pulse oximeter and heart monitor. She checked the blood pressure and watched the oxygen concentration rise to 96%. She smiled. "That's good."

"Who will be the doctor taking care of him?" Marla asked.

"I will."

Marla spun around and saw Dr. Wilson standing in the doorway. They both stared at each other, waiting for the other to apologize first.

"Dr. Wilson is one of the best neurosurgeons in town," the nurse said.

Marla crossed her arms in front of her chest. "We've met."

"Mrs. Adams. I am the neurosurgeon on call today, and I am just as happy as you are about being in this room."

"I'm not so happy," Marla snapped back.

"Neither am I."

The nurse raised her eyebrows and backpedaled out of the room.

"We're stuck with each other until you sign him out AMA again, so tell me what has happened since you left."

Crosby slurred his words. "I'm better, Doc."

Dr. Wilson spun around toward the bed. He turned Crosby's head where he had surgically removed a sizeable chunk of his skull days ago and touched the shaved scalp. There should have been a void under the skin, but it felt full. He fished for a penlight from his lab coat and shined it into Crosby's eyes. "Open your mouth...stick out your tongue...close your mouth...smile...look right...left...close your eyes...close them tight.

His penlight clicked off. "This is impossible. I've never seen anything like this." He turned toward Marla. "This is your husband, Crosby Adams, who was shot in the head, and the man I performed surgery on?"

"Now you understand why I took him from this hospital. Dr. McCollum, the man you said was a lunatic, did this."

Dr. Wilson turned back to Crosby and said, "Squeeze my fingers."

Crosby squeezed and muttered, "Weak—as—a—new-born—calf."

Wilson checked the reflexes in Crosby's arms and legs. "Astonishing. What did McCollum, Dr. McCollum do? I must talk to him."

"That won't happen."

"Yes, I must. He has done something no one has ever done."

"He was murdered," Marla said.

"Murdered? How? Why?"

"Does it matter?"

Dr. Wilson stuck his penlight into his pocket. "Mr. Adams doesn't need to be in ICU. I'll transfer him to the rehab unit and consult Dr. Yamamoto."

An hour later, inside the rehab unit, a nurse explained the whiteboard with doctors, nurses, and rehab technician names to Marla. She smiled and thanked the nurse before moving to the doorway. Pausing, she studied the medication carts aligned on the wall near each room entrance. They looked like Craftsman rolling tool cabinets. "Are these here all the time, or are they moved?"

"They are specific for each patient and stay until released."

"Good," Marla said.

"You must have some heavy-duty pull around here," the nurse said. "Only the VIPs get room 814 and this view of the city."

Marla had lost track of time with the sun already setting. "I'm sure it is beautiful when the sun comes up." She changed the subject. "Tell me what the plan is for my husband."

"Dr. Yamamoto's program is quite intensive. We start at seven in the morning with speech therapy, then move to small motor skill therapy, followed by acupuncture and massage. After lunch, he does large muscle therapy and occ med, sorry, occupational therapy. Since your husband needs everything, Dr. Yamamoto schedules upper body one day and lower body the next."

Marla thought about where she would sleep since her house burned down and the trailer sat in the city police holding area. "May I stay with my husband at night?"

"No, I'm sorry. The rooms are not set up for overnight visitors. This is the long-term wing of the hospital. He may be here for weeks, but you can visit during the day and watch his therapy on closed-circuit television." She glanced at Marla's bandage around her hand. "You should have someone look at that."

"Thank you, I will."

Marla waited for the nurse to leave before removing three items from the grocery bag. She bent down to eye level with Crosby. "You see me, right?" He smiled back at her and nodded. She gently kissed his lips. "I love you, big guy."

He struggled with the words. "Me too."

"These are mini-cameras, and I am placing them on the windowsill, so I can watch you and anyone else in here." Next, she pulled out what looked like a garage door remote. "When I am not here, keep this clipped to the waistband of your pajamas." She touched the red button. "Push this for an emergency. It goes right to my phone. You push it, and I am here ASAP."

"Okay," Crosby said.

"Promise me, if you see something you don't like, you'll push the emergency button."

He nodded.

She held a long chrome letter opener with a Velcro strap. "Next is this." She gently strapped it to his wrist. "Use this if all else fails."

He half-smiled and barely shook his head. "Too weak."

Marla took his hand and wrapped his fingers around the handle. "Got it? Swing it."

He moved at the speed of a sloth.

"We'll work on it. You seem to be a fast healer. Tomorrow you will be quicker." Marla removed it from his wrist. "They won't let me stay with you at night, but I'm here until they run me out."

His eyes glazed over. What little facial expression he had disappeared. His fingers twitched before they turned into tight fists. His body jerked, arms and legs tremored. A nurse rushed in and called out, "Seizure protocol." They pushed Marla into the hallway, and the room filled with hospital personnel.

Marla sat in the tiny waiting room and stopped watching the hospital propaganda loop on the television after the sixth time. There was no remote to change the channel or turn it off. The smell of floor wax lingered. She picked up one of the four magazines on the table.

A young woman in her twenties sat in a chair, knees pulled to her chest, staring at her phone. She wiped a tear off her cheek with the sleeve of her hoodie.

Marla stood when Dr. Wilson entered the room. "Mr. Adams has a problem. His kidneys have shut down. His heart is twice the size it should be."

"The man you called a quack diagnosed it yesterday, or it might have been the day before."

"And how did he do that?"

She shrugged her shoulders, not revealing their clinic break-in. "He was a genius."

"He needs dialysis, but ultimately needs kidney and heart transplants."

"Do it. When?"

He scoffed at her question. "Not that easy. Everyone wants a transplant tomorrow, but nobody wants to donate their organs at death."

"I don't care about easy. I want it done as fast as possible."

"It will take weeks if we get lucky with a match. The problem is that all his organs are growing disproportionally large. The stem cell therapy has doubled your husband's heart, kidneys, and liver, and almost twice the amount of blood he should have. He may have a working brain, but everything else is near end stage."

"Is he?" She scuffed the sole of her boot across the carpet. "I mean, is he going to die?"

Dr. Wilson softened for the first time since Marla threatened to take Crosby out of the hospital. He placed his hand on her shoulder. "He's stable. We're starting him on anticonvulsants. I don't believe he will have another seizure, especially after dialysis starts. Go home, shower, get some clean clothes, and eat. Your husband needs you to be healthy."

✦

It was past midnight. Marla hadn't eaten since breakfast, which seemed like days ago. Eating was the last thing on her mind, but she turned into the convenience store across the street from the hospital. An electronic bell rang above her head when she entered. Neon beer signs shined brightly inside the building. Standing in front of the soft drink fountain, she stared at her favorite drink emblem. She didn't deserve it. She deserved something terrible, something disgusting, like today, tonight. Her hand tugged an extra-large cup out of the dispenser and pushed it against the lever. Ice cubes clattered inside. After tapping every drink on the long fountain bar and adding all the flavors; Dr Pepper, Pepsi, Coca-Cola, Orange Crush, Cherry Bomb, Sprite, root beer, lemonade, sweet tea, whatever, she set the drink on the counter and dropped a five-dollar bill close to the cup. The cashier didn't move as he stared at her.

"What?" she asked.

"I watched you. You're not going to drink that, are you?"

"How much for it?"

The cashier chuckled. "It's free if you take a drink and tell me what it tastes like."

"No."

"Come on. One sip and tell me."

"No, I said." She put both hands on the counter and looked down. The gauze on her hand was red. "Sorry, bad day. How much?"

He reached under the counter and handed her a fistful of paper napkins. "Two dollars and seventy-nine cents."

Inside the pickup, she placed the drink in the cup holder and buckled her seatbelt. Even after midnight, the traffic was still heavy. Quinton was right. San Antone buzzed 24/7 on the roads. She touched the lid and straw, not ready to try it yet. Staying in the center lane the entire time, it took over an hour to circle Loop 410 twice. Stomach acid slithered its way up into her subconscious. A bead of sweat wormed from her temple, past the front of the ear, and down her neck. It's the first time she allowed the thought to stay longer than a second. *What if Crosby is not here? Gone. Forever.* Her chest felt heavy. It hurt to breathe. She wanted an asthma inhaler, but her doctor in Hildebrandt said it was not asthma. It was plain old, in your face, anxiety. Good ol' Dr. Sanborn. She hoped he was not too upset with her about the break-in. After lowering all her windows, the cool night air twisted her hair. She grabbed the drink, ready to pitch the liquid out the window, but on second thought, she placed it back in the cupholder.

Before the next exit, a bright blue and white Walmart sign hovered above the fuel station. She turned and stopped at the edge of a fuel pump. While filling her tank, she watched the store's automatic glass doors open, and a woman exited with a fountain drink in her hand. *That probably tastes better than mine.*

Four semi-trucks had shut down at the far end of the parking lot for the night. After filling her tank, she snaked between the trucks, raised her windows, and killed the engine. She lifted the drink cup and tasted the concoction. It was not good, but better than some of Crosby's Cowboy coffee she had tasted in the past. She climbed into the back seat, tired of it all, and fell asleep.

Chapter 47

After dressing the next morning, Suzie called her agent. "I have an idea. How about I place a recording device inside my boss's office, so I can hear everything he says?"

"Suzie, I can't condone that. I'm sure that's illegal, besides, with that in the book, the Feds would come after you whether it was legal or not."

"Talk about publicity. They try that, and I'd be on every national talk show in the country."

"We should talk to our attorneys first, but how would you do it?"

"Borland has a routine. In the morning, he unlocks his office door, hangs his jacket on the coat rack, goes to the mini fridge, takes a cold bottle of water, drinks half while looking out the window, and then sits at his desk. I could put it on the top shelf behind his chair when he's drinking water across the room. That's all. Easy, quick. It wouldn't take but a second."

Suzie drove to a small electronics store called Spy On You and bought a recording pen. She sat in her chair at her desk, spinning it on her desktop, while waiting for Borland to arrive. When footfalls bounded down the hallway, she covered the pen with her hands.

"Good morning, Suzie." Borland stuck his key into the lock and opened the door.

"Good morning, sir." She wiped the pen with a facial tissue to remove any prints.

Like a lion at the circus, Borland performed the expected repetitive actions Suzie had described.

She entered the office and slid the pen behind a set of books on the top shelf. "Is there anything I can get for you, sir?"

Borland screwed the top back onto the half-full water bottle while continuing to stare at the horizon. "Not now. Give me a head's up when Agent Adams arrives. She's scheduled to be here at eight o'clock."

"Yes, sir. I have her on my calendar."

When Suzie turned away, Marla was standing next to her desk.

"She's here, sir. Are you ready for her?"

He glanced at his watch, 7:48 a.m. "Sure. Send her in."

Suzie motioned for her to come closer. When Marla stopped, Suzie lightly held Marla's wrist. "Do you need a minute to freshen up in the ladies' room?"

"No." Marla gently removed Suzie's hand. "I don't care about that right now."

"Yes, I can see that." Suzie closed the door when Marla entered Borland's office.

Marla sat across from her boss's desk, hair disheveled, eyes red-rimmed. She tried to hide her little finger nub freshly wrapped in gauze. A well-placed box of tissues and a room temperature bottle of water sat on the end of the desk.

Suzie listened to their conversation on her cell phone.

Borland leaned back in his chair. "That intel about The Blue Lily panned out, except that is not the official name. It's an English translation."

"Sir?"

"The Azucena Azul is a slaughterhouse eighty miles north of Laredo, near where we found the Camaro your husband was driving. We raided it last night and found bundles of hundred-dollar bills, semi-automatic rifles, pistols in the office with Illegals sleeping on the killing floor, and the same capsules of heroin sealed in fifty gallon barrels."

Damn. Crosby said ocean with an a. Acean. He was trying to say Azucena. I was stupid. Azucena, Spanish for lily.

"That's great, sir. I'm, uh…I have something to say."

Borland remained seated, waiting for her to speak. He had always believed that if you give a criminal enough leeway, they will confess. He wanted to blurt out questions about the doctor but waited.

"I'm sorry about all this, sir." She twisted the cap off the water bottle, drank about a third, then stared back at Borland.

"That's it? That's all you have to say? Adams, you killed another man, and you're sorry?"

"Well, I mean, no." She twisted the cap back on the bottle. "Is it just the two of us in here?" Marla asked. "Microphones? Recordings? Two-way mirror?"

Borland stared without a single facial movement. Was she confessing to something? He waited.

She jerked several tissues from the box and held them against her finger nub. "I have information only you can hear."

He continued to stare.

"You have a problem in the district," she said.

Incredulous. She's not confessing to anything or about the doctor. She's complaining about my employees. He stared her down. "My district? You better believe I do. I have a problem with two agents. One is shot in the head, and the other sits in front of me. And one of them is definitely a pain in my ass."

Marla forced a light cough to clear her throat. She looked around the room before speaking in a muffled voice. "No recordings, no other ears in this room?"

Suzie turned the volume up.

"I record nothing in this office. If I have nothing, lawyers can't get it. President Nixon taught us that fifty years ago." Borland picked up the phone receiver. "No calls, Suzie, and no one enters while Adams is in my office." He hung the receiver back on the cradle. "Satisfied?"

Marla drank from the water bottle again. It tasted better than the concoction from last night. "I had cameras on the outside and inside of my trailer at the RV Park." She retrieved her phone, tapped a video, and let him watch Bird stab the doctor.

"Why would he do that?"

"Dr. McCollum was a genius. He had Crosby talking and drawing."

"Drawing? Adams? The man with a bullet in his brain drew pictures?"

"Not quite. He had Crosby's brainwaves send words and pictures to a computer tablet."

Borland tilted his head like a curious dog. "Brainwaves?"

"Crosby drew a picture on an electronic tablet...you sure no one else is listening?"

"Yes. I don't want anyone listening to this heedless conversation."

"Crosby drew a picture of Bird, Alejandro Torres-Hernandez, holding a gun against his head."

"He did this before Bird killed the doctor?"

"Yes, before."

"This is why you asked me about recordings? Why didn't he tell you instead of drawing a picture?"

"He wasn't talking at the time. Well, he was, but mostly electronically through the tablet. A robotic-sounding voice."

"Brainwaves did that too?"

"Yes—" She slumped back in the chair. "You don't believe me, do you?"

"More like confused, and so far, it's a stretch."

"He also drew another man behind Bird."

"With brainwaves?"

Marla nodded. "Right."

Suzie sent a text to her agent. *OMG, more to come very soon.*

"You've piqued my interest, Adams, but you need to get it out."

"The other man, behind Bird—I took a picture of the tablet screen." She turned her phone toward Borland, sitting across from her. "The man watching Crosby get shot in the head looks like Special Agent Quinton Wales."

He grabbed her phone and gazed at the image again. "Your evidence is an electronic drawing from an unconscious man's brainwaves?" Borland pitched Marla's phone back at her. "This picture is worthless."

"Not unconscious. At that time, Crosby could speak a few words. He moved his head and looked around."

"Where is this tablet with an image of a man looking like Special Agent Wales? Or is it like an Etch-A-Sketch, turn it upside down, and it's gone?"

"Police have it in their evidence room."

"You mean the San Antonio Police Department has a computer tablet with a possible image of a DEA agent from my district standing behind Torres-Hernandez, aiming a gun at another DEA agent?" He pushed his chair away from the desk. "Adams, there is so much sci-fi bullshit going on here, the district attorney would never accept it. He would laugh in my face. How do I know you didn't draw this on the tablet and want Wales out of the way so you can work your way up?"

"I have nothing against anyone," Marla said. "I'm trying to be a team player."

"A team player accusing a DEA Special Agent with ten years experience and an outstanding record, conspiring with a Mexican cartel of attempted murder. If he's in with Bird, he's in on the drugs and trafficking."

"Sir, I did not draw this."

"Right. You said an unconscious man did with his brainwaves."

"Almost correct, sir."

"That's enough. You are way over the line." Borland said. "You're off the case. Go to your husband and take care of him."

When Marla opened Borland's door, Suzie laid her phone on her desk.

"Don't forget, you signed a nondisclosure when you were hired," Marla said as she left.

Chapter 48

I nside a small restaurant on the east side of San Antonio, Torres-Hernandez and Quinton Wales faced each other across a table near the front door. Both were utterly out of place, one wearing a five thousand dollar suit and the other an off-the-rack *Men in Black* suit.

Three men from a construction company, still wearing white hardhats and bright orange and yellow jackets, came in and sat at a table. In the back, small children chased each other around their parents' table, who seemed to ignore them while they ate. Arturo sat alone in a booth not far from the front door, staring at Quinton Wales.

"You need protection from me?" Wales kept his voice even. "I'm your boss and don't forget it."

"I always have someone close by." Bird sipped his coffee, ignoring the dramatics.

"Someone told me Borland removed Agent Adams from the case." Wales ate the last of his bacon. "My guess is she's being processed for a transfer to a bottomless pit." He had to put a scare in Torres-Hernandez. "What will you say to Juan Carlos when he wants the money next week? The feds took three cases worth almost a million dollars each." Juan Carlos Moreno was the Los Zetas Plaza Boss in charge of drug and gun distribution in South Texas. "The police in Texas will pull over every livestock trailer for weeks. You won't last a day after he finds out how you messed this up."

"And you were paid for our protection," Bird said. "Watch your back because you didn't hold up your end of the bargain, either."

Bird considered this for a moment. The only way to convince Juan Carlos that he should live was to kill Wales and blame him for the debacle. He drank the last of his coffee, then placed the cup on the table. "Los Zetas is not our chief concern." He gently withdrew the handkerchief from the front pocket of his expensive coat and meticulously dabbed his forehead. "If this doctor does what he says he can do and Crosby Adams talks, he'll identify both of us. We won't have to worry about the cartels. The United States Government will kill us."

Wales laughed and wiped his mouth with the back of his hand. "The police and Sheriff's office know about you, not me." He thought about how to convince Borland that Marla had gone full-blown psycho from grieving over her near-dead husband.

Killing Alejandro Torres-Hernandez, the notorious Bird, could make me a hero in the DEA. He sneered as his plan coalesced. *I arrest Bird for shooting an undercover DEA agent, but unfortunately, he would be killed in an escape attempt.* He glanced at Arturo in the booth, then the two other occupied tables. *Too many witnesses. Not here, but soon, very soon.* Quinton placed his coffee cup on the table. "I know where both DEA agents are."

"Where?" Bird asked.

"A nurse I supply coke to called me and told me Adams is on the eighth floor of the Bexar County Community Hospital."

Bird snapped back. "That Adams woman will never back off. Too much at stake for her."

The waitress slapped a check on their table. Neither reached for it.

"We should talk somewhere else," Wales said. "Can't go back to the slaughterhouse. More eyes and ears there than flies on stink bait." He tapped the tabletop. "Remember Cardinal Regional Airport?"

Bird moved his head slightly. "Sure."

"It's been abandoned for a year. I still use it to chill, pretend I'm working, and hide out for a few hours. I have a bottle of good scotch in the drawer. He scooted out of the chair and stood. Meet me there in an hour." He glanced at Arturo, still lounging in the booth. "Your buddy is invited."

Quinton stepped outside to the sidewalk and called Suzie. "Hey, baby. I'm ready for that vacation. I'll send you the location to meet me."

Bird stayed at the table and sent a message on his phone.

While standing near Crosby's bed, Marla's phone dinged. She glanced at her sleeping husband before opening the text.

MARLA, MY DEAR. IT HAS BEEN A MIXED DAY FOR YOU. I'M SURE YOU ARE RELIEVED THE HOSPITAL TOOK YOUR HUSBAND BACK AND HE IS SAFE EXCEPT WHO IS EVER REALLY SAFE? EIGHTH FLOOR? IT IS A SHAME YOUR BOSS HAS REMOVED YOU FROM HUNTING ME. I SO WANT TO MEET YOU AGAIN AND DISCUSS GUNSHOTS OF FRIENDS AND FAMILY. I HAVE A PROPOSITION FOR YOU. LET ME GO BACK TO MEXICO AND I WILL HAND YOU QUINTON WALES. MEET ME AT THE OLD CARDINAL AIRPORT PRECISELY IN NINETY MINUTES. IT WILL BE A COZY MEETING OF JUST THE TWO OF US WITH WALES IN HAND-CUFFS.

Marla's face flushed, and her eye muscles twitched. How did he know about Borland's meeting and Crosby's room so quickly? Who was in on this? She wanted to rid herself of this man, his bullshit, and his ability to always stay two steps ahead of her. Her finger almost touched the delete button, but it was evidence, so she put her phone back in her pocket.

"Everything all right, Mrs. Adams?" Dr. Wilson asked.

"No. Everything is not all right. I have to leave. With one attempt on my husband's life in this hospital, what can you do to ensure his safety?"

"There's nothing I can do. All that is through hospital security, and albeit what happened, I don't believe the hospital will place their security officers at his door side. I would suggest calling the San Antonio Police Department."

Marla waited until Dr. Wilson left the room before leaning over the hospital bed rail and whispering in Crosby's ear, "I'm going to Cardinal Airport to arrest Torres-Hernandez and Wales."

Crosby struggled with his words. "No. One road. Setup."

"That's not how I'm going in." She reached for the letter opener across the bed, strapped it to his wrist, and then pointed at the mobile camera on the windowsill. "I'll be watching you. If you need me, push the emergency button, and I'll be here ASAP. Button and mini sword, okay?"

"All good." Crosby rubbed his thumb over the red button on his waistband. He tightened his hand around the improvised weapon and swung it across his body. "I'm faster."

She kissed him on the lips and then on his forehead. "I love you, Crosby Adams."

"Love you too." He raised his hand while holding his weapon. "Ready."

It had been over two years since Marla last visited the airport. A friend invited them to Breckenridge, Colorado, for a ski trip. It was a fast flight in his private plane. Remembering the layout with a single narrow road a quarter mile long, she would be a clear target from the tower or the top of the building. Knee-high scrub brush and cactus filled the area east of the runway, with rugged hills to the west. Impossible for a vehicle to traverse, but a horse could get through.

Chapter 49

Wales drove his black Tahoe to the abandoned airport and waited for Suzie. It didn't take long for her as she turned onto the road and headed toward him. He smiled and waved as she slowed to a stop in front of the double glass doors of the single building.

Suzie sent the recording of Borland and Marla's discussion to her agent but was surprised she didn't reply. She had to be careful being in the presence of a murderer. Smiling at him, she lowered her window, revealing pink hair, a thin print blouse unbuttoned and tied at the bottom, and white shorts.

He smiled back at her while keeping his black-gloved hands behind him. "Love the hair. I am so happy you decided to come. The beach will be fantastic." He looked in the backseat and noticed no luggage. "Where's your bag?"

"My suitcase is in the trunk."

Swiftly shifting his hands to the roof, he asked, "Suitcase? I was hoping all you brought was a bikini and champagne."

Suzie pulled the blouse open to show her bikini top and laughed. "You mean this old thing?"

"Drive around to the back. There's VIP parking alongside the building."

Suzie glanced around. "I don't think I have to worry about finding a parking spot."

"Follow me." Keeping his hands hidden from her, Wales paced around the corner and stopped near a metal back door. "Back up the car, pop the trunk, and I'll unload the suitcase."

Suzie backed the car near the doorway and stopped.

The trunk lock clicked, and he opened it, removing a small case.

When she climbed out, he held the door to the building open for her. "You are such a knockout."

She swiped her palm across his chin. "You look pretty studly yourself. Why the gloves?"

"Cleaning stuff." He dropped the case beside the back wheel.

She entered the building with no furniture inside. Before she could turn around, Wales grabbed a handful of her pink hair and punched her in the neck. She fell to her hands and knees. The metal door closed behind them.

"You think you can get a story about me?" He kicked her in the abdomen.

Suzie yelled as she rolled onto her side and cried, "Stop!"

"Bullshit." He knelt beside her while holding onto her hair. "Sticking a bug in my phone was stupid." He backhanded her across her face, and she fell flat on her back. "Did you think I wasn't going to notice it?"

"I'm an author. My agent has a copy of all my recordings and my notes. She has it all. You can't do this. Everyone will find out what you're doing."

Wales stood over her. "You mean your New York agent, Anastasia Bradley? I should let you go because your small-time agent has your work?"

"How do you know her name?"

With his phone, he showed her the news flash on the screen. Her hands shook while reading the headline. *International best-selling author turned media agent Anastasia Bradley died in an automobile crash this morning.*

He bent down and grabbed her neck. "Don't fuck with Los Zetas, you pathetic bitch."

She tried to turn away. The last thing she felt was a fist hitting her face.

He rolled Suzie onto her stomach, handcuffed her wrists, and jerked her upright. Inside, there was no handle on the back door, only a key in the lock chamber. He turned the key and pulled the door open, then dumped her in the trunk of her car and slammed the lid closed. After unrolling a short garden hose hidden near the door, he shoved one end into the exhaust pipe and the other into a small hole at the base of the wall. He started the engine, and fumes poured inside the building.

A vehicle rolled to a stop at the front of the building. "Perfect timing, asshole." He snapped off the gloves and tossed them on the ground before marching around the corner, smiling and waving hello. He opened the door for Bird and held out his hand. "I'm glad you came," Wales said as they shook hands. "Together, we must fix this problem. I found a way to get the drugs and money from the sheriff's department."

"How would you do that?" Bird asked.

Wales retrieved a single key from his pocket and unlocked the front glass door. Not touching the glass, he used his shoulder to push open the door. "I have someone on the inside who is desperate to help us."

The two entered the building minus the lobby furniture, followed by Arturo holding an AK-47.

"Everything is gone," Bird said.

"Sold it all."

Bird eyed a solid wooden door with Manager's Office printed across the top. "Different door from the last time I was here."

"Yes. Someone kicked a hole in it, so I replaced it with a solid one with a pneumatic closure at the top. I've always liked those. Easy open, easy close." He stepped toward the door.

"Where are you going?" Bird asked. "We can talk out here."

"Have you forgotten the scotch in the desk drawer? Come on. There are chairs for everyone. I'll pour us a drink for old times' sake. We ran a lot of drugs through this airport."

"You're right. Until your DEA shut it down," Bird said.

"And I warned you to get out before the raid."

Bird smiled and nodded in approval. "True."

When Wales leaned in toward the door, he slipped out his pistol from the shoulder holster, spun around, and fired once, hitting Arturo in the chest. He staggered and fell, bouncing his head against the concrete floor. Wales aimed his weapon at Bird.

"What is going on?" Bird yelled.

He stomped on the AK rifle before kicking it across the lobby. "Hands behind your head and turn around."

"Are you going to arrest me? I'll take you down with me."

In a quick, standard police action, he snapped handcuffs on Bird's wrists behind his back. "This is where it gets a little tricky. Does Rafael Villegas sound familiar? Playing two cartels for extra cash on the side is stupid. When I tell Juan Carlos you fucked everything up, I will be guaranteed to be on his good side."

Pulling out a handkerchief, he used it to turn the knob on the office door, then shoved Bird inside the empty room and shut the door. "What an idiot." Quinton picked up the spent cartridge from the floor and put it in his pocket.

Inside the room, next to the metal back door, at the baseboard, a garden hose stuck out like the head of a snake, pumping fumes. "Let me out, you fucking pendejo!" Bird yelled. He kicked and shoved his shoulder against the wooden door. With his hands cuffed behind him, he tried to turn the doorknob. "Damn it. Let me out."

Quinton laughed and said loud enough for Bird to hear. "This is so much more fun than shooting you. I get to hear you suffer."

Bird coughed from the fumes and fell to his knees. "The cartel will figure this out. Me dead and you alive? They'll kill you for that."

"You're not living up to your name. Let's see you get away this time."

Bird noticed the back door had no handle, but there was a key in the lock. He tried to reach for the key, but it was too high. He slumped down the side of a wall, then in one movement, slipped his hands from behind his back, under his buttocks, and the back of his legs. With his cuffed hands in front of him, he drew a .22 caliber revolver from his ankle holster and fired three times at the wooden door.

Wales dove to the floor.

Bird yelled, "When I tell Juan Carlos what happened," he fired twice more at the door, "he's going to laugh at your dead body." Bird fired again.

The car's engine pumped more exhaust into the room.

Bird coughed harder from the fumes. "Answer me, you fuck-head." He spun toward the back door and turned the key. *I'm a fucking bird flying away.* He swung the door open.

Outside, Wales smiled as he fired his gun at Bird's stomach. "I must say, I'm surprised you opened it."

Bird dropped to the floor, and Quinton kicked the gun across the room.

"You kill me," Bird yelled, "and Juan Carlos will—"

Two shots fired point-blank into Bird's chest. "I'll finish the sentence for you. He will congratulate me for killing an idiot."

Wales turned Suzie's car engine off, then picked the spent cartridges off the ground. Using the handkerchief, he pushed the outside door wide to let the exhaust escape.

A pool of blood grew under Bird. A foot away, his phone lay on the floor.

"Looks like you dropped your phone. People do that all the time. So frustrating when they lose their phone." Wales picked it up. "Let's see who you have been talking to." It was locked. He tapped 1234. Nothing. "What's your birthday, asshole?" He never cared what it was until now. Pushing 7277 (PASS) didn't open it.

When Quinton pushed the sole of his shoe on Bird's stomach, he screamed.

"Hey, dipshit. Tell me your password."

"Fuck you."

Refocusing on the phone, Wales tapped 5679 for LOSZ, Los Zetas, and the screen lit up. "Too easy."

Most of the phone calls listed first names of livestock drivers, but there was one yesterday to JCM, Juan Carlos Moreno, cartel boss. He wondered what the two talked about. Him?

He read text messages sent to Marla Adams. "You are screwed up in the head." He checked his watch. "So, she is coming here in about forty-five minutes." He leaned down toward Bird lying in a pool of his blood, growing larger as he bled out. "You have made my day even more perfect. I get to set up the newbie for a major fall." He shot Bird in the head.

Noise rumbled out past the back door. "Suzie? Almost forgot about you." When he opened the trunk, she swung her foot toward him. He grabbed her ankle and slammed his pistol against her knee. A gush of blood spewed from the gash in her leg. Screaming at him, she tried kicking his hand. Blood poured from her broken nose.

"Time's up, girl."

She spat blood at him when he reached for the handcuffs behind her. He punched her in the face again, then yanked her out of the trunk. Dragging her over Bird, her leg streaked blood across the floor.

"You're like a gnat buzzing around my face." He aimed at the center of her chest.

Suzie's face was swollen, with a bruise growing under her left eye. She stared at him and yelled, "Bastard!"

He fired a bullet into her heart.

More blood smeared the floor as he dragged Bird's body beside Suzie's. He heard a grunt behind him.

Arturo charged, wrapping his arms around Wales's neck. "I'm going to kill you."

Quinton ran backward, slamming Arturo against the wall and releasing his grip around Wales' neck. He spun around and punched Arturo in the stomach. Curling into a ball, Arturo moaned and rolled to his side.

A bullet ripped into Arturo's skull, and he went limp.

Quinton picked up the last of his spent cartridges and chuckled. "Adams, you are going to have a lot of explaining why you killed all three of these people. He dropped four of Marla's cartridges he had taken at her firing range days ago. "A gift to you from the cartel. May you spend the next forty years in prison."

He traipsed outside and looked down the road toward the main road. "She's a smart girl, never leaving herself wide open and driving down the only road to the airport." He cut around to the back of the building again and surveyed the hills. "She would come from there and come early."

Marla sat on a horse at the top of the ridge. "Well, I'll be damned. There you are, DEA Special Agent Wales."

Wales tapped 911 on Bird's phone. "There is gunfire at the old Cardinal Airport. Someone is hurt." He wiped the prints off before pitching it into the dirt.

Marla stopped at the top of the ridge and adjusted her black cap with DEA letters on the front. Her leather-gloved hand patted Daisy's neck. "Good girl. We can do this. Not much further." She clicked her tongue. "Easy does it down the hill."

It took a few minutes for them to sidle down to the front of the building. Marla recognized the backend of a black Tahoe driving down the road. "Quinton Wales, you sack of shit."

Daisy's horseshoes clomped on the concrete as she trotted alongside the empty minivan that looked just like the ones at the stockyard. She dismounted and slid her hand over Daisy's head and nose before checking the inside of the vehicle. It was empty.

She stuffed her gloves in her back pocket, then pushed the front door open and aimed her pistol inside the lobby. Fresh blood was on the floor and near the wooden door.

Refusing to call him Bird to his face, she said, "Torres-Hernandez, come out with your hands above your head." After clearing the entryway, she counted six bullet holes in the Manager's wooden door, all exit holes.

When she pushed the door open, the odor of exhaust fumes almost overwhelmed her. Three bodies were sprawled across the floor.

"Damn. Borland will be pissed if he thinks I have anything to do with this."

Marla checked the man on the far side of the room, dead with bullet holes in the head and chest. She recognized the woman lying beside the other male. "Oh, girl, what are you doing here?" A puddle of blood surrounded Suzie. The second man wore a colorful jacket and pants and had been shot in the chest and stomach. She reached inside the jacket pocket, removed the wallet, and opened it. She stared at the name on a Mexican driver's license — Alejandro Torres-Hernandez.

Crosby rushed through her mind, his smile, laughter, hands wrapped around her, his promise to love her forever. Quinton Wales took away her closure. She wanted to bring Bird in and stop the injustice, but Wales, the son of a bitch Wales, who doesn't deserve to be called anything but a murderer, stole that from her.

Marla noticed four spent cartridges on the floor bunched together like someone rolling dice against a building. It made no sense. Cartridges eject from a gun in random directions. She tilted her head and bent down on one knee. There was a black dot on the back of a cartridge. This was not evidence; it was a plant with cartridges from her practice range. She pocketed them.

Her eyes burned from the residual exhaust hanging in the air. A garden hose stuck through a hole in the wall. There wasn't a handle at the back door, only a key stuck in the lock. She turned it and pulled open the door. The other end of the hose was stuffed in a car's exhaust pipe, and the trunk was open and empty.

Sirens cried in the distance. Marla bolted around the side of the building and saw flashing lights turn into the airport. "The asshole must have called the police." She whistled, and Daisy clomped around to her. "Is Wales going after Crosby?" Marla plucked the gloves from her back pocket, stuck her boot into the stirrup, and galloped toward the hills.

Four police cars surrounded the airport building. Movement past the airstrip caught the eye of an officer, and he called out, "Somebody on a horse riding toward the hills."

Another officer watched the horse race away and pushed the microphone button on his shirt. "Suspect escaping west of Cardinal Airport."

The dispatcher answered, "West of Cardinal is hills, no road for vehicles."

"Rider on a horse."

"A horse, of course." There was a pause for a moment. "Will contact sheriff's department. They have readily available four-wheelers."

❖

Dr. Wilson sat behind the eighth floor doctor's counter and reread Dr. McCollum's last published article about a protein catalyst and stem cells. If he got his hands on the catalyst, he could patent it and mass-produce a potential gold mine. This would change everything, neurosurgery, orthopedic surgery, rehab, athletes, the elderly, and congenital deformities.

Quinton Wales paced down the hospital hallway until he reached the rehab nurse's station. He flashed his DEA badge while holding his coat closed to block the view of his gun.

Crosby pushed the red emergency button when he recognized a voice.

Marla crested atop the hill, and her phone rang like a nuclear reactor alert.

Chapter 50

Marla slapped Daisy's flank and spurred her boot into the horse's side. "Go, girl."

The hospital was two miles away. She had a choice: zigzag over frontage roads, six intersections, and too many traffic lights or a straight shot through two enormous, shoulder-high cornfields. The major problem with the cornfields—crossing a busy four-lane road between them.

When Marla pulled the reins and turned Daisy, her hooves romped between rows of corn. The stalks and cobs pummeled Marla's thighs like a piñata. Electric shocks shot through what was left of her little finger. Blood splattered her hand. "Come on, girl. You can do this."

Marla's cap flew off. She leaned forward, closer to the horse's neck, and Daisy charged straight ahead, not missing a step in her gallop. It didn't take long to get to the other end of the cornfield. Ahead of her, the hospital roof line towered above the stalks. Traffic sounds grew nearer.

An engine roared near her left side and caught Marla off guard. The tops of cornstalks dropped like spectators at the Running of the Bulls. An ATV with a sheriff's deputy on top raced behind her, and the engine slowed. Marla kicked Daisy's haunches and cleared the last row of corn. They veered right along the fence line abutting the 4-lane road. She needed to get across, but a continuous line of vehicles zipped by them. A fuel truck roared past. A hundred yards ahead, there was an opening in the fence. An engine roared to her side.

An ATV pulled out of the cornfield between her and the fence opening. It was Deputy Keene. He revved the engine. "Marla," he yelled. "Stop. Get off the horse, and let's talk about what happened at the airport."

"I don't have time for that." Marla tugged the reins to the right, and Daisy headed back into the cornfield. Jeffrey followed. Daisy plowed through a row, then another. Jeffrey's ATV charged through the stalks, corn bashing his body. He honked his horn. "Marla," he yelled again. "Stop."

Marla turned. When Jeffrey tried to follow, another ATV sideswiped him. She turned again back toward the street. The opening in the fence was straight ahead. She told herself she could make it out before Jeffrey knew where she was.

An ATV slid to a stop near the opening. Jeffrey waved his arms above his head and yelled, "Come on, Marla. Stop. We have to talk."

Marla was ten yards away and swung her arm wildly at him. "Get out of my way."

She's too close to the fence. Turning would be impossible, and hitting the ATV would kill Daisy. She kicked the horse again. "Go, girl." Marla swung her hand at Jeffrey to move out of the way. He jumped off the ATV and rolled on the dirt.

Marla gripped the reins and leaned forward. "Do it, Daisy. Please." She closed her eyes and prayed Daisy did the right thing. Hooves pounded the dirt. Marla's hair stood on end. When Daisy squeezed through the fence opening, Marla's right leg slammed into the post like a sledgehammer striking a railroad tie. She looked down at the bloody gash above her boot.

Car tires screeched as they slid to a halt. A dump truck blew its horn long and loud, missing Daisy's head by inches. Police sirens screamed. Emergency lights spun in the air. She took what little luck she had left. With no fence along the side, Marla snapped the reins against Daisy, and they charged across the road, disappearing into the next cornfield.

Rhythmic whomps in the sky caught her attention—a helicopter. She couldn't hide anymore. Riding through the field slowed her down. She pulled the reins and turned onto the road toward the hospital. Hoofbeats clopped on the concrete. Automobiles aligned bumper-to-bumper with their windows rolled down and people waving and cheering.

Half a block away, a traffic light changed to red in all four directions, and a mass of pedestrians entered the intersection. When she fired her gun, people scattered out of the way. Marla charged through the crossway and raced by startled people. A block ahead, another traffic light, red with too many cars waiting to go. She glanced back as sirens grew louder and police cars closed in. Marla couldn't wait for the light to change. She turned Daisy toward oncoming traffic. A rider on a motorcycle slammed on the brakes and slid to the ground. Daisy reared back, and Marla grasped the reins with one hand as she held her pistol in the other. Her phone blared another alert from Crosby.

ATV engines and sirens came from every direction. The helicopter hovered above with a voice calling from the P.A. system. "Stop the horse and raise your hands."

Marla turned Daisy at the intersection, and she galloped down the middle of the road. There was a creek between her and the hospital, but it was too wide to jump and too steep to climb down and back up again. A hundred yards away stood a footbridge over the water the police hadn't covered, the last obstacle before the hospital. She kicked the horse's haunches, and Daisy veered toward the bridge. People stood, frozen in place like statues.

Marla pulled back on the reins. "No. We can't do it."

Daisy paid no attention like she understood this was for Crosby and sped forward. People stared and refused to move. Marla fired her pistol in the air again. Instantly, people scattered, and the footbridge cleared. Daisy ran her heart out as she raced over the bridge, hooves hammering rhythmic sounds on wooden slats.

One intersection to go. Marla felt lucky when the light turned green and snapped the reins against the horse. "We got it, girl." Daisy charged through.

A car horn blew, and tires screeched. Marla didn't see the car running the red light. Daisy reared back, front legs raised. Marla leaned forward, grabbed the neck, and squeezed the saddle with her thighs. When Daisy lowered, the hooves hit the car's hood. Marla pulled the reins and Daisy ran toward the hospital. The automatic glass doors opened. Marla lowered her head as they entered the lobby. Daisy's hooves clip-clopped on the linoleum floor. Marla quickly dismounted and pitched the reins over the horse's neck.

Chapter 51

Quinton Wales flashed his DEA badge toward the nurse. "SAPD. What room is Crosby Adams in?" The nurse paid little attention to the badge, and Quinton quickly covered it. "He's one of us."

Unknowing about the activity outside, the nurse gestured toward the end of the hall with a smile. "Third room on the left near the stairwell door."

He ambled down the hallway without a limp while holding the cane.

Dr. Wilson stopped typing on the computer at the doctor's counter near the nurse's station and called out, "Who are you?"

Wales smiled. "I'm...um, Lt. Smith, SAPD, and I'm here to see Adams." He took a step toward the patient room.

Dr. Wilson hopped from his chair and stopped the man unknown to him. "It's about time someone came to stand guard. The hospital doesn't have the personnel to do that, and the wife has been up our ass about the whole thing."

Wales stood at eye level with the doctor. *I can play this game.* "Right. That would be me. I should check on him. Won't be but a minute."

"Wait. It doesn't happen often, but I know the administration requires a hospital badge to stay in the ICU. Go down to security and get one. By the way, SAPD sent a guy with a cane?"

From inside his room, Crosby turned slowly toward the commotion. His head was still fuzzy, but he had heard that voice before.

Wales didn't know Marla was almost there or that Borland saw an image of him standing behind Bird shooting a DEA agent.

I should throw your ass down on the floor, walk to Adams' bed, and shoot him, but that would blow my cover. Wales glimpsed at the door to the stairs. "Twisted my foot a few days ago. All good now. I'm officially on duty here, so let me give you my number if you need anything in the next thirty minutes while I'm downstairs. Do you have a piece of paper I may use?"

Dr. Wilson stared at him momentarily before pulling a scratch pad from his white coat pocket. He tore off the top sheet. "Here."

"Thank you, sir." Wales leaned over to Crosby's medication cart in the hallway, laid the hook of his cane over his forearm, and dropped a small Bluetooth microphone inside a box of gloves as he touched the ear pod in his right ear. He wrote a fake phone number as he gazed at Crosby in the bed. Ripping the top third off, he handed it to the doctor. "This is my direct number."

Holding his cane, he stepped toward the metal stairwell door as he wadded the rest of the paper in his hand. He pushed the panic bar and opened it. Blocking Wilson's view, Wales shoved the paper into the strike plate.

"Don't go out that way," Dr. Wilson said. "All the doors are locked with keypads. We keep the riffraff out that way. Besides, it's eight floors down, and with your cane, I don't believe you should try that."

"I wanted to work the muscles a bit, you know, up and down the stairs."

Dr. Wilson pointed down the hallway. "Go back down the elevator and return with a hospital badge."

Wales closed the door. "Absolutely. No problem." He glanced at the patient identification next to the room: C. Adams, Dr. Wilson.

Crosby couldn't understand the conversation but recognized the man. The one who stood behind Bird. Their eyes met, and Crosby pushed Marla's alarm again.

Dr. Wilson followed the man to the elevator until the doors closed, then dropped the number into the wastebasket before returning to his desk.

Distant sirens caught his attention. Dr. Wilson was still on trauma call and liked the possibility of more surgeries. He had a sudden distaste at the possibility of never needing to perform surgery again if the new stem cell therapy became widespread. He turned and entered Crosby's room.

"How are you, Mr. Adams?"

Crosby dragged his sheet up to his shoulders, hiding the red button. He nodded.

"Still not able to talk?"

Crosby kept his progress to himself and stuttered, "Some."

"Any sensations returning in your arms and legs?"

He knew he shouldn't say yes. "Some."

The doctor moved around to the left side of the bed and slipped on gloves. He removed the bandage from Crosby's head. "I removed a large section of your cranium during surgery. Most people don't realize it, but we keep it in the freezer. When we are ready, we put it back, and the patient has a full skull again." He touched the hole. "You, on the other hand, had this stem cell thing done, and the bone has regenerated, almost closing on its own. The hole," he touched the wound, "is slightly larger than the tip of my finger. I believe it could fit all the way into your brain."

Wales exited the elevator on the first floor while listening to Dr. Wilson speak to Adams on Bluetooth. He marched directly to the stairwell and opened the door. Stagnant air hovered inside as he charged up the stairs and stopped after the fourth floor. The infection in his leg had dissipated, but the pain lingered, especially after four flights. The doctor was right. A keypad was attached to the wall close to the door. He shook his head and trudged on.

Dr. Wilson smiled at Crosby. "It's quite surprising this doctor could inject his concoction into your brain and not cause an infection." The doctor stepped back and clasped his hands. "The body is a miracle. A million years ago, the brain developed a sack around itself for protection against infections. But a few days ago, a hot piece of metal punctured your sack and shredded your brain. With all that necrotic tissue in your head, you should be septic—dead by now, but as we can see, you are not." Wilson stopped smiling as he touched the hole in Crosby's skull again. "This bone is firm. Newly formed bones are soft, like an infant, and yours should be the same, soft, pliable. What am I saying, before today, I would never believe you could have any bone. You went from no bone to hardened. That should take months, not a few days." The doctor stopped touching Crosby's skull. "Dr. McCollum was a genius. Maybe a mad genius, but your brain survives. It continues to restore function and memory, and all that is left is this one-inch wide hole where McCollum injected his stem cell formula."

Under the sheet, Crosby slid his left hand holding the letter opener near his leg while staring at the doctor's face.

Dr. Wilson grabbed Crosby's chin and turned it toward him. "Did you know there are no pain receptors in the brain?" He scoffed. "No, of course, you didn't. How could you?" He released his hold and smiled again at Crosby. "That is why no one feels pain until a brain tumor expands and puts too much pressure inside the skull." His smile left. "This crackpot British doctor did more than I expected. I thought he was some quack that humiliated himself in the eyes of the world's medical community." Wilson shrugged. "But this changed my mind. Your brain tissue has almost completely filled in. In less than a week? New tissue! Think of it: if we injected livers, kidneys, and hearts, we could eliminate transplants. We could stop all the trauma surgeries and simply inject stem cells with this miracle catalyst into damaged tissue." Dr. Wilson tapped his chest. "I would be out of a job. No need for a neurosurgeon if the ER doctor shoots up all the trauma patients and sends them home to recover on their own. That's not even outpatient surgery."

He clicked his tongue. "I could start a new research program, bring in millions of dollars, maybe even get a Nobel prize, but that would take too long, and what if it didn't work? If I didn't mix it correctly? Would I be like McCollum? A clone? Disastrous." He pointed at Crosby and raised his voice. "You're a freak. Why are you alive?" He pointed his index finger toward Crosby. "This would take the world back to normal. The way it was, the way it should be." Wilson grabbed Crosby's head and turned it to the side. "As I said, you are McCollum's freak, and a madman's ghost won't drag me down. Don't worry. You won't feel a thing when I shove my finger into your brain and turn you back into an invalid."

With every particle of strength Crosby had, he lunged the letter opener toward the doctor.

Wilson froze. Glaring at the weapon stuck in his chest, he barely got the words out, "You freak." He yanked the metal blade out and raised it above his head. Blood poured onto the bed and floor.

Crosby bent his knee and pushed his foot against the doctor's abdomen. When he fell backward, the weapon clattered to the floor. Crosby pushed the red button again with his thumb.

Wales reached the eighth floor and heard the doctor ranting in the room through the microphone in the medication cart. He cracked open the door. Nurses stood at their desk. One stepped toward a room, so he closed the door and waited.

Wales turned toward the stairs when he heard footsteps below. He chuckled. "Marla Adams, you seem to be about five minutes late to everything today."

Marla rushed the steps, swirling around each corner, charging up each floor two steps at a time. She felt blood inside her boot down to her toes. Adrenaline killed her pain. Visions kept popping into her head; Crosby was in trouble, and someone was in his room. Wales with a gun? Someone else? Huffing hard, she called out as if he could hear. "I'm almost there, Crosby."

She stopped at the eighth floor door, dropping to one knee and gasping for air. Warm blood covered her right hand. She felt her finger nub and the side of her leg throbbing. Red drops splotched the concrete.

Wales quietly sat above her at the top of the stairs with his gun pointed at her. It would be difficult to explain why he shot another DEA agent, but if she turned around, he'd have no choice but to shoot.

She twisted the handle, wincing from the finger pain. Opening the stairwell door startled a nurse nearby.

"Have to see my husband."

The nurse caught sight of blood on Marla's hand and pants. She wrapped her arm around Marla's waist and helped her to the room. "Oh, my Lord, ma'am, you're bleeding. Let me call for the doctor." When they entered the room, Dr. Wilson was sprawled on the floor, chest covered in blood. The nurse released Marla and screamed for help.

Wales stood behind the stairwell door and smiled. From the listening device, he couldn't tell who killed who or if both men died. Did Wilson do him a favor?

The doctor's blood covered the sheet on Crosby. Marla flung it off his body and felt for any wounds. "Are you hurt?"

Crosby's lips curled up in satisfaction that he had resolved the problem. "No. Not me."

The nurse knelt over Dr. Wilson with her hand covering the puncture wound. She yelled, "I need a doctor."

Another nurse ran into the room. "Dr. Wilson?" She hurried around the bed to start chest compressions.

The first nurse said, "No, no. Push the emergency call button. Get help."

Marla focused on Crosby, her face inches from his. "What happened?"

"Stop right there, Marla."

She turned to find Deputy Jeffrey Keene red-faced, eyes dilated, lips dry...and his gun pointing at her.

He glanced at the bloodied floor and then back toward Marla. "Did you kill him?"

Several nurses and a doctor rushed in.

"No, Jeffrey. I did not kill Dr. Wilson, and I did not kill anyone else today."

Jeffrey shook his head. "You mean the three inside the airport." It was more of a statement than a question. "Who were they?"

"Torres-Hernandez, another man, and a girl from the DEA office. It was Wales who did it."

"Come on, Marla. He wasn't there."

"No. I promise. It was Quinton Wales. Check for fingerprints and footprints. I saw him drive away. I think he's somewhere nearby to kill Crosby."

Other deputies entered the room with their guns aimed at Marla. Jeffrey stared at her for a long time before he holstered his pistol. "Lower your weapons. She didn't do it. Go back to the airport and check for evidence." He turned back to Marla. "Who killed the doctor?"

"I stabbed Dr. Wilson," Crosby said as he pointed at the bloody letter opener on the floor.

Jeffrey turned toward Crosby. "You're supposed to be, like, almost dead."

"Almost, once upon a time."

"It had to be self-defense," Marla said. "He's lying in his bed."

"What happened?"

Crosby's words were clear but slow. "He wanted to kill me and stop the—" He turned his head away, eyes glazed, fists tightened, and arms and legs stiffened.

"Wait," Marla cried. "Don't do this."

Crosby's head extended back before his body jerked a hundred times.

❖

Bright lights shined on Crosby's face. His muscles ached. "What happened?"

Marla's finger nub and thigh were wrapped with clean gauze. She slid the IV pole closer to the wall. "We're in the emergency room. You had a big seizure this time, lasting forever, and you stopped breathing." She held Crosby's hand.

"Wilson?" Crosby asked.

"Dead." She shook her head. "Looked like the blade punctured his heart." She snickered. "At least Borland will be relieved that I didn't kill him." Holding up her phone for him to hear the audio from the camera she placed on the windowsill, they both listened to Dr. Wilson's threats and accusations. "I showed it to Jeffrey. It was self-defense."

"Keene?"

"He left to report what happened and said he would return to check on you."

Crosby concentrated on the words he needed to say to her. "Where to now?"

"You're not returning to rehab. They don't want you there until you stop the seizures."

"And Wales?"

"I don't know. Out of town, state, country? In Mexico? Hopefully, out of our lives."

He didn't know what to say to her. Even with the seizure, his thoughts started clearing, but his speech slacked. "Muscles weak." He smiled as he swung his arm. "But deadly."

A young doctor entered the room after a brief tap on the door. He stood several feet away from the bed. "Mr. Adams, your lab tests are not good. You need a kidney and heart transplant. The sooner, the better, but we don't do those here. You will be transferred to Methodist, but they are full today and won't accept anyone until tomorrow."

Marla stepped toward the foot of the bed. "Where will he go tonight?"

The doctor moved back and held the metal patient chart in front of him like a shield. "Cardiac ICU. Sit tight. It may take a few hours to get him there." He backed toward the door and slipped out.

She sat by Crosby and leaned her head against his hand. "Not the life I expected." She kissed his hand. "I don't think I can do this." Laying her arm across his chest, she turned her face into the blanket and held back tears.

Crosby laid his hand on top of her arm. "We'll get through this."

Marla raised her head and gazed into Crosby's eyes. "I want you out. Both of us. We can raise cattle, something besides this." She put her head back down against his hand. "You can't die and I go on. I can't do that."

Marla's family flashed in her mind. Stainless steel tables in the morgue. Not mentioning anything about Daisy or the house, she was frustrated with herself for not telling him everything and exhausted from carrying all that loss herself. "I'm going to the bathroom."

Crosby's arm drifted toward a door. "We have one here."

"Hmm, so we do." Her hands wrapped around his face, and she kissed him. "Rest your eyes." She needed a hard cry. "I'll be back in a few minutes."

Marla pushed the room door open and slowly closed it behind her. She trudged around the corner, slumped against the hallway wall, and sobbed.

Two nurse's aides trooped past Marla. One spoke, "Every day is different here. Nothing is the same."

The other said, "Crazy about someone killing Dr. Wilson. That bastard should go to jail."

The first one said, "Killing a doctor? They need to throw away the key." She looked at Marla kneeling against the wall in street clothes and wearing a gun belt. "Not supposed to have that unless you're a cop. Are you a cop? If so, go arrest the guy who killed our doctor."

Marla wiped her red eyes and tried to smile. "I'll make a note of that. Where's the bathroom?"

The second aide said, "Down the hallway, third door on the right."

Marla slid up the wall and walked away.

Quinton Wales came from the far end of the hall wearing a white lab coat, entered a room, and calmly shut the door. Crosby lay on his back with his eyes closed and an IV bag hanging from the pole beside his bed. Wales smirked at the tray of food near the bed. *Like this guy is going to eat dinner.*

Crosby opened his eyes and shoved the tray table toward Wales, but he stopped the tray from falling to the floor.

"There's a rumor you are doing better. Looks like it's true." He grabbed a cup of water and poured it on Crosby's head. "You have been an unbelievably bad person, DEA Special Agent Crosby Adams. You don't die when you are supposed to."

Crosby pushed the emergency button, then flung it at his assailant.

Marla's phone blared in the bathroom. "No. No. No. No. No."

Crosby rolled out of bed and bounced on the floor. Trying to crawl away, he felt the hospital gown tighten around his neck. Wales wrapped his arm around Crosby's neck and pulled him up. Crosby swung his arms out but felt himself being dragged toward the bathroom.

"I'm tired of you not dying. Shot in the head, almost killed in the trailer. Even that dumb shit Wilson screwed it up." He dragged Crosby to the toilet and flipped the seat up. "With you and Torres-Hernandez dead, Juan Carlos will believe I am the hero." He shoved Crosby's face down into the toilet bowl. "But first, you have to die."

Crosby tried to hold his breath, but he was too weak.

Marla kicked the door in. She pointed her gun toward the bathroom. "Let him go, Wales."

He raised Crosby's face out of the water, arm still wrapped around Crosby's neck, holding him like a shield. Crosby coughed and hacked, spitting out water.

Watching Marla's face, he scoffed. "What happened to calling me Quinton? Your friend, your mentor."

"You're a murderer. Murders in my book don't deserve a first name—Wales." She winced. Her wounded finger screamed in pain.

"Hand hurts, doesn't it?"

"Stop right there," Marla said. "You're under arrest."

"I believe your accuracy is gone with only four and a half fingers wrapped around that pistol." Wales drew his weapon and stuck it against Crosby's ribs. "We are leaving this place, and you will let us walk down the hallway, all nice and easy."

"Nobody is going anywhere." Marla kicked the door closed. "Drop your weapon. I swear, I'll kill you."

Wales pushed the barrel harder against Crosby and yelled at Marla, "Move!"

Crosby wrapped his feet around one of Wales' ankles. They both fell to the floor. Marla tried stomping Quinton Wales' hand, but he grabbed her ankle and twisted it. The sound of his pistol firing was deafening in the closed room. When she rolled away, he raced out into the hallway. Marla sprang to her feet and chased after him. He shifted back and forth, shoving people against the walls.

Marla yelled, "Everybody down! He has a gun!"

People dropped like flies.

Wales grabbed a young hospital employee around the neck and spun toward Marla. He caught sight of her gun barrel aimed at him. The girl screamed and tried to free herself. He fired a shot at the ceiling. In a knee-jerk reaction, everyone on the floor covered their heads with their hands.

"I'm leaving this place," he pointed the firearm at the girl's head, "or she dies." He backed up. "Lay your gun on the floor, Adams."

The girl begged. "Please do what he said."

He peeked around a corner and then back at Marla. She moved closer.

The girl cried out, "I promise I won't do anything. Just let me go."

"Shut up," Quinton yelled.

She cried out more. "Please. I don't want to die. I'm going to vomit. Let me go, or I'll vomit."

Marla shuffled her feet closer.

"Stop, or she's dead." He tightened his grip around the girl's neck. "Drop it, Adams. Now!" He tapped the barrel on the girl's head. She winced and screamed.

"Please, lady. Help me. I don't want to die." She stomped on his foot. "Let me go, you bastard."

"Shut the hell up." He gun-butted the top of her head.

She screamed and cried more.

"Adams. Drop your weapon on the floor. I swear I'll shoot her."

Wales didn't hear the stairwell door open behind him.

In her periphery, she saw Jeffery and holstered her weapon. "No. I'll put it right here."

With a high-pitched laugh, he confirmed what he knew. "You think you can quick draw me with mine out already? Once upon a time, you were fast, but not with an injured hand."

Deputy Jeffrey Keene eased around a corner. He aimed at the DEA agent's back. "Sheriff's department. Stop right there and put the gun on the floor."

Marla said with an even voice, "Stay back from him."

Jeffrey stared at the man. He stepped closer. "Drop the weapon and put your hands behind your head."

Wales turned toward the deputy with the girl in front of him. "You drop it, or she dies."

Jeffrey froze. He couldn't take the chance.

Wales fired, and Jeffrey's gun went off as he fell to the floor. Blood spurt from Wales' thigh. He released the girl and grabbed his leg. He faced Marla and raised his weapon toward her.

She drew and fired twice into his chest. He staggered backward, but she knew he wore a vest.

"Drop it, Wales," she said.

Crosby's smile crossed her mind, and this man standing in front of her had taken that away.

Wales raised his gun toward her again. She fired two more into his chest, and he landed against the wall, sliding down onto his buttocks.

"Damn, that hurts."

"Drop your weapon. You are under arrest for human trafficking and murder."

Jeffrey sat up and touched his vest where a bullet had lodged. He aimed his service weapon toward the man. "Weapon down."

Wales sat on the floor, still holding his gun on his lap. "I can't." He yelled at Marla. "I can't go to prison!" He sighed. "You know what happens to police officers in there?" He mumbled, "Damn." He turned his gun barrel toward his temple and pulled the trigger. The body slumped to the floor.

A burst of frantic yelling came from behind Marla. Medical staff rushed into Crosby's room. A nurse pushed a red medical cart with a cardiac defibrillator on top and wrestled it into his room. Someone yelled, "Clear!" A machine screamed with a long, loud, high-pitched sound—a siren of help. The voice yelled again. "Clear."

Marla turned the corner and entered the room. Six people knelt on the floor over Crosby with blood pouring out of a bullet hole in the side of his chest. An EMT did chest compressions. Crosby laid flat, still, motionless. The high-pitched sound of the defibrillator screamed in Marla's ears. The screen scrolled a straight line of death. No heartbeat.

The doctor said words she never wanted to hear. "Stop compressions."

For Marla, the world stopped.

The nurse removed the Ambu bag from Crosby's mouth. Another nurse pulled the sheet off the bed and laid it over Crosby. Blood crept through the white sheet near his chest.

"Time of death?" the doctor asked.

A nurse replied, "5:14 p.m."

Chapter 52

A fire with four logs crossed over each other burned bright with a branding iron buried in the embers. Marla withdrew it from the fire and held the head against the new barn door. The iron sizzled against the wood. She eased it away, revealing the same heart brand Crosby made the day they married. Steam rose from the water when she lowered the iron into a bucket. Leaning against her fifth-wheel trailer, her living quarters until the house was finished, she tugged on the visor of her black cap with red stitching, HILDEBRANDT F. D.

A neon yellow sun separated itself from the horizon. With a crisp morning, Marla opened the corral gate, and the two horses stood majestically and nodded in the morning light. "Good morning, guys." Marla scratched behind their ears.

Behind her, front loaders with buckets shaved over dirt, scooping blackened wood and ashes from the burned house, and loaded dump trucks. Repetitive high-pitched beeps filled the air from construction vehicles backing up. The sounds of jackhammers machine-gunned in the air, breaking concrete. A dozen firefighters, some coming to help after their shift and some before, pitched remnants of the chicken coop and barn in a pile.

Marla gazed at the men helping clear the destruction of her home and accepted her blessings and misfortunes. She wore a Wrangler long-sleeved shirt and jeans with leather work gloves stuck inside her back pocket. After saddling the horse, she guided him past the corral.

Don Verdon wore his red Fire Chief helmet and waved at her. "Wait, Marla. Stay there." He rushed to her. "Glad I caught you before you took off." He looked back at the front loader beeping, then back at her. "Can't believe the insurance company. They should write you a check today. Pretty obvious what happened."

"Not much else it could be besides arson. Thanks for coming in and doing this. I promise to pay when I can."

"Don't worry about it. Everyone raised their hands when I asked for volunteers at the fire station. Whatever they pay you, we'll stick it in the indigent fund and help someone else. I've got two men at the fence where the arsonists broke in. They should have it repaired by now. We don't want Daisy and Blackie slipping out."

"They aren't going anywhere. They know where their bread is buttered. Thanks, but you don't need to do any of this."

"You know this entire town will help you in any way it can, and the congregation at church will be out here bringing food."

She chuckled. "And where am I supposed to put all of it? My fridge in the RV is the size of a dishwasher."

"Oh, almost forgot. Wait here." His hand kept the helmet from falling off his head as he jogged to his truck and opened the door. A border collie jumped out of the front seat and joined Blackie.

"Well, aren't you a beautiful dog?" Marla asked.

Verdon stopped beside the dog. "His name is Festus because I love that old television show, Gunsmoke. I wanted to call him Chester, but he doesn't have a limp. He loves running and needs a big place like this."

"I can use a dog." Marla bent down and patted the happy dog on its head.

"Heard you bought some cattle," Verdon said. "He's great with animals."

"I did. Fifty more head, and not from Mexico." They both laughed. She gazed across the land. "I wasn't expecting to own three hundred acres by myself. Crosby and Ricardo, his ranch hand, took care of everything. When I left, they sold off the herd because we wouldn't have time with both of us," she slipped the cap off and swept her hair back, "both of us working at the DEA." She cleared her throat. "Anyway, Ricardo moved on, and I'm here ready with the new herd needing another ranch hand. If you hear of one, send him my way."

"I have the perfect person."

"Yeah? What's his name?"

"Cassandra. She goes by Cassie."

"A woman?"

"My wife's niece and her husband in Oklahoma let her go last week, and she's looking for a job."

"Let her go? A troublemaker?"

"She was the assistant boss, or whatever they call themselves at a ranch, and she beat up a hand who slapped her on the butt. It was the second time she pounded someone for doing that."

"A no BS woman. Sounds like she would be perfect for me. Send her my way."

Verdon patted the horse on the backside. "But we could use you at the police station."

Marla nodded. "Thanks. After Crosby..." She stopped and held her breath for a few seconds while she smiled at the dog. "After Crosby..." Her eyes watered. "Anyway, my days of law enforcement are on hold. After all that, my boss, ASAC Borland, and I went through, tussling over Crosby's injury, my stubbornness about the doctor, and the eccentric stem cell treatment, he was kind enough to give me an extra month of leave on top of the ninety days the DEA normally gives. Guess he wasn't as hard-nosed as I thought. I have time to decide which direction to go, the DEA or staying in Hildebrandt." Marla threw a sad smile at the dog. "And now, Festus."

Verdon held out his hand. She grabbed it, pulled him toward her, and hugged him. "Thank you, Don, for saving my life." She let go and held her arms toward her new house. "And all this."

"It's our pleasure to do this for you and an honor to do it for Crosby." He smiled and pointed back toward the destruction. "I must get back up there." The jackhammer slowed down. "See? Those guys, you leave them for a few minutes, and they go on break."

Marla's phone rang as Verdon jogged to a front loader. It was SAC Roger Davies on the line. "Hello, sir. What can I do for you?"

"I'm checking on the most head-strong, charge up the middle, newbie in the DEA."

Marla smirked. "I'm here at my ranch watching men rebuild my house and barn."

"I wanted to let you know about your girl, Kata. Her DNA didn't match anyone on record in Mexico or the US. You were right about her story of the cartel killing families, stealing minors, and hundreds of teenagers kidnapped. They did the same to almost every teenage girl and boy we recovered from the trafficking cases. Thanks to you, dozens have been recovered, and that hole under the Rio Grande is full of concrete and will never be used again."

"I'm honored to have been part of the operation."

"Take your time and rebuild your life. Your husband was a brilliant agent. His undercover work broke the back of several large Mexican operations."

"Yes, sir," she scraped her boot across the dirt. "His undercover work that I didn't know about while we were cops in Hildebrandt."

"We are very proud of him."

"He's the greatest man I will ever know." She waited a moment before saying anything else. "Thank you for the call. I will stay in touch."

When Verdon left, Marla looped a velvet bag holding Kata's cremated remains around Daisy's saddle horn. After the autopsy, no one wanted the body. The Mexican government refused to take it with no family still living, and Bexar County would have placed it with others in an unmarked grave. She couldn't allow that to happen. With the blessings of the sheriff's department, the health department, and a gracious county judge, she brought Kata to the ranch. Marla remembered the night they came to the house. Kata said, "It is so beautiful. Please let me stay forever." And so, she shall.

She placed the phone in her back pocket before slipping her boot into the stirrup and mounting Daisy. Leaning forward, she patted the horse's neck and gently kicked the sides. Unsaddled, Blackie followed beside them with Festus close behind.

A few weeks back, almost every person in Hildebrandt attended Crosby's funeral, with standing room only in the church and more outside watching and listening to the service. The local florist had thousands of flowers shipped in to manage all the orders. The mayor declared that day Crosby Adams Memorial Day.

The Hildebrandt Cemetery stood halfway between the Adams' ranch and the edge of town. She rode there yesterday, the day before, and every day since the funeral, talking to him about rebuilding the ranch, adding more cattle, and everything and nothing. Could he hear her because she couldn't hear him anymore?

The media couldn't decide if they should declare her a hero, a victim, or a criminal by helping an unlicensed doctor perform unconventional medical procedures that produced accelerated tissue growth far beyond any research agency ever predicted or bringing down a multimillion-dollar sex trafficking and drug ring, second only to what DEA Special Agent Ronald Borland did a decade before.

In her last meeting in the DEA office conference room, she again observed the jungle pecking order. She didn't want to be an impala or a lion, but Borland asked her to stay with the administration. She didn't say no or yes.

They stopped at the creek bank, and the horses bent down to drink. Five hundred yards away, cattle chewed on grass.

She had the time and space to work through her grief and not run from it. And that's all there was left. Marla lost more than half of her life. That's the price you pay when you fall in love and marry and then suddenly lose that person, that magical fulfilled life.

Marla climbed off Daisy and tied the reins close to the two large oak trees with trunks just ten feet apart, their crowns intertwined as one. Removing the velvet bag off the saddle horn, she opened it and scattered the ashes along the creek bank. "And so, Kata, you will have your wish and stay forever with me."

Crosby loved to watch the sun disappear under the horizon. A ray of light pierced through the branches with the warm radiance hitting her face. Stepping in front of a tree standing strong above the ground, she pressed her palms on the trunk and felt the heart brand he left her, and the tears were unstoppable.

Her phone rang in her pocket. She cleared her eyes and saw BOSS on the screen. She answered, "Adams."

"Adams, this is Borland. Where is it?"

"Sir? Where's what?"

"That stuff your doctor had in a vial."

Marla stepped beside Blackie and rubbed his neck. "Are you talking about the protein extract? It was supposed to have been destroyed. Not thrown away, not held, destroyed."

"A Colonel from the Pentagon showed up at the SAPD and wanted it."

"The army?" Marla nodded. "That extract made stem cells grow ten times, twenty times faster than normal."

"They want to militarize it. They said it could heal deadly wounds in days. Make muscles bigger, stronger."

While holding the phone in one hand, she stuck the toe of her boot into the stirrup, grabbed the saddle horn, and flung herself onto the saddle. "Last I heard, it was in the Hildebrandt evidence room."

"Well, it's missing," Borland said. "Someone stole it."

The End

About the Author

Patrick Hanford has lived in Texas most of his life. He graduated from the University of North Texas, Texas College of Osteopathic Medicine and recently retired from family medicine after more than thirty-five years. He interjects his past experiences of daily medical clinic life throughout his stories.

With two novels published and *The Creation of Marla Adams* reaching Amazon best selling status in four countries, he has continued with the Marla Adams series. A third in the series is planned to be released in the Spring of 2024.

He lives with his wife, plays golf, walks in West Texas wind, and travels from one end of Texas to the other visiting children and grandchildren.

Acknowledgements

Thanks to all my family, friends, critique partners, beta readers, and arc readers for their help and direction in writing and rewriting multiple times of *The Desperation of Marla Adams*. It's wonderful to have people encouraging me to pursue a second career.

I am indebted to my editors, Cameron Chandler and Audrey Mackaman. I hope we stay connected for all my future novels. Once again, thank you to the participants of the Write Right Critique Group, Texas Tech HSC physicians, the city of San Antonio, and Bexar (pronounced bear) County.

A special thanks to KJ Waters for pointing me in all the right directions and Jody Smyers Photography for the amazing book cover.

If you travel to San Antonio, you will find the highways mentioned to be real, but the RV Park, wheat fields, farm equipment sheds, barns, medical clinics, livestock tractor-trailers, and convenience stores are fictitious.

Keep in Touch

Please visit my website at www.patrickhanford.com. You can find me on social media at:

Facebook: PatrickHanfordauthor
Instagram: @patrickhanford
Twitter: @patrickjhanford

If you'd like to receive the updates, contests, and exclusive excerpts, please sign up for my newsletter on my website. I'll share occasional updates on my writing, upcoming releases, sales, and special offers.

www.ingramcontent.com/pod-product-compliance
Lightning Source LLC
Chambersburg PA
CBHW071233300726
48975CB00002B/398